THE GREY LIST

GREY HUFFINGTON

huffington*socials*

Instagram: Instagram.com/greyhuffington
Instagram: Instagram.com/huffingtonhq
TikTok: TikTok.com/@greyhuffington.com
Pinterest: https://pin.it/695pEOV9m

sub*stack*

The Huffington Note column by Grey Huffington.

Discover the works and writing of Grey Huffington in a different form of Huffington publication. ***The Huffington Note*** emphasizes the slowness, softness, and stillness Black women desire and deserve while also taking a deep dive into the beauty of womanhood (sex,

love, marriage, liberation, self-care, elevation, wealth,
and mindset) in its entirety.

Substack: thehuffingtonnote.substack.com

trigger *warning*

PLEASE READ THIS SECTION!

Seeing this note means the book you are about to read could contain triggering situations or actions. This book is subject to one or more of the triggers listed below.

Please note that this a universal trigger warning page that is included in Grey Huffington books and is not specified for any particular set of characters, book, couple, etc.
This book does not contain all the warnings listed. It is simply a way to warn you that this particular book contains things/a thing that may be triggering for some.

This is my way of recognizing the reality and life experiences of my Romance friends and making sure I

properly prepare you for what is to unfold within the
pages of this book.

violence
sexual assault
drug addiction
suicide
homicide
miscarriage/child loss
child abuse
emotional abuse
mental illness
infidelity
infertility
cancer
criminal activity

TO NOTE.

*a*huffington*note*

Between the covers of this book is **my** art piece —
beautifully paired words structured for **my** creative
satisfaction and later consumed by others for
enjoyment.

It's **leisure for you**, it's **life for me**.
This is just a book to most. **It's art for me.**
My art. I've had *my* time. Have **yours**.

happy reading

GREY**HUFFINGTON**

CONTENTS

GREY**HUFFINGTON**

Royce

NEVER GIVE *a man a second time to waste yours.*

The thought rolled through my head as I rubbed the mascara wand across my lashes. The instant lift and visible thickening forced my hand down as I gazed at my reflection. A smile creased the corners of my lips. I shifted my weight from my right side to the left. Instinctively, my head lifted and fell.

"Oh, she's good."

There was hardly anything Roulette managed to screw up, but beauty finds were her specialty. Suggesting the new stick of mascara wasn't enough for the newlywed damsel. She'd contributed to our ever-growing vanity collections by purchasing one for every woman in her circle.

Bzzzzt.

Bzzzzt.

My cell vibrated on the vintage wood. I was brought back to my initial thoughts. *Men.* A mundane subject that didn't quite deserve the few minutes of recognition it managed to acquire from me daily.

Bzzzzt.

Bzzzzt.

My thumb pressed into the side of the phone, forcing silence. The unknown caller was no secret, nor were the digits that combined to form his cell number. They were blocked.

Second chance.

Second wind.

Second attempt.

Second nothing.

The music resumed. I swayed my body slowly.

Because it's incredibly likely they didn't deserve the first. Red flags will still be red no matter how many times they are forgiven.

I leaned toward the mirror of my antique vanity, applying a second coat of mascara to the same lashes I was head over heels for. Once satisfied, I began brushing the wand across the lashes of my left eye, promising to return once the second coat of the left eye was semi-dry.

Men will beg you to disappoint you again.

I kissed the skin of my teeth at the thought.

Righting their wrongs is hardly ever their objective.

Not for most men.

Victory is.

They can't stand to lose.

It hardly has anything to do with you and everything to do with their fragile egos.

They inherit a sense of urgency to be in the good graces of women that should be grounds for insanity. Mainly because it is improbable they've changed anything within hours or days of their exile.

Chuckling, I considered the facts.

They feel like the heroes of their lousy friend group when they're expressing the dirty things they've done to their partners. Cheating. Lying. Manipulating. Gaslighting. Harming. Hurting. The list goes on.

Yet, when the gift of that woman stops giving, those loose lips are sealed. There's silence amongst that circle. And, the mission is to retrieve what they've lost before the realization hits those around them.

Explaining they've lost the person they joked about cheating on, lying to, manipulating, gaslighting, harming, and hurting feels incriminating, embarrassing, and impossible.

With a shake of my head, I inched the wand from my lashes.

One.

Two.

Three.

Four.

Five.

I went in for a second coat.

Bzzzt.

Bzzzt.

Giveon was silenced on the Bluetooth speaker once more.

"Fuck."

Inhaling slowly, I shoved the mascara wand into the tube and set it on the vanity. I replaced it with my cell, swiping the screen to connect the call. Until I answered, he'd continue calling. Interrupting my music again would send me to a place I wouldn't be able to return from before the night's end. In an attempt to remain level-headed, I decided to give the caller the attention he craved.

"Leland, let's make this the last time you dial my number. I'd hate to turn those talented fingers to nubs to make sure you never press another digit on that cell of yours again and think three times about telling Siri."

"Royc–"

"Your unforgettable, curved dick and your knowledge of use are the only reasons I'm giving you the courtesy of a warning. This will not happen again. *Should it…* Then, I will not be on your line, Leland. I'll be in your home, turning every warning into your reality."

"Please. Just hear me out," he begged.

"Your excuses are trash. Your explanations are trash. Your head is trash. Your frame is trash. Your choice in clothes is trash. Your chains are trash. Your watch is trash. Your vocabulary is trash. Your lack of awareness is trash.

"Your choice of guns is trash. Your outlook on life is trash. Your resources are trash. Your connections are trash. Your conversation is trash. Your circle of friends is trash. The thread count of your sheets is trash. And, your apology method is trash.

"Had it been a direct deposit of six figures for all the trash I've endured since encountering you, maybe this call would be going a lot smoother. But, since it was a measly twenty-thousand-dollar Rolex, *product of more trash*, here we are.

"Leland, you don't represent my standards. I'm doing us both a favor by ending what should never have begun. It was fun while it lasted, but your time is up."

My cell slammed against my vanity as anxiety crept up my throat.

"Ugh."

A shake of the head led my eyes upward with a roll. I instantly regretted the number of words I'd shared with Leland. He wasn't worth even the first four, let alone the rest.

It's the curve. I reasoned, recalling the way it touched the corners that no one before him had discovered.

I closed my eyes, sure not to smear the damp mascara on the rest of my perfectly polished face.

That fucking curve.

It was lethal, giving Leland a chance he likely didn't deserve. Our first encounter in the gym was my downfall. There was hardly anything he could do to conceal the weapon between his thighs. It kept my lips bumping much longer than usual as he struck up a conversation at the water fountain.

His dick was as long as his money. However, his qualities ended there. They rewarded him with six weeks of my time. That was too much in my opinion.

Bosses only.

The words of my brother toyed with my thoughts. I didn't take any of his advice lightly, but this advice I took to heart.

Not all of them deserve the time of day, Teddy.

Leland fit the mold, but things ended there for him.

I coated my lashes a final time and stood back to admire my handiwork. Satisfied, I grabbed the custom fan and waved it in front of my face.

*Enough about **that** nigga.*

There are a hundred more waiting.

I placed the fan in its rightful place and turned on the tips of my toes after a final look in the mirror. The naked makeup routine was becoming my favorite. While there were hints of the enhancements coating my skin, the thin layers created the illusion of its nonexistence.

Plush carpet crept between my toes as I strolled across my bedroom. I pressed my hands against the wall as I slid into the fluffy slippers near the threshold that led me to the full-sized closet.

The moisturizer had melted into my damp skin and dried beautifully. Slippers were prohibited during the process. They'd only soak up the oils and lotion on my feet and ankles.

Brent Faiyaz's voice replaced Giveon's. A chuckle fell from my lips.

Seriously?

My cell had become a traitor. I was convinced. I wasn't opposed to hearing the voices of men at the moment, but as unpleasant thoughts of them circulated, I would've rather listened to the voices of fellow women. Instead, the men confirmed my accusations with each word they spewed.

Still, I couldn't deny the hit. Instead of trying or changing the song, I entered my closet and began the hunt for perfection in a gown. Preferably thin. Easily removed. Brown in color. And, flowed like lava with each move I made.

An assortment of fabric grazed my skin. It wasn't until I reached the silkiest that I halted. The coolness raised fine bumps on my arms. I closed my eyes briefly, savoring the buttery softness.

The array of colors was exciting, but I was only after one. *This one.* My fingers landed on a chocolate one with black trimming. *Or, maybe this one.* A beige dress caught my eye.

Or– I thought, looking at the fawn-colored dress.

Shaking my head, I returned to the original choice. *This is the one.*

The lace trim elevated the piece a few notches, placing it on a completely different level than the others. It was out of their league but right on point for the occasion.

Occasions. I corrected, taking the velvet hanger and heading for the dressing stand.

Pebbled nipples stared back at me in the oversized mirror that surrounded me. With my gown for the evening hanging next to me, my hands were free to roam. The light sheen of my skin was a compliment of *The Sevyn Summers Duo,* a combination I'd fallen in love with over time. It was the sweetest treat for my dark skin.

I ran my hands down the length of my upper body, ending at my expanded hips. The expansion was subtle and petite and perfect for my frame. My chocolate nipples that had turned to stones resembled the color of my dress. I tilted my head, attempting to get a closer look at my hairless mound.

The space between my legs allowed the observation, making it slightly easier. Admiration sped my heart rate. I gnawed on my bottom lip as a thought occurred to me.

I know she's good. I summed. *Damn good.*

The repeated unknown calls this evening wasn't evidence.

Because, again, men are just egotistical assholes.

"I'm Royce. Royce Childers," I announced softly. "Everything about the Childers is good."

I shrugged, ending the daily session of self-validation that boosted my confidence every day on God's green earth. It displaced my need for validation from those around me, especially men.

My body jerked forward and my jaws fluffed.

Men. Validation. Urgh.

I gagged at the thought. My fingertips touched my lips. I was fearful that something might actually breach them and spill over onto my floor. When the feeling subsided, I grabbed the dress of choice and unzipped the side.

With ease, it slid down my well-glazed skin, ending near my ankles. It was such a pleasure when the clothes I acquired were tall-girl-friendly. I rejoiced inside, tilting my head rightward as I pulled the zipper up. My hands smoothed the invisible wrinkles.

"Perfect."

I lifted my hair from my shoulders and turned from side to side.

"Hmph."

The decision was hard. I wasn't sure if I wanted to wear it down, showing off the perfectly trimmed layers, or pull it up into a beaded claw clip.

Or a quarter up and the rest framing my face.

Or maybe a high ponytail. Loose. Messy.

I shifted my weight, staring at my reflection in the mirror as the options were being weighed.

"I don't know," I admitted.

Whap!

My hands slapped against my thighs. I wasted little time getting to my vanity and retrieving my cell. I dialed in the board of advisors, knowing that the answer to my question was not far away.

As the FaceTime call began to ring, I peered at my reflection in the vanity mirror. Tonight's itinerary rolled through my thoughts. Though my timeline was risky, I was certain everything on my calendar would be checked off before I returned to bed and rested my head.

"Who called? Is everything okay?" Rather answered, concern dripping in her tone.

"Hi," Rome joined.

"Hi, everyone," Roaman added.

"It was me. I called. Hi, Rugs."

Rugger remained silent, waiting for the reason for the call to be mentioned.

"Everything is fine," I explained. "I just don't know if I want to wear my hair up or down or half up and the rest down or what– I just– I don't want to disrupt the beauty of this dress."

"It's bomb, baby," Roulette finally joined the call after Range.

"Isn't it?" I scoffed.

"I love it," Range admitted.

"Let's see our options," Rome suggested.

So many parts of her had changed over the last year. As we got more acquainted with the new layers of Rome, I was falling head over heels for her. Rome would always be Baby to us, but she was no longer a baby.

"Yeah," Rugger sighed.

"Everything okay?" I asked her, wondering if all was well in her world.

"Yes. Just tired," Rugger yawned. "Options."

Her demand urged my movement.

"Oh. Yes. Right."

I set my cell on the vanity and pulled my hair into a messy ponytail.

"This."

I let a large portion fall down my back.

"This."

I then let it all fall.

"This."

Lastly, I used a pearl claw clip to hold it together at the back of my head.

"Or this."

"Definitely not that," Rome said.

"I'm torn between some of it being up and all of it hanging. Something about that twinge of hair being up, though. It gives an innocent but very lethal bitch," Roulette explained.

"Well–" Range chuckled, "I mean– there's truth there."

"Where are you headed anyway?"

"On a date with the guy Brandon I have been telling you all about."

"Finally giving that man a chance?" Roaman joked.

"I guess. He's asked enough. Bought enough." I shrugged. "I'm not optimistic. There's this thing to be noted about guys who have been trying to get your attention for long periods."

"First chance you give them, they will–" Range tittered.

"Exactly. But, trust me, sister… the chance to play with me will never surface," I assured everyone.

"That wasn't even considered. Not even a little," Roulette claimed. "Niggas know."

"If they don't, then I can surely inform them," Rugger replied.

"Hey now," Rome interjected, "We don't have to take it there."

"The door is always open," Rugger told me, ignoring Rome.

"Up or down guys?" I asked, toying with my hair so they could see the final options.

"Up."

"Down."

"Down."

"Up."

"Up."

"Up."

"Well, that settles it. I have a date and then another date after that, so I must get going."

"My type of party," Roulette cheered. "Why not together, though?"

"It's not that type of party, Rou. I have business to handle after my date. It happens to involve a date as well."

"Call me tomorrow, I was thinking lunch."

"Lunch sounds doable, baby. I'll call you."

"I look forward to it." Rome's smile lit the light in the dark tunnel I often found myself headed down.

"Alright, ladies. Love you *all*. There's not a lifetime I won't."

"Find me first. Leave the others to their madness for a minute," Range proposed.

"That's not fair," Rome murmured, "But I can wait. Hopefully I've found the love of my lifetimes and I don't have to wait alone."

"Later."

"Have fun."

One goodbye after another came as the ladies left the call. I did the same before removing hairpins from the drawer of my vanity. There was a way to merge both styles without sacrificing the beauty of either.

I pulled my hair up as if I were forming a ponytail and placed bobby pins along the area meant for a hair tie or rubber band. My reflection revealed the marrying of the two options. Rome preferred my hair up. Range preferred it down. I couldn't disappoint either, so I made it work in both of their favors.

There.

Bzt.

Bzt.

My vibrating phone garnered my attention. I gazed at the screen. Pleasantries lulled me. I tapped the name at the very bottom of the blurred image of Jru.

A familiar text thread appeared. The face of a beautiful baby, less than a few weeks old, graced me. My heart sagged from the weight of the adoration I was overcome with.

Mercer, she's beautiful.

My brother, from another mother and father, had a sure way of gutting me. Seeing him reacclimated with the public and flourishing was music to my existence. While I loved Malachi, Milo, and Makai, it was Mercer who held the most special place in my heart.

I could hardly think of Malachi without being overcome with emotions. My eyes welled as his face roamed in my head. I shook away the tears that surfaced.

Maylei. Another text came through.

A smile tore through my face. She was the perfect balance between Mercer and Vallei.

Kiss her cheeks for me. Stay well. I love you... in every lifetime.

I shut down the screen, certain there wouldn't be a response. All that Mercer had to say had been said. He'd given me his quarterly life update through an image. It was fitting for him, and I looked forward to more updates. They always warmed me to the core.

Vallei had our daughter.
Her name is Maylei.
She's precious.
I'm in love.
We're all well.

His message was clear. I could only hope my joy was evident.

"Baby, I need your love. I need your love–" I sang along to Tink as I shifted gears.

Clarke's skyline followed me like a narcissistic ex who couldn't fathom the fact I'd moved on with my mind, body, and soul intact. As if I wasn't supposed to. Not without him, at least.

"We've been fighting the urge. Holding it in–"

My head swayed in the wind. I silently thanked everyone who suggested pulling my hair up. The ponytail was serving its purpose. The few pieces hanging fought the wind until I slowed down to a creep at the red light. The roof of the Lamborghini was missing. So was my filter tonight.

And my patience.

And my kindness.

And my tolerance.

And my consideration.

I entered the parking garage at full speed. My wheels came to a screeching halt at the door. Once they split open, I pulled forward, slowly. Inside the large circle painted on the floor, I pressed the round button on the remote that was clipped to my visor.

I was instantly enclosed in a glass container that pierced the red line of the circle. I rested my head on the seat, exhaling deeply. The idea of ceilings gripped me by the lungs and squeezed.

No height is too high, baby.

Not even the sky is our limit. We're in that motherfucker every chance we get.

Whatever you think your ceiling is, it's not. Ceilings don't exist in our world, baby.

We don't make goals, baby. We break them. And rules. And boundaries. And, anything that puts a limit on our capabilities.

Teddy's words echoed in my heart. I could no longer hear Tink. All I heard was Chemistry. My belief that there were no limits to my life had left me with a slight struggle with claustrophobia. I hated enclosures, ceilings, roofs, and walls.

"Thank God."

I stepped out of my car and allowed the door to close behind me. The door of my family's loft opened for me without resistance. The full body scan had been in motion since my wheels stopped in the large circle, and my car was placed in park.

The new upgrades to our common space were impressive. Chemistry wasn't a fan of technology. However, Malachi had been bitten by the tech bug and convinced him to look into some changes he thought would work in our favor. Better security for the sake of his girls was the winning phrase. He was down for it. All of it. Any of it.

"Hello, home."

It was the closest thing to our family's home as I'd

get since the passing of my dear Richie. I tilted my head rightward at the thought of his corpse decomposing in the grave we'd dug for him. The saliva dried in my mouth. My shoulders tried gathering at the center of my body. I closed my eyes, begging the heaviness to bear with me.

Please.

When I opened my eyes, my spine straightened and my shoulders pulled apart. A deep breath allowed me to let go of what once was and focus on the tasks ahead of me. My eyes narrowed to slits as a smile swept my lips backward.

"I've got shit to *handle.*"

As the words exited my mouth, my attention departed. Footsteps near the door forced my hand against my thigh, clutching my Glock.

Knock.

Knock.

Knock.

Knuckles against the door reminded me that I didn't come to sit in solitude. In fact, I hadn't come to sit at all.

Click.

Clack.

My heels collided with the floor as I unlocked my cell. The notification on my phone alerted me and all the others to the lurking presence. Dressed in black from his head to his toes, awaiting an answer, was Brandon Stemmons.

I pulled my bottom lip into my mouth. Not much

had changed about him since the first time he'd asked me out, eight years ago. If there was one thing I'd learned about choosing a man, it was that you never chose the man who had been after you for far longer than you'd like to remember. Because, once they had you in their grasp, they would secretly seek vengeance for the wait they endured and the men you allowed in your space before them.

Ninety-five percent of them will, at least. Though I hated to give men any type of credit, it was true that a handful used the opportunity to lock in and lock it down.

I wasn't sure if I was ready for either, but Brandon was still here upon my return.

Asking.

Inviting.

Hinting.

Spending.

Hunting me down.

Naturally, I was curious. Curiosity and boredom had led me to this moment. He didn't have much of my time to waste tonight. Business was calling. The second I felt anything but comfort in his presence would be the second our time together would end.

I pushed the button to shut down my screen and wrapped my hands around the doorknob. Simultaneously, I smoothed my hair to refresh my style.

"Good evening, Kimberly."

My brows furrowed at the sound of the name Kimberly. I squeezed the knob, prepared to shut the door before realizing Brandon wasn't calling me by my government name because I hadn't given it to him.

Chuckling, lowly, I rolled my lips together, smoothing out my lip gloss. I wanted to share the news that he had the wrong name, but decided against it. The handsome, dark, and buff ex-NFL player had spent nearly fifty thousand on Kimberly. Royce was worth so much more. I wasn't sure if he was ready to meet her yet, so it would be Kimberly for now.

"Good evening, Brandon."

"For you," he said, extending his right arm to hand me the beautiful bouquet.

Though my face remained pleasant, my thoughts were the farthest from it.

I hate flowers.

And dates, actually.

Men as well.

Talking stages, especially.

"Thank you."

"Is it really that bad?"

"Elaborate."

"Getting flowers. This must be your hundredth bouquet this year." He chuckled.

"I had intentions of reserving my thoughts, but since you insist— I hate flowers. Don't bring them again unless you don't want me in your company. And, make this your last time mentioning what another man has done for me. Because then we'd have to talk about how you aren't touching their gifts with a ten-foot pole. Let's try a bouquet of checks next time. Flowers don't do shit but die."

The words were at the tip of my tongue. Instead of letting them fly, I smiled with flared nostrils.

"If we're going to hint at what other men have done for me in the past, I will have to mention how much of their budgets they reserve for me. Let me know when you're ready."

"Just like that?"

I accepted the roses.

"Yes, love."

I eased the blow with a word frequently used on women after a bunch of bullshit had been spewed.

"I think I'm in love already." He laughed, placing his hand across his heart. "You ready?"

"Yes. One second. I need to put these in water."

"I'll be right here."

The door closed behind me.

Click.

Clack.

Click.

Clack.

I strutted toward the kitchen. The top of the bouquet met the lining of the trash bag before toppling over and finding its way to the bottom. I squared my shoulders and twisted my body by the heel of my shoes.

Click.

Clack.

Click.

Clack.

I reopened the door. Brandon was still standing behind it.

"Ready?"

"I am."

He lifted his hand, beckoning for mine. I stepped forward, knowing the loft's door would lock behind me. So much had changed. I was still adjusting, but the changes were proving to be beneficial.

Hand-in-hand, Brandon and I obliterated the space between our bodies and the elevator. Not much time passed before we were in the rectangular cart waiting for the doors to reopen.

"You smell good," he complimented.

"Thank you."

"What are you wearing?"

"Oak."

"I'm going to have to find that and buy you a life-time supply."

"It's a limited edition."

The elevator doors opened, urging us to exit.

"And you wore your precious fragrance for me?"

No. I wore it for me.

"Feel special yet?" I asked, stepping forward.

"I felt special the minute you agreed to go out with me. It only took eight years or some shit."

Chuckling, I shook my head. "I was occupied."

"The wait wasn't all that bad," he lied.

"Well, that's good to hear."

Brandon sealed those pretty lips of his and stepped

ahead of me, forcing the doors open with his presence alone. The automatic timer forced them closed once we were in the parking lot. My nostrils flared as the flesh on the inside of my mouth rolled between my teeth.

Loud music welcomed me into the night. The sound of my heels came to a halt near the awaiting vehicle. A time would be had tonight. This, I was sure of.

The pearl black ride was sickening. Its beauty was ravishing. It blended so well with the night. The crimson-colored brake pads were the perfect touch.

"A Lamborghini?" I asked, forging my surprise.

There wasn't much I didn't know about Brandon. I'd done my research. Nothing was impressive, not even his choice of vehicle. I had the same car. However, mine was reserved for the following year. The public didn't have access to what I had. Not yet, at least.

His was pearl. Mine was matte. It was ghostly in the late hours. While it was hard to spot past eight-thirty at night, one could hear me coming from a mile away.

"It's beautiful."

"Been in one before, Kimberly?"

I shook my head, lying through the perfect teeth God had given me.

"I haven't."

Play sheep. Preserve the wolf.

It was the method to my madness when involved with men. I chose to appear harmless, helpless, and clueless as a boost to their ego. I was rewarded well.

You catch more flies with honey.

It wasn't until those inflated egos needed to be *handled* that I unleashed the wolf within.

"First time for everything, *love*."

I lowered my body into the car. Brandon raced around to the driver's side. The second his foot touched the pedal, he revved the engine. The hairs on the back of my neck stood. The sound was so familiar. It was the reason Teddy made the purchase. He loved seeing the smile on my face as I watched Roulette race down the freeway.

The liberation I felt was inexplicable. I'd tried to put it into words a hundred times, but couldn't. Fortunately, I didn't have to. Chemistry just knew. He always did.

I pulled the seatbelt across my body, preparing for takeoff. It was swift and rightfully so. In my opinion, there was no sense in having the engine if you weren't going to use it. We put so much of my family's past behind us, clearing the lot of the loft and heading straight for the freeway.

My right hand caught the fierce wind, welcoming the turbulence it offered. With my eyes closed, I etched the feeling of limitlessness in my brain for the eighteen hundredth time. My body swayed to the sound of Future and Sza. The collaboration was an instant hit in my head.

Four songs played on the stereo before we pulled into the parking lot of *Prime House*. The chophouse was a true staple in our circle, owned by a business associate and someone Chemistry was rather fond of.

Hadn't I known better, I would call Abel a friend of Teddy's, but Teddy didn't have friends. He had sisters. There were too many emotions to manage and too much work involved with us to have any more friends. His brother-in-laws were the closest he had to friendships, yet they were still connected to his sisters. All of them.

"Ma'am–" the valet attendant urged my exit by extending a hand in my direction.

I accepted his offer and stood on my feet right beside him. He was merely five foot nine inches. Effortlessly, I towered over him. Height was a given in my family. My father's legs were long like stilts. My mother was nearly five eleven. My siblings and I had it honest.

"Thank you."

"Kimberly," Brandon called out, beckoning for me.

By his side, I allowed his fingers to rest between mine.

Physical touch. I studied him like an open book.

"Good evening, Ma'am. Sir," the hostess greeted us with a brimming smile.

Her eyes landed on Brandon and never left.

Stand the fuck up.

I bit my tongue, pushing my words deep down my throat. If I'd been sucking his dick for three years without a commitment, ring, or compensation, my orbs would automatically program themselves to avoid him and anyone who even favored him. However, Brittany wanted to be acknowledged.

Her pride was bruised. Validation was riding her coattail. And, she was still in love with a man who only loved what she offered his life–*not her*. It was the downfall of so many great women. She was obsessed with the potential of them, not the reality of it all.

Nothing in his past was off limits during my search. My findings proved to be interesting. It confirmed what I already knew about most men. They deserved hell.

"Evening, Brittany," I responded.

Her attention parted ways with Brandon, momentarily, as she stared at me. Openly observing me. Closely. Harshly. As if I gave a damn.

"How–"

I tipped my head toward her name tag, though I knew her name long before I'd read it.

Chuckling, she loosened her limbs. Her spine curled slightly as that beautiful smile came into full view.

Thinking she'd ever be a topic of conversation for a man who could give two shits about their rendezvous was quite optimistic for her. Unfortunately, it wasn't the case.

Her heart broke at the realization. Her smile faded. She swallowed back the lump in her throat and rounded the podium.

"This way."

"I'ma hit the men's room right quick," Brandon informed me, planting a kiss on my left cheek.

"Okay."

"I'll find you when I come out."

"Okay."

I continued behind Brittany, catching up to her with ease. Heaviness kept her feet from moving as fast as they normally would. I was sure. Defeat was written all over her frame.

"Don't do that," I demanded, stopping her in her tracks.

"Excuse me?"

"That."

"What is that exactly?"

"Give a man a chance to darken your spirit."

Continuing, she sniggered. "I'm not sure what you're referring to."

I wasn't easily swayed. We reached the table and before I had a seat, I turned Brittany's body toward mine with a single hand to her shoulder. I entered her personal space, wanting to make sure she heard every word that came from my mouth.

"The next time you decide to suck dick until your nose is snotty and your cheeks are stained with tears, make sure it's for a man who would turn the city red behind you. Brandon isn't that man. You're a pretty girl.

"And, from what I have discovered, you've got a good head on your shoulders–literally and figuratively. He will run his play when he leaves the restroom, just in case this date doesn't work in his favor. Just for you, love, I will make sure it ends on a shitty note. But, not before I eat.

"Tonight is when you take your power back. I don't

want to find out you were sliding down his dick by sunrise. I'll be very disappointed in you. Deny him. Confidently. Surely. As a matter of fucking fact. You undersand?"

"I– uh–"

"I don't care, Brittany. Do you understand?"

She nodded. "Yes."

"Good. And, congratulations on your nursing degree. Expect a gift at your door by the end of the week for your accomplishments, *including regaining the upper hand*. Never give that to a man again. Not even the pastor at your church."

Her head was still lifting and falling. She was picking up everything I was putting down.

"How'd you know?"

"Know what?"

"About Brandon and I?"

"There's not much I don't know. Enjoy your night."

"Uh... you too. And, thank you."

"The deed isn't done. Thank me once you've managed to make it through the night without giving into his advances."

"How?"

"How what, Brittany?"

"How will I thank you?"

"By finding someone worthy of your time. You'll be around incredible suitors between those hospital walls. Take your pick. Goodnight."

"Okay, but I didn't get your name."

"I didn't give it to you."

"I–"

"Goodnight," I finalized.

"Goodnight."

With her tail tucked behind her, she took off in the other direction. I shook my head as I released a sigh.

She's definitely going to fuck him tonight. I thought. *Hopefully I'm wrong.*

I settled with my own company as I waited for the inevitable. *Brandon's return.* He wasn't obligated to me as I wasn't obligated to him. Whoever and whatever he wanted to do or pursue he could and vice versa.

The respect he showed during his quest was most important to me. Hadn't I known his history in lengths, I would be clueless at the moment, and that's exactly how I planned to move throughout the rest of the night. Until it was my turn, at least.

"Sorry about that," he apologized as he approached the table.

I shrugged with a smile, admiring his handsome features. Brandon was far from slim, yet I doubted there was a crumb of fat lingering on his body. He visited the gym as often as he visited the restroom. His results were staggering.

Bulging arms.

Wide back.

Chiseled midsection.

Thick thighs.

It was all covered in dark chocolate that I would

like to assume tasted as well as it looked. I wasn't sure I'd ever find out, but I was certain Brittany could attest to the facts if I inquired.

"There was a little line forming or whatever. Had to wait that out."

Brandon lied straight through his teeth. Still, I leaned in closer, placing my elbows on the table and bringing my shoulders inward. Rhea would have a fit if she saw me.

"It's fine. Have you been here before?"

"Yeah," he responded with a nod.

"Good, I was hoping you could tell me about the menu and where to start. I feel so lost. There are so many options."

I hadn't opened the menu tonight because I knew it by heart. I knew every starter, salad, soup, steak, side, and drink on it. I'd tried almost everything.

"You have to go with the shrimp for your starter. It's a given."

"Then that's where I'll start. And, have a French Tart."

I split the menu open and casually scrolled the papers bound in a leather case. It was to do nothing more than keep my eyes and hands busy. Nothing had changed since my last visit with Range five weeks prior—*other than the hostess at the podium.*

"So, the lovely Kimberly finally carved out some time in her day to entertain me."

I shook my head as I closed the menu, giving Brandon my undivided attention.

"I'm no circus act. I don't strive to entertain. I prefer chasing enjoyment."

"Then you're in luck. I'm going to make sure you enjoy our time together."

"Good evening, ma'am. Sir. Can I get you two started with some water? Tap or house? We also have sparkling."

"I'll take house," I answered the question of our waitress.

"And for you, sir?"

"I'll take the same."

"Alright, any starters? Champagne? Fou–"

"I'll have a French Tart."

"I'll have tequila. Your finest reposado. Chilled. And, uh– two orders of your volcanic shrimp."

"Anything else?"

"Nah. That'll be it for now."

The waitress turned to leave, gracing me with her gracious backside. Her brown skin and natural curls were already the closest things to perfection. Knowing she had a body to match her light spirit and fluffy hair forced my head up and then down.

She's easy on the eyes, but I hope she's hard on the men. They deserve it.

"She's beautiful," I said, barely above a whisper.

Still, Brandon heard me. He snapped his neck in my direction.

"Hm?"

I nodded toward the waitress as I reopened my menu.

"Our waitress. She's beautiful."

"Yeah. She is."

Her beauty had led his eyes and head in the opposite direction. I didn't blame him. My position gave me the upper hand. I didn't have to maneuver in my seat to make sure my eyes weren't deceiving me.

"I don't get that often," he sniggered.

"Get what?"

"A woman complimenting another woman. Usually it's claws out the moment a woman sees another beautiful woman."

"I hate to break the news, Brandon, but it seems as if you attract jealous women."

"I won't deny it." He chuckled, flashing his pearly white, surgically enhanced teeth. "They can be a bit jealous."

"From the sound of it, you find out later than sooner."

"That, too, is true."

"All of them?"

"All of the ones I'm truly interested in. The others, I don't care enough to tell."

"Sounds like you have a type." I chuckled.

"Maybe so. I see now that you're different."

"Maybe." I lied. He was accurate. I was unlike anyone he'd encountered, unless he'd bumped into a Childers other than me.

"Nah. I, for sho, ain't met nobody like you."

"I'm going to take that as a compliment."

"You should, because that's exactly what it is and

that's exactly why I've been patient. Waiting you out, hoping to wear you down until you agreed to a date with me."

"Now that I'm here–"

"I'm hoping this isn't the last date. I'm hoping you enjoy my company. I'm hoping tonight goes well enough for you to start picking up the phone when you know a nigga on the other end of it."

My heart fluttered with anticipation, waiting for the words to fall from his lips one after the other. I was genuinely smitten by people who could hold a conversation. Good conversationalists could hold my attention for hours. Nothing more was required of Brandon tonight.

If he could capture my attention with his words, there would be no trouble on my part. It didn't mean I'd answer the phone when he called or agree to a second date. It meant we'd get through this one just fine and see what the future held.

"I'm going to enjoy the night, Brandon. And, so will you."

"No doubt about it. I'm already having the time of my fucking life." He laughed, forcing me to do the same.

His smile was contagious, and so was his laughter. I rolled my eyes upward, wishing I could admit to hating everything about him like I did most men. But, I didn't. If nothing else, I knew Brandon was decent company. The rest was still up for debate.

"A French Tart and a chilled tequila."

Our drinks were set before us. Instantly, I began wishing I'd chosen a glass of champagne instead. Though I loved a good mixed drink, it was champagne that allowed me to sip more slowly and not overly indulge. Martinis were tasty. Champagne wasn't.

"And, our house water."

"Your name–" I asked, peering up at the waitress as she poured water from a glass bottle.

"Amanda. I apologize. I thought I started with that."

"You didn't, but I understand. Busy night?"

"Yes. I'm swamped. Can you tell?"

"By the beads of sweat on your forehead and the breathlessness, yes," I confirmed.

Chuckling, nervously, she continued. "This uniform. I still think short-sleeved collar shirts should be an option."

She paused, taking a deep breath.

There you go, girl. I encouraged. *One more.*

As if she could hear me, she inhaled slowly and then exhaled even slower. Amanda then put the water on the tray beside her.

"Maybe it was your beauty," she stated.

"Excuse me?" I asked, unsure of what she was pairing it with.

"Maybe it was your beauty that took me by storm," she snickered, "Had me forgetting my lines and things. I feel awful for walking away without leaving you with my name."

"I could say the same about you," I explained, "I was telling my date that you're gorgeous."

"Thank you."

She pulled out her notepad and pen. She pulled in another breath and then exhaled.

"Now, do we know what we're having, or do we need more time?"

"She's been studying the menu since we got here, so I'll keep her ideal entree in my head. Save it for next time. Maybe she has something she's decided on."

I shook my head, staring at Brandon.

"I don't. Please– do the honors."

I watched quietly as he took the lead, placing an order for us both. The remainder of our time at dinner was more of the same. I sat back and allowed Brandon to manage the conversation as well as everything else around us. I was interested in his leadership skills as I was with any other man I sat across the table from.

I was born into a family full of women. We had two Kings. Both demonstrated how a leader operated, thought, handled partnerships, analyzed situations, and made connections.

When my glass was running low, Brandon made sure another drink was on the way. When my water was low, he made sure Amanda refilled it. And, when I'd eaten enough, he made sure my plate was taken away.

Attentive.

It was one of the most attractive traits in a man. Brandon had it. And, it earned him a few points in my notepad.

. . .

By the end of dinner, my lips were attempting to touch my ears. I admired my ability to compartmentalize my feelings and emotions. It was a lesson Chemistry and Richie taught us as children. Some of us at least. Rome and Roaman were not his subjects.

They understood very early that they'd both display their feelings proudly. It was in their wiring, and there was nothing anyone could do to change that. Honestly, I don't think Chemistry or Richie wanted to. Rome gave Chemistry reason to believe his heart worked.

Roaman gave Richie reason to believe there was more good in life. Our mother, Rhea, was his first encounter with it. He needed more confirmation it was real, and Roaman was just that.

"I'm not so sure I'm ready for the night to end," Brandon revealed as he leaned down into the car I had just lowered my body into.

"You should get inside," I responded with a smile.

"Ahh," he sighed, "The rejection is already settling in."

Playfully, he held a hand to his heart and shook his head.

"Elizabeth, I'm coming to join you, honey," he joked.

Chuckling, I tilted my head toward the passenger seat, urging him to get in. Noisily, he rounded the car and took his place next to me, hand still on his heart.

"Brandon, please."

"Kimberly, please," he countered, lowering his hand onto the steering wheel as he sped through the parking lot.

"A bar?"

"A rooftop?"

"The strip club? I know a good place."

Me, too. My sister owns it.

"A hookah lounge?"

"A fucking library? You look like you'd love a library."

"I would," I admitted.

"Then which one? I'll have them open it right now."

Four blocks over, and the conversation continued. Hadn't I made plans, Brandon could have a few more hours of my time. However, that wasn't the case, and I wasn't interested in prolonging the inevitable for the sake of an empty schedule. I had shit to handle.

I shook my head. "Not tonight."

"I just got you in my world and now you're trying to skip planets."

I shrugged, unable to soothe his ache.

"What's at home for you right now? Real shit."

"You're not taking me home."

"I'm not?" He asked cheerfully.

"No. You're taking me to The Balgaria."

"The hotel?"

I nodded. "Yes."

"For-"

"For whatever reason I am going. I'm not obligated to answer that question."

"I'm just trying to make sure I'm not taking you to the hotel to-"

"To the hotel bar."

"And I can't join you?"

"You can't. Someone is waiting for me."

There was a discomforting silence lingering.

It's time to exit. I summarized.

Discomfort was a non-negotiable for me, especially in the early stages of partnership. Be it a man or a woman, the rules were the same. It didn't matter if it was someone auditioning to be a friend, a potential client, or someone trying to buy more of my time.

"A nigga?"

I gnawed on my bottom lip as my lips stretched backward. With each passing second, another layer of the sheep's wool fell onto the seat underneath me. The wolf had been activated. And, as soon as the shed was complete, visibility would no longer be a hindrance.

"Kimber–"

"I am a single woman who is dating. Instead of getting dressed date after date, I put on my good clothes and line you niggas up, because that's what works for me. I don't live in a world where I try to make men's lives easier. I'm all about saving myself time, energy, and free days on my schedule.

"So, I wouldn't give a fuck if there were three or four niggas at the bar waiting for me, it isn't and won't be you. That's the bottom line, and that's what I need you to get over. Clean some of the wax from your ears so you won't be so hard of hearing.

And, maybe go see your doctor to get that wide head of yours scanned. Obviously, they crashed into you too many times on that field. You deserve compensation, but I'm not it."

We came to a screeching halt at the stoplight.

"Yo– you–"

The door lifted with ease. I didn't bother closing it behind me.

Don't want to hear it. I thought, deleting the space between me and the sidewalk. With my purse in hand, I trekked across the large white lines.

"Bitch!" Brandon spewed, fuming as he dealt with the trauma rejection triggered.

That's between him and his mother. That's not my problem.

I'd seen it too many times. Women making the problems of men they barely knew theirs. This wasn't *Project Y Chromosome.* I was well into my thirties. Therapy and meditation should've been things of the past for any man I dated. The work should already be done, because I refused to strap up my boots for anyone or anything but late autumn and winter.

"I'll be a bitch," I breathed out, "As long as I'm not a dumb bitch, a broke bitch, or Brandon's bitch."

I stepped up onto the sidewalk as the sweet melody of burning rubber played in the background. It was Brittany's chance to reclaim her power. I was praying she didn't slip and fall on that man's dick before dawn or any time after.

Limited fabric and lots of legs reminded me where I was. My goal wasn't to come between anyone's money, so I continued down the street lined with bars, restaurants, and a car garage or two. I weighed my options, taking every business within walking distance into account.

The Balgaria was a mere three miles from Lamaz, the strip with concrete far too rough for my designer heels. I regretted every step I took, hoping my soles were still intact by the end of the night. Nevertheless, the night air was gentle against my skin. Liberation was at the tip of my tongue, nose, and fingertips.

God, I feel good.

"Pretty, babes!" An unfamiliar voice complimented.

"Thank you." I tossed over my shoulder without looking behind me.

I peered in each direction before stepping into the road. My strut intensified as the thought of Brandon's audacity resurfaced in my head. I tittered, unsure where he'd stolen it from, but I was hoping he would return it soon.

Wrap it up.

He wasn't allowed to take up space in my head. There was no room for foolish men. Not in my thoughts, memory, presence, or future. Forgetting him and his ignorance was simple.

Besides, he hasn't spent nearly enough to linger.

I rolled my eyes, ridding myself of that man and the false hope he carried.

Scrrrrrrrrt.

Screeching tires startled me. I froze, placing a hand on my thigh. My Glock was underneath my palm when I met the deeply troubled orbs. My heart collapsed into the seat of my panties. I observed the intricate details of the stranger's profile, wondering who he was and where he'd come from so suddenly.

I'm sorry. He mouthed.

I could feel the heat from the Aston Martin's engine. It wasn't until it mirrored my body's temperature that I realized my hand was on the hood and my thigh was just inches away from the grill.

The door of the SUV swung open as a haunting baritone echoed in the dark.

"My apologies. I– The– didn't– *Shit*. Listening to this fucking GPS will have my Black ass in a ditch somewhere."

Or shot.

"Or dead," I said, clearing my throat.

I pressed the camera icon on my screen. Secretly, I snapped an image of the license plate just inches away from me. Without taking my eyes off the man in front of me, I forwarded the photo to my second cell. It buzzed in my handbag, letting me know the message had been received.

He tipped his head rightward and nodded. The few words he'd spoken would likely be the only ones I heard from his mouth so swiftly and so plentifully. I knew his type. After fixing what he assumed he'd broken, he retreated.

His spine straightened. His hands folded in front of him. His eyes stilled. So did his body.

The creases in my forehead softened. Though he was a total stranger, I recognized him. Not wholly, but parts of him. The rigid ones. The reserved ones. The quiet ones. The analytical ones. The observant ones. He was out of his comfort zone.

Teddy.

"You're lost."

He nodded. "I am."

"Where to?" I sighed, loosening the grip on my Glock.

I, too, straightened my spine. His reservation was magnetic, pulling words and thoughts from me that I, too, wanted to reserve.

"*The Balgaria.*"

My face fluffed with a smile as I nodded.

Of course.

I didn't pour from my mouth. Instead, I lifted the bottom of my dress for a better range of motion. My strut resumed, ending as I lowered my body into the driver's seat of the foreign ride.

Tonka.

Cedar.

Vanilla.

Vetiver.

Orange.

I quietly admired the fragrance on his skin and the clothes he wore.

Black on black on black.

His skin was as crispy as his fabric. A hood was pulled down over what I knew were deep waves. As he turned around to face me, dipping his head into the car, he pulled the black shades from his head down onto his eyes.

"You driving, I'd assume?"

He didn't smile. Not outwardly, at least. His face remained stoic. Unreadable. Unforgetful. It was dazzling.

"You'd be accurate."

He rounded the car and opened the passenger door. As he settled in, so did his scent. He didn't fuss. He didn't put up the slightest fight.

Myrrh.

I finalized my findings. The combination was tantalizing, prompting me with the idea for Teddy's next gift. It didn't matter that he hated them; I'd continue giving them to him anyway.

He was deserving. Always had been.

As he adjusted the seat for comfort, I pressed my foot against the pedal. The weight of his body stopped his back from crashing into the seat. The stiffness of mine kept me upright.

"Did that image go to your friend group?"

Half-enthused by his attention to detail, I shrugged.

"It went to me," I confirmed, hiking the volume on the stereo.

The smoothness of the drive led my mind to other places. I considered the gift for myself.

Maybe for Christmas, I thought.

Or tomorrow, I countered instantly.

Every day I walked on Earth was a special day for

me. I didn't need to wait until the calendar told me it was.

Nas pumped through the speakers. Though I didn't listen to the tracks he laid in solitude, I was no stranger to his words, knowledge, or his voice. He was on rotation quite often in my family's home.

A dagger went through my chest. I'd been secretly yearning the moments spent around the dinner table with smiles touching my edges as I experienced unfiltered joy just being in the company of those I loved. When we were all living, breathing, and free were the best years of my life.

I turned one corner after the other, making my way back to the main street. Lamaz. Once on the stretch, my feet grew heavier on the gas. We sped down the street in pursuit of our destination. The odds of us being headed to the same place was in my favor. Though I wouldn't have had trouble getting to *The Balgaria* a solution sat in my path at the perfect moment.

The handsome stranger, whose name I didn't even know, stretched his legs and expanded his arms. He consumed an ungodly amount of space, making the passenger seat look and feel like a toddler seat. A booster chair of some kind.

I pulled the inside of my lip between my teeth as my nostrils flared. My curiosity was alarming. So was my quietness. I'd been known to be one who accepted her fate and the forwardness that caused it. But tonight was different. This moment was different.

I became the avoidant presence I despised. I didn't want to waste words on a man who was running from something. Hiding from someone. Or the world itself.

Black clothes.

Black shades.

Discomfort.

All the signs aligned with my analysis. He was incognito.

Doesn't want to be seen.

Doesn't want to be noticed.

Doesn't want to be bothered.

Doesn't want to be outed.

I'd been him before. Hiding in the shadows. Lurking. Hoping my discovery didn't manifest. Praying my presence was obsolete.

I inhaled deeply, pulling my thoughts from the abyss they were headed down. There was an eventful night ahead of me. I couldn't bear that load right now. It was too heavy.

I made a left into the well-lit lot. The wheels of the car bounced on the rocky roundabout. The red bricks that paved the space for vehicles were large and beautiful. They were held together by cement, with the names of the hotel investors etched on their surface.

The Balgaria sign sat atop the building, shining brightly with the backlighting as its source of energy. Fine bumps lined my skin. It didn't matter how many times I visited the establishment; it always felt like the first.

"Good evening, ma'am."

The door swung open. An attendant met me on the driver's side. Another met the handsome stranger on the passenger side. I lifted my butt from the seat, but electricity stopped me from exiting the car.

"Good evening, mister."

The wave of shock pulled me back onto the buttery soft leather. I searched for the source. I didn't have to search very long. A hand rested on my arm.

His hand rested on my arm.

"Thank you."

I remained silent, lowering my gaze to his hand. He did the same. I waited for him to release me. The moment didn't surface.

"Maybe we should keep in touch," he said, clearing his throat.

"I hate donuts and I'm not much of a coffee drinker. It gives me diarrhea."

I wasn't waiting for him to unhand me any longer. My exit was swift as my words resonated with him. By the time I reached the doors of The Balgaria, his voice raised the hairs on the back of my neck and the ones beneath my lasered pores.

"I'm not a cop."

Yeah, that's what they all say.

I clenched my walls together, wishing the handsome stranger didn't smell so much like pork. It would've been an honor to ditch my workload for a little fun.

"*Ugh.*"

My family had been down that path already. I

wouldn't take them down memory lane. Those moments were too unpleasant, too painful, and too real. Our perfect world was snatched from beneath us.

We were handed an alternate one instead. And, for the first three years, I hated it just like I hated almost everything else. But, slowly, I was coming around.

One day at a time. I reminded myself.

"Evening, welcome to The Balgaria."

"Welcome to The Balgaria."

"Welcome... The Balgaria is happy to have you this evening."

Like a broken record, the staff remixed the same line three times. With my lips sealed and my eyes straight ahead, I located the elevators.

Chatter surrounded me, but I was in no mood for words. Greetings. Goodbyes. Or games. I sharpened my shoulders as I stood in front of the doors. I watched them close as a couple expanded the room around them by pressing their bodies against each other.

The intoxicated man halted the door's movement with his left hand.

"Getting on? There's room."

I shook my head, hating the idea of disrupting my thoughts with words.

"No."

"You sure? There's room."

I'd already declined. No further action was necessary on my behalf. As he waited for my response, he realized it was highly unlikely he'd receive one. The doors closed shortly after. A sigh followed.

People.

I was starting to hate those, too.

Seconds later, I leaned forward and pressed the upward arrow. As I stepped back, I flattened my palms against my thighs.

Eyes trained.

Attention undivided.

A melody began to play in my head as the words seeped from my lips.

Slowly.

Lowly.

"Is it bad that," I whispered, "I never made love."

Ping.

The elevator sounded. I stepped inside and pushed the number twelve.

"But I sure know how to fuck. I'll be your–"

The singing quickly turned to whistling as the words continued. I reached my designated floor in a matter of seconds.

Click.

Clack.

Click.

Clack.

"Twelve twenty-eight."

I counted down the numbers as I ambled down the hallway, sure not to pass the room waiting for me. Upon approach, I removed the key card from my handbag and laid it on the keypad. A green light flashed, prompting my entry.

Cool air brushed against my skin. I raised the

temperature on the thermostat by four degrees. Satisfied with seventy displayed on the small screen, I scanned the room for my belongings.

A black duffel bag rested on the bed. I sighed with relief. Though I knew it would be here waiting, it was a relief to lay my eyes on it.

Time was of the essence. I unzipped the large compartment and removed the silk bonnet from the bag. It slid onto my head with ease, officiating the start of my transition. The Bluetooth speaker was next to be removed.

I powered it on and connected my cell.

"Do you mean it when you say it. I believe it because you're my fucking favorite," Sza sang as I dug deeper into the black duffel.

One by one, I removed the items inside, laying them out neatly on the bed before placing the bag they'd come from on the table behind me.

The suites at *The Balgaria* were stunning. Numbering of the guest floors began on the fourth floor. Because the first three floors were full of amenities, eateries, spas, salons, and shops, every room had at least a partial view of Clarke's beauty.

At night, the city's skyline was undefeated. Tonight was no exception. With the curtains drawn and the lights low, I witnessed Clarke's glow from fifteen stories high.

I peeled my dress from my body and spread it across the bed, sure not to wrinkle or fold it. Next to go were my panties. I replaced them with a black leather thong and garter belt. The matching bra snapped on with ease. Pantyhose slid up my moisturized legs, stopping above my thighs. They clung to the suspenders of my garter belt.

"Definitely not budging."

I loosened my hair, letting it all flow down my back. It made getting on the full mask a simpler task. I strapped on my accessories one by one. Time was on my side. It wasn't often it wasn't.

I'll be there when I get there. He'll be waiting.

It wasn't something I'd surmised without evidence of its truth. Undoubtedly, I knew the person awaiting my arrival wouldn't budge until he had me in his line of vision. There were rules, and he followed them well.

I pulled the trench coat over my body, concealing the details of my night. My exit from the room was simultaneously swift and slow. Had one blinked, and they would've missed me.

A long blink. I clarified, pressing my back against the cold steel of the elevator.

The letter P was bright and red, illuminating the keyboard. I watched closely until the red faded and the doors opened.

Ping.

I pushed my body off the wall of the cart and left the smell of freshly baked goods behind me. I wasn't sure what scent The Balgaria used on their elevators and hallways, but each had a different fragrance. Yet, they all smelled delicious.

Caramel.

Brulee.

Vanilla.

Cranberry.

Nutmeg.

I tried summarizing the combination but knew I was missing something. Possibly some things. Nevertheless, I put the essential oils behind me as I met the lettering on the double doors before me.

Presidential Suite.

I lifted my fingers and rammed them into the hardwood.

Knock.

Pause.

Knock.

Pause.

Knock. Knock.

I twisted the knob and entered the suite as the combination of knocks resonated with the hotel guest. Nothing was improvised. Everything had been discussed, strategized, and confirmed.

Click.

Clack.

Click.

Clack.

My heels slammed against the marble flooring. I untied the string holding my coat together. I placed the ends between my thumb and index finger, pushing the fabric backward to reveal what was underneath.

Heat soared through my body, letting me know an open trench simply wasn't enough. I proceeded to peel the fabric from my skin, allowing it to fall onto the floor as I met a pair of enamored orbs.

Every move I made, he lost another breath. His body shook with anticipation. Intrigue. Lust. Secrecy.

I was here for one thing and one thing only. I symbolized the forbidden. I was the awakening of his fantasies. I became his quest.

I removed the necessary contents and then placed the small bag on the grand piano just before I descended the two steps that led me to my task for the night. Just like everything else put on my desk, he would get handled. And, by any means necessary.

"On your knees," I instructed.

Slowly, my subject lowered his body to the ground. One knee at a time. Eyes still on me. Spine still straight. Shoulders still squared.

"Open your mouth."

He complied. I was close enough to smell the desperation on his skin. My feet didn't stop moving until my thighs met his cheeks. I dug my gloved hand into his hair and pulled his head backward. A bright light flashed in his face, blinding him temporarily. The sound of the churning film roll was empowering. Things were aligning.

"Suck it like the nasty little gobbler you are."

He slipped his hair from between my fingers, anxious to put the eight-inch, girthy dildo that was strapped to my waist inside of his mouth.

The obnoxious light flashed again. This time, he wasn't startled. Neither was he affected. He continued to roll his neck and enjoy the plastic tool he'd talked about at great length through texts on a secure line.

"That's it. Just like that."

I folded my lips into my mouth, hardly able to wrap my head around the idea of the well-connected, well-respected man on his knees with a dick lodged in his mouth. It wasn't the act itself that left me befuddled. It was his stance on the very subject. His distaste for those who were openly gay or bisexual was the reddest flag of them all. It was the reason this was my angle, and I didn't explore any others.

"Up."

His lips were covered in his own saliva. So was the veiny, thick dildo.

He stood up, attempting to clean the mess he'd made of his face.

"Leave it."

His hands fell. I pressed the button on the side of the black leather mask, starting the recording.

Click.

Clack.

When I turned around, my subject was on my heels. Upon entering the bedroom, I smiled. He'd followed all the rules. Chains dangled from the contraption. Leather filled the spots where they were separated.

"Get over there."

Hastily, he moved toward the structure, stepping inside and waiting for more instructions. I placed the camera on the bed and began attaching the chains to his body, strapping him completely.

Hands.

Arms.

Legs.

Neck.

Mouth.

Head.

Back.

Nothing was free. Not even the erection he managed. My lips turned upward, wondering how satisfied his partners must've been in bed. He'd requested an eight-inch dick because he likely hadn't seen one off-screen or beyond the urinals.

I removed the strap from my waist, placing it at his lips. Hungrily, he accepted it. His skills were impressive. His hunger was apparent. He wanted more. He needed more. He was interested in crossing every boundary known to the heterosexual male. And, unfortunately, I wouldn't be crossing them with him.

"You like that?" I questioned.

"Yes. Yes. So much."

"Where else do you want this big dick? Hm?"

"Inside of me."

"Where?"

"In my asshole."

"Will you take it like the boss you are or cower like a sucker?"

"Take it," he muttered, sucking the tip.

"I can't hear you?"

"I'm going to take it– like the boss I am."

"Good. I want you to show me."

I grabbed the camera, leaving the dildo shoved in his mouth. Two final images were taken and printed immediately. I stared at my subject, considering the rules we'd made. It was clear to him that all of my subjects were under surveillance for my arsenal of evidence. Even the idea that he'd be given proof this moment existed intrigued him.

He wanted to be reminded of the time we had and asked if I would provide footage and photos I wasn't very fond of. I obliged. But, unfortunately, I lied. It wasn't the first time, and neither would it be the last.

I pressed the button embedded in the mask and gathered the photos from the bed. I exited the room, leaving him clueless.

"Mmmm–"

I continued through the suite, collecting my things. With the trench on my shoulders, I gathered it at my waist and tied a knot to secure it.

"Mmmmmm!"

The door closed just as I pressed the down button on the elevator. I was entering it as quickly as I was exiting it. Before the steel doors reopened, welcoming me to the fifteenth floor, I snapped an image of one of the instant films in my hand.

I forwarded it to the starred contact and shoved my second phone back into the small handbag. As I stepped off the elevator, I removed the mask from my head. Relief consumed me.

Bzzt.

Bzzt.

The cell vibrated the bag it was in as I laid the keycard on the door for entry. Cool air touched my skin. I placed my back on the door, catching my breath. One blink and I had gathered myself.

Click.

Clack.

I removed the vibrating phone just as the caller ended their attempt to connect with me. Bypassing the missed call, I pressed one button after the other, dialing the latest number I had on the person I needed to hear my voice.

Once.

Twice.

My brows furrowed as the phone rang for the third time. Shortly after, there was silence on the line.

"Phase two has been **handled**."

I moved to end the call, but heard the deep baritone just before the call ended.

"Be careful."

"In every lifetime," I responded, heart melting in my chest.

The line died. I inhaled slowly and exhaled even slower with the phone pressed against my skin.

Bzzt.

Bzzt.

It vibrated in my hands. I didn't need to see the caller ID to know who was calling.

"Speak."

"This is insane," Odessa cried.

I strutted toward the bed, removing piece by piece.

The sound of her tears reminded me of our meeting just a few months prior. I'd given her time, yet she was still sitting on her hands, and her lips were still sealed shut. That didn't work for Teddy. That didn't work for me.

Tears stained her engorged cheeks. Sniffles inflated and deflated her chest continuously. The lengthy lashes on her eyes were soaked. She was a complete mess. But, still, I didn't give a single fuck. She had something I wanted... something I needed.

And, I didn't want to leave without it. Otherwise, this entire situation would go from bad to worse. The ball was in her court. I just needed her to dribble and pass it. I'd make sure it hit the basket.

"I can't–" Odessa whimpered. "I just can't."

From one side to the other, she shook her head. Her expression remained the same. Botox had taken away her ability to maneuver her facial features with ease. If the tears weren't as plentiful, I wouldn't have known she was upset.

"A million solid, Odessa and you're free to go. No attachments. No worries. Just freedom."

"I know. I jus–"

"A million on top of whatever is in his accounts. I'll see to it, personally, that it is all transferred to yours. A few buttons on my computer and it's all yours."

Adamantly, she shook her head, declining the offer she'd been given.

"Fine." I sighed with a shrug.

My feet were on the ground and my back was turned toward her within the blink of an eye. Wasting time was never on my list of things to do. I was out of the door before she could bat those thick lashes a second time.

With my phone pressed against my ear, I slipped into my ride. Leather seats welcomed me. Cool air pushed through the small holes of the fabric, decreasing my elevated temperature on contact.

I hate a dumb bitch. *I scoffed.*

"Have a great nigh–"

Yeah, yeah. *I thought, switching gears. My engine roared loudly, announcing my departure as I slammed my door. The valet attendant was too slow to his job.*

"Speak."

Naturally, my slightly arched spine straightened and the tips of my ears began to tingle. I swallowed the air pocket that had formed in my throat and prepared to dish the not-so-good news.

"She isn't budging."

"Next steps? Therapy?"

"No. She doesn't need The Therapist. She needs to be taught a lesson."

"What's your plan?"

"Make her regret ever having me to ask her twice–"

"By?"

"Unless you want to consume your dinner for the next few nights, I suggest you not ask questions like that."

A heavy sigh left the lips of the man that likely grew a new strand of gray hair every time we conversed.

"Just handle it," Teddy responded.

Those words were like a sweet song on a difficult day. It was everything I needed to hear.

"That was the plan, anyway."

As the suspenders loosened the pantyhose, I sat on the edge of the bed. I pushed my hair from my face and reminded Odessa that nothing had changed. And, she had been warned.

"I don't ask twice, Mrs. Raines."

"He's my husband."

Her tears weren't moving me.

"You were warned."

"What am I supposed to do with this? Why can't you just leave us alone?"

"Your husband still has breath in his body because he has precious information that belongs to us. Know that we do not give a fuck about you or his offsprings. Fortunately for you, we promised our mother there would be no blood shed during her birthday month, and we like to keep our promises.

"Should you find yourself in doubt before you see my face again Tuesday morning at eleven, then understand I will not hesitate to detonate the explosions we have in the arsenal for you and your husband. That includes the release of my archives."

"Bu–"

"Same place as last time. Tuesday. Eleven."

I ended the call and opened the camera roll.

There it is.

Derrick, Odessa's husband, trying to suck the polish

off the plastic dick as he told me how well he'd behave as it was lodged in his asshole.

"Hypocite!"

Sexuality, in my opinion, was far too critical and sensitive of a subject. I didn't give a damn who the people I loved were fucking or sucking unless they were detrimental to their health or our family's wealth. Beyond those parameters, I hoped they got the ceilings sucked out of their pussies every chance they got by whoever they chose.

Solitude quieted my thoughts. I stripped down to the body that God had given me. My feet glided into the slippers near the bed. I stalked the suite's floor until I reached the bathroom. My things lined the shower. A smile rearranged the features of my face.

My nipples hardened as the bathroom's coolness rested on my skin. Painfully, they stretched, protruding without apologies. I pressed them against the glass as I reached over and twirled the gold knob.

"Mmmm."

Water poured from the showerhead. The pleasurable pain I was suffering from subsided as heat began to warm the space around me. I straightened my spine and spun around, facing the mirror.

As it began to cloud from the steam, I peered at my reflection. My hands pulled together, palms covering my breasts. I tilted my head, admiring all the wonderful parts of me. My pussy was bald. My thighs expanded slightly. My frame was thin. And lean. And long. My belly button was just that. A button. It was neither protruding or sunken. It was circular. Perfectly round.

Rhea and Richie had paired well. I was a combination of them both, but I was my father's daughter. To my core, I was Richard Childers. I bled his blood. Thought his thoughts. Said his words. Took his lessons to heart. Strategized as he had taught me. And, kept my head on straight as he'd required.

I pulled my bottom lip into my mouth as my emotions surrounded me. Deeply, I drew in a breath. And, slowly, I released it. A smile pulled at my lips as I shook away the heaviness creeping into my spirit.

"There's no time, baby. There's shit to handle."

I snatched the silk hair dressing from the counter and slid it on my head, sure not to destroy whatever the full face covering hadn't.

"Hey, Ria."

The small, round ball on the bathroom counter lit up a golden brown.

"Yes, Miss Raines?"

Chuckling at the alias I'd used when booking the room with Derrick's hard-earned cash.

"I'd like to hear soft Jazz by Black musicians like Louis and Miles and Duke and Ella."

"Black Jazz now playing."

"Thank you," I whispered as I stepped into the warm shower.

I emerged from the stairwell with the black leather bag on my forearm. The thought of the elevator's doors closing on me for the twentieth time today was repulsive. I couldn't bear it.

"Besides," I reasoned, "I needed the steps."

My heels collided with the floor beneath me. My chocolate-colored dress swayed with each step I took. The door of *The Balgaria* was so near but felt so far away. And, frankly, I wasn't ready to end my night in the bed, under the covers.

The night was still so young. I'd collected all of the infinity stones and had Derrick by the balls, quite literally. A celebratory drink sounded so much better than the wine waiting for me at home.

I'll still have it though. I chuckled as the thought crossed my mind.

There wasn't a day on earth I'd turn down a cool glass of wine. It was my energy source. It fueled my thoughts and my ability to handle any fucking thing on my plate.

Anything.

I ambled toward the front desk. The line for check-in was lengthy. I bypassed those waiting, taking the first available receptionist.

"Excuse m–"

As the words of the impatient fella spilled from his lips, I turned on my heels. With a penetrating gaze, I encouraged him to continue whatever it was he was about to say. Knowing what was best for him, he quieted.

"Good evening," I greeted the receptionist, placing my bag on the counter.

"Good evening, ma'am. How can I help you?"

"A girl can't quite explore this beautiful building with luggage weighing her down. I thought maybe you could hold it for me until I'm ready to depart."

"Sure. The name?"

I didn't have one to give. By the time the question had rolled off her tongue, I was near the entrance of *Bar Balgaria.*

My feet halted at the entrance. Nearly every seat in the house was filled. Because the owner of the hotel was a friend of the family, it brought me great joy to know his establishment was still thriving.

"Welcome to Bar Balgaria. How many tonight?"

I was whisked from my thoughts and brought back into the moment by the lovely host waiting to seat guests. She smelled divine. I turned in her direction, finding a petite, brown-skinned beauty with a sleek bun to the back. I clenched my walls and swallowed back the adoration quickly building in my system for the stranger.

Hmph.

"Just me."

"Alone, huh?" She asked, "Anywhere in particular you'd like to sit?"

"Never alone," I clarified, knowing there were eyes on me. There were always eyes on me. "And, save your menus. I'm going to have a seat at the bar."

She shoved the menus back into the pocket of the podium she was standing in front of.

"Enjoy your evening."

"You do the same."

The path was paved for me. Not literally, but figuratively. Bodies moved aside to accommodate my presence. My journey to the bar was seamless, uninterrupted, and quite the breeze.

"Thank you."

I sat in the chair that had been pulled out for me.

"My pleasure," responded the nice gentleman who'd just paid his tab and was on his way out of the door. "Hey, Justin."

"Yeah?" The bartender looked up at him as he typed numbers into the computer.

"Open that tab back up for me. Give this pretty lady anything her heart desires for the night."

"Sure thing, man."

"Appreciate you," the hotel guest called over his shoulder.

I didn't bother wasting my time telling him he didn't have to reopen his tab for me, because he understood his role well. He was a provider, a man. And, I was a receiver, a woman. There was no need to complicate things, not even with a stranger.

"What can I get for you?"

"A bottle of your finest champagne."

Justin's eyes bulged. My shoulders lifted and fell.

"You heard the man. Get me whatever my heart desires."

He nodded, chuckling. "That'll be seventy-eight hundred dollars, ma'am."

"He looks like he has it to spare."

Justin said nothing more. He placed his hands in the air, surrendering.

Smart man.

I surveyed the area, taking note of everyone and everything. *Bar Balgaria* was no hole in the wall. Neither was it a sunken place. It was lively and vibrant, full of life and full of wealth.

Connections.

Money.

Drugs.

Illegal activity.

Bosses.

CEOs.

Leaders.

Lenders.

All in disguise. Their thousand dollar suites concealed their true identities. While eighty percent of the guests were legal, tax paying citizens, the other twenty were deep in the dirt.

Sparkles began to pop behind the bar. Fire danced on the sticks in the bartenders' hands. A gold bucket of ice holding a gold bottle headed in my direction. Justin's eyes found mine. I placed a hand near my neck and swiped it across my throat. Mid-stride, he halted, forcing everyone behind him to do the same.

I wasn't interested in a light show. In fact, I wasn't interested in lights, at all. Being seen was hardly ever my mission. I only desired to be felt, experienced, and remembered.

Quietly and now alone, Justin set the bucket on the bar and removed the bottle of champagne. He placed a champagne flute in front of me and cocked his head leftward with a smile.

"Little Miss Simplistic."

"Nothing about me is simplistic, Justin. Enough eyes are on me, already."

"All the eyes are on you, and I don't blame them. You sparkle alone."

"Mm hm."

Pop.

Bubbles slid down Justin's hand as he lifted the glass.

Clink.

The bottle and flute kissed. I was poured a generous amount before he retreated. I pulled the champagne toward my nose and inhaled. Small bubbles popped against my skin.

"You know," I began, still admiring the aroma of my drink, "You should be more careful. I've found the same set of eyes on you since I arrived."

Curiously, the hooded man with the glass of brown glued to his fingertips turned his head from one side to the other. As his features became more visible, I was reminded of his radiance. The darkness he possessed was consuming.

A shrug lifted his shoulders as he lifted his drink up to his mouth. Words wouldn't wash ashore. He didn't have any. His type hardly did. They were so guarded. So reserved. Cautious. Observant. Always in their head.

But, he was intoxicated.

Senses slightly disabled or possibly delayed. Either way, he wasn't the man whose car I'd sped off into the night in hours ago. He was merely a shell of him. The night wasn't kind to him. From the snigger that left his lips as he shook his head, I could sense the bitterness.

Disappointment.

The vulnerability.

"You've had too much to drink," I acknowledged, sipping from my glass.

A heavy sigh pushed from his body.

"Or not enough," he tittered.

The hair on my arms lifted, standing straight up at the sound of his voice. I lost the silent battle inside my head. Involuntarily, I twisted my neck, finding him hunched over the bar.

Defeated.

Drunken.

And, handsome.

No words were exchanged as our eyes met. His through a pair of dark shades. Mine through a lustful haze.

God doesn't make them like him anymore.

I guzzled the champagne in my flute and reached for the bottle. The fizzing liquid filled my glass again.

"I'm no cop," he revealed, facing forward.

Losing his gaze felt too much like torture to admit. Still, I retrieved my pride and did the same.

"That's usually the first thing a cop says."

I bit the inside of my bottom lip, unsure how to feel about the displacement of my emotions.

Time to go home, Royce.

I removed the envelope holding the hotel's key card from my purse and placed it on the bartop. Slowly, I slid it in the stranger's direction.

"Sleep it off."

Without another word, I emptied the glass of champagne I'd just poured and stood. The parts of my dress that had hiked as I sat flowed down my legs, grazing my skin and forcing small bumps to rise.

Click.

Clack.

Click.

Clack.

His eyes burned holes in my back. Still, I continued out of *Bar Balgaria*. My head tipped back a bit. My nose pierced the air. My shoulders squared. My spine was as straight as a stripper's pole.

He's the law. I surmised. *It doesn't matter which department or which field. Go home.*

We'd been there and every Childers and Domino had felt the consequences of Teddy's happiness. It looked so damn good on him, but it had cost us all.

Click.

Clack.

I floated across the open floor. His scent lingered.

So did his depth. There was so much more to the lone wolf at the bar. And, as a person with a fetish for digging, probing, and discovering new information about situations and people, it was hard to leave him at the bar without asking the questions that would sooth my natural desire to be knowledgeable.

"Uh hm." I cleared my throat as I swallowed the unspoken words.

The line didn't interest me the second time either. I stepped up to the desk where a guest was waiting to be checked in. The long, slim, and chocolate-colored stiletto nails tapped against the counter.

The young lady who'd taken my bag paused momentarily, peering in my direction. Nervously, she smiled back at the man in front of her. She was unsure if she should continue serving him or tend to me. I made her choice an easy one.

"Sir–"

My attention departed. My line of vision weaved through the hotel guests in search of the source of the small commotion that others were anticipating. It wasn't long before I spotted it.

Of course.

I glided across the lobby, nearing the bar, again. Just as the hooded stranger stumbled forward, I looped my arm underneath his and held him upright.

"Sir, we're going to have to as–"

"He's fine," I exclaimed, squaring my shoulders and pulling my lips apart with a smile.

I patted his chest, sure to stand him upright.

"Hmm? You're fine, right?"

An exaggerated nod confirmed my claims.

"You two have a great night."

"You do the same, sir."

The fragile, easy target went about his way as I started toward the elevator with the handsome stranger on my arm. I pressed the button upon arrival. It opened instantly, relieving us both.

Inside, he retreated to the far left corner. I took the right. Starting from his shoes, I analyzed his frame. Inch by inch.

Six three. Four, maybe.

Two fifty. Two sixty. Two fifty, surely.

Single-parent household.

A product of poverty.

Hungry for change.

Secrets.

Skeletons.

Regrets.

Revolver.

He's a Revolver man.

I kissed the skin of my teeth as a chuckle rolled off my tongue.

The clearing of his throat silenced me. I rolled my inner lip through my teeth, waiting for words to follow. There were none.

Ping.

He gathered himself as best he could and stumbled off the elevator. I was close behind. Even in his drunken haze, he was still glorious. His legs were slightly bowed.

His frame wasn't thin nor thick. It was perfect. He wasn't too tall, but he definitely wasn't short.

He's capable of making long, Black babies.

I closed my eyes as I reached the hotel room.

Many cops are.

"Right here."

I pushed the door open after gaining access. His legs finally stopped moving and backtracked after realizing he had gone too far. I held the door and my breath as I waited for him to pass me. And, once he did, I still didn't let it go.

Quietly, I closed the door behind me. His silence was as peaceful as it was agonizing. Drunks were loose at the lips. He hadn't said a word.

I deepened my presence in the room, finding him sprawled out on the bed. He'd gotten rid of his shades, but the hoodie was still tied around his neck. His focus was upward. His eyes were fixated on the ceiling.

Slowly, I blinked, hoping to erase his aesthetics from my memory. He would be a *pretty* big problem for all I loved. Every law enforcement was… no matter the division.

"Check out is at twelve. Pull yourself together by then. Maybe your spectator will have decided to call it quits."

I didn't wait for a response. I knew there wouldn't be one. And, I had shit to do. Lusting over a piece of pork that feasted on donuts and was fueled by coffee wasn't going to get it done.

As my hand touched the cold metal, a deep, uneven baritone stopped me in my tracks.

"Thank you."

Simple.

Straight to the fucking point.

He didn't use more words than necessary and I didn't plan to waste more seconds than necessary. This time, I didn't bother looking back or acknowledging him. I pulled myself up by the spine and raced to the opposite side of the door.

Once there, I pinned my back against the wood and closed my eyes. I swallowed warm saliva. As it slid down my throat, I tipped my chin upward. By the time it reached my belly, I was on the elevator, again, forgetting the existence of the hooded man.

As best I could, at least.

With my eyes trained on the hotel receptionist, I neared the front desk. The bottom of my black bag collided with the countertop. Wordlessly, I retrieved it, turned, and beelined for the door. Too much of my time had been spent in *The Balgaria*. It was never my intention to overstay.

I removed the valet ticket from the side of the bag as I exited. The midnight breeze welcomed me with a whistle. It kissed my cheeks and patted the tip of my nose.

"Good evening, ma'am. Your car?"

I nodded, extending my hand. I'd return to the loft another day to retrieve my other set of wheels.

Tonight, I'd be in the set that got me to *The Balgaria* hours before my date.

"Right there."

The SUV hadn't moved much. It was nestled between a navy *Phantom* and a white *Maybach*.

"One second."

"There's no need. Keys, please."

My patience was thin and my bedroom was beckoning for me.

"Are you su–"

"Keys."

"Sure. Sure thing."

I observed as the young, vibrant valet attendant opened the small cabinet full of keys. He retrieved those linked to the ticket in his hand. As he placed them in my hand, one foot was already in front of the other.

I pounded the pavement, making my way toward my vehicle. Confliction carried me all the way. I pressed the proper button on the fob to unlock the doors. Before I could grab the handle of the rear driver's door, the attendant snatched it open.

He slid the bag from my hands and placed it on the backseat. I slid into the driver's seat and started the engine. My reflection in the visor mirror was interrupted by the tumbling of the bill it once held. I caught it just before it fell into my lap.

"Thank you."

The young man accepted the one hundred dollar bill with a nod of his head.

"Thank you, ma'am. Goodnight. Drive safely."

He shut the door, closing me inside with my thoughts. I pulled the seatbelt over my body and stuffed the buckle into the connector. Everything behind me blurred as my wheels began turning. Nothing more mattered than getting home… *safely.*

THE **GREY**LIST

Phase three.

I watched from across the bar as Odessa's body turned in every direction as she attempted to locate me. After satisfaction soothed me, I stood on my feet and headed toward her. Still, she was clueless, unaware of her surroundings.

Reddened, puffy eyes met me just inches away from her body. They swelled with surprise as her hand went over her mouth.

"Oh God, you scared me."

"This way."

She scurried behind me, attempting to keep up. Her five foot frame was no match for my six foot frame. She was falling behind drastically. I took my seat and waited for her. Breathlessly, she slid in across from me.

In her hand was a brown envelope. I watched as she slid it in my direction. I did the same with the file in my possession.

"Is this it? Is this everything?"

"It's never everything. But, it's enough."

"You told me—"

"I don't care what I told you. You have the images. There are no copies. You won't get everything."

"There's more?"

Ignoring the question, I slid the folded papers from the envelope. The four numbers on the first sheet were enough to save Odessa's husband's life. Phase four was next and my involvement would cease if we made it to that point.

Rhea's request would be overturned just before the clock struck twelve on the final night of August. Teddy would handle it from there. And, Range would be left to clean the mess he made. It was simple. And that's how we preferred it. Unfortunately, we respected our mother's wishes.

No bloodshed during my birthday month.

"Thank you."

I sipped from the glass of wine. It was my third and it was as lovely as the first. Once the glass hit the table again, I leaned forward and released a steady breath. I'd seen Odessa's kind far too many times than I wished.

Pretty.

Innocent.

Gullible.

Untrained.

Hopeful.

Loyal.

All she wanted in return was to be loved and cared for. Those desires ran deep. Too deep. Consuming her identity and turning her into a magnet for men like Derrick.

Narcissist.

Cheaters.

Hypocrites.

Misogynists.

An unpleasant human with enough money to help the helpless and hopeless forget just how unkind he was.

His financial firm was a huge asset to the triad. However, his business was no longer wanted. He was becoming a liability. *Sloppy. Loud. And, again, very unpleasant.*

The retrieval of his ledger was detrimental to the success of our departure. He held too many of our coins to end his life. Therapy required bloodshed. Even if it didn't start that way, it would end that way. It always did.

The contacts, codes, and passwords Odessa had taken from his computers would allow us to operate at his capacity without his help while simultaneously funneling our money through the systems he created so that every dollar was washed clean and stored in more secure accounts that he didn't have access to.

"You're far too pretty to be so fucking stupid, babe. Tighten up. In that folder is the best divorce attorney in all of Huffington. They owe us a favor. Use the contact. Take everything."

Tearfully, she shook her head.

"He's worked so hard for everything he has."

"And your stupidity has helped him build every brick he's used to get to where he is now. Take it all, Odessa. You deserve it."

"I–"

"I've read your medical records. I don't want to hear what he's trained you to believe. Whatever beliefs he pounded into your skull has to be dismantled. Right now. Right here. This is your opportunity to run. And, run far."

Quietly, she stared at me, eyes tearful and heart heavy. Her nostrils widened as she tried not to release the tears in her eyes.

"He's all I know."

"You have to become all you know. For you– for the children–"

"He'll just find me. He always finds me."

"The month is drawing to a close. I can be certain he won't find you. Eve–"

"No. Please."

Sucking my teeth, I tilted my head.

"I don't mean it that way," she clarified. "I just want him alive. If I make it out of this marriage, I want him alive to see it. To feel it. To feel my absence."

I nodded. "Understood."

"I'll call the attorney."

"And, if they can't get you what you need from him, I will handle it."

"I don't understand. I thought we–"

"Everything that was once his will become yours, down to the pennies."

"You could do that?"

"I can do anything, Odessa."

I stood up, placing two one hundred dollar bills on the table. Before taking off, I stopped beside the booth Odessa had slid into.

"The moment you start believing it, you can, too."

My exit was as swift as my entry. However, my progress took a direct hit as I made it on the other side of the doors. The scent of the beautifully aging woman stopped me in my tracks. I paused, trying to grasp its origins.

Long gray hair flowed down her back. She was swimming in a powdery blue dress. The wrinkle lines near her eyes revealed a lengthy life of leisure. She was stunning. Her caramel skin was glowing.

"You ready?"

"Yes, honey."

The diamonds that lined her husband's wedding band were evidence of their privilege. They weren't facing financial annihilation. Their money was old and long. So were his legs.

Just like Richie.

And Rhea.

I was punched in the heart. The blow forced me to place a hand on my chest, attempting to rub away the soreness. There was hardly any use. It didn't subside.

Not when I started my engine.

Not when I made it to the expressway.

Not when I pulled into the garage of my home.

Not when I sent the text canceling the lunch date with Range.

Not when I pulled the curtains and pretended the sun wasn't beaming out.

Not when I undressed and flung my body on the bed and wrapped my sadness in my comforter.

THE GREYLIST

Bzzzt.

Bzzzt.

Bzzzt.

I patted the bed, feeling for my cell. It had been silenced. However, the vibrations meant that the person trying to reach me had repeated their calls enough times to get through to me. I pushed the eye mask up onto my forehead once it was located.

Mindlessly, I swiped the screen. Blurriness wouldn't allow me to make out the name, so I didn't bother trying.

"Yes?"

"Good evening, Royce."

My curled lips matched the smile of my heart as I slid up in the bed. Rubbing my eyes, I cleared my line of vision. Nothing and everything made sense at once. The soreness in my chest subsided finally. It bloomed with new breath and didn't pain me as I exhaled.

"Mercer."

"I woke you, huh?"

"Yes. What time is it?"

"Seven, baby."

"Gosh. Your call was right on time."

"Long nap?"

"Too long," I yawned.

Silence trailed my revelation. I waited for Mercer to speak again. My heart thudded against the nippy air of my bedroom as I anticipated what was next to fall from his lips.

"I need your help."

"You have it."

"A favor–" he breathed out.

"I'm listening."

"It's in Berkeley."

"Interesting."

"When should I expect you?"

I sighed, considering my responsibilities to the triad. My responsibilities to Teddy.

"I'm handling things," I admitted, "But I will see you soon."

"Royc–"

"Forty-eight hours, Mercer."

"Thank you."

"Don't. Kiss the babies and make room in their closets for me. Their aunt has a tab to run."

"I will, but keep your money in your account. They have far too much already."

"I wasn't asking."

Chuckling, Mercer quieted briefly. My heart ached for him. For them. The things they'd lost at such young ages were etched in their identity. It didn't matter how many years got in between them and that tragic day, I could still hear the pain of it in their voices.

"Goodnight Royce."

"Goo–"

The line died. I pressed the phone against my chest and released a shaky breath. The love I held in there for Mercer, Malachi, Makai, and Milo was immeasurable. Visiting Berkeley would be my pleasure.

Clink.

The sound of glass kissing startled me. I braced myself for impact while simultaneously gripping the Glock underneath my pillow. In the darkness, I aimed the pistol toward the sound of movement. Though stalled, my memory was impeccable. But, still, I halted. Hesitation stalled my trigger finger.

My nostrils bloomed. A familiar fragrance gripped me by the throat. Security. Comfort. Warmth. It surrounded me, promising one thing.

You're safe.

"Shoot!" Teddy demanded.

I lowered my gun. Complying wasn't in my interest. Neither was possibly harming him. Or worse, ending his life. I couldn't. I wouldn't. It was a chance I just wasn't able to take.

"Teddy."

"You're emotional."

"I'm lonely," I groaned, sliding my gun underneath my pillow case.

I slid from the silk sheets. Though my brother had

changed my diapers, I wasn't a kid anymore. He didn't care to see me unclothed or in my under garments. It was one of the reasons he didn't mind the darkness. The other was because it resonated with him.

Everything about Teddy was dark.

His humor.

His thoughts.

His mental state.

His eyes.

His skin.

His heart.

I slipped into the robe hanging from the edge of my bed. I hadn't put it there. But, I had an idea who had. He always did. Feeling for it wasn't necessary. I could count on it. I could count on him. While unpredictable to most, he was the most predictable to the ones he loved. He was the most consistent piece of our worlds.

"Berkeley will be good for you."

"Some dick and a decent suitor would be, too," I confessed, making my way toward my side table.

I turned on the lamp, slightly illuminating the six hundred square foot bedroom with a golden glow. The sight of Chemistry was wavering. I tightened my robe as I headed in his direction.

Upon reaching him, he extended his hand. I accepted the wine glass, knowing that his offer was for celebratory purposes. He picked up the glass he'd poured himself.

Good job.

Well done.

Thank you.

They wouldn't fall from his lips, but I knew how much he meant each. His presence and the risk of his freedom was his way of saying everything without saying anything.

I sipped from the glass after a swirl and sniff. Chemistry did the same.

"I'm assuming you already have the envelope."

He nodded, his chin flattening and his bottom lip pulling upward. I closed my eyes, accepting my fate. He would be a figment of my imagination in the next few minutes. He'd always come but he'd never stay. That part of our lives were over.

"I'm listening."

I opened my eyes and tilted my head. A snigger crept between my teeth as I rolled my eyes.

"Are you?"

"Always. You aren't ready for me to leave, so I'm listening."

"I never said that."

"You didn't have to. I heard your heart—"

"Because you're listening."

"Always, baby."

"It's nothing, Teddy."

His eyes never left mine. Silently, he waited for me to spill. I hated his ability to make me do so. He was privy to my darkest secrets. Things I wouldn't tell a soul, not even the women I shared blood with, Teddy knew.

I sucked in a healthy stream of air and then let it out

slowly. The thought of facing him as my confessions rolled off my tongue was agonizing, so I turned on the tips of my toes and headed in the other direction. Absentmindedly, I began pacing my bedroom.

"I despise men."

I swallowed back more wine as the truth revealed itself to me and Teddy simultaneously.

"I've been trying to avoid saying that, but it feels so good to finally let that out."

"There's not much you don't despise, Royce."

"True. True. But, men are at the top of that list."

"Mm."

"But–"

I exhaled.

"I'm beginning to despise being lonely as much. I'm getting older. I don't like having the entire bed to myself. Or the entire closet. Or the entire bathroom. I want someone to take up space with. Someone to comfort my emotions. Understand my morals and feelings and how much I truly despise. Someone who keeps choosing me every day no matter how out of touch with reality or insufferable I am."

"You're not insufferable."

"Because we're so much of the same. All of us. But, to the average person, Chem, we're insufferable."

"Your husband won't be an average person, baby. We don't fall in love with that kind. We don't run in the same circles as them. Walk the same paths. Head in the same directions. Dine at the same restaurants. Shop at the same stores. Catch the same flights. Vacation on the same beaches. Know the same people. Have the same resources."

His accuracy forced a nod from me.

"You're right."

"So, don't worry yourself with that part of it all. Just like you have shit with you… your person will have shit with them. Our kind comes with all kinds of luggage. Just make sure you don't hate them in a week."

"I probably will."

"Egypt hates me sometimes. It's the fact that her love runs deeper than any other feeling she's ever experienced that keeps me around. That's what matters. That's what saves me."

"She belongs to you and knows that any man after you would have hell. That's what saves you."

"That man would be *in* hell the first time he looked at Egypt, baby."

"Exactly." I chuckled.

While Teddy didn't share a laugh, his face lit up with a smile. That was more than enough for me. That look on his handsome face healed a bit more of me. Parts of me that were hurting somehow vanished altogether. Just for a moment. Just for a second.

"I want love," I exclaimed. "That kind of love. It doesn't have to be fairytale. Perfect. Or, even gentle. I'm no gentlewoman. It just needs to be real. And consistent. And unpredictably predictable. And true. And honest."

"As it will be."

"When?" I scoffed, taking another sip.

"When you're ready."

Teddy stood on his feet, breaking my heart into pieces. Everything he'd fixed he'd broken again. I released an exaggerated sigh.

"Don't give me that look, Royce."

He sat down his glass and obliterated the space between us. His hand was around my head in an instant. His lips were on my forehead, bidding me farewell. A single blink and he'd shifted positions again. His body was no longer in front of mine. My head was no longer in his hands.

"Turn away."

Nothing had changed. When it came to Teddy, they hardly ever did. I turned my back and closed my eyes. With my heart, I listened for his footsteps. With each second they grew more faint and my heartbeat grew louder.

Just like when I was a little girl.

I couldn't stand to see him leave then. I couldn't stand to see him leave now. I swiped the lone tear from my right eye and then lifted my head.

Chin up. His words stuck with me. *I can't see that pretty face when it's down.*

"In every lifetime, Royce," Chem tossed over his shoulder.

"Wait for me. I'll find you," I called out to him, reminding him of the promise I'd made to him.

I didn't hear the door close.

I didn't hear an engine start.

I didn't hear tires on the pavement.

Chemistry's presence had always been the eye. His absence had always been the storm.

I placed the glass up to my lips again. The heaviness returned as I slipped slowly. I was feeling every fucking thing. Past. Present. Future.

"Berkeley," I whispered. "Berkeley doesn't sound too bad right now."

I ran down the mental checklist of things that I needed to handle.

"Twenty-four," I concluded. "I'll see you in twenty-four hours, Mercer."

And Makai, I remembered, rolling my eyes. The headache he'd caused had already began and my journey hadn't.

And Milo. I smiled.

And Malachi. My heart smiled.

to the girls who are afraid of the unknown
to the girls who need it as much as their next breath
to the girls who can't function without it
to the girls it tried to swallow whole

—lose control.

GREY**HUFFINGTON**

ONE

Ishmael

MY FOREHEAD CREASED as weariness parted my eyelids. Darkness penetrated every inch of the open floorplan. The city's lights served as the secondary background, hardly glistening in the distance because of my level of elevation.

Slowly, I pulled my body from the breathable fabric of the cooling sheets. My feet touched the floor, sending a chill up my spine. I rotated my shoulders, working out the kinks that stillness resulted in each morning. Instinctively, I searched for the glowing numbers on the nightstand.

4:24a.

I shuffled my feet, moving them from one side to

the other, until I located the black slides used to transport me from one part of my condominium to the other. The idea of bare feet on the floor was repulsive.

Bzzzt.

Bzzzt.

Just as I slid into the shoes, my cell vibrated. I peered at the nightstand. Uncertainty pumped my heart three miles a minute.

Nothing good ever came from a call at this hour. Not even pussy.

I pushed out a nervous breath as I leaned forward and wrapped my hands around my cell. My mother's call was one I dreaded in the wee hours. With Indigo still knee deep in the trenches, I loathed the day I'd hear my mother cry on the line while trying to explain how gruesome it was seeing his brain matter on the pavement.

Even the thought of someone bringing harm to the boy I'd helped raise into a man was gutting. I mourned my career whenever it crossed my mind. Because, Berkeley would bleed. And, Berkeley would bleed uncontrollably. My freedom would be revoked and the light of day would hardly see me.

Unknown.

I rubbed my eyes, taking another look at the screen. Nothing changed. Unknown was still planted there for me to see. For me to acknowledge. For me to wonder.

I decided not to do either and silenced the call instead. My legs stretched as my arms reached for the ceiling. I was up on my feet and headed for my think tank. Sleep wouldn't find me again. Not any time soon, anyway.

My feet spread shoulder width apart. My right hand leaned against the metal connecting the glass of my floor to ceiling windows. My left hand tugged at the hair on my chin. Deep thought forced me to stare aimlessly out into the darkness.

Berkeley's skyline was impeccable, but all a blur. Most times it was when I stood in this very same spot at an ungodly hour like this one. My alarm was set for five thirty. Though only about sixty minutes away, it wasn't four in the fucking morning.

My chest swelled with disappointment. The time of the morning was a distraction. It was something to blame other than myself for the depths of my frustrations.

"Should've fucking known."

The whispers echoed in the silence. Their accuracy penetrated my bones with despondency.

Should've fucking known that ni–

I shook my head as the incomplete thought turned over and a new one began developing. The journey to Clarke was well-planned and poorly executed. Not on my part, but that didn't change the circumstances.

I flexed the muscles in my back as my muscles began to tighten. My heart was heavy but my head was heavier.

Because you knew better. I chastised.

I'd waited for the same man to show his face for thirty-two years. Thinking anything would change after a few phone calls and a text thread we visited every few weeks was reckless of me.

The lies.

One after the other, they tumbled from the lips of my sperm donor. But, still, I found myself questioning why. It was pointless. So was the deep yearning I suffered every time I accomplished something extreme or was on the verge of it. Somehow, I became vulnerable and open to receiving love from a man who never truly loved me before.

He put three sons in my mother's womb and left her to birth the last one alone. Indigo was the youngest of us all. Isaías was the second.

Neither of them were aware of my plans to visit Clarke. Neither one of them were aware of my plans to meet up with Pops. And, neither of them were aware that he didn't show. But, the last bit was more believable than the others.

Absence had become a character trait of his. Optimism was one of mine. Together they crashed and burned, leaving me in the dark hotel room of a stranger with a splitting headache and drunken thoughts.

A beautiful stranger. I recalled.

Much of the night was a blur, but she was far from it. Her presence was magnifying. It enhanced every part of me.

I wonder if she knows she has superpowers?

I shook the question from my thoughts and unlocked my phone. My erection gradually stiffened and threatened to squeeze through the fabric of my briefs.

Asia.

Her image flashed in my head, provoking me with nudity. She was the perfect candidate to deflate my dick. It didn't matter the time. With certainty, she'd come.

And cum.

And cum again.

Her complex was a few feet away. It was the sister property to *Morehouse*, the condominiums built for ownership. She lived in The Evermore, the apartments built for short or long term renting.

Bzzzt.

Bzzzt.

Asia slipped my mind as my forehead wrinkled with lines. Bemused by the unknown caller again, I stared at my vibrating phone.

Who the fuck is calling me at this hour?

I turned away from the window and headed for the kitchen. The lone glass on the counter was in my right hand within seconds. I pushed it against the dispenser. Cold, filtered water began to fill the glass.

"Yeah?" I answered.

The call was on the verge of rolling over to voice-mail. This time, I didn't plan to miss it.

"Good morning, Mr. Mayor."

I felt my eyebrows attempt to center on my face, pulling inward and downward. Not only was the prediction unprovoked, but the voice was unfamiliar.

Bullshit is to follow.

The polls wouldn't be open for nearly ninety days. I still had an uphill battle. And, nearly every rich, prestigious motherfucker in Berkeley was waiting on my demise. They wanted this boy from the projects to prove his worthiness of their mayoral vote in spite of my credentials and the work I'd put in to get my name on that ballot.

"I'm listening."

"I'm privy to your extra curricular activities." The caller chuckled. "Admittedly, I didn't think you were into that kind of thing but I don't blame you."

"Say what the fuck you mean or get the fuck off my line."

I was prepared to end the call as much as I was prepared to find out who was behind it. Within an hour of my discovery, they'd take their last breath. I was certain because it would be me who squeezed the life out of them.

Ish. Chill.

I reminded myself how far I'd come, but in the same breath I was reminded how far I'd go.

"No need to get your briefs in a bunch. I've paid for a little pussy, too. There's no judgement on my end, but I can't say that for the voters of Berk–"

"Pussy is the only meal I will never pay for. You have me confused."

I didn't wait for a response. I ended the call, hating that I'd answered it despite my apprehension. I tossed my cell on the counter and sniggered with disgust. The audacious claim made my chest inflate with air.

"Paying for pussy," I tittered, "*Nigga.*"

Bzzzt.

Bzzzt.

I snatched the phone from the counter, answering on the second ring.

"Speak."

"You'll find something interesting in your email. Goodbye, Mr. Mayor."

The dull, distorted voice riddled my conscience with uncertainty, confusion, and chaos. I ended the call for the second time. Only this time, I didn't place my cell on the counter, I opened my mail app, expecting an email from the person adamant to ruin a day that had barely gotten started.

Nothing.

I scrolled for thirty seconds. Nothing was out of the ordinary. I made a mental note to reply to Julie's email about my itinerary and wardrobe as I exited the application.

Water raced down my throat, attempting to cool the heat growing inside of me. Its efforts were in vain. I returned to the window seal. This time, Berkeley wasn't a blur. Everything was crystal clear.

Beep.

Beep.

· · ·

Beep.

Beep.

Beep.

Beep.

The five-thirty alarm sounded. Without urgency, I moved to shut it off. I lowered my body onto the bed as I realized how long I'd been standing.

Staring.

Stalking the sun's rising.

I ran a hand down my face, still trying to make sense of the call I'd received.

You'll find something interesting in your email. Those words rang out for the twelfth time in my head.

Loud.

Disturbing.

Thunderous.

Disruptive.

Loaded.

My nervous system remained tactless.

A prank call?

This didn't feel like a joke. Neither did it feel staged. Something was brewing. Something sinister had been planted in my path and before I stepped foot in my office this morning, I needed to find out what it was and who was behind it.

I returned to my email application, desperate to find something.

Nothing.

Frustrated, I tapped the tip of the cell against my temple.

You'll find something interesting in your email.

As I dissected each word, I sifted through my thoughts to discover their true meaning.

"Shit."

I slid the drawer of my nightstand open and pulled out the cell I hardly saw much of. It was considered my personal cell before I ended up with two more and a business phone. I tapped the screen, hoping God was on my side.

"Fuck."

As suspected, it was dead. I followed the white cord from the wall to my pillow. Once retrieved, I shoved it into the cell, hoping for a speedy recovery.

As the wait began, I pulled in a deep breath and then released it slowly. My fingertips massaged my temple as I planted my cheeks on my thumbs. I could feel a migraine approaching.

Again, I was up on my feet and in the kitchen within seconds. I twisted the cap of the meds and poured two in my hand. I recapped the bottle and tossed it back into the drawer it had come from.

Two pills entered my system with the help of cold water. I retreated to my bed. As the cushion attempted to comfort me, the Apple logo appeared on the black screen.

846200

It had been nearly a year since I'd typed in the code, but muscle memory kicked into overdrive. I bypassed the notifications that came in one after the other, storming the screen. I navigated the applications, landing on the one I was most interested in.

Fuck!

My heart stilled as I stared at the email I'd been alerted to. As I tapped the message, it restarted, beating erratically with each scroll of my finger.

It was her.

*The **perfect** stranger.*

*The **pretty** stranger.*

In front of my car.

Next to me on the driver's side.

Taking the wheel.

Beside me in the car at The Balgaria.

At Bar Balgaria.

Arm looped through mine in the lobby.

At the elevator.

In the hallway.

At the hotel door.

Entering the room.

Leaving the room.

I stiffened in my briefs at the sight of her. Since she'd entered my line of vision, she hadn't left my mind. Thoughts of her felt baseless staring at the images.

Her long legs journeyed for miles, finally reaching her round ass.

She was lean, but it was obvious she hadn't missed a meal.

Just like everything else in her life, food was plentiful.

She had everything. Everything she needed.

I zoomed in on the image. My pupils focused on her hand.

Except a ring.

A woman of her caliber deserved unwavering support, security, and a soft place to land when the world felt like too much.

I scrolled until the images ended. A heavy sigh landed between my cell and I. Disappointment followed the threads extinction. I pulled a hand down the back of my neck, selfishly wishing there were more.

Of her.

"Ish," I chastised, bringing myself back to the matter at hand.

And, it wasn't her. Not exactly.

"You should be more careful. I've found the same set of eyes on you since I arrived."

Her words resurfaced. While the night was a total blur, she wasn't. In the back of my head, she'd held a spot and she was crystal clear.

My fingers wrapped around my main cell. Instantly, it vibrated in my hand.

Unknown.

"What is it that you want?"

"Terminate your campaign or your opponent will receive this shiny email I have."

Their words were like blades across the belly.

"Not a fucking option."

"You're not the one calling the shots here."

"Then why the fuck are you on my line?"

Silence swept over the line. The caller's steady breaths are the only thing left to be heard.

"Name your price."

"I–"

"Price or I'm hanging this phone up. I will not be responsible for what happens to you after my offer expires."

Malice laced my words. As much as I wanted to regret them, I didn't. I wasn't too far removed from the same streets Indigo was still running. We were one in the same at many points of our lives. However, I cleaned up my act and pledged to be a part of the change I wanted to see happen.

"Is that a threat, Mr. Mayor."

"It is whatever you want it to be."

"2.5 million."

"Don't hold your breath, motherfucker."

Venom spewed from my lips as I ended the call. There was nothing left to be said. That $2.5 million would still be in my account when this was all said and done. Whether or not the bitch on the other end of the line still had breath in his body, I couldn't be certain of.

The phone rang again. I didn't hesitate to answer.

"Speak, bitch."

"Twenty four hours to decide or–"

Chuckling, I asked, "Or what?"

I wasn't making light of the situation. Neither did I

think it was humorous. I stood on my feet and began pacing the floor, hoping the fire from my body didn't burn a hole in my mattress and the expensive ass sheets covering it.

"Your friend and you– *all over the news.* And, you can kiss that office goodbye."

My jawline grew rigid as I drew in a slow, steady breath. Every muscle in my body tightened as I halted. Nostrils flared, I pulled a hand over my mouth.

"We should me–" I paused, "We should meet and talk about this face to face. Man to man. You want the money and I want every image in your camera ro– matter of fact, I want the entire fucking camera."

Taking a page from my book, the caller chuckled. His laughter awakened parts of me I promised to allow rest.

"Just like I know your future... I'm privy to your past. I'm not that stupid."

"*Gots* to be. You're on my fucking line."

My eyes bulged as my head nodded. He was contradicting himself.

You should fucking know better.

"Twenty-four hours, Mr. Mayor."

I squeezed the cell in my hand. The chunk of titanium didn't bend or break.

"Fuck!

The call ended, leaving me in the middle of my floor, steam emitting from my nose and ears. My teeth pressed into each other. The sun's light did nothing to cure the darkness inside of me.

I pressed forward, bypassing the living room, the guest bedroom, the third restroom, and my office. I took the steps of my condominium to the first level. I went through the main kitchen, pulling the pantry door open. Behind the glass jar of granola, I pushed aside the small cut out to reveal the keypad.

842212.

Double doors parted the pantry in two. I step inside of the bunker. Revolvers of all kind welcomed me into the room. I wasn't in search of them. Not yet, anyway.

On the desk, near the computers, I retrieved the flip phone. Beside it were six SIM cards, all unused but prepared for use. I slipped one into the back and laid the battery on top. Once the cover was back on, I powered the cell on.

Numbers. Numbers. Numbers.

One glance at a number...

One recital...

And, I'd never forget it.

Once in my head, I knew it backward and forward and then backward again. A number I knew by heart rolled off my fingertips. I pressed the phone to my ear and waited for the line to connect.

"Speak to me."

Indigo answered on the first ring. I didn't expect anything less. A soldier by default, there wasn't a second of the day he wasn't ready. Willing. Able.

I cleared my throat, trying to suppress the tension I was feeling.

"Got a call this morning."

"Who I need to shoot? My trigger finger been itching all fucking night."

"If I knew, I would be scratching my own finger."

"A coward, huh?"

"At his finest."

"What he talking about?"

"Pictures. Pictures that insinuate something that didn't happen."

"Like?"

"I was paying for pussy."

"Wrong nigga."

"Wrong fucking nigga. But, that doesn't matter. The pictures say otherwise."

"Understood."

"Pictures of me picking up something I'd double take on even the darkest night out and I can't see shit. *I'ma see her.* I was fucking around in Clarke on some other shit," I confessed, "Lost my way and needed directions. Instead of giving them to me, she hops in my ride and makes me get on the passenger side. We were both headed to the same spot."

"And this nig–"

"Picture after picture," I confirmed, knowing exactly where he was going.

"Say less. I'll handle it."

"If it were that simple I wouldn't be calling you, Indie. I'd have someone at the office handle it. But, this isn't that type of–" I struggled with my words. It was uncharacteristic of me, but here I was.

The last thing I wanted was that perfect stranger's

images plastered over the news stations, insinuating something that wasn't remotely close to the truth. She didn't deserve that type of scrutiny. Slander. Judgement. She deserved to be showered with compliments. Designer threads. Handbags. Jewelry. And, as many martinis as her system could handle.

"Not me, Ish. I know somebody that knows somebody."

"I need that somebody in front of me within twenty-four hours."

"I'll see you at your office, bro," he confirmed.

"My office? Indie, thi–"

"They're legit. Legal. Whatever the fuck you good niggas call it."

"Good niggas?"

"The kind the law ain't looking for."

"They aren't looking for you either."

"Not right now. Not as long as I stay out of their way. But, maybe they will be if I bump into whoever the fuck was on the other end of that call."

"We're not taking that route."

I massaged my forehead.

"I need to get my day started. Goodbye, Indie."

"Stay ready."

"Ready right now."

I closed the phone and flipped it over. I removed the battery and then the SIM card. It cracked under the pressure of my fingers. I tossed it into the graveyard with the rest of the broken cards and placed the phone back in its rightful position.

TWO

Royce

BEEP.

Beep.

The metal detector sounded. I gnawed on the inside of my bottom lip as I watched the eyes of the resting security guard reach me. My legs didn't stop moving. I continued ahead. In a flash, he was standing in front of me, blocking my path.

"Excuse me, ma'am. I'm going to have to pat you down."

"That won't be necessary."

"The detector alerted me of–"

Quietly, I spread my arms. My blazer shortened at my wrists as they rose. The guards' unkempt fingers patted down them simultaneously. My abdomen was next in the search, followed by my waistline.

His brows furrowed as he discovered the Glock on my hip. He paused momentarily before continuing.

Down my back.

Down my thighs.

"Oh," he exclaimed as his hand made contact with the one strapped to my leg, underneath the flowy skirt that stopped at my ankles.

He'd found the gold he was searching for in the mine. Our eyes met as his mouth slackened with astonishment. Bemused, he tried conjuring words. They, too, weren't necessary.

You've met the twins.

I tilted my head leftward.

"Ma'am, you can't br–"

"They go *wherever* I go."

"You ca–"

"Jerald," I said, stepping deeper into his personal space and straightening the collar of his shirt. "Don't lose your life for a job that barely pays you enough to take care of your family. You're barely surviving on two incomes at the moment."

I placed a hand on his right cheek.

"Don't play savior today or you won't make it home to your wife. You'll be forced to watch her struggle off one income from the grave and there won't be a thing you can do about it."

He swallowed the lump in his throat.

"I'm a girl's girl through and through, but before

that, Jerald… I'm *my* girl. So, home to your wife or attempt to retrieve two of the three firearms on my person?"

Slowly, Jerald stepped backward. He returned to his seat with his eyes still planted firmly on me.

"Have a nice day, ma'am."

"I will."

With squared shoulders and an elevated chin, I strutted across the lobby of the high-rise complex. It was brimming with businesses of all kinds. I could still feel Jerald's eyes on me as I pivoted, turning the corner where the elevators were.

I stilled at the wondrous sight before me. My cheeks swelled as my lips spread across my face. My heart shattered and recovered simultaneously.

"Royce–"

Dressed in all black, Mercer held open the elevator door.

"This way."

I stepped on, greeting him in the process.

"Well… hello, sir."

Though his smile was hard to come by, I was rewarded almost instantly.

"What's up, sis? How was the journey?"

"Pleasant. Swift."

"I was expecting to get downstairs before you made it. You're early."

"I'm on time, Mercer. Don't insult me."

With a nod, he agreed.

"Thanks for coming on such short notice. A partner

of mine hit me up yesterday morning. I lost track of time. It had been on my mind to call you all day but– life. And kids and shit."

"No need to explain. I'm here. I'm sure whatever this is won't take too long. I'll be back on a flight to Clarke in a few hours. I can resolve this virtually. All I need is a little Wi-Fi and–"

"A lot of wine." Mercer sighed.

"Who's paying for that?"

"Me if you want, but I'm sure their account can handle it."

Smiling, I folded my hands in front of me. I readjusted my briefcase for the maximum level of comfort. Mercer reached for it. I stepped to the side, dodging his hand.

"How is the family?"

"I have to get back to them. I wanted to make introductions."

"I'm a big girl," I assured him.

"I'm aware, but that doesn't change anything, Royce. I'm not here because I think otherwise. I'm here because there's no other place for me to be right now. Pretty can hold it down for a few."

"How is she?"

"Incredible. Brilliant. Steady. Glowing. Happy. In her element. She's so amazing. I– I couldn't ask for anyone better."

The depth in his tone emphasized the depths of his love for the mother of his children. I smiled inside, knowing he was head over heels and Vallei couldn't have asked for anyone better either. The two were created for each other.

"And you?"

"I'm as good as I'ma get."

"So am I, Mercer. And, I can tell by the void in your eyes you want to be wrapped in newborn bliss. Go. I'll be fine."

Quietly, he leaned against the steel of the elevator. A hand covered his mouth before tugging at the hair on his face. He was retreating. Returning to himself. His reserved self. His quiet self. His mental imbalances were landing. And sticking. And submerging him in their uncertainty. I couldn't let him stray. Not even for a second.

I stepped in front of him, handing him my briefcase. A snicker crept from my lungs, up my throat, and out of my mouth. I eyed the handsome fella, still appalled by the resemblance to Teddy. Catherine's DNA ran deep.

"You miss me, don't you? That's why you aren't ready to leave."

His smile wrapped me in warmth like a blanket by the fireplace on a winter night. It quickly transformed into the most gratifying sound I'd heard all day.

His laughter.

His head lifted and fell. His confession was silent but I heard it loud and clear. So did my heart. Instinctively, I wrapped my arms around his body. Unlike Chemistry, Milo, Makai, and Malachi, Mercer had meat on his bones.

My head rested on his chest.

"I've missed you, too."

His body stiffened. Affection was difficult for him. *For them*. Nearly all of them. They were men and life had hardened their shells. Naturally, the affection of a woman who wasn't their partner brought back memories they tried burying with the woman who created them.

Ping.

The elevator invited us to the thirty-fourth floor. I released Mercer. His chest deflated as his limbs loosened.

I was the first to step off. Mercer followed close behind. My spine straightened, extending my length. Mercer took the lead. Though I was conquering the distance between me and my destination, I didn't know where the hell it was.

Click. Clack.

A glass door pushed open, allowing Mercer and I to bypass the keypad that required a code.

"Good morning, ma'am. Welcome back, sir."

No words were shared. I followed Mercer through the office.

Grayson for Mayor.

Vote Ishmael Grayson.

Grayson for Greater.

Ishmael Grayson for Berkeley.

"Good morning."

"Morning!"

"Hello, sir. Ma'am."

"Morning."

As the greetings poured in, I took note of the variations of messages on the sign. It was clear that Ishmael Grayson was campaigning for the mayoral chair. And, my assistance was needed in his efforts to secure the spot.

It's as good as yours, I thought as excitement crept up my spine.

Consider it handled.

It was best he began packing up his current office in preparation to relocate. If he had Mercer's vote, then he had mine. The seat was already his. I knew it and so did the man in front of me.

We stalled at the door of the office closest to the end of the large suite. Eventually, both of our bodies halted. My nostrils widened with suspicion. A familiar scent pushed them apart.

Mercer's frame obstructed my vision, forcing me to step around him. As I collected myself, standing mere inches away from the brother I'd inherited through Chemistry, I searched for the source of my curiosity.

"Royce, Indie. Indie, Royce."

"Nice to meet you, Royce. I've heard good shit about you."

Immediately, I understood the man in denim with at least two hundred thousand dollars worth of jewelry on at nine o'clock in the morning was not running for mayor.

No.

Still, I accepted the hand he extended. He was easy

on the eyes. There wasn't a visible flaw. He had skin most women paid thousands for. Though seemingly mature, youth was evident in his eyes.

"A pleasure, Indie."

"Indigo. You can call me Indigo."

Though I was speaking to the man in front of me, it was the one with his hands shoved into his pockets staring out the floor to ceiling window that my eyes were trained on.

"This is my brother–" Indigo revealed, "Ishmael. Ishmael Grayson, the next mayor of Berkeley."

At the sound of his name, Ishmael turned on the heels of his loafers. The breath I didn't know I was holding tumbled from my body as the remainder in my lungs dissolved. My mouth dried completely. A fire began in my throat, consuming me within seconds. My fingertips became lava, melting the briefcase Mercer managed to return upon our entry.

There wasn't a hoodie or shades masking the beauty that plagued me for the last five days. It was untamed. Raw. Refreshing. Riveting. Far better than I'd imagined. It deemed me speechless. Rendered me breathless. And, dismantled my claims of being heartless.

I had a heart. But, I wasn't sure for how long. It was expanding in my chest by the second, threatening to explode. I'd be left with pieces. So many pieces. Too many pieces. And, a hole in my chest that would serve as a memorial for what that handsome stranger destroyed.

It's him. I internalized.

"It's her."

Ishmael wasn't looking at me. He was looking through me. His gaze penetrated me, searching for parts of me I'd tucked away because I hadn't stumbled upon anyone deserving of them.

"Yeah, the person I was telling you about," Indigo explained. "She's going to be handling th–"

"No–" Ishmael countered.

Ishmael. I let roam in my head. *Ishmael.*

The name was fitting.

Firstborn son. Promised to father a great nation with descendents spread across the desert. Preserved in the wilderness. Destined for greatness.

"God hears," I whispered, barely above a breath.

"He does," Ishmael replied.

Taken aback by his sudden closeness, I collected the oxygen he provided. He'd taken all I had. It was only right that he replenished me.

"You know her?" Indie asked.

Without taking his eyes off me, Ishmael unlocked the cell that appeared in his hand. He scrolled before handing it to Indigo. His brother's eyes swelled. They bounced between my face and the cell.

Baffled, I cleared my throat and dug deep for a suitable response.

"Oh damn," Indigo gasped.

"Would you like to fill me in on why I'm here or keep passing around a cel–"

Thoughts of his occupation claimed me. Inwardly, I found it amusing that I wasn't too far fetched.

Mayor.

Cop.

Same difference.

On the other side of the law, regardless. I could smell his political ties from a mile away. It wasn't pork but it was close enough.

"I received a call this morning. Someone *was* following me that night. And, unfortunately, they captured our entire night."

Mercer's movement caught my attention. With furrowed brows, he requested an explanation.

"Mr. Grayson," I began, witnessing the disappointment on Ishmael's face.

He wasn't fond of the name that rolled off my tongue.

"Was lost. I helped him find his way."

"And someone caught it all on camera, claiming I was paying for pussy."

Disgust replaced the disappointment on Ishmael's face.

"Untrue."

"But, could easily be assumed. You picked me up on the same block they're selling pussy by the pound in Clarke. At least twenty-four thousand dollars are spent on that very stroll every night. Thirty six on weekends."

"And you know this because?"

"There's not much I don't know about Clarke. Now, back to the call. Male or female?"

"Male."

"Figured."

"You saw him?"

"Possibly, but I doubt he was working alone. Could've been a partner."

"Maybe the cameras at The Bal–"

"Finding him doesn't make the evidence disappear. He could easily have everything scheduled and ready to go in the event of his death or imprisonment. I'm certain he's thought this through. We need him alive."

Ishmael nodded. So did Mercer. So did Indigo.

"Maybe you're right."

"I'm right," I stated as a matter of fact.

Ishmael began pacing. I made the mental note. He was unraveling at the seams. Weariness weighed him down, slowing his stride.

"How much is he asking for?"

"Two point five." His brother spoke up.

"Million?"

"Yes," Indigo responded.

"How much to make this go away?"

"Two point five," I demanded.

"Million?" Indigo asked.

Ishmael stopped in his tracks. Eyes trained on me, he watched as I nodded.

"We might as well pay him for the images," he reasoned.

I agreed, "Yeah. You should."

I turned on the balls of my feet. Mercer didn't hesitate to follow me. I didn't need his leadership. I remembered every corner we'd turned to get to the office we were in. Just as I crossed the threshold, the thunderous baritone I remembered so vividly made the hairs on the back of my neck stand at attention.

"Royce!"

My eyes grew in my skull. My heart imploded. My chest caved. Everything around me roared with silence. All that was left was the unsteady breaths of mine, each armed with jagged edges.

One.

Two.

Three.

Four.

Five.

"One second!" Ishmael yelled across the room.

His fragrance washed me ashore as his words attempted to submerge me in his limitless realm.

"Yes?" I inquired, turning to face him.

"I–"

"I'm not in the business of convincing anyone of anything, especially not my worth. I will never explain or justify my price. It is whatever I decide it is. You can pay or not pay. Either way, both sides of my silk pillow will stay cool and I won't lose a minute of sleep."

"Understood. I'm not questioning your worth, but can you please fill me in on why you chose that number after hearing that was the number we're working with on the other end?"

"Because, you can pay him the money and it become a total waste… because he's going to release the images anyway. Or, you can allow me to handle it. Make it go away completely."

He nodded.

"Next steps. What are the next steps?"

I slid the phone from his hand and searched for his banking application. Once locating it, I turned the phone toward him. His credentials were verified through face recognition. I confirmed the availability of the funds before sliding the phone back into his hand.

"The wire."

I opened my briefcase and handed him the slip of paper with my banking details.

"And, after that? I was given twenty-four hours. I'm past that deadline. He's going to releas–"

"Let him."

"Let him? Let him do what?"

"Release them."

With that, I headed out of his office again. This time, my exit was successful. Not because Mr. Grayson wanted it to be, but because he was too stunned to speak. To move. To demand more information. Or to cuss my Black ass out.

Click.

Clack.

My Prada pumps collided with the floor. Each step I took I regained a bit more of my power. Ishmael had stripped it all from me at once.

"Good day, ma'am. Sir."

Mercer trailed close behind. Still, he hadn't said a

word. He wouldn't. He knew me well enough to know that there was nothing to worry about. I'd handled enough for him. For Chem. For our family. His trust was unwavering.

We entered and exited the elevator quietly. Mercer began in my direction, but I stopped in my tracks.

"I'm fine. Go home to your baby girl. I will be around."

"Seems that way, huh?"

"Yes. I'll see you later. I love you."

"In all of them lifetimes," he responded, wrapping his arm around me.

He pulled back and broke contact. His truck was on the opposite side of the large parking lot. I observed until he disappeared behind the trees planted for shade.

The journey to my car was short. I was two rows away from the building's entrance. I stretched my arm to open my door, but my effort fell short.

Ishmael's presence was announced by his aroma. He confirmed it with the swatting of my hand. I turned to face him, pressing my back against my car.

Steady, Royce.

He was unearthing. I hadn't met a flaw of his yet.

"Yes, Mr. Grayson?"

His nostrils widened.

"Ishmael. My fucking name is Ishmael," he grunted.

"Can I help you?"

Unbothered by his discomfort, I waited for a response to my question.

"Are you insane?"

"I'm not following you here."

"Release the images? You want him to release the image? Your face will be planted all over the news. Every station from here to Clarke."

There.

My spine curled toward him. The root of his dilemma was revealed. It wasn't his race he was most interested in saving. It was me.

From the scrutiny.

The embarrassment.

The shame.

The lies.

I peered into the darkness that surrounded him.

My God he's gorgeous.

His skin was black like tar and smooth like a newborn's backside.

And troubled.

His hair was perfectly lined. His teeth were perfectly aligned.

"Never let someone feel like they can dangle something over your head that's absolutely nothing at all."

It was a double entendre.

"Royce…" He sighed.

"I would've made sure you didn't get in that car in your condition regardless. You don't owe me anything but the $2.5 million dollars I've requested as my retainer. I can handle a little press and being called a whore. I've been called worse… *I've been called a man.*"

For years, the agents working our case considered us a syndicate full of men. The thought was repulsive.

"I've said I'll handle it. Let me do my job."

"Right. Right."

"What phone has he been calling you on?"

He held up the one in his hand. I slid it from his fingers and threw it toward the ground. The collision caused irreparable damage. Ishmael watched in horror as it shattered.

"Consulting will begin once the money has been wired. Goodbye, Mr. Mayor."

I slid into my Lamborgini, leaving Ishmael standing with his breath stuck in his throat, darkness in his eyes, and worry lines across his forehead.

Ishmael

I SHUT the door of my office and closed the blinds. Fury and fascination were both fighting to consume me. Indie leaned against my desk with his face planted in my cell. I snatched it away from him, knowing exactly what he had his eyes on.

"I thought you said she would help!" I yelled, garnering his attention.

Shrugging, Indie stood straight like an arrow.

"Man, Mercer is as solid as they come. If that nigga says she's going to handle it, then she's going to handle that shit."

"Who is he anyway?"

"The nigga I did time with. The one with the res–"

"*The M?*"

"Yes. We went to his grand opening."

"And I've been back four times since. The steak is just– the shit is ridiculous."

"Me, too." Indie chuckled. "I'm in that motherfucker at least once a month with something bad to the fucking bone."

"I'm sure."

My loafers were pinned to the ground and lifted rapidly. Over and over. My hand pressed against my forehead.

"She destroyed the phone he's been contacting me on."

"Damn. Did you at least get the SIM out that bitch?"

"Yeah. Yeah. I got it."

"Hand it here. I'll put it in the one you're holding."

I handed Indigo both the SIM and the older cell. For now, it would have to work. I knew Royce wanted him to lose contact but so many more important calls came through that line. I didn't need to miss either of those.

"Make sure she gets her money," I breathed out. "Make sure it doesn't trace back to me."

"Say less."

"Fuck, she's high as hell. Charging me two poin–"

"You should look into her."

"Have you?"

A pain shot down my spine as I twisted my neck, planting my eyes on my brother.

"I did while you were downstairs."

His mouth knotted and his forehead slid backward, shortening his hairline.

"And?"

"Shiiiid–I'm happy that's all she charged us."

"I don't understand."

"The Chemist."

Indie's eyes grew bigger as he explained. I searched my memory but didn't have to dig far.

"*Chemistry Childers?* Most wanted man in all of Huffington?"

"Fucking right."

"Royce Childers. She and Mercer share a brother."

"That's why she's not afraid of being in the public eye," I whispered.

The wheels were turning. The facts were linking. The vague was becoming very fucking clear. Royce was no longer a beautiful blur.

"She doesn't give a fuck about what motherfuckers think of her. She wants a mess to be made so she can clean it up. That's what they do."

I continued pacing. Nearly every explanation I'd conjured was dismantled. Royce wasn't just impressive by the beauty standards. She was smart and resourceful. Wealthy and reserved. Tantalizing. Deemed untamable. Her type wasn't conquered or controlled.

They had the mental strength and capacity of an elephant. Their memory never failed them. Neither did their resources or capabilities. Their reach was beyond the comprehension of a law abiding, tax paying citizen. Just like me, they were above the law. In fact, the law didn't exist in our worlds. It was a nuisance.

I've been called far worse... I've been called a man.

My brother's chuckles startled me. I turned in his direction. A fist covered his mouth.

"What the hell you laughing at?"

"Nothing man." He shook his head, handing me the phone.

It rang immediately. I pressed the button on the side to silence it. I wasn't interested in taking any calls. Not at this moment. I'd return it as soon as Indigo told me what the fuck was so funny.

"Nah, nigga, what's funny?"

"You!"

"What about me?"

He shook his finger in my direction.

"I know that look, Ish. I know that fucking look," he sniggered.

"What look?"

Baffled, I lifted my shoulders and leaned in closer, dropping my head to the right as I waited for an explanation.

"I have that same look when I see something I can't go too much longer without having a piece of. I have that same goddamn look when I'm thinking about how I'm gon' take that shit down and nail it to the nearest mattress. And, if ain't naan around, then the nearest fucking couch, counter– *whatever, wherever* nigga."

"I'm more concerned with my luck," I lied, "What are the odds of the woman in the images being the woman who is supposed to help me wiggle my way out of this situation and secure the votes of Berkeley."

"You're going to be the mayor, Ish. Ain't no denying that. If you ask me, that's good luck. You have somebody on your side that will make sure you're in that seat November twelfth."

"At a hefty price."

"You act like you ain't got it to give."

I do and I want to give it to her. Just not for the work she's about to do. I want to give it to her because she asked. Because she's ready to start a consulting firm. Or because she wants to buy a small private plane. Or because she's depleted her savings. Or because what's mine is hers.

"I do and I will."

"That's the spirit, my boy," Indie howled, laying his arm across my back. "And, maybe when she finally lets you slide into her heavenly gates, it'll all feel worth it. That nigga wasn't too far off, my brother. You're about to pay for what might be the most expensive pussy in the world. Two point five."

He slapped his hand against my chest and rushed toward the door.

"Fuck you," I retorted, knowing that everything he released was accurate.

I had never paid for pussy but today, I'd be settling a debt on the most expensive piece I'd ever have the pleasure of tasting.

And, that motherfucker better fall right off the bone.

My cell chimed, beckoning for my attention.

"Is that a yes, Mr. Grayson?"

It had been twenty-four hours since hiring Royce. This was her first point of contact. I stared at the message, rereading it six times as I attempted to pull words from her brain that she hadn't placed in the text.

It was too simple.

Too formal.

Too cold.

Too straightforward.

Too meaningless.

A sigh sliced through the cold, brittle air.

Tomorrow.

The M.

7:00 PM.

Royce.

Three lines. Three numbers. Three punctuation marks. Fourteen letters. I tipped my head rightward, realizing how little effort was placed in the message. My chest tightened. The skin around at the corners of my eyes bunched as my fingers grew restless. I massaged my beard, hoping to bring solace after such a disruption to my nervous system.

Let it go, Ish.

While the lack of effort shouldn't have bothered me, it did. The entitlement I possessed for the woman who was no longer a stranger was on the rise and it had little to do with the money wired to her account. But, it had everything to do with her.

All of her.

"Mr. Grayson."

I was plagued with the unknown. I was weighed down to my seat like an anchored ship. My hands moistened around the cell as I read the message again.

And again.

Hoping more words magically appeared on the screen. Or her voice on the line.

"Mr. Grayson!" Matte was no longer across the room.

She was beside me with a hand on my shoulder, forcing me out of my head and back into reality.

"Mr. Grayson, is everything alright?"

"Uh– yeah. Yeah. Everything is fine."

"Is that a yes on your end?"

I didn't recall what the conversation was about. Neither did I recall what I was agreeing to. But, the smile on Matte's face assured me it was the right answer.

"Yes."

"Good. Good. Now, we just have to get these papers

filed and hope for the best. I have a great feeling about this."

"Wrapping this campaign up in less than two months. We're in the home stretch. No hiccups and we're all good. Keep doing what you're doing, Mr. Grayson, we're almost there," Cameron cheered.

Applauses from around the room rang out. I lifted a hand to settle my team down.

"Listen–" I blackened the screen of my cell and stood on my feet.

The broad smiles began to fade. Curiosity spiked the temperature in the room. I loosened my tie and unbuttoned the first button on my shirt.

"At any minute, a shit storm is coming our way. I've been contacted several times regarding images taken in an attempt to falsify their origins. A few days ago, I traveled to Clarke to catch up with someone from my past.

"I got lost and the GPS was of no use. I stopped to ask a young woman for directions and turns out we were headed to the same place. She took the wheel and got me to my destination safely. After my night ended at the bar of the hotel I was meeting this person at, I bumped into the young lady again.

"She realized I'd had one too many drinks and it probably wouldn't be a good idea to drive home in my condition. So, she was kind enough to make sure I got into one of those hotel beds safely. I didn't speak to her again after she left me there on the bed, fully clothed and intoxicated. Well, not until yesterday.

"That woman walked into my office. I'm sure you all seen her. She walked into my office prepared to handle the scandal that she happens to be the center of. I was sent a slew of images that misrepresents and undermines both of our characters. Her name is Royce. Royce Childers and you will be seeing a lot of her until this campaign ends."

"Mr. Gr– How do we know she's not the person behind the bla–" Matte asked.

"Because she's not."

"Okay, but what abou–" Cameron started.

"I am in no mood to say more on the matter at the moment. Just know that it is being handled. I need you to keep working hard. Eyes on your computer screens. We've got this."

I exited the conference room without another word. Upon entering my office, I closed the blinds. At one point I knew I had this election by the balls. In the last forty-eight hours my perspective had been shifted.

While I was still confident in my abilities to head Berkeley, I wasn't very confident in the people who were tasked with getting me to that point. The voters would be in an uproar the second those images released.

"FUCK," I shouted, slamming my palm against the desk.

Papers flew off the edges, landing on the floor. I had faith in Royce's resourcefulness, but it didn't change the fact that someone was willing to sabotage everything I worked hard for to obtain on a measly two million. Two million had touched my fingertips by the time I heard my mother's voice on my line for my twenty-second birthday.

Sixteen fucking years ago.

The money was insignificant. The principle, however, was abhorrent.

Unshakeable.

Repugnant.

My ringing cell did little to resuscitate my sanity. I answered without second thought.

"Speak," I barked into the phone, uninterested in exchanging words with anyone.

But her.

"Ishmael."

I removed the phone from my ear and held it in front of me. The human who'd gifted my mother with his sperm was on the line, adding more wood to the fire I was struggling to tame.

My limbs stiffened. I ground my teeth together, inhaling. I pushed out the oxygen I'd pulled in with hopes of releasing the tension in my body. I failed miserably.

"What the fuck do you want?"

"I–" he coughed out, "I was calling to apologize about the other night, Son. I took a tumbling down the steps at my apartments. I was headed to you. My neighbors found me on the ground the next morning. I can't remember a thing. I'm still in this here hospital.

"I'm sorry, Son. I was looking forward to seeing you. You know– catching up. I was thinking we could reschedule when I don't look like the stairs used me as their punching bag and my ribs have healed up a bit."

"Fuck you, your ribs, and your schedule."

I pressed the red button, still fuming. His absence was the reason I was in the predicament I was in. I didn't care to hear his apologies about continuing his tradition and possibly causing me the election.

My fingers massaged my temple. I closed my eyes, desperately needing to catch my breath. Settling felt impossible. My chest rose and fell as I took in and released deep, steady breaths.

Fuck.

I snatched the jacket of my suit from the back of my chair and headed for my office door. Without a word, I ambled through the suite.

"Mr. Grayson," Matte called out. "Mr. Grayson."

The sound of her footsteps grew closer.

"I'm taking the rest of the day," I tossed over my shoulder, never slowing my stride.

"I– I was wondering if I could get your approval for the donors f–"

"Tomorrow, Matte."

"Okay, but what about th–"

Halting completely, I turned, finding Matte behind me.

"Tomorrow."

I fought to keep the darkness inside, but this situation made it extremely arduous. Matte's quivering frame made it evident I wasn't victorious. I was falling deeper into the abyss.

I continued down the hallway. The elevator's doors parted almost instantly. I stepped inside, grateful for the solitude. My spine flexed as my head rested against the steel.

A chime from my cell reclaimed my thoughts. I dug into my pocket to retrieve the chunk of titanium I was beginning to despise. The number in the notification bar forced me to straighten my posture. I tapped the screen to find the words I'd searched for just minutes prior.

There's no one more suitable for the seat than you, Mr. Grayson. It's yours.

I peered at the message as Royce's voice rolled around in my head. All that had gone up in flames quietly settled and became nothing more than a smoldering pit of desire.

So are you, Ms. Childers.

It became apparent that there was a job I wanted a bit more than the mayoral position. I wanted to be things to Royce that no man had been before. When my plate was clear and my attention was undivided, I would seek the opportunity to do so. For now, I had an election to win.

T H E   G R E Y L I S T

"Front door open."

I entered my condo to the sound of my alarm system. Six numbers silenced it, keeping it from alerting the local authorities of my presence. I slipped out of my loafers as I pulled my tie from around my neck.

One button at a time, I loosened my shirt. One stair at a time, I got closer to my destination. The secondary kitchen was my first stop. I removed a bottle of water from the fridge. My fingers wrapped around the top of the only glass in the cupboard. I emptied the bottled water into it after a swift rinse.

Back against the counter, I chugged the cold liquid. The glass collided with the marble as I exited the kitchen. I removed my shirt, lessening the distance between me and the lovely bar that had sold the condo itself.

Though it was small in size, its beauty was something to behold. Olive green tile lined the wall, forming a distinct separation between the bar and the rest of the second floor. A marbled top and small gold black sink paired perfectly, beginning where the tile ended.

A wine cooler stretched to meet the edge of the marble. Shelves occupied the space the tile didn't, leading up to the ceiling. Olive decor filled the spaces it was humanly impossible to reach on any given day.

I lifted the top of the decanter and placed it at my mouth. I sipped slowly. The cognac began to numb my heart and head at once. Lowering the liquor came without hesitation. Intoxication wasn't my objective, forgetfulness was.

Numbness.

Insensibility.

Carelessness.

Thoughtlessness.

I slid another glass across the bar. The cognac filled the bottom rim. At the quarter mark, I recapped the decanter and claimed the glass. The bathroom was my next stop. It didn't matter that it was just after five-thirty. It was time to wash the day away.

Warm water poured down on me. My right hand rested on the showerhead as my thoughts ran rampant. The to-do list sitting on my office desk lengthened with each day. However, I couldn't even begin to scratch the surface with the unwarranted scandal lingering like a bad cold.

I wasn't sure if it was the anticipation of the images being released or the fact that they would be released troubling me most. Either way, I was suffocating from the unknown. My lack of control was humbling. I despised the feeling.

Finding out who was responsible and forcing them to kiss the butt of my bullets felt much more logical. Easier. Obtainable. Actionable. Yet, here I was, waiting for the inevitable. Struggling to keep from fading to black. Trying my hardest to keep my trigger finger moistened so it didn't itch too often or too much.

Yes, Mr. Grayson?

I squeezed my eyes together. Everything beelined for the center of my face. There was a noticeable shift in my breathing. My heart drummed against my chest. I stiffened between the legs.

Quietly, I etched her frame in my memory, demanding it stayed for the rest of my time on earth. While I wanted to forget the last few days, I never wanted to forget her.

She's unforgettable.

And impressive.

And tall.

And pretty.

And knowledgeable.

And mean.

And confident.

And strict.

And striking.

And dark. Just like me.

I shut off the water and stepped out of the shower. A white bath towel was waiting for me. I patted my face, neck, shoulders, and chest dry before wrapping it around my waist. Two minutes after entering my closet, I'd switched it out for a pair of black briefs.

7:06p

I reentered my bedroom with my eyes trained on the nightstand. My mattress sunk under the pressure of my bodyweight. I slid the drawer open and removed the natural butter my mother supplied me with monthly. She'd been making it for us since we were kids. Our limbs were long and our skin ashed easily. She vowed to keep us moistened and she hadn't broken that vow yet.

Her days were lighter, giving her the opportunity to enjoy the things she once discovered while in survival mode with three continuously growing boys. Like sewing our clothes because she couldn't afford the pieces we truly wanted. Like making our moisturizer because we ran through bottles of lotion weekly. Like thrifting. Like gardening because a pack of seeds were cheaper than whatever vegetable or fruit we wanted.

There's no one more suitable for the seat than you, Mr. Grayson. It's yours.

I polished my skin as Royce rejoined me. She crossed my mind so often I was beginning to wonder if she ever escaped. Images of her manicured nails tapping the screen of her phone lulled me to steadier ground.

I twisted my neck, stretching it until it popped. Everything tightened at once. My vision was perfect according to the optometrist. I recognized things that belonged to me. Royce was no exception.

I placed the butter in the nightstand. The drawer never closed. My sudden need for gratification wouldn't allow it.

I rested my head on the pillow behind me, elongating my body until I was flat on my back. My erection fought for relevancy in the wake of my desires. Sexual tension plagued me.

I fisted my dick, coating it with the Vaseline from my nightstand. Involuntarily, my eyelids sealed themselves. My chest caved. My stomach stiffened. And, my breaths deepened.

There she is.

The grip around my tool tightened as Royce appeared without even a hair out of place. And, it wasn't her phone her fingertips met continuously. It was my shoulders. The heels that she conquered any fucking thing she put her mind to in were planted on each side of me, giving her the stability she needed to rise and descend.

"Shit," I whispered, clenching every muscle in my body.

High cheeks, large almond eyes, slim frame, pearly white teeth, kissable nose, full lips, and an ass that had no business being so unforgettable, promised me a life of unpredictability.

Up.

Down.

I stroked my dick as I watched our bodies connect. I disappeared in her wetness.

Up.

Down.

She was sloppy. In bed was the only time the adjective deserved the right as a descriptor. Otherwise, it didn't belong in the same sentence as Royce.

Up.

Down.

"Fuck," I breathed out.

The curling of my toes signaled my undoing. I wasn't prepared. The air was too nippy. The silence was repulsive. The solitude was unbecoming.

I released my bone. Its steadiness remained as I

grabbed my cell. I scanned the contact list and landed on Asia. One tap on the camera icon and FaceTime was initiated.

Her pretty face appeared after the second ring. I was certain it wouldn't make it past the third one.

"Hello, Ishma–"

Her bottom lip folded into her mouth. Those light brown eyes of hers glistened with desperation. I resumed, massaging my dick for her viewing pleasure.

Up.

Down.

"Asia?"

"Yes, baby?" Pouty lips questioned.

Asia was ready. Asia was always ready. Her contact should've been *Ready* instead of her government name.

"Come put him down."

"I'm coming."

I ended the call. The exchange of words had reached its cliff. I tossed my cell on the bed and closed the drawer of my nightstand. Its contents were secured.

My feet carried me back into the bathroom where I cleansed my dick of the greasy substance. There would be no use for it where it was headed.

In her mouth.

Down her throat.

Deep in her pussy.

I tossed the warm towel as the doorbell alerted me of a visitor.

. . .

7:45p

Four minutes. Flat.

That was a new record for Asia. I wasn't complaining. My erection had yet to relieve me of the aches from the rigidness.

She was heavy on my mind.

Royce. Royce Childers.

I doubted it subsided on its own. I'd need assistance. I'd need Asia.

"Good evening, Ishmael."

Her lips moved slowly.

"Front door open." The alarm sounded.

I searched her big, light brown eyes for the unknown. I was only met with the desperation that pushed her forward, into my pad.

I secured the lock and turned on my heels. Asia's feet were no longer on the floor. Her knees had replaced them. The tube dress she wore pooled beneath her. She was pantiless. Braless. Senseless.

My towel was no longer around my waist. And, my hard dick was no longer kissing the air. Asia was kissing it. Longingly. Lovingly. Gently.

"Good evening, Asia," I groaned, placing my hand on the back of her head.

Darkness filled every pixel of my vision as my head fell backward, leaning against the door.

Good fucking evening.

FOUR

Royce

MY SHOULDERS SQUARED as my heels met the polished wood that covered every corner of *The M* that was reserved for staff, management, and vendors. I straightened my spine. My finger ran the length of my dress.

Their journey ended as swiftly as it began. The black dress stopped just beneath the cheeks of my ass. A white collared shirt with winged cuffs at the end rested under it. I hadn't fastened a single button. My little black dress that flared so subtly was holding it together.

Stockings that matched the tone of my skin brushed against the smoothness of my legs. Prada pumps met them near my ankles. Three anklets dangled just above them. A diamond bracelet, pink diamond studded Rolex, and a diamond rope all danced in the dimness of the small hallway.

I pulled my briefcase in front of me. Thoughts of Rome curled my lips upward. Gifts from her always touched me deeper than I cared to explain. There was something about them.

Something about her.

Snap.

"Focus, baby."

Chemistry's fingers appeared in the back of my brain. I collected myself as I closed my eyes.

Ishmael possessed every quality I searched for in a man. However, he wasn't mine to have. Business and pleasure never mixed well. He wanted the election. He couldn't have both me and the election.

I wanted his business. I couldn't be his handler and his partner. My line of work didn't include sex on the job. It blurred lines. It broke codes. It crossed boundaries. And it complicated the work relationship with clients.

I'd made that mistake already. I couldn't repeat the same misstep I'd considered a lesson. Jason was the greatest misfortune of my thirty one years on earth. His dick was as long as his money. However, his capacity wasn't forgiving enough for a girl like me. It was small. So was his mind. And, his refusal for growth beyond his finances forced me to end a year long commitment. I lost four clients the day I ended our union.

Jason.

His father.

His uncle.

His business partner.

I wasn't willing to leave money on the table by falling victim to feelings that could be as temporary as a tag from the dealer.

"Baby, that dress would be on the flo out there. Only cloth my ass would know is the linen of that damn table," Kleu exclaimed, fanning her face. "That's a fine motherfucker."

Her presence was startling, forcing my eyelids apart. She was stunning in all black. Kleu didn't miss a meal and it all went to the right places.

She was thick.

And pretty.

And confident.

And witty.

And her energy was good.

Every time I'd encountered her she was in good spirits. Mercer kept her around *The M* for more than her management skills. She lit up any room, and Berkeley was no stranger to the temptress. She brought in customers by the droves. Kleu was good for business. She was also good for the soul.

Chuckling, I nodded.

"Hello."

"Nah, fuck hello. Let's talk about that man out there waiting on you. He can't keep his eyes off that damn door. Heart in his dick. I know that look. Lawe still has it. He–"

"This is business, Kleu." I shook my head. "Can't leave that much money exposed because he's handsome and likely knows how to use his tongue well."

"Business. Please. Same thing."

She twisted her mouth and rolled her eyes.

Her beauty was breathtaking. She reminded me so much of the woman lying across the bed under the blue tint of the film *Belly*. Her skin was just as dark, as smooth, and as shiny.

"Is Mercer here?"

"If you're here, then you can expect him to be."

"Right," I chortled, nodding.

"He's in the kitchen. His safe place."

"I won't bother him. My guest is waiting."

A sigh pushed from my lips. I pulled a piece of skin between my teeth, silently praying my sanity was intact by the time dinner ended. I stepped forward, prepared to enter the main floor.

"Um hm," Kleu mumbled behind me.

I shook my head as a smile surfaced. It vanished as the door swung open, welcoming me to the five-star dining room that displayed every award it had earned since opening. Mercer's growth was rapid. So was his success. Both were inevitable.

My attempt to scan the room failed miserably. He wouldn't allow it. My eyes landed on his handsome face the moment I exposed myself to the public. His were fixated on me. Beckoning for me without even a word. Gesture. Nothing.

Just those dark eyes. Those dark eyes I knew far too well. Those dark eyes that mirrored mine.

One hand rested on the table. The other rotated a toothpick between his teeth. His mouth was slightly ajar. His attention was undivided.

Slowly, I placed one foot in front of the other. The magnetism was invigorating. I was unable to disrupt the motion of my body as I floated toward the source of the current.

Boom.

Boom.

Boom.

Boom.

As if it was on the loudspeakers around the restaurant, my heart beat loudly in my ears. My hands tightened around my briefcase as I watched the lengthy man stand on his feet. He moved around his chair, pushing it in slightly to make more room for himself.

For his ego.

For his pride.

For his masculinity.

For his politeness.

For his haughtiness.

My fingertips danced in the air, awaiting his touch. He extended both hands. Taking my right hand into his left and covering it with his right. An indication of endearment.

"Mr. Grayson."

My chest collided into his. Naturally, as if it had happened a hundred times over, my left hand slid up his shoulder and around his neck, pulling him closer.

Fuck.

My body's response to his presence was displeasing. My lack of control was repulsive.

Divine.

I inhaled, programming his scent in my head. My heart wanted parts, too.

I can't.

Pulling away posed an issue. Ishmael held me near, refusing to release me from his grasp. His hand lowered onto my back, keeping a safe distance from my treasured parts. My eyes were growing tired of the constant exercise. I'd closed them more in the last twenty-four hours than I had in the months leading up to this moment.

His chest was firm. His gym regime was apparent. So was his hygiene. His cleanliness reminded me why he felt so heavenly.

Ishmael.

His mother was no fool in naming her son. She understood his power. His future was written before Mercer dialed my number. My presence was only to ensure his journey was as seamless as possible.

Mayor Grayson.

Another unsuccessful attempt to pull away forced me to submit, acknowledging Ishmael's leadership. Establishing my trust.

In him.

The handsome stranger.

"Don't ever wear this to work again, Royce. I won't be responsible for my actions."

His whispers raised my skin. Fine bumps pained me from my neck to my ankles.

As his statement drew to a close, so did our connection. He loosened his hold on me, handing me to the crisp air that was once warm.

Once.

Twice.

A third and fourth time…

My lashes batted. My neck drew back slightly. The corners of my eyes tightened. He'd thrown off my entire nervous system. I didn't know what to say… what to do… what to feel. So, I followed up with what felt most accurate.

Simple.

Vivid.

Free of confusion.

"Good evening, Mr. Grayson."

Ishmael's right hand disappeared into the jacket of his suit as his radiating smile proved to be a hoax.

"That's not my fucking name." He chuckled.

A walking contradiction.

"Don't let me tell you that again, *Royce.*"

Warmth rode my spine to the tippy top. My nipples hardened. The rings that pierced them caused a pain that rested in my pussy.

She's alive.

"Ishmael. Ish. Take your pick, but Mr. Grayson ain't it. Sit down."

I hadn't noticed the chair he'd pulled out. Neither could I comprehend how he'd disappeared from my line of vision. Or how his breath grazed the back of my neck.

Maintaining a smidget of self-control, I remained standing.

"I can pull out my own chair, Mr–"

"Ishmael."

I clipped my statement to allow him to speak. A smirk turned my lips upward as I shook my head.

"Go ahead. Sound it out. You're a smart woman."

I turned to face the eligible bachelor that was too close for comfort, yet right where he needed to be, simultaneously.

"If you'd have a seat, we could get down to business."

"I'm not sitting down until you're seated, Royce. Don't make this difficult."

"I'm not easy," I blurted.

Regret sealed my lids. My nostrils flared. My chest rose.

"Neither are you cheap."

I took my seat. Words failed me. It didn't matter how extensive my vocabulary was. Ishmael adjusted it before settling in his.

Those eyes.

Those dark eyes.

They unclothed me. Exposed me. Left me naked

and vulnerable as I tried fleeing their grasp. It was pointless.

"Cognac, neat. And a mango sour."

I snatched all of my things that Ishmael was after and managed to stretch my line of vision across the floor. Mercer held a hand to his head and pushed it outward. I placed a hand on my heart, expressing my gratitude for more than the drinks he'd sent our way.

It was for his love.

His light.

His life.

His presence.

His victories every time his mental health slipped.

The first sip was surreal. It placed so much back into perspective for me. The crown that Ishmael had tipped during his extended hug was upright now.

"The images," Ishmael exhaled, "It's a mess."

"It's nothing I can't handle. I didn't come to dinner to be insulted."

"Why are we here? I'd love to hear how you plan to han–"

"We're a couple."

"Excuse me?"

I swallowed back, securing my hammering heart in my chest.

"You and I. We're a couple. As of eight months ago."

Chuckling, Ishmael shook his head.

"That's your bright idea?"

I took another sip, waiting for the wheels that I knew would begin to turn in his head. Words weren't necessary. I'd said all that needed to be said for now. It was up to Ishmael to use that pretty head of his for something other than taming the untamable.

"A couple?"

His brows raised as he posed the question. I nodded.

"Tell me more. Royce."

A black tray stopped in front of us. An array of dishes were set in front of us.

"Compliments of Chef. Enjoy."

As quickly as the waitress had appeared, she vanished. I observed the servings we'd been complimented. I knew the menu of The M by heart.

Literally and figuratively.

"Royce–" Ishmael called out, bringing me back to the topic at hand.

Speaking while eating wasn't in my interests, so I avoided digging into the food. Ishmael hardly wasted time.

"We are scheduled for an eight o'clock photoshoot that will depict our life as a couple. Twenty sets. Twenty-six outfit changes. And a slew of scenes that will contradict every image that will be published to the public soon."

"Eight? It's after seven, already."

"Which means you don't have long to eat. The location is twenty minutes away."

"Then why didn't we meet there instead of her–"

I nodded, pointing my head toward the patrons.

Ishmael nodded his head. Those white teeth were on full display.

"You don't think at least six of them have snapped a picture or recorded us?"

"I'm sure they have."

"So am I. Our images won't be enough to convince the public you're in a healthy, happy relationship. But, they can convince each other."

"Why the relationship route?"

"Because it will win the election. You're a single man. Your opponents are all married and have been for years. It's part of their campaign. Their rings are in every photo they've taken since announcing their run. And, frankly, it will win them the votes of many women here in Berkeley.

"You can't afford to lose any more of them when these images come out. You'll leave a bad taste in their mouths—but not if the poor woman whose images are on every news station they turn on for weeks is actually just your girlfriend who found herself stranded as she tried making the reservations for the mini staycation you spent hours planning."

Ishmael didn't speak. Neither did I. Instead, I picked up one of the forks in front of me and stabbed a few cucumbers from the cucumber salad in front of me.

"Eight o'clock?"

I swallowed my food.

"Eight o'clock."

"Then, we'd better get going."

"I agree."

I forked a few more cucumbers before I stood on my feet. Ishmael did the same. My job here was done. *The M* would get the exposure it deserved and so would my *faux* relationship with the future mayor of Berkeley.

THE GREY LIST

My nipples pebbled against Ishmael's chest. Slowly, I blinked away the lust that was evident in my eyes. A quick search and he would learn the truth.

"The camera, Royce."

I lost myself in his smile. His arms encased me, surrounding me with comfort. The same white shirt he wore rested against my skin.

"Perfect. Perfect," Dexter called out. "Perfect. Now, Mr. Mayor, do me a favor and kiss her forehead. Royce– your eyes closed, sweetie."

My instincts didn't need instructions. Ishmael's lips against my body, any part of it, ended with the same results.

Lids sealed.

Center throbbing.

Heart racing.

Fine bumps rising.

Thoughts jumbled.

Words lost.

"Hold it right there. Perfect!"

The camera flashes halted, letting me know Dexter had exactly what he needed.

"Change of clothes," I demanded, lifting my body from the California King bed.

I'd created a total of twenty scenes in a secure location. We had gone through twelve of them. The last eight of them were intimate, depicting our home life and capturing our downtime on film.

Upon my request, Dexter had traded his professional lens for a simpler one. The last thing we needed was hi-def images that all looked as staged as they were. Some images, he took straight from the cellphone to fully commit to the vision. It was beneath him but it wasn't beneath our vision or the hefty payout in route to his account.

I shoved the cover toward my feet before swinging my legs over the side of the bed. I was dressed in a pair of briefs and a white shirt from the pack I'd purchased for this purpose alone. Ishmael was dressed the same.

I scurried to the dressing room and closed the door behind me. My back collided with the steel. Its coolness chilled my warm frame. I rubbed my hand across my forehead.

This isn't real, Royce.

Snap!

I inhaled a slow, deep breath and released it even slower. My head lifted and fell continuously as I separated fact from fiction.

The publicity that came with political relations and affairs, my family didn't need it. We strayed from cameras and visibility. We thrived in the darkness. In the underworld. In the underbelly of Huffington.

It's all made up. I reminded myself as I stripped down to my thong.

The beige silky gown slid up my body with ease. I paired it with a robe that matched. Tulle gathered at the sleeves, giving the illusion of a performance by the robe with each sway of my body or movement of my arms. Vintage Gucci mules adorned my feet, showcasing my freshly pedicured toes.

I spritzed on what was becoming my favorite fragrance. It held a subtle power that commanded every space I entered, furthering my ability to do so alone. Together, we turned every head and widened every pair of nostrils within a seventy-five foot radius of us.

We left a lasting impression for all to gnaw on until they closed their eyes for bed. We were the first thing on some people's minds when they opened their eyes. Others lost us in the awakening of their fears and desires that happened in the form of dreams and nightmares.

I checked the mirror for the fourth time. The person staring back at me was admirable. I clipped my hair in the back and allowed carefully trimmed pieces to frame my face as they were designed for. The thick yet bouncy curtain bang wasn't my usual style, but Flo, the stylist I'd brought on for this task, had customized four wigs in twenty-four hours.

I rotated them throughout the shoot. This one,

however, happened to be my favorite out of the few. I would circle back in the months to come. But, for now, I was happy with the under curls that flipped, giving me the old school nineties beauty that I adored.

Kenzington Cosmetics coated my lips. Chanel balanced the skin of my face and neck. Mascara enhanced my lashes. Everything was where it needed to be. Nothing was out of order. Not even a strand of hair.

With my chest protruding and my chin high, I returned to the set. Cooking utensils awaited me near the stove. So did Ishmael, sitting at the table with a newspaper in front of him that was published five months ago. The cuffs on his shirt were undone. So were his top four buttons. A loose tie dangled from his collar.

God took his precious time.

His eyes pinned me to the counter. I rolled a piece of my flesh between my teeth.

"Uh mm."

The clearing of my throat didn't break his stare. Neither did the shuffling of utensils. It wasn't until I turned around, folding my hands across my hardened nipples, and matched Ishmael's gaze that his concentration was interrupted.

"You have to actually lift the paper if you care for the camera to catch it," I advised.

A titter made his shoulders rise and fall.

"Hmph."

Sarcasm dripped from his biceps. His beard. His hands. And, his words.

"Noted."

As the word tumbled from his lips, he removed his cell from the pocket of his slacks. His features grew more rigid with each vibration.

"Ishmael–"

He held the phone up, turning the screen in my direction.

Unknown Caller.

"Answer."

"You told me–"

"Answer it," I suggested.

Silently, he slid the bar across the phone.

"Speak."

The depths of his baritone pierced my pussy. I squeezed my walls together to compress her pain. She was aching with desire.

"Speakerphone," I whispered.

"... might have forgotten who is in charge here. I've made requests that you haven't met. Two m–"

"Come get it if you want it."

Chuckling, the altered voice on the other end raised the hair on my shoulders. My index finger itched with as much desire as my pussy was thudding with.

Not the answer, I reminded myself.

"You and I know that's not the answer I was looking for. It seems like I'm going to have to release these photos, Mr. Mayor. You leave me no choice."

"Do you what you need to do, my nigga."

Ishmael's jawline flexed as he suppressed his truest emotions. He didn't allow the caller to respond before he ended the call.

"How much longer do we have?"

"Another hour."

It wasn't what he wanted to hear, but nothing would change the facts. In order to build a solid story, this step was crucial.

"The images will release soon."

"How do you figure?"

"He knows he can't corner you. He will find the next best option."

"Daniels," he scoffed, calling the name of his competition.

Daniels was the only person in the running who could possibly take the election from Ishmael. Not because he was more qualified. He wasn't. However, one scandal and it would lead Berkeley to believe otherwise.

I nodded.

"So, unless you want Daniels in your seat in November, hold that paper in front of you and tuck your tail for the next hour. You'll be home soon."

Ishmael quieted. He parted *Berkeley News* and began his pointless observation of the publication.

"We're ready, Dexter," I called out, never taking my eyes off Ishmael.

I couldn't.

The activity of his magnetic field was at its peak.

FIVE

Ishmael

I ROLLED OVER, silencing the alarm on my nightstand. The blackout shades filtered the sunlight from the condo. Aside from the internal lights from electronics, I was in total darkness. I patted around the bed, searching for my cell.

Sunday was rest day.

Business didn't get handled. Calls went unanswered. The cell was on *Do Not Disturb* until Monday at eight sharp. Saturday had offered me nothing more than restlessness, leading me into the wee hours of today. I didn't close my eyes until five this morning. Sleeping the day away wasn't an option. I needed to burn some stress and calories in the gym.

10:01a

The screen was littered with notifications. One after the other, I swiped through them, face pinched and stomach in knots. An incoming call made everything vanish. All that was left was a choice I didn't want to make at the moment.

Red or green button.

Answer or decline.

My mother's name crossed the screen. Movement was beyond me. I was paralyzed with uncertainty.

Once the line rung out, the new notification appeared.

Missed call.

Pain ran up my spine. My thumb hovered over the screen as I contemplated returning a call I'd never missed. Not until today.

"Fuck."

I tapped the screen, bypassing the message to open the text from Matte. It was followed by messages from Cameron, Julius, and Sarah in our group thread. As the phone rested in my palm, more messages filed in.

And then the phone rang again.

And again.

And again.

Matte.

Cameron.

Sarah.

One after the other, the calls flooded in. I ignored them one by one. Before I heard anyone's voice from the office, I needed to educate myself on what was happening. I scanned the messages for the source.

The header from the first link made it apparent.

Mayor Hopeful Buying More Than the Voter's Loyalty.

My skin grew tighter as my body expanded with despair.

Could the Mayoral Candidate, Ishmael Grayson, Be in the Center of a Prostitution Ring?

Ishmael Grayson Using Campaign Money to Fund Unshakeable Habits?

Mayoral Candidate, Ishmael Grayson, Picks Up Prostitute.

The headlines filled the screen.

Bold.

Big.

Lie after lie.

And there she was. In the midst of my shit. Remorse pumped through my veins as I stared at the image of Royce.

Head high.

Chest out.

Spine straightened.

A fucking force to be reckoned with.

I leaned my head leftward until my neck popped. My eyelids found each other, consuming me with darkness. I inhaled deeply.

And there she was. In the midst of my madness. Joy exuded from her frame as she stared at the images of us.

Lips pulled backward.

Teeth on full display.
Shoulders curled inward.
Chest caved.

Admiration and disbelief tiptoeing around the business persona she had coated her desires in from the moment she stepped into *The M.*

The black socks on my feet caught the dust the robotic cleaning tool that was a gift from my realtor after closing hadn't. I scanned my contacts, settling on the one I yearned to connect with most. If it wasn't Royce's voice on the line, I didn't care to hear anybody's.

I didn't only need her to handle this.

I needed her to handle me.

My head was in an uproar.

So was my heart.

The first ring sounded off like explosives in my ear. The second ring caused a tightening in my chest. The third ring forced me to halt in the middle of my condo. The fourth disabled me.

"The caller you—"

I ended the call and retried the line.

Five rings.

"The call—"

I couldn't remember a moment in life I'd tried anyone a second time. Neither did I remember a time when my call went unanswered. There wasn't anyone in my life who didn't value my existence and vice versa. The missed call from my mother was the first in history and it would be the last.

Another text vibrated my cell. I dismissed it, regretting the decision almost instantly. It wasn't Sarah or Matte or Cameron or anyone from my team.

It was her.

I opened the nearly empty thread and fixed my eyes on her message.

You're late to the party, Mr. Grayson.

I didn't respond. Instead, I exited and pressed her contact from the call log. This time, a regular call wouldn't suffice.

"Hello, Ishmael."

Her body was dripping with sweat. Her dark, perfectly even skin shined from the moisture. And those fucking lips. I'd imagined them wrapped around my dick too many times for them to still be unbruised and on her pretty face. Untouched.

Disbelief silenced me. Royce was resting against a wooden bench with her eyes closed. Contentment consumed her.

"Ishmael–"

Her comfort disturbed me in ways I wasn't ready to admit. My world was going up in flames and she was in the sauna, sprawled out like a piece of meat on the grill during a summer cookout.

Unbothered.

Unphased.

Not worried about a fucking thing.

. . .

I ended the call. Waiting for Matte to send another text or try my line again was absurd, suddenly. I hit her contact and waited for her to pick up. It wasn't long before she was on the line, sighing with relief.

"Mr. Grayson… the images… the imag–"

"Matte–"

"Yes?"

"I'm aware."

"What– what should we do here?"

"It's Sunday. You rest."

"We're all at the office, waiting for you–"

"I won't be there, Matte, neither should you all be there. Sunday is rest day. Nothing has changed."

"But, Mr. Grayson."

"It's being handled," I assured her, ending the call.

I didn't have answers for the team. For the first time in history, I wasn't sure what the next step was or if it would suffice. I knew that Royce had promised me the seat and somehow, I believed her.

The red dot on my cell was idle. Unmoving. My target was immobile and I doubted that would change any time soon.

Stay put.

I flipped on the lights throughout my condo as I stalked my closet. Once inside, I was dressed in under two minutes. I had no time to waste and rest could wait.

I made it out of my home and into my car without incident. My GPS called out one turn after the other, leading me to the newest spot on the city's rave list.

According to the voters, it was a must everyone visited. Truthfully, not everyone had the budget to visit. Upon arrival, I knew that you'd need at least a band to touch their marble floors.

"Good evening, Mr. Grayson. Welcome to *Hydro-Oasis*. How are you today?"

The entire city knowing my name and face was something I was still getting accustomed to. If I could run a faceless race, then I would've. My actions would speak for me. They always had.

While most preferred visibility, it wasn't on my list of priorities. I'd much rather be felt than seen. Valued than viewed.

"Unfortunately, the entire complex is res–"

"Nancy, his pass is under the keyboard," the older gentleman informed us both.

"Thanks, Harold."

Confusion plagued me. Still, I remained silent, allowing Nancy to take heed, because the complex being reserved didn't have shit to do with me. I would be inside whether it was her that granted me access or not.

"Here's that pass, Mr. Grayson. You'll wear this around your wrist until you end your time here. This bracelet will give you access to every pod in our facility, including special services and VIP soaks."

I laid my arm on the counter, allowing Nancy to strap the cloth bracelet around my wrist. There was a large piece of metal wrapped in plastic in the center. As she fitted it to the circumference of my arm, my eyes were on Harold.

Sensing my inquisitive gaze, he looked up from the stack of papers in his hand. Towels piled on the counter. A robe rested in my hand after the bracelet was secured.

"Here are your towels and a new pair of slippers just in case you choose to wear them. Your rob–" Nancy explained.

"Where is she?"

Harold froze. I observed as he contemplated his next set of words. He'd chosen wisely. After a brief pause, he released the breath he'd been holding.

"Ending her soak."

I didn't respond. I waited for more. He'd given me her location. I wanted her destination. If she was ending one service then it meant she was headed to another.

"Headed to the massage pods," he continued after a few seconds.

I left both towels, slippers, and robe on the counter and headed toward the double doors. On the other side, a digital board displayed a map of the entire spa. I zeroed in on the pods marked with a massage graphic and a large M.

One left.
Two rights.
The breezeway.
Another right.

One left.

I locked the directions in my cerebral cortex and followed them to a science. Still, they didn't result in Royce. I stood in front of ten doors, all labeled with a number. Slow, calming sounds played on the speakers. They contradicted everything I felt at the moment.

"Can I help you, sir?"

"No," I responded, continuing through the parlor.

Nancy's spill about the entire spa being reserved quickly resurfaced. I twisted the knob of the first room.

Empty.

The second room.

Empty.

The third room.

Empty.

Growing impatient, I twisted the knob and entered the fourth room.

My heart settled in my chest. The music that had little to no effect suddenly began to transport me to another place.

There.

Royce was stretched out on a velvety-soft bed with her arms flattened beside her. I folded my arms across my chest, admiring the Glock her right hand was wrapped around. She was magical.

Far beyond belief.

Implausible.

Mind-blowing.

Without a doubt in my mind, I knew she wouldn't

hesitate to fire her weapon. And, neither was there a doubt in my mind that she didn't shoot for shits. Royce would certainly shoot to kill. That Glock wasn't an accessory. It was a warning.

A towel covered her from her neck down to her thighs. Her face was hidden, buried in the head rest that formed a circle. Beside her was an empty bed.

She was irresistible. Magnetic. Alluring. And, I was fully engaged without the ability to control myself. Royce felt too much like mine. I felt too much like hers.

Small hands rubbed her body. I observed, taking note of the movement, pressure, and direction. When time permitted, my lengths to please Royce would be immeasurable.

She was quiet. Content. Relaxed.

I lowered my body until my mouth was ear-level with the woman who was slowly stealing my power and my sanity.

"My world is crumbling and you're face down, eyes closed, and without a care in the world. Royce–"

I was hardly here because I needed her to do any more than she'd already done in preparation for the inevitable. I was here because I needed her. And, it ended there. Seeing her clothed me in content. Disturbed whatever was going on up in that fucking circus of mine. My brain was a complex place... one that she simplified with one word. One look.

Still, I didn't reveal the true nature of my presence. But, somehow, I had a feeling she knew that already. She lifted her head. Things inside of me shifted.

"Get undressed, Ishmael," Royce demanded.

After the words left her mouth, she lowered, disappearing without as much as a glance in my direction. Perturbed and tantalized at once, I stilled. Unmoving and completely consumed, I considered her bare-faced beauty. It was staggering.

Her side profile left me gobsmacked. I wasn't prepared for the full image. Not mentally, physically, or in any way I could be. I rested my eyes and shook my head from one side to the other, slowly, as I attempted to collect myself. Or as much of me that she hadn't yet stolen.

I rubbed a hand down my chin and neck. Royce was becoming as much of my stressor as she was my reliever.

I didn't protest. Instead, I laid my naked body on the table next to her sixty seconds later, smothering my hard dick with the weight of my body. *Revolver in hand.*

THE GREY LIST

A warm, damp towel cleansed my skin of excess oil. My lungs and chest had loosened. So had my limbs. The sound of water crashing against the shore swayed my thoughts.

An hour and a half of my time had been well spent. The noise was behind me. Anxiousness was beneath me. Contentment was before me.

At thirty-eight, I had never taken the time out of my

day to rest my body and mind on the table of a masseuse. That changed today, and I was contemplating fitting a monthly maintenance in my schedule.

"Ma'am. Sir. Have a blessed day."

"Thank you, Hailey." Royce sighed.

The weight she was carrying had been freed from her shoulders. She sounded much lighter and utterly refreshed. I couldn't deny the difference I felt either.

I was the first to rise, considerate of Royce's discomfort. Remaining respectful, I held both ends of the towel around my waist as I stood. I lifted my left foot, attempting to put it forward. However, I halted midstride.

Royce was on her feet in a flash. Unclothed. Uncovered. Unphased. Her body glistened from the remnants of oil. Her face radiated from the effects of the hour and a half long massage. Her cheeks rose as my erection followed suit.

Down, boy.

Dark areolas housed hardened nipples. They were small, round, and suckable. I swallowed the saliva forming in my mouth at the thought of all parts of her touching my tongue.

Her breasts were only the first perfect parts of her I noticed. However, she was perfection at its finest. All of her.

Those chiseled abs.
Defined waistline.
Hips that spread like mayo on a slice of bread.
The slight gap between her legs.

And the way her legs rounded out so perfectly.

Even her toes were flawless. All aligned, no signs of the work I knew she had done to acquire her title and become a walking resource.

Slowly, she located one piece of clothing after the other. Her speed was agonizing. She moved without haste. On her own time.

First, it was her top. She was braless underneath. Next was her panties. The fabric clung to her bald pussy. It was as beautiful as she was.

Smooth.

Hairless.

Thick.

And, undoubtedly, creamy.

I didn't need any more evidence than the moisture that darkened her panties where her lips started. Darkness came quickly. Light surrounded me again, almost immediately, as my eyes reopened.

A thigh strap clamped around her leg. She shoved the Glock into the holster. In pure bliss, I observed every detail of her makeup.

"Clothes, Ishmael."

"Don't dangle meat in front of a starving beast and expect him not to eat at some point."

My warning had come. Destruction would follow.

With a smile, Royce pulled a silk skirt up her body. She was enjoying the turmoil she was inflicting.

"Clothes."

I released my towel. Royce's efforts to redress concluded, simultaneously. Her eyes found my center, where my rigidness sliced the air. I pulled my briefs over my ass, feeling the tension thicken in the room.

Undoubtedly, Royce would suffocate before I did. Her gaze told me so. She hadn't calculated the risk factors before jumping into the boiling water she'd placed on the stove herself.

The fabric did little to conceal my hard dick. Though caged, it still had an audience. I followed with additional clothing. Once I was clothed completely, I placed both hands in front of me and rested my weight on my legs.

"Shoes, Royce," I commanded.

"I– Ye– Right."

She tripped over her words as she began scrambling. She slid into a pair of heels that only had a strap over the front. They were black in color, tall, and had a red sole. I knew the designer without mention.

I allowed her to exit first. She stepped into the hallway, making her presence known with the sound of her shoes colliding with the floor.

And, that shit…

That shit did something for me.

Something to me.

There was something about a woman announcing her presence without a fucking word that lit a fire within me.

Like a lost puppy, I followed behind Royce. I didn't mind her taking the lead because it meant I had a full view of what was waiting for me post-election.

We reached the double doors far too soon. Our

time together was coming to a screeching halt. The tightening in my chest returned. I wasn't prepared. I needed more time.

More time with Royce.

More time not worrying.

More time not thinking about a damn thing but her.

"Royce," I called out as we reached the doors that led to the parking lot.

"Yes, Ishmael?" She asked, stepping outside.

Flashing cameras met us. Indifference gripped my heart, squeezing until it was near explosion.

"Smile, your annoyance is showing, *honey*." Royce chuckled with her back toward the cameras.

"You knew?"

"I always know," she assured me.

I pulled her inside.

"Royce, your face will be all–"

"It's already all over Berkeley, Ishmael."

Protecting her image was the main source of my indifference. Exposing her to the public at the current capacity was unsettling.

"I'll be fine. I promise. I just– well..."

She slid a hand across my shirt, clearing meaningless dust particles.

"Well what, Royce?"

She was mesmerizing. Naturally and utterly spectacular. A piece of hair hung in her face, next to bangs that covered her forehead. Her identity was partially concealed with black Prada shades. Her lips were shiny and she smelled like something in a summer catalog.

"I was wondering if I could catch a ride," she asked, gnawing on her bottom lip.

In the next breath, Royce pushed the door open, forcing me to grab ahold of it. She had planned this spa visit down to a science. No stone was left unturned.

Flashing cameras sealed my lips. I took Royce's hand into mine, shielding her from the group of reporters with microphones pointed in our direction. She leaned into me.

More things inside of me shifted. Moving to make space for her.

Because for the first time since I'd encountered her, I didn't feel like I was chasing the intangible. Something I wanted was at the tip of my fingers. In my hands.

Victories had been few and far apart since that night in Clarke. However, Royce's head on my shoulder as I covered her face from the cameras deemed me victorious. Her submission was far more invigorating than any part of my mayoral campaign or the idea of heading an entire city.

Truthfully, leading Royce had become my ultimate goal. But, I had a feeling Berkeley would be much easier. Simpler. Less entertaining. Still, I wanted both seats. I deserved both seats.

SIX

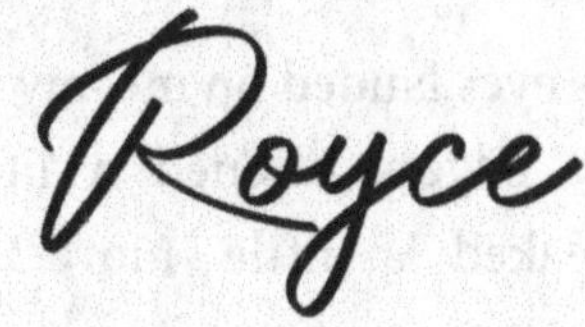

THE DAMSEL IN DISTRESS.

The role was well-rehearsed, well-played, and would bring about pleasing results. With the visor down and a suit jacket from his passenger seat, Ishmael obstructed the cameras views of me.

Slowly, he reversed the Aston Martin. It wasn't the same as the one from that night. They resembled, but weren't the same vehicle.

The interior was different. So was the motor of the SUV. Red accented the tires by way of the brake pads. Black coated nearly every surface beyond his wheels. Wherever black ended, gun metal gray began.

Speed mounted me against the seat. Every possible

path was etched in my memory. I'd taken the route six times before confirming the location was perfect. I wasn't wrong. We were on the expressway within seconds, leaving the crowd of hungry reporters behind us.

Sunlight greeted me. Ishmael's anguished eyes condemned me. Worry twinkled in his irises. He altered his line of vision.

Me.

The road.

Me.

The road.

Me.

Each time his eyes landed on me, my heart quieted a little more. My edges softened a little more. My vulnerability peaked a little more. My rigidness dissolved a little more.

"What is it, Mr. Grayson?" I asked.

My words were loaded. So was my heart.

His nostrils didn't spread. His chest didn't enlarge. His jawline didn't stiffen.

"Don't call me that, Royce." He paused with a sigh.

His gaze felt intrusive. It violated so many regulations in my book. But, it felt as good. As pleasant. As reassuring, and I wasn't a woman who needed assurance.

Me.

The road.

"Are you okay?"

Me.

The road.

Me.

"I'm okay, Ishmael."

The road.

Me.

"You can, uh– just take this exit. I'm not very far from here."

The road.

Me.

"I didn't ask you where you were staying, Royce."

This time, he didn't take his eyes off the road. His gaze didn't slice right through my core. His dark rounds didn't open my soul's portal.

"Ishmael– I–"

"You are going to sit back and shut up, love."

He turned the volume up on his steering wheel and increased his speed. I didn't object. I couldn't.

I pressed my back deeper into the cushion. My lips met with promises not to part.

I wasn't sure what sounds were coming from the speakers. My ears were flooded with one sound in particular.

Boom.

Boom.

Boom.

Boom.

My heart beat wildly. My thoughts ran too far too fast. I closed my eyes, desperate to regain control of my nervous system. It was shattered and the cameras weren't the culprits. It was him. It was the time we had on our hands. And, it was the uncertainty of what was next for either of us.

I wasn't a woman who went with the flow. I was the flow. I created it and I ended it. Somehow, I was no longer in a position to do either.

"You knew they'd be there."

I hadn't heard the volume of the music lowered. But, I heard Ishmael clearly. He commanded my attention. Listening wasn't a choice I had to make. It was made for me each time he parted his lips to speak.

"Yes."

"How?"

"Because–" I paused, running a hand through my hair, loosening the curls. I stared out of the window. "I knew you'd come. And, I knew they'd follow you."

"How'd you know I'd come?"

"You're not too far removed from your past, Ishmael. You try to remain level-headed, but that fire inside of you is the same fire I fight every day."

"Every day?" He sniggered.

I nodded.

"Besides, I didn't disable the tracker on my car to be sure you found me."

Silence trailed my statement. The small black tracker was hardly noticeable. However, no stone was unturned. I discovered the device the same day it was attached to the barrel of my wheel.

"Have you eaten, Royce?"

"I haven't."

His handsome face was angled perfectly. I lost my

way in the intricacies of his perfect skin, thick beard, and beautiful Black features. There were parts of the Black man that were significant to us. And, there was hardly nothing more I loved witnessing on a man than those features that distinguished us from the others.

"What is it?" He asked, taking his eyes off the road for a brief second.

"Since I'm your woman now, I assume you can feed me."

"I have every intention of stuffing you, Royce."

I clenched my pussy muscles. My walls pulled inward, tapping against each other. My stomach knotted. My throat thickened. And all the air in the SUV was sucked right out.

The volume of his stereo heightened again. I melted against the seat. My elbow rested on the door handle. I peered out of the window, praying peace rescued me. Ishmael refused to let me have any in his presence. It was as much of a gift as it was a curse.

No parts of me desired companionship with a politician, but this man was making it abundantly clear he was not the average politician. Ishmael was a refined street dweller in a black suit with an extensive vocabulary who observed more than he spoke. And, it was no secret that I was a sucker for a street nerd. I just couldn't have this one.

My fingertips grazed the olive green tile. There wasn't a single one misaligned. Neither was there a flaw in sight.

Perfect.

The bar was incredible. Pots mingled in the background, disrupting nothing more than Ishmael's nerves. I was unbothered by his culinary struggles. Though I loved exploring dishes, Ishmael's kitchen was no place for me.

Don't be a wife to a boyfriend.

Don't be a girlfriend to a man you're dating.

Don't ever give a man more than his actions have shown you he's capable of reciprocating.

My mother's words stuck like glue. They never left me. I recalled them more often than not.

I wouldn't be found in a man's kitchen barefoot with breakfast on the stove. Not until my finger was sore from acclimating itself with the weighty diamond that was a result of our vows. I wouldn't become a homemaker for a man who hadn't built a home for us. A life for us. And, established a trust for us.

There were rules.

There were guidelines.

There were stipulations.

And there were requirements.

They didn't bend, fold, or disappear for anyone. Not even the politician.

I stopped near the window, overlooking a slightly gloomy Berkeley. The city had birthed my greatest gift. My Teddy. The city had also broken his heart.

His spirit.

His head.

And his bond with the men that meant the most to him.

I placed a hand on my chest to relieve the pain I was experiencing.

"You seem to know your way around. You sure it's your first time here?"

"Is it yours?" I asked, never releasing Berkeley's skyline from my line of vision.

Ishmael's grunt was low, sultry, and sex-filled.

Or maybe it was the thudding between my thighs that translated everything that fell from his lips.

"I've moved things around a bit and forgot where I put everything."

"Hmph."

"Your explanation?"

"I'm not a woman who explains herself much."

"Royce–" he called out.

Giving into his demand, I turned around. I headed toward the kitchen where he stood near the sink. His home was impressive. Another kitchen was just beneath us. The architect was superior. So was the interior decor.

"I'm starving. Takeout sounds like a better idea."

"You're pivoting."

"I am."

"Don't."

Smiling, I exhaled. "I studied the blueprints."

"Plural?" Ishmael asked, partly surprised.

"All of them. Every address that belongs to you."

He sniggered.

His smile rearranged my insides. It was darling. It was dark. And it was sexy.

"That is possibly the furthest from the truth, Royce."

"Hm." I didn't care to elaborate unless he did so himself.

"Not *all* of them."

"78123 K Street. 32982 Parnel Drive. 86120 Butcher Road. Those three sound familiar to you?"

"They shouldn't."

"I'm aware. You don't frequent them and they're not in your name. Neither are they in your mother's name. Or your brot–"

They were his secrets to keep, but now they were mine, too.

"So, how did you find them?"

"I'm good at what I do."

"Still curious. How?"

"A lot of wine and a little Wi-fi."

He tittered. His curved smile straightened swiftly.

"You make it sound easy."

"Because it is. *For me*."

"Shrimp and broccoli? Side of soy noodles?"

"I'd like that."

"I won't be long in here. The bar is that big green slab you were just admiring, but I'm certain you knew that before stepping foot in this motherfucker. The glasses are waiting. Take one and pour yourself some wine. Take your pick from what's in the cooler in the first cabinet."

"Now that, I didn't know."

Sarcasm dripped from my lips. Ishmael's abdomen jolted from the sharp air pushed from his nose. He didn't share more words with me. I didn't need him to.

Because, the wine would never get opened and it would never get poured. My mouth would never greet its greatness. And, my nerves wouldn't take the hour-long break they needed. I'd be right here. Listening. Waiting. Anticipating every syllable he released.

Absentmindedly, I revisited the bar top. So many parts of me were left behind. Abandoned by my desperation to be freed from Ishmael's grasp. He had me by the neck, demanding things from me that I didn't have to give. *Not to him.*

"This one, Royce."

He was alarmingly close. His voice. His warmth. His hands. His pounding heart. His chest. His mouth. His eyes. *Him.*

Our lips were mere inches from each other. Silence settled between us as I struggled to catch my breath. My world was casted into the darkness while I fought every urge in my frame.

I could taste his minty breath on my tongue. I could feel his long, thick arms around me. And, his dick, his veiny and sizable dick, I could feel it inside of me. Digging into me, extracting my creaminess.

My God.

"Maybe I should go hom– back to the place I'm

stay– I should." I couldn't form a full thought. I couldn't conjure a full sentence. My face flushed with shame, a feeling I wasn't accustomed to. I turned on my heels, needing to put Ishmael in my rearview. Because, he was wrecking everything standing in front of me.

I didn't recall when he'd left the kitchen. When he'd passed me by. Or when he'd removed the wine from the cooler. But, I knew exactly where he was now. And, it was too close for comfort. Yet, comforting. The conflict was clear. Defeat was upon me.

"Stay where the fuck you are, Royce."

His baritone dissolved the bones of my spine. My skeleton was missing so many pieces. I was spineless. Mindless. Completely dependent on what was to come from Ishmael's lips next.

I listened as the cork of the bottle in his hand was removed. My mouth watered as the wine hit the bottom of the glass. And, when Ishmael rounded my body with the glass in his hand, I knew that I'd be in the bathroom the first chance I got.

Removing my drenched thong.

Discarding it in the trash.

And, using the first towel I came across to clean the parts of me he'd extracted without laying a finger on me.

"Ishmael."

"You're not leaving."

"Why no–"

"Because I said so. You have your wine. I have two

iMacs and three MacBooks here. Take your pick. The Wi-Fi is yours."

I shook my head, accepting the wine he was handing me.

"It's not that simple," I explained.

"Then let me make it simpler. What else do you need?"

"I prefer working on my own devices. It's possible yours is compromised. I can't risk my entire client... Ishmael– please. Distance."

His feet were planted. Unmoving.

"Have a seat, Royce. I am not against cuffing you to the pipes to help you better understand your current situation. But, I'd much rather you just sit your pretty ass down, drink your wine, and tell me more about yourself while watching me cook. I said I'd feed you. I meant it. I'll have you a brand new MacBook at the door in the next thirty minutes. Be patient, my baby."

My baby?

I swallowed nothing. The air pained me as it slid down my throat. Ishmael didn't repeat himself. He didn't elaborate further. He disappeared.

Back into the kitchen.

Back to banging pots.

Back to preparing a meal.

Back to the forefront of my brain.

Back to the center where my yearning was so deep it hurt with each step I took toward the sofa.

The day a man can tell you what to do and you actually fucking listen, Royce, that is the man. 'Cause, you're one hardheaded ass child. You do things your way. It doesn't matter what anyone else says or how it affects them. You march to the beat of your own drum. You're hell. But, I'm okay with that, because it was my intention to raise hell. Eight different pits of it.

Richie lulled me as I sunk into the couch. Its warmth welcomed me.

The television rose from the compartment in the floor that I had difficulty figuring out on the blueprint. It made sense now. The 75-inch screen powered on. Pandora began to play. 6lack was the first artist on the list. I couldn't deny his ability to set the ambience.

I crossed one leg over the other. The right mule dangled from my foot. Wine slid across my tongue. It's sweetness paired well with the dryness. It was expected with the reds of its caliber. The glass would be emptied much sooner than later.

I lowered it. Ishmael's presence was startling. On his knees, he peered up at me. My ankle was impossibly small in his hand.

Slowly, he slid the right mule from my right foot. And then the left. But, his eyes never left me.

His touch ignited the smoldering fire inside of me. My chest rose as I pulled in more air than my lungs had the capacity to hold. Yet, and still, I was breathless.

"I'm not ready for you to leave, Royce."

I parted my lips to take another sip.

"I've gathered that."

"And, your feelings toward that?"

"You wouldn't have the chance to cuff me to the

pipes, Ishmael. You'd be dead before you could properly open the first cuff. If I wanted to leave, I would've. I don't need permission to do what I want. I'm capable. Well-capable. But, I'm telling you things you already know."

"You'd shoot me?" He chuckled.

"I'd kill you. But, you've given me no reason."

"How'd you get into this? This occupation?"

"I'm hungry. You can either stay right here and talk to me or make me food, but you can't do both."

"Not right here, but both can be done."

He stood on his feet and made his way to the kitchen. It wasn't until he vanished that I noticed the bottle of wine on the table in front of me. I leaned forward, my bare feet touching the plush rug beneath me. I uncapped the wine and poured more in my glass.

"I'm listening," Ishmael called out from where he stood.

I tucked my feet behind me and turned my body in his direction.

"I was born into it."

"That doesn't explain much."

"It explains enough."

He cleansed the shrimp in one bowl and the broccoli in another.

"As much as I admire your strength, I want you tender, my baby."

I gasped, choking from the wine on the way down my throat.

"Ishmael. This is business."

"Until it's not."

"I–"

"We're a couple now, according to this plan you've made." He sniggered, "So I'm just telling you how I like my shit. I expect the same from you. I'm a team player. I'll oblige."

"That's hard to believe."

"When a woman has my attention, you'd be surprised at how obedient I can be."

"Hmmm. Sounds like a lot of women have had your attention."

"If that's your way of asking if I've had a plethora of women, then yes. I have. But, as of late, nah. One woman has my attention. Besides, there's a difference in capturing and keeping my attention. No one has had that power yet, but I can bet my last dollar this one does."

I rolled my eyes as a smile ripped through my face.

"Mayor… what led you to the point of wanting to run that race?"

"I'm for my city. I'm overly qualified for the position. Daniels is crooked. He doesn't deserve the seat the city has given him. And, each day he proves it a bit more. Right now, he's scrambling knowing that someone who actually deserves the seat is running against him and has a chance at winning this thing."

"Daniels is dirty," I agreed.

"And doesn't play fair. Neither does he win fairly."

"You've heard the rumors, too, huh?"

"I don't think they're rumors."

Chuckling, I sipped from my glass.

"I want this. There's only one thing in life I've wanted more than this. I'm going to win the election. I have to. And, I can't let this little mishap ruin that chance for me."

This disappointment in his tone was gutting. His passion poured from his lips and his posture and his movements and his eyes.

"I won't let it."

"I'm counting on it. Quite literally. I've run a scandal-free race until now. Shit sucks but it is what it is, ya know. I'm a firm believer that everything happens for a reason. Everything happens as it should. And, what is for you will find you. That is for me. It will find me."

"I think so, too."

T H E **G R E Y** L I S T

Time was lost between laughter and glasses of wine. My cheeks hurt from laughter. Though few words had ever come from Ishmael's mouth, I learned he was full of so many unsaid things. And, unintentionally, he was comical.

Bright.

Knowledgeable.

Innovative.

Politically correct.

Two strangers were a little less stranger with each passing second. A few things were evident from our conversation on the living room floor where we opted to dine on the coffee table over the dining table.

His mother meant the most to him.

Indigo was his heart.

He was Berekely bred, to his core.

Change was his motivation for the race he was running.

My heart made its presence known with each beat. Everything slowed to a creep, even time, as I marveled at the man before me. He was resilient. He was reserved. He was ravishing.

His beauty and his brains.

As he stood over me, arm stretched, awaiting my dish, I lost myself again. He was so easy to escape within. I forgot it all. Everything. Nothing mattered at the moment. Nothing had mattered since that night. Not when he was around. Not at the sound of his voice or the comfort of his world.

"I'm going to clean the mess I've made and I'll set you free, Royce."

The sun would settle soon. Time had gotten away from us. I'd forgotten about the laptop that had been delivered three hours ago when we'd sat down to eat. I'd also forgotten about my cellphone. My tasks. My schedule. *Everything.*

"Thank you, kindly, sir."

With my wine in my hand, I slid up onto the couch. My cell hadn't moved an inch. It was right where I'd left it. Notifications had been pouring in. I pressed the proper buttons to unlock the screen and began to scroll through them all.

Looking like you're that bitch! Roulette hyped.

Your face is all over the news in Berkeley, babe. Rome's concern could be heard through her text.

I'd risk it all for a man that fine, too. Range stated the known.

He is a shooter. Rugger notified me, though I'd already done my research.

He hunts. Well. She elaborated.

You look good together. Roaman's smile was obvious through her words.

My books are open. A session to welcome him into the family sounds good, right? Rather was serious.

I love that look on you, Egypt added.

It's just business, babes. But, I agree. He is mesmerizing. With a seven-inch, veiny tool between his legs. Let's pray I keep my tongue and pussy juices to myself. He writes big checks.

I chuckled as I pressed the blue arrow to send my message. I placed my cell back on the couch and stretched my legs, preparing to wait for Ishmael to finish cleaning his kitchen. A shower, some good tunes, and a bed was calling my name.

SEVEN

Ishmael

ANGELIC.

Gentle.

Magical.

Mystical.

She was a long-legged fairy. She didn't feel real, but she had to be. She was on my couch. In my home. Asleep.

Peace had found her.

Calm had lulled her.

Food had filled her.

Laughter had exhausted her.

I didn't want to disturb her. Night had fallen, and I wanted nothing more than to transfer her to my bed.

However, the thought was repulsive. Before Royce touched sheets or a bed I'd nailed another woman to, I'd burn in hell.

I'd placed the order for a new bed, new linen, and a deep clean of my entire condo. Still, I felt I wanted her elsewhere. Not at my pad, but at the address I'd built from scratch. Out of the city. Out of the way.

Not in hiding, but in privacy. Somewhere no one else had been. No woman had entered. No intimacy was established. No bodies had been taken down.

She can't stay.

The reasoning left a bitter taste in my mouth. But, I knew better. My heart did, too.

"You're staring at me."

Royce's voice was soothing. She hadn't opened her eyes. She was trying to regain consciousness.

"You're asleep on my couch. And, you're quiet. Not making demands or quietly disagreeing with me. It felt nice."

She sniggered.

"You could've had your space all to yourself."

"I wanted to share it with you."

"Well, that gets you back talk, disagreements, and—"

"But, not when you're asleep."

She quieted, finally opening her eyes. Her arms stretched and her body uncurled under the blanket I'd placed over her an hour ago.

"How long have I been asleep?"

"Two hours."

She shook her head, disappointed.

"I don't nap."

"What's wrong with naps?"

"They keep me up all night. I cherish my rest hours."

"Maybe your body needed it."

"Yeah, but now I'll be up all night long."

"Me, too," I admitted.

She remained quiet as she sat up.

"Thank you for the blank—"

"You don't have to stay up alone tonight," I pushed out much faster than I could stop myself.

She placed her elbows on her knees and ran her hands through her hair. A sigh parted her lips.

"I've enjoyed myself, Ishmael. But, I should get home to get ahead of this thing. We have a campaign to win. We won't win it if I'm not in front of my computer every chance I get. You paid me for a service. I wouldn't be well if I didn't approach it with excellence. That's how I operate. I don't know anything else. I don't want to either."

"Understood."

"Give me five minutes and I'll be ready."

"I'll be waiting."

The ride to the gated community of condominiums was silent. Though well-rested, Royce was reserved. Quiet. Completely soundless.

Admittedly, I missed her voice. I anticipated the next time I'd hear it. The low sounds playing in the background wasn't enough to fill the space in the whip.

My wheels stopped at the door of the address I'd been given. Royce's hand touched the handle. My hand rested on her thigh. Her head twisted, eyes meeting mine.

"*Don't do that, my baby.*"

She lowered her hand, signaling my exit. I was out of the SUV in a flash. The night air was calm. Its warmth wasn't surprising. It would be November before Berkeley cooled down.

Royce stepped out of the car. Even in the darkness, she was radiant. I closed the door behind her. Hating to see her creep away.

Click.

Clack.

Her heels collided with the concrete beneath us. My body pressed into the passenger door as I shoved my hands in my pockets to keep from hindering her escape. She didn't make it very far before her legs stopped moving and her backside was no longer in view. It was that pretty face of hers.

Still, she said nothing. I watched her body stiffen with uncertainty and possibly regret. She smiled and began toward me. I didn't budge. My limbs were anchored. So was my heart. And my ears. And my thoughts.

"*Thank you.*"

There it was. Her voice serenaded me, quieting things that I'd been trying to lower the volume on for years.

She was close enough for me to smell the peppermint on her breath. She'd twirled it around in her mouth on the entire ride over. For the first time, I wanted to be a fucking peppermint. I wanted to be that pepperment. I wanted my hardness to dissolve on her tongue, too.

As quickly as she'd come, she'd gone. But, this time, I couldn't resist. I removed my hand from the pocket of my jeans and gripped the back of Royce's neck, bringing her back to me. Where she belonged. Where I needed her. Where she needed to be.

Her softness was heavenly against my rigidness. I lowered my hand, wrapping my arm around her waist.

"Ishmael–"

Sultriness toggled with her tone.

"Couples usually end their time together with a goodbye hug. I can't have you leaving without giving me mine."

Relaxing against me, Royce succumbed to her defeat. It didn't matter what her head or heart were screaming. Her body was willing to do what they were unsure of. In my arms, she maneuvered, facing me.

She was so close.

Still, she wasn't close enough.

Her arms wrapped around my neck. Her chin lifted, barely clearing my shoulder. Naturally, I surrounded her. Pulling her as deep into my web as humanly possible.

Everything was supple. She was loose at the limbs. Comfort coaxed her. Elevated her degree of softness. She was like putty in my hands.

"Goodnight, Ishmael."

She wasn't breathing. Not even when she pulled away. This time, I didn't disrupt her. I allowed her to walk away. I had to. Our night wouldn't end here if I didn't. And, too much was at stake for us to explore each other's sacred quarters.

Each other's private real estate.

Each other's precious gems.

Buried treasures.

"Goodnight, Royce."

. . .

I rubbed my hand through my beard. My jawline flexed as I watched Daniels go on and on about the images that had recently surfaced.

"My concern isn't only with his obvious addiction to escorts and sex workers, but if he'll use the taxpayer's money to support it when he's in office."

Brain matter coated the screen as I fired a single kill shot. Straight to his dome. From a mile away. At a secure location. With no chance of being discovered. My skills were far too advanced for the authorities' small, limited capacities.

"That campaign is being funded by private donors. It makes me wonder if that money is how he's managing his expensive habits and if the donors are aware of where their money is going," he continued, reminding me that I was far removed from my past and trying to build a better future for Berkeley.

Sex worker.

The term made my blood boil. Royce was not in the business of selling her pussy. She was selling her talents. Her resourcefulness. Her ability to turn messes into miracles. Her gift. Her knowledge. Not her pussy.

Matte's fists clashed with my office door as she pushed it open.

"Sixty seconds, Mr. Grayson."

"Headed down."

The office building was littered with reporters. Every inch of the press conference room was filled with those dying to hear more about what was happening in my world. The part of it that wasn't their concern. The private part.

I was up from my desk, sliding my cell in my pocket within the next few seconds. Three minutes of my time was all the press was allotted and I wouldn't be in front of them a minute more.

I took the elevator with Cameron, Matte, and Sarah surrounding me. Together, we stepped out into the lobby, greeted with the flashing lights of cameras. Microphones were angled towards us, but distance was maintained. It was evident I prioritized my personal space. Reporters had learned it earlier on in my campaign.

The chatter in the conference room quieted upon my arrival. I stepped up onto the platform, stopping at the podium where the microphone was waiting. The clock on the back of the wall began. I was down to two minutes and fifty seconds before I opened my mouth.

"Uh mmm." I cleared my throat.

Two minutes and forty-five seconds.

"I want to start by thanking everyone in this room who have taken time out of their day to address such a senseless, baseless matter. It has been brought to my attention that parts of my life that are reserved for my eyes and ears only have been plastered across your screens in an effort to tarnish my name, credibility, character, and smear my campaign.

"For my first point, fuck whoever you are who put the face of an innocent, loving, and incredibly smart woman who was simply experiencing a string of unfortunate events one evening and fully expected the man she shares personal time with to be of assistance on the screen of people who have real life issues they're facing daily. Like hunger, childcare needs, low wages, declining test scores, housing–real life crisis that my opponent isn't doing much about because he has his head too far up his own ass."

Gasps followed my candid thoughts. Matte's hand on my shoulder did little to steer me in the direction we'd discussed. Royce's face was fresh in my memory. It wasn't my image I cared to protect today. It was hers and the women around the world under the scrutiny of the male gaze.

"Secondly, what I do in my spare time is none of your concern. I'm human–just like you all. I'm not perfect and I've never made that claim during this campaign. However, out of all the pleasantries I've paid for in my life, a woman's body has never been one. I find their value to be far beyond the limits of our financial capabilities. But, speaking of the bodies of women, I'm led to my next point.

"Aren't we tired of policing them? By them, I'm referring to the very real estate of a woman. It's not ours. It's not ours to make rules or laws or assumptions or decisions about. Just like my spare time shouldn't concern you, neither should their bodies. Using sex worker or escort or prostitute as derogatory terms when men quite literally walk around each day trying to prove they have bigger balls than the next man is idiotic.

"Fourthly, my significant other is a lot of great things, but she's nothing she's been referred to as for the last few days. Next time she crosses your screen, be sure to remember that she's a beautiful, well-educated, resourceful, entrepreneurial, witty, adventurous, brave, and confident Black woman who cares little about what the world thinks of her and everything about what she thinks of herself.

"She's not afraid of her reflection in the mirror. I can't say the same for Daniels, Herd, or the person who turned a tender moment into a public display of malice and ill intent."

I had nothing further to say. Neither did I care to answer questions. There were forty seconds left on the clock. I didn't have those to spare.

I was back in my office, bathing in solitude, by the time the time ran out. Outside of my door, hands came together, sounding off in the silence. I peered out of the glass to find my staff in celebration.

I waved a hand, letting Matte know it was okay for her to come in. She rushed inside.

"Oh shoots."

She tripped over her feet, landing face first in front of my desk. She'd disappeared. I waited patiently for her to rise again. This was typical of Matte. She was working with two left feet.

"You good?"

Chuckling, she nodded. Simultaneously, she pulled

her dress down. She was no longer apologetic for her clumsiness. And, everyone in the office had gotten accustomed to it.

"I've never been better, sir."

"What's with the celebration?"

"Your speech, Mr. Grayson. It has social media buzzing. Especially the parts where you used profanity. And, the parts about policing women's bodies. Oh, and, about sex work or escorts not being derogatory terms. And, of course, Royce."

"Royce? They've mentioned her name?"

Matte nodded.

"Um hm. It seems as though they've discovered who the mystery woman is."

"And?"

"Uncovered pictures of you two. Is there anything you haven't told us?"

I shook my head, "Nah. I told you she was handling it."

"If this is her way of going about things, then– well– I like it."

"She's good at her job."

"She's pretty darn impressive."

I nodded.

"And, pretty."

I nodded, again.

"I mean– they're loving her! They're loving you all. They've given you a hashtag already."

I hated social media. It was such a wild place. It gave so

many powerless people ammunition. So many people lost their souls in the midst of strangers. Too many people had a microphone. Everyone wanted to be a main character. No one wanted to sit the socials out or simply enjoy them for the entertainment they were designed to be. Everyone wanted in. Everyone wanted a voice. Everyone wanted a platform. Everyone wanted a network.

Aside from my campaign, I didn't have a social media presence. I didn't have a personal page. Neither did I have any of the applications downloaded on my phone. Posting felt too much like providing evidence to the public and authorities in the event they needed to use it against you.

But, as Matte turned her screen around and Royce's handle was tagged next to the hashtag Rayson, I reconsidered my stance on the platforms.

Maybe one day. I reasoned.

Not for posting. Not for entertaining. Not to become the main character of anyone's story. But, to become a supporting character in Royce's story. Her number one fan. The first comment on her posts. The first one to tap the red hearts. The person to hype her. The person to praise her. Openly.

"Click her page."

@CCRoyce

Six posts.

Her beautiful face was obstructed in them all. Three fully clothed photos were between three vacation photos. Her page said many things without saying anything. It proved many things without proving anything.

I slid down slightly, placing a hand underneath my chin as I stared at the images. Royce was as close to heaven I'd ever reach. I had to have her. If not now, then eventually. Soon. In the next ninety days. I couldn't fathom waiting longer.

"This is not a hoax for you, huh?"

I didn't look up from the phone. My eyes were still pinned on the screen, still pinned on *her* when I responded, "No, Matte. It's not."

"You're starting to like her."

"This is no start. I've felt this way since I met her."

"That night."

I nodded.

"That night."

Matte said nothing more. She waited in silence as I studied every detail of Royce. It wasn't until I was ready that I returned the cell.

"If you need me, I'll be in my office."

"Noted."

The door closed quietly behind her. As it did so, I picked up my cell. I flipped it from one side to the other in my hand, contemplating my next move.

There was an overwhelming urge to make contact with Royce. Too many hours had passed since I'd seen her face or heard her voice. From the lack of movement on the tracker, I knew she was no longer in Berkeley. She was back home, in Clarke.

That's exactly where I wanted to be. Right beside her.

I unlocked my cell, deciding that a text would be best.

Thank you.

I kept it simple. There was no need for an explanation. She had her eyes on the prize. She might've been in Clarke, but her ears were on Berkeley's soil.

I didn't close our thread. I ran a hand around my neck as I waited for gray bubbles to appear. A yawn cut through my concentration, forming tears in my eyes. Sleep hadn't been easy to come by last night.

I ruffled my sheets with the constant tossing and turning. Insomnia twiddled with my sanity all night. I rose just before sunrise, feeling quite shitty. However, duty called.

There were three communities to visit and a school's book fair where I purchased every book the children's hearts desired. I remembered not having the funds to splurge during the yearly school book fair. No kid should suffer that level of heartbreak at such a young age.

You owe me. Her reply was accompanied by a winking emoji.

My account is in great standing. Two point five has been satisfied.

I slid my index and middle finger across my lips, awaiting her response. One minute turned into two.

Two minutes turned into three. Ten minutes slipped away from me before I noticed how tightly I was gripping the phone. Eyes still locked on the screen.

My stomach flipped. My head spun. My chest expanded with entitlement. Daniels was accurate when he noted my addiction. A new habit. A good habit. Royce was quickly becoming the source of my obsession.

Blanche's Steakhouse.
  Tonight at 7p.
  Send the address. I'll have a driver at your door by 6:30p.

My fingers were moving at the speed of lightning. I couldn't deny it any longer. It was Royce who I wanted to end my night with. The victory didn't feel as victorious without her to celebrate with.

My schedule was clear after three. I could be in Clarke by nightfall and at Blanche's by seven. It was one of the many restaurants I'd found in Clarke while tossing and turning last night. A note in my cell listed the places I found interesting and wanted to visit with Royce. Traveling to Berkeley wasn't a requirement. Clarke was calling me. If that's where she was, then that's where I wanted to be.

  Sorry, Mr. Mayor. I have dinner plans already.
  Cancel them.

I can't, unfortunately. I've canceled on him three times already.

Him?

I felt my eyebrows creep to the center of my forehead as I read the message twice more before responding again.

Royce.

Yes, him. As much as I love playing in pussy, it's not my preference.

I could feel the heat raging in my body. My blood was no longer flowing with ease. It was boiling.

That's not a good idea. You're all over the screens. You could easily be recognized and there goes the campaign.

I'm careful, Ishmael. This is a private dinner. No one will be in the restaurant but the staff, owner, and a waitress. NDAs have been signed. Any more concerns?

Cancel the date, Royce.

My client's need comes before mine. Always have. It'll be fine.

Then why the fuck do I feel like I need you and you're not here? I erased the message as it appeared in my head and decided against replying. She'd made up her mind and so had I.

EIGHT

Royce

I SMOOTHED the wrinkles of my dress, sliding my palms along the soft, cool fabric. Clarke's air was moist and muggy. Still, it was breathable, and perfect for September. I hadn't expected much less.

My key fob slid into my bag with ease. I buttoned it and lowered it to my side. One foot in front of the other, I ambled toward the door of Georgio's. The secondary entrance was reserved for those who valued their privacy.

It swung open upon my arrival. A young, dark-skinned fella with gold covering his front teeth offered a smile and a hand to help me up the four steps. I took him up on his offer.

"Good evening, ma'am. Welcome to Georgio's."

"Good evening. Thank you for having me."

"Right this way. Your guest and your table are waiting."

I obliged, following the handsome fella through the restaurant. We reached the private quarters where Hakem was waiting. He hadn't taken his seat. Neither had he sipped from his water. He was awaiting my arrival.

"Royce."

Arms extended, he pulled me into his embrace. It was bone-chilling. The warmth I anticipated left me cold and concerned.

Hakem was the first profile I'd actually considered on *Prestige*, the dating app for the wealthy, well-respected, and untouchable. Our schedules never aligned. Not until tonight. Something always came up on my end. But, after spending time with Ishmael, and experiencing the beauty of partnership, I was determined to make the next date a success.

Hakem was born into wealth. He didn't obtain it on his own. He was spoiled rotten as a child and became the head of his family's oil company after the sudden passing of his father.

There wasn't a rough edge to be noted about Hakem. He went to the best schools, had the best tutors, and hung with the filthy rich children of his family's immediate circle.

Our stories nearly resembled each other. However, our upbringing was incredibly different. I could hit my target with my eyes closed. I doubt Hakem had ever fired a weapon for anything other than the sport of hunting, *if that.* Bodyguards were trained to handle situations that required heavy fire power so he wouldn't have to. And that's where I was struggling.

He's no soldier.

Tonight, there were no guards. It was only Hakem. And, the burgundy suit that adorned his frame made the decision to see him tonight make so much sense. He was long, slim, and as suave as they came.

Hakem was the color of charcoal. His eyes were the brightest things on his frame. And, still, not a detail of his makeup could be overlooked. Everything was bolded. Italisized. And highlighted.

Hakem reminded me of royalty. And, rightfully so. His family was as close to royalty as Clarke would ever see. The legals, anyway. The underbelly was an entirely different beast. They didn't belong down there. Their kind couldn't withstand the heat emitting from the steam pipes.

"Hakem."

Though he was nicknamed Kem, hardly anything about him reminded me of Chem.

His height.

His wealth.

His reach.

It didn't go beyond those parameters.

He smelled like cedarwood and pepper. Vanilla was the link between the two, rounding out the fragrance extremely well.

"You smell divine."

"You look the same," he complimented, loosening his grip on me.

"Thank you."

"I was beginning to think I wouldn't catch up to you. Busy, busy."

"Yeah. It happens."

"Your face has been all over my screen lately. I thought I'd lost my chance."

"I'm here. You're here. Let's not worry about anything more."

"I agree."

I took my seat and Hakem took his.

"Evening, ma'am. Sir. I'm Grace. I'll be taking care of you tonight. Anything from our drink menu piques your interest? We have incredible wine."

"I'll have a bottle of your finest red and two glasses for my date and I."

Hakem was quick on his toes. Grace scurried off to fulfill his request hastily. I stared at the regal gentleman before me, waiting to feel what I'd been feeling over the last few weeks.

I quieted my thoughts to hear the beat of my heart. It wasn't as loud or as thunderous as it had been lately. It was meek and somber and slowly beating in my chest.

"What have you been up to, Royce? What's been keeping you lately?"

Ishmael.

The hammering began as his name crossed my

mind. I placed a hand on my chest to keep my heart from escaping. It beat against its cage fiercely, wanting out. Wanting more. Wanting *him*.

"Work," I admitted.

"You ever considered putting your briefcase down to enjoy the fruit of your labor?"

"Sounds torturous."

A smile from Hakem had my lips curling upward as well.

"I, too, am addicted to the thrill. The rush. The multitasking. The risk. The uncertainty. It's thrilling. Much like you."

I closed my eyes.

Ishmael.

His name was like sugar on my tongue.

"Thank you."

Hakem's gaze was wavering. He rescued me from deep waters, bringing me back to safer grounds. Back to the moment.

"Tell me," he paused, "Your profile has been active for months. I can't help but wonder what it is you're looking for in a partner."

Ishmael.

I inhaled, closing my eyes again. Only briefly, as I tried shoving his name down my throat. He was every-thing I was in search of.

"Me."

Gosh. I'm losing my mind.

I heard his voice so clearly. So closely. I forced my

eyes open and tried pinning the smile Hakem was responsible for back onto my face. I failed.

I wasn't losing my mind. And, Ishmael wasn't in my head. He was standing before me with his hands gathered in front of him. His lips were rolled inward, tucked into his mouth. Veins sprouted from his hands. His nostrils were spread so wide I could see what he was thinking.

And feeling.

And neither were comforting.

Ishmael was dressed in black from his neck to his feet. He reeked of wealth and confidence. Lust oozed from his orbs.

But so did disappointment.

Anger.

Frustration.

And impatience.

His robe was short. His fuse was even shorter.

"Dismiss your guest, Royce."

"Ishmael." I chuckled, finding his presence rather comical.

Just hours ago, he was in front of cameras telling men to stop policing a woman's real estate. Tonight, he was at a private dinner, policing a woman's time.

"A walking contradiction, you are, sir."

"I'm Hakem." Hakem began to rise from his seat. "Nice to me–"

"Move another inch and I will empty the entire clip in your chest for even thinking about getting close to something that belongs to me."

Hakem stilled.

It was at that moment that I remembered the unforgettable flaw.

He's no soldier.

"Dismiss your guest, Royce, or I will fold his shoulders and head together with one blow to his neck. If he's lucky, he will survive a crushed windpipe, but the chance is highly unlikely."

I turned my head in the opposite direction. Collecting myself felt impossible.

"Royce."

"Goodnight, Hakem."

I faced my date, who was partially confused and fully unprepared for the hell I knew Ishmael would bring.

Hakem was a very smart man. He stood, quietly making his exit. I lowered my gaze, fixing it on the contents of the table. As much as I wanted to call Ishmael's bluff, I didn't want Hakem to lose his life because of it. There was a chance he would.

Ishmael took the seat Hakem once occupied. The wine was delivered as his bottom touched the cushion. Grace was perplexed, but poured a glass of wine for us both anyway. Ishmael refused his. I pulled my close for comfort, placed it at my lips, and took a big sip.

I didn't bother with the proper etiquette. I didn't give a damn how the wine smelled. For now, I cared about its potency. I needed it to numb the nerves that were splitting rapidly and uncontrollable.

"I'll have cognac. Neat."

"Yes, sir. Can I get you two started with appetizers?"

Ishmael nodded. His orbs were fixed on me.

Unmoving. Unblinking. Unchanging.

"Bring us the best in the house."

"I can do that for you."

"Thank you."

Grace disappeared, leaving us alone again. I matched Ishmael's gaze. My heart was unsteady. So was my breathing. Fine bumps riddled my skin. Everything quieted around us.

"What are you doing?" I didn't recognize my voice. Neither did I recognize myself.

"I'm pretending to be your man, Royce. Isn't that the route *you* chose instead of paying to make this shit go away?"

Ishmael leaned forward.

"I've never been one to half-ass, my baby. As my woman, I'm expecting your undivided attention, unwavering support, and faithfulness. I can't have the word on the streets being that the future mayor can't keep his woman on a leash."

As Ishmael sat back, I pulled his glass of wine closer. It would be silly to allow it to go to waste.

Admittedly, I was amused. But, undoubtedly, I was smitten. I could listen to Ishmael talk shit for hours without growing tired.

He was egotistical, but not too much.

He was haughty, but not too much.

He was confident, but not too much.

He was cocky, but not too much.

He was possessive, but not too much.

He was entitled, but not too much.

He was foolish, but not too much.

Ishmael was just the right amount of everything.

"Why didn't you cancel the date?" He asked, crossing his right leg over his left and bringing his hands together.

He hadn't looked over his shoulder once since he'd sat down. Rugger's claims sat with me. He wasn't worried about dying tonight, because he knew he wouldn't. He wasn't going to allow it and neither was I.

I didn't have an answer to his question. So, I didn't respond. I kept my eyes fixed on him, falling deeper into his trance with each breath I took. Lovingly, hopelessly, I adorn his handsome face.

"You are aware that this is all make believe, yeah?"

Ishmael uncrossed his legs, leaning forward again. He hesitated, choosing his words ever so carefully.

"Then make me believe it," he demanded, "Because the shit happening in my head and heart ain't made up. It's real."

I quieted, expanding and shrinking in my seat, simultaneously.

He'd said everything I'd been thinking. He'd unrooted everything I'd been burying.

"Here we have stuffed shrimp, smothered in our seafood bisque sauce. We also have our lobster spinach dip with seasoned, freshly fried garlic chips, and cognac. Anything else I can get you right now?"

"No. Not at the moment," I assured Grace.

"Alright. I'm going to get out of your way. Let me know when you're ready to order."

Suddenly, my appetite had vanished. So had my vocabulary. I had nothing to say. Just big, unprecedented feelings that I hardly knew what to do with.

Ishmael dug into the spinach dip.

"Eat your food," he demanded.

My fingers moved faster than I would've liked had I had control of them. Still, everything was in slow motion. I used a fork to slice open the stuffed shrimp.

"You're not allowed to date, Royce. Not unless that nigga's name is Ishmael Grayson. Anybody else getting beat the fuck up or a bullet right where it ached at the realization that you didn't take heed to my warning."

"I'm a grown woman, Ishmael Grayson."

"Grown and free are two very different terms. Please understand you're not both."

I filled my mouth with an array of flavors. They were all pleasing to my tastebuds, receiving a nod of approval.

"Are you going to stare at me the entire night?"

"I am."

I chuckled, knowing Ishmael was no liar.

"I think you're stunning, Royce. What better is there for me to sta—"

"Why were you at the hotel?" I blurted before stuffing my mouth again.

Discomfort covered him completely. His posture changed. His limbs loosened. He bit into another tortilla chip with dip on top. He was in no rush to respond. I was in no rush to hear his response either, because it would only mean I was next up to speak again. I wasn't ready.

"I went to meet my father. He didn't show."

My chest rattled with despair. His words were riddled with pain. Unresolved pain that was likely the purpose of his visit to Clarke.

"Has he ever?"

"Ever?"

"Shown?" I asked.

He shook his head.

"Nah."

"Will you try again?"

"Fuck 'em," he tittered with a shrug.

"Understood."

"Your father?"

"Dead."

He nodded, accepting my indirect request to move on. My suffering since Richie's passing would not be the subject of dinner. It hurt too much. It bruised too much. It shifted too much.

"Your mother?"

My smile lifted my cheeks.

"Rhea– her name is Rhea. She's heaven on earth."

"Yeah? Sounds like my old lady. Life would've been a shit show without her in my corner."

I nodded.

"I feel the same about my father and my brother. Rhea has been the softest place to land since I can remember. But, I've never been a girl who wanted to land softly. I've always wanted to hit the ground running. For that, I had my brother and my father to count on."

"Most girls– it's their mothers wh–"

"I'm not most girls, Ishmael. Have you not taken note?"

"I have. My notepad is running out of space and my pen is running out of ink. I've been making notes since I met you."

"Good notes or?"

"Notes. There's not much that isn't good about you, Royce. Aside from the fact that you don't listen."

I shrugged, sipping from the wine glass.

"I'm waiting to be given instructions worth listening to."

Ishmael's lips turned upward as his head lifted and then fell, numerous times.

"That won't work for us."

His index finger pointed from my chest to his.

"Us?"

"Don't insult me, my baby. You heard what the fuck I said."

Ever so gently, he released his next set of words. Never raising his voice. Never altering his position. He was fully in control of himself. Of me. Of this moment.

"When you open your mouth, I listen. When you give instructions, I listen. That's how this shit is supposed to work," he explained.

"You're my client."

"If you thought that was the reason, then you're sadly mistaken."

"Then, why is it?"

"The bottom line is you can fall in line or you can fall in line–voluntarily or involuntarily; makes me no fucking difference."

"Is that your favorite word?"

"What?"

"Fuck? Fucking?"

"It's my favorite action," he clarified.

My pussy spat onto the seat of my underwear. My walls pulled together. My stomach muscles clenched. Saliva rushed into my mouth, pooling around my teeth and tongue.

"But, I'm a man of great discipline. I thought I was." He chuckled, pulling his hand over his beard. "Until…"

"Until."

"You."

"Before deciding to be a changemaker, what were you doing in Berkeley?"

"You know the answer to that question. You have the blueprints to my homes. I'm sure my background is in whatever file you have on me, too."

"I asked you a question."

Slowly, Ishmael leaned forward. Hands on the table.

"A killer."

A chill ran through my spine. My throbbing center salivated. I batted my lashes and squeezed my thighs closer to suppress the aching yearn that was becoming insufferable.

"You're no stranger to that kind of crazy, are you?"

"I'm that level of unreasonable myself. But, you know that," I breathed out, tilting my head with a smile.

"So is your family."

"So is your brother."

"And yours," he replied, popping the end of a chip in his mouth.

I folded a hundred times inside. It didn't matter what Ishmael was doing, he was unrealistic while doing it. Downright fine. Ridiculously sexy.

"Which is why this couldn't–it shouldn't work."

I placed a hand on my chest and then pointed across the table.

"It will."

This I knew. So, I didn't disagree. I forked more shrimp and slid the fork across my tongue.

"You belong to me, Royce. Do whatever it is you need to get that through your pretty skull. Until then, I'll be at every dinner date, every lunch date, and every coffee date. You won't be able to escape me or whatever the fuck this is happening between us."

"How'd you find me?"

"I'm a hunter, my baby. In case I haven't made it clear, you are on the top of my hit list."

"I'm flattered."

Truthfully, I was. Ishmael was aware.

I unlocked my screen and found the last note I'd created. I slid the phone across the table and turned it in his direction.

"You have an Instagram account. Since the press conference, it has amassed over twelve thousand followers. Sign in. Make them believe what you're trying to make me believe."

"Which is—"

"This will work."

As if he'd accepted my challenge, he unlocked his cell and downloaded the application. He didn't attempt to mask his code. I watched carefully as he logged in with the credentials on my screen. Once in, he scrolled through the photos already on his profile. There were only three.

"This is your personal page. Careful what you share."

"I'm not a fan of social media."

"Your voters are. They want to know Ishmael Grayson. The campaign page has served its purpose. They want more."

He nodded.

"Understood."

"I was heading to Berkeley in the morning, yet here you are."

"I plan to have you in Berkeley tonight."

I swallowed the air pocket in my throat.

"Would you like to order, Royce, or have more wine?"

I shook my head.

"Neither," I admitted.

It wasn't anything on *Georgio's* menu that I wanted in my mouth at the moment. It was Ishmael.

Ishmael Grayson.

"Well then."

He stood from his seat. Four hundred dollar bills magically appeared, falling onto the table. Ishmael was behind me, pulling out my chair in a flash.

"You before me."

I stood, feeling my slippery center become the source of discomfort. If I didn't clean up, my juices would be running down my legs, ruining my clothes.

"I need to stop by the ladies' room."

He pointed his head toward the restroom sign. It was inside of the small area designated for private dining. Ishmael was on my heels as I made my way across the room.

He pushed the door open upon arrival. I stepped inside, happy to have freed myself from his trance. He was breathtaking. I breathed out, releasing the breath I'd been holding.

Click.

The sound of the door locking behind me stiffened my frame. Within a millisecond, I'd become immobile. I couldn't move. I couldn't speak. I couldn't think.

Ishmael's hands were on me at once. My back was against the door. And, my thong was a torn piece of drenched fabric.

His fingers touched my sensitivity. The sound of my arousal against his extremities was nauseating. His breath against my skin was intoxicating.

"Ridiculous," he whispered under his breath.

Still, I heard every word. Every syllable.

"Please," I begged, needing to feel parts of him I'd deemed off limits.

"I'm trying my hardest to respect you in public, but you're making it impossible, my baby."

Three fingers entered me. They turned toward him, and then pulled forward.

"Ish—uhhhhh."

"I can't keep letting you walk away from me with all this shit pent up inside of you. You need to clear your cache. So you can clear your head. And your ears. And get a better understanding of who the fuck is in charge here."

He spoke to me calmly, yet firmly. His fingers hadn't moved another centimeter. I desperately needed them to. He knew it as much as I did.

"Ishmael."

"I like the way you call my name, but that ain't gone work, my baby."

"Pleas–"

"Are you ready to listen, Royce?"

I nodded, rubbing my walls against his fingers. He ejected his fingers, leaving me powerless. I was feeble, weak, and withering by the second.

I needed Ishmael. Not later. I needed him now. He'd turned on my facet and then folded the hose, causing build up at a rapid rate.

Desperate, I caught the tail end of my dress and shoved my fingers into my wetness. The pressure around my wrist forced me to reconsider.

"Uhhhh–"

Ishmael removed my fingers from my center. He lifted them up to his mouth and opened slightly. One finger at a time, he cleaned the traces of my intrusion from each extremity. His eyes were on mine, chastising me for my disobedience.

"Keep your hands," he demanded, placing another finger in his warm mouth.

"Off shit that doesn't belong to you."

He placed another in his mouth.

"Ishmael, you're killin–"

He pushed into me again.

"Yesssssss."

"Are you ready to listen?"

I nodded, head scrubbing against the door.

"I need words, Royce."

He twisted his fingers inside of me.

"Yes. Yessss."

"Yes what?"

He pulled them forward, toward him.

"I'm ready."

"Ready for what?"

He curled them forward a centimeter more.

"I'm ready to listen."

"That's my baby," he whispered against my ear.

Beckoning for my orgasm, he stroked my G-spot forcing my arms around him, pulling him closer.

"Ishmael. Oh Go– Yesss. Yessssss. Yesss."

"Shit is pathetic," he mumbled.

It was. I was. This was. I hadn't been touched this way. Not before him. And, I doubted I'd be touched this way after him. Ishmael was staking his claim. Ishmael was unraveling me so effortlessly.

His skillset was apparent. He was a pleaser. A fucker. A man after a woman's whole heart, starting with her pussy and working his way up.

"I'm gonna cum–"

"That's why we're here, my baby."

As the words left his mouth, my soul left my body. I slammed my eyelids shut and leaned my head against the door. I lost control of my limbs. A gush of my gratification led way to my undoing.

My sprinkler was ignited. I wet my threads, Ishmael's threads, the floor, his fingers, and my bottom half.

"Oh fuck. Oh fuck. Oh fuuuuuuuuuuck."

He continued extracting my pent up frustration, pain, loneliness, disappointment, despair, sexual tension, and desire.

"Ishmael. Please. Please."

My stomach knotted. My abdomen tingled with pleasure. My legs grew numb.

His lips crashed into mine, silencing me. He tasted so sweet. He tasted like he belonged to me. I tried removing his tongue from his mouth. My hunger would be the rebirth of me. A newer me. One that wasn't afraid of what Ishmael had to offer me. One that wasn't afraid to risk it all for a love I knew he could offer. One that understood Chemistry's choice to love Egypt in spite of everything. One that had chosen to listen, learn, and fall head first for the man before me.

Ishmael ejected his fingers. As I released him from my mouth, I came to the realization that nothing would be the same beyond this moment. Silence coated the uncertainty swelling my chest. My vulnerability was on the shoulders of my fabric. My emotions were all over the place. I was tender. Just as he wanted me. Just as he had made me.

Ishmael wet a napkin. He cleaned the mess he'd made as best he could. He patted my skin gently, hoping not to miss a spot. I didn't move. I couldn't move. Something was happening inside of me. Something was changing. Something was altered. I felt things shift in my chest, making room for him. Saving a spot for him. Expanding to accommodate him and all that came with him.

He cleansed my hands with a soapy towel and then followed up with water. He did the same for himself. His eyes were penetrating my sensitivity. They searched me as he moved about the restroom. I didn't have anything to give, except everything. Every part of me. I was defenseless. He could have it all. All of me.

He discarded the paper towels as he had my boundaries.

"Feel better now?" He asked, readjusting his rigidness.

I swallowed back my tears. "Yes."

Without another word, he grabbed me by the hand.

Click.

The door unlocked. So did my heart. We stepped out into the restaurant. Ishmael took my purse, understanding of my inability to carry anything but the heaviness of my heart at the moment. He slid his hand up my arm, neck, and check, pulling me closer. He planted a kiss on my forehead.

"I'll have you home soon, my baby."

THE GREY LIST

Ishmael sat inches away. The private plane featured a small main cabin, fit for a family of six or less. It was intimate. It was dark. It represented so many parts of our night.

"You are beautiful, Royce."

I inhaled, but quickly forgot to exhale. It wasn't until his phone camera was in my face that I noticed I was turning blue. I released the oxygen.

"Thank you."

My cheeks flushed with gratitude.

I unlocked my phone and found the pinned texts from the people in my world who meant the most to me.

"Don't be too harsh on me in that recap. I mean well, Royce."

I looked up from my phone, a smile tearing through my face.

I didn't bother responding. Ishmael caring how I presented him to others sat with me.

I know. I responded internally. *I know.*

I skipped the messages I'd missed for the evening. Instead, I started a message of my own.

When I said this is just business, I, wholeheartedly, meant his business. My businesses. Our business.

I know that's the fuck right. Fine as he is, he better have a big dick or this is just a waste of all of our excitement. Roulette was the first to respond.

She pushed a chuckle from my lips. It was low. Hardly notable.

I saw it. I saw it on the screen. Some things we aren't able to pretend. Range noted.

I can feel it through the images, babes. Egypt claimed.

Maybe I'm in love. A heart emoji followed.

I didn't care to see their responses tonight. I'd revisit them when the sun rose. For now, I wanted to let my thoughts run wild. I wanted my attention undivided. I wanted Ishmael in my line of vision. And, Ishmael only.

I lost track of time in his eyes. In his smile. In his presence. Ishmael was consuming. In the best ways. In the richest ways. In the most pleasant ways.

Shortly after we'd boarded miles and miles away, I slid into the Aston Martin. He closed the door behind me. My eyes were planted on the private plane. Grayson was sprawled across the tail. It was a small detail I hadn't noticed as we approached it on the tarmac in Clarke. So much was clearer now that we'd landed.

Ishmael settled into the driver seat. The pressure he applied to the gas pedal glued my body to the seat. His hand snaked across the center console, landing on my knee. He rubbed upward, finally finding comfort mid-thigh. Naturally, my fingers wrapped around his hand.

I rested my head and my heart, unsure of where we were headed. However, it wasn't my concern, not as long as Ishmael was leading. I found comfort in his touch, his guidance, and the twinkling lights of the Berkeley night sky.

I couldn't recall a moment that felt better than this one. Not even the first time seeing Teddy after he'd treaded those waters with his bare hands, back, and legs. Not even the birth of Jru. That had all been a part of their stories. This was mine. And, this would be a memory that forever stuck with me.

NINE

Ishmael

THE SMELL of her sweetness lingered on my lips. As I rolled my tastebuds across the roof of my mouth, extracting whatever was left of her, my thoughts escaped me.

Honey.

Her pot was overflowing with the sweet thickness. Her hive had been neglected over the years. As her keeper, I made a personal promise to drain her combs and keep her producing the richest, finest honey in all of the land.

So beautiful.

So beautiful.

So beautiful.

I whistled along to the lyrics of *Beautiful* as the base from the track filled the whip. My sentiments had been bottled in a chorus. Royce embodied the description effortlessly.

Physically.

Mentally.

Emotionally.

Conflict plagued me. My condominium had become my source of comfort. However, the condo Royce called home while in Berkeley, was closest. Still, the idea of taking her to either was loathsome.

A glance in her direction put my mind at ease. She simplified everything in my world. Exhaustion was slowly defeating her. She was the prettiest when rest was within reach.

The city's lights danced across her skin. A sly smile spread across her lips as she stared back at me. Her safety was the only thing that reminded me to keep my eyes on the road. I wanted her alive and well to experience her in every fashion.

I squeezed her thigh.

"Mmm." A groan tumbled from her lips before a yawn disrupted it.

"Almost home, my baby," I murmured. "Almost home."

Her exit approached and disappeared. A decision had been made and I'd hardly made it myself. The moment had. Her eyes had. The feel of her fabric underneath my hand had. The night had. It wasn't my decision to make. Neither was it hers.

Royce didn't protest. She turned toward me, knees against the center console. Both hands surrounded mine. One wrapped around my wrist. The other never changed position. She held me closely. *Tightly*. As if I'd vanish.

I'm not going anywhere, Royce. Cross my heart, hope to die.

I continued down the expressway, applying pressure to the gas pedal. My baby was ready for our night to end. And, my baby would get exactly what she wanted. Exactly what she needed.

The gates of my Colonial-style home. The seven bedrooms and nine bathrooms were fit for a large family. I didn't have one. My plans weren't to create one either. In addition to the bedrooms and bathrooms, there was a game room, a basketball court, a gym, a theater room, a family room, and a tactical room.

It was in the tactical room where I found most peace. But, as Royce and I walked through the front door, I realized I'd find peace anywhere in my home. As long as she was there.

"The restroom, please," she announced with urgency.

"This way."

I rounded the corner and made two rights, showing Royce to the guest restroom right underneath the back staircase. It was the fourth and final set in my home.

"Is there anything in particular you'd like to drink?" I asked as she stepped inside of the restroom.

Already, I was missing her and she hadn't disappeared behind the door yet.

"Wine. Your finest bottle of red."

"I'll have that for you when you come out."

"Thanks."

Her voice was light, low, and gentle. Pulling away from the door to give her privacy proved to be harder than I'd anticipated. Silently, we gazed at each other. A soft smile tugged at her lips. I took a deep breath, understanding I would hardly be any good without Royce.

Not just for the moment but for the future.

I closed the door, giving her the space she needed to handle her business. I busied myself in the cellar, searching for the finest wine amongst my small collection. I wasn't home much and it was evident. Still, I located a well-aged red that I hoped she loved before heading back to her.

She had emerged, yet she was nowhere in sight. I turned to my right, wondering where she'd gone. My heart pumped loudly in my chest. It settled the moment my eyes witnessed her glory again. She descended the stairs with bright, curious eyes.

I held the red wine in my hand, trying to make sense of Royce's perfection. I couldn't. But, I knew that it wasn't the bottle I wanted to drink from. It was her fountain.

"You have a gorgeous home," she complimented.

She settled in front of me. Her beauty was taunting me. Controlling me. Demanding things of me I shouldn't have been agreeing to.

Breathlessly, I shook my head from one side to the other. I was struggling to place my feelings, thoughts, and words. Everything was misaligned. She was destroying me and piecing me back together at the same fucking time.

"What if–" I huffed, short of breath.

"What if what?"

"What if I don't want to pretend anymore, Royce? What if this is no longer a game for me? What if this is real? What if we are real? What if it was never a hoax and simply the path that would lead us to each other? Not until this election ends, but forever."

Royce stood twenty-five feet away from me, soundless. I waited for her words. Her smile. Her movement. Something. *Anything.* There was nothing.

"I don't want to pretend anymore."

"Then how do you proceed, Ishmael?"

"With intention. With devotion. With dedication. With determination. With resilience. I run your race just as I am this race. I conquer your heart and win the election. We spend our lives debating about the temperature of our home, *this home*, instead of what time we'll meet to stage more images of a life I want to create instead of imitate."

"Sounds like a fairytale. I've learned that those aren't real."

She was jaded. I wasn't sure who hurt her but it wasn't me. And, I wasn't going to allow their mistakes to hinder our progress.

"You're right, my baby. This is no fairytale, because I am no hero. I am a killer. And, the moment those dirty lies were spread about you, I wanted blood. I wanted everyone who indulged, shared, liked, or believed that bullshit to bleed. I wake up every morning suppressing my urges to turn Berkeley into a cemetery.

"You're no angel, Royce. You're not a damsel in distress. You're a natural-born leader with a Glock bigger than most niggas attached to your thigh. You can't sleep without it. You can't eat without it. And, you won't hesitate to empty that motherfucking clip.

"You're stubborn and hardheaded, sure to get some niggas hurt, because you love the reward risk brings. It makes your pussy leak. It hardens your nipples. It turns your faucet on.

"So, again, this is no fairytale and I'm not interested in one. I want something real. Something solid. Something impenetrable. Something to last a lifetime."

I demolished the space between us, hammering away at it with each step I took.

"Everything about you assures me I can have that with you."

I was no longer holding the wine. It was Royce between my fingers.

"And, I want it."

I cupped her chin.

"No pretend."

I pulled her closer while lowering my lips to hers.

"No make-believe."

She gasped.

"No games."

I took her into my mouth. She was as sweet as I remembered. Her body collided with mine. As if I was her favorite tree, she began to climb me. I placed both hands underneath her, deepening our connection.

She was soft. Supple. So fucking sweet.

I ran my tongue across her mouth, sure to touch every surface. I was leaving my mark. But, simultaneously, I was learning parts of her with every part of me. My senses were active. Every one of them.

Royce accepted her fate. Her ability to do so revealed another layer to her. One I wanted to peel back with time. With care. With caution. With my bare hands. Or tongue. Or dick. They were all hers to have.

As a classic iconoclast, her submission was invigorating. Opposition was comforting. Disagreeing. Disobeying. Royce was rebellious by nature. That very nature kept her employed. She wasn't afraid to do or say what others were. She fought for sport. Taking on big names, brands, and companies didn't intimidate her.

It stimulated her. Aroused her. Kept her hands and her head busy, because deep down inside, she'd rather be in the boardroom than the bedroom alone. Solitude was not her safe space. Companionship was.

The cool countertop pressed against the back of my

hand as I lowered Royce's body onto the custom marble slab. My insatiable appetite determined each movement of my spine. I wasn't in control of my limbs. Hunger was.

The soft fabric trailed up Royce's skin under the influence of my fingertips. Her perfectly smooth seventh layer was riddled with small bumps. Her panti-less, hairless pussy appeared from underneath the threads.

So pretty, my baby.

I slid a bartop chair backward and planted myself on the beige fabric. With ease, Royce's legs parted. A rich, rosy pink connected to the darkness of her thick lips. Her pearl was swollen, confirmation of her sexual inclination.

The contrasting, partially translucent cream seeped from her center. Royce was demanding so much without saying a fucking thing. My tongue ran across my lips as I prepared to grace the meal in front of me.

I drove two fingers inside of her wetness. Royce's body lifted from the counter.

"Dear God, keep me from killing a nigga 'bout my shit," I whispered.

"Issssssshhhhhm–"

"Help my baby understand that I'm not the nigga to play silly games with."

"Uhhhhh."

"Her search ends here. I'm everything she needs and if I'm not yet, I'll become whatever she's missing."

"Uh– Fuuu–"

"Amen."

I placed my mouth on her most sensitive parts. Her legs drew inward, attempting to join. I removed my fingers and sat back in the chair. Royce's chest rose and fell as she tried catching the breaths that were running away from her.

"Please."

"Open your legs, Royce."

She obliged. Simultaneously, her right hand met her center. Jealousy crept up my spine.

"Don't do that, Royce."

"Ishmae–"

I observed as she disobeyed my order. Her fingers glided across her center. Disappointment subsided. It was swiftly replaced with curiosity. And calm. And fascination.

"Go ahead, my baby. Let me see."

With my permission, Royce dipped her fingers into her slit.

Fuck.

She brought them both out, slowly. Her nectar dripped from her fingertips onto her clit. She lowered her middle and index fingers, touching herself again. She rolled them counter clockwise, applying the slightest pressure.

I wasn't sure when my belt was undone or when the hole of my briefs expanded. Neither did I know when my hard dick got in my hands.

I leaned forward, returning to Royce's sloppiness. I

inserted my fingers, opting for natural lubrication. She had so much of it. *Too much* of it.

I twirled her pussy's saliva around the head of my dick. My eyes never left her. She was too demanding. She commanded my attention. All of it. All of me. All-consuming, my baby was.

My hand fit around my dick like a glove. The first stroke was jolting. My stomach imploded.

Fuck.

My lids were desperate to touch. However, the thought of missing a second of Royce's self-pleasuring was torturous. Bliss was upon me.

She circled her sensitive nub. Her hips rolled, meeting her fingers when they roamed too far.

"Uhhhhh."

Those dark, doughty eyes of hers were no longer facing the ceiling. Still at the edge of the counter, she rested her weight on her left elbow.

"Mmmmmm."

That pretty pussy and pretty face were mere inches away from each other in my narrowed vision. Between her thighs were a set of top and bottom lips. The lines of reality began to blur as one disappeared into her mouth.

Lapsed judgment and an attempt to keep my semen in my sack led me to the darkness behind my eyelids.

Fuck. Fuck.

I stroked my dick ever so gently. Yet, I grew closer to my ending with each movement of my hand, each movement of her.

"Open your eyes, Ishmael."

Royce's demand twisted my nose, mouth, and eyebrows.

I can't. I admitted inwardly.

"Ishmael."

Hearing my name fall from her lips pulled my skin apart. There she was. In all her glory. Fingers dripping with her nature as she pulled them from her pussy.

Royce leaned forward, closing the gap between us.

"It's yours," she claimed, coating my lips with her cream.

Greedily, I cleaned them with my tongue. Unable to contain my thirst, I parted her legs wider and buried my face between them.

So fucking good.

"Yesssssssss."

Royce's spine curled as she took my head into her hand. Her rotating hips were gracious with their servings, feeding me pussy with each twirl.

I pulled her clit into my mouth. My tongue flickered across it rapidly. With each flick of my tongue, Royce's body curved a centimeter more. Her grip on my head tightened.

"Mmmmmmmmm. Ish— Uhhhh."

I wasn't ready. I wasn't ready for her climax. Abruptly, I disengaged. Royce's chest swelled with anticipation.

"Continue."

The silent, extremely complicated power dynamic between us was exposed with each decision we made.

Every moment of submission was a precursor for the dominance she was inherent in. It was in her blood. It was in her build.

She was struggling to keep it at bay. It was satisfying experiencing her struggles while I had every intention to nail her ungodly ass to the cross every fucking day my dick stood and her pussy welcomed it.

For now, I'd allow the quiet battle. Because, undoubtedly, the war was already won. I simply wasn't prepared to be the bearer of bad news. Not while her pussy was this wet and my dick was this fucking hard.

"Ish–"

"Play with that pussy, my baby. Show me how well you take care of my shit."

Edging Royce had become the highlight of my evening.

And to think, I believed shooting a nigga would be.

I traveled to Clarke with a full clip, hoping to be missing one upon my return. But, the nigga sitting across from Royce was as pussy as the one I was enjoying the kneading of.

"That's it," I coaxed, taking my dick into my hand again. "That's it."

I tilted my head, sure to get every angle of her meatiness. Royce was unbelievable. I wanted all parts of her. The good. Bad. Pretty. Ugly. Problematic. Hardheaded. Emotional. Toxic. Tamed. Untamed. Disciplined. Determined. Sassy. Sad. Sweet. Salty. All of her. No discounts.

"Uhhhh. Fuuuuuuck."

Royce's rhythm was steady, unchanging. She was aiming for her mountain's top. Her climax was within reach. I wanted to tear her down, breaking her concentration. However, my limbs were unreachable.

"I'm gonna— oooohhhh, Ishmael."

The way she said my name like that. So softly. So deeply. So surely. So pleasantly.

"Mmmmm. Uhh. Fuc– Uh."

I lost my way again. Darkness surrounded me. Warmth consoled me. Royce's hands found me. So did her voice.

"Open your eyes, Ishmael."

Her request was granted, but not without cost. She was no longer on the counter. She was on me. One foot in the chair to my right. One foot in the chair to my left. Her pussy hovered over the head of my dick.

"Look at me."

I didn't have any other choice. All I could do was look at her.

So pretty. So perfect.

She lowered her contracting pussy onto my treetop, disregarding my tightened fist. I released my shaft, allowing her the freedom to slide down until her ass touched my thighs.

I released a shaky breath. Heaven and earth joined beyond the seams. Part of my world intertwined with hers.

Simultaneously, the glasshouse I'd built around my heart shattered. Shards of glass promised to draw blood should I dare try piecing it back together. I didn't want to. I wanted whatever the terrain presented. *Whatever Royce brought my way.*

Plush walls engulfed my hardness. Contractions protested for the extraction of my semen. And, I wanted out. But, just as much, I wanted in.

Forever.

This moment never had to fade. As we were, we could remain.

Nothing mattered right here. With her. In her.

"Ishmael," she moaned, placing both hands on my shoulders.

Stabilization would be the death of this moment. I despised and desired it simultaneously. Royce's lips pressed against mine as her body lifted.

"Fuck, my baby," I grunted, feeling her gushiness as she slid up my shit.

My eyes closed, involuntarily. Royce was far from reasonable. Her voice. Her pussy. Her presence. Her body. *Her.* Keeping my composure was impractical.

"Look at me," she demanded.

I nodded.

She slid down my shaft. Everything tightened. My heart rate quickened.

Oh Royce. You do not play well, my baby.

A hand released my shoulder. It gripped my chin, lifting my face.

Up.

"Look at me."

I did as I was told. The shift was upon us. Royce was

empowered. I could do absolutely nothing. If I did, I'd bust all in her shit.

She peered down at me. Her sinful gaze was a forewarning. I didn't have much time to prepare for the extraction of my soul. But, it hardly mattered if I had. Royce would take it anyway. Even if it wasn't already hers to have.

Down.

There was so much in those irises. They said so much without Royce saying a word. They were full of so many things.

Greed.

Need.

Pleasure.

Pain.

Confusion.

Fear.

Fearlessness.

Understanding.

Sadness.

Pride.

Selfishness.

Selflessness.

Openness.

Vulnerability.

Submission.

Power.

She was my pretty contradiction.

"Tell me I feel good."

The validation she sought wasn't a requirement of

hers. Yet, it was paramount. She **knew** she felt like everything I needed. Still, my words were necessary to add cushion to the fall she was taking for me.

For us.

Royce was self-indulgent. And because she spent her days handling everything for everyone else, it was imperative I was as permissive as her heart needed me to be in order for her to understand that it was my job to handle her.

And all of her things.

And all of her needs.

And all of her desires.

And all of her fears.

And all of her troubles.

And all of her tears.

And all of her good.

And all of her bad.

"Tell me," she begged, vulnerability peaking.

Up.

"You feel like a fuck– a fucking dream, my baby."

The exchange was swift. Her submission consumed her. I pulled her tongue into my mouth. I was no longer privy to her orbs. Dark, flawless skin lowered on top of them.

Down.

I lifted my hands, placing them on both sides of her face to make sure she understood every word I was preparing in my head.

Up.

"You feel like everything a nigga needs, Royce."

Down.

"Everything a nigga wants."

Up.

"I'm completely and utterly obsessed with your presence in my life."

Down.

"I want you here."

Up.

"Fucking me like this."

Down.

"Touching me like this."

Up.

"Riding this dick."

Down.

"Just like this, my baby."

"Uhhhhhhhhhhhh."

The suppressed moan was released.

"Whenever you want it. Whenever you need it."

Up.

I lowered my hands. One to her neck. The other to her waste. My lips abandoned hers, sliding toward her ear.

"Because it's yours, Royce."

Down.

"I'm yours."

Up.

"All yours."

Down.

"Same as you are mine."

Up.

"Don't make me have to prove it."

Down.

"I'll keep the funeral homes in business doing so."

Up.

Down.

"Understood?"

Up.

"Understood?"

I released her neck. My free hand fell down to her waist. With her in between my fingers, I lifted upward, meeting her where she was.

"Uhhhhhhh. Fuck."

Up.

Down.

I stroked her from beneath. Her breasts bounced. Her hands pulled her hair up on her hand. Those pretty eyes never exposed themselves. But those teeth did. That tongue did. Just before she folded her lips into her mouth, attempting to accept the painful pleasure of our connection.

"Understood, my baby?"

"Yessssssssssss."

Up.

Down.

"Yessss."

Smack.

Smack.

Our skin collided. The well oiled machine was slippery to the touch. Her insides were spilling out onto my thighs. Her pussy was talking, saying all the things I wanted to hear.

"Yes, who?"

"Ishmaaaaael."

"That's it."

In.

Out.

I extracted my dick before plunging back into her. Full force.

Royce was a rider. She didn't try escaping the brutality of her walls. She snaked her arms around my neck and dug her fingers into the back of my arms.

"Oooooooohhhh yesss. Yes. Yesssss."

In.

Out.

I loosened my grip. Giving into my intrusive thoughts, I placed my thumb against the tip of Royce's crack. I slipped my index and middle fingers into her ass.

"Oh fuck."

She melted against me.

Up.

Down.

I drilled into her. She was dripping wet. Sounds of our connection promised to end me.

"Yesssss. Yesssss. Yessss."

Up.

Down.

My movements slowed to a creep. I wanted to hear more of what her pussy had to say to me. It was loud and quiet at once. Sloppy yet maintaining its structure. Slippery yet suffocating. Soft yet hard to fathom more days without.

Up.

Down.

"Shit feels too good, my baby."

"Um hmmmm." Royce moaned against my mouth.

"Kiss me."

Her lips parted, pulling me in. I was preparing for my end. As our tongues touched, I understood I was near my ending. At any given second, my dick would be spitting out my minions. I prayed her womb could withstand the weight of my military.

"You 'bout to make that dick spit up, Mommas."

Up.

Down.

"Um hmm."

She was climbing a mountain of her own.

"Where you want it?"

"Uhhhh."

"Hm? Where you want it?"

I tightened my grip around her neck. Her pussy tightened around me.

Fuck.

On the tips of her toes, she placed both hands on my chest. I was no longer driving into her. She was rolling her pussy while bouncing. Completely dismantling me, one stroke at a time. Her eyes were open. Wide with wilderness.

The final shift awakened the beast within me.

"Royce–" I warned, "I'm about to cum all in this mot– mother– fuc– ker."

I didn't finish my statement before my clip began to unload in her womb. My ass bounced off the chair. My limbs grew stiffer with each pump.

"Fuck, my baby," I panted.

Uncontrollably, my seeds continued painting her walls.

What the fuck?

"Ohhhhhhhh fuuuuuuucc–"

Royce's body slammed into mine. She was no longer bouncing on my pole. Her hips rolled, grinding her pussy against me. The contractions within drew more semen from me, forcing me to question the actual capacity of her pussy and just how extensive her pussy's power truly was.

Fuck.

I tongued her down as I tried stifling my flow. My efforts were in vain and her pussy runneth over with all that had been stored in my sack.

THE GREYLIST

She smelled like spices, oak, butterscotch, and myrrh. Like me. I'd cleaned her from head to toe without a single light in the bathroom to guide me. Dark showers weren't an indulgence of mine, but it didn't take much convincing from Royce.

I had her from behind in the glass encasing.

Then, I had her against the tile.

And, underneath the showerhead.

Though her hair was wrapped in a towel and one of my plain white shirts adorned her body, she was still unbelievable.

A gem.

I loved so many parts of Royce already, I wondered if time was a systematic flaw or a forgotten phenomenon in our universe. The screen of my phone obstructed my view. But, just as quickly, her body appeared on the glass rectangle. I snapped a photo.

Then another.

And another.

And others.

My obsession was growing at an alarming rate. I exited the camera application and opened the Instagram application. The page that Royce had created for me wouldn't be a personal outlet or way for the world to keep up with my life. It would only give them the false sense of closeness. It would also make them feel as if they knew and understood me. They never would.

The page would be dedicated to the woman in my life. Not the one presented to them with scandalous images. But, the one in my bed. The eighth wonder of the world. The narrative that was being written about her needed to be rewritten. For me, it was fuck every news outlet and blog who'd reported false information. This would be our outlet.

A well-tailored, carefully curated outlet. One that emphasized Royce's beauty and my falling–*head first.*

I uploaded the image I'd just snapped to a story, sure to end it where the white shirt stopped at her thighs. Most parts of her would be reserved for my eyes only.

I scrolled through the tunes, settling on *Everybody's Business* by *Kehlani*. It was most fitting. Because what we were building was nobody's fucking business, but a coward had made it Berkeley's business, and as a result I'd won.

I'd won her.

I'd won at life.

And, eventually, I'd win the fucking race.

"Sleep tight, my baby."

I lowered the light and exited. The thought of her leaving in the morning made my stomach turn. She had business to tend to. She'd made that clear. But, the first time her fine ass was free again, I'd be in her space.

Mouth on her clit.

Dick all up in her.

I searched my contacts, finding one I used more often than not. Indigo's last text reminded me that I'd ignored his foolishness and decided not to respond.

Maybe you were right. I won't miss that two mill.

Pointless ass message. Knew damn well you'd find your way to her. She had you whipped from the moment you met her.

Fuck you. I chuckled. It wasn't often Indigo was right and I was wrong.

Just know we're both wearing Burberry shirts to the baby shower. I'll even let you walk in first.

Won't be no baby shower.

One of us has to give our old lady some grandkids.

You've got that.

Ain't ran into nobody worthy of her presence yet. You have.

You will.

I shut down my screen and took a seat in my study. With my thumb against my chin, I pondered on my next move. Everything was aligning as it should. And, there was a sleeping beauty in my bed who I refused to become background noise as I ran the last leg of the mayoral race.

It was critical that she understood her vote was just as essential as the votes of the Berkeley residents.

TEN

Royce

SUNLIGHT BEAMED into the fifteen foot windows. Its heat warmed my skin to the touch. The smell of black coffee stretched my nostrils. Nothing was familiar about the space I occupied.

Mentally.

Physically.

Or emotionally.

Still, content parted my lids, welcoming me into a new world of possibilities. I uncurled my spine, straightening my limbs in the process.

"Oooouch," I yawned.

Everything hurt.

"Good morning, *my baby*."

Ishmael's voice lured me to unsteady waters. His loafers collided with the wood flooring. His steps drew closer, increasing the rate of my heartbeat.

Black loafers.

Black slacks.

Black button down.

Black blazer.

Black tie.

He was gutting. And well-groomed. And handsome. And alert. And curious. And quiet. His beauty was staggering. His silence was unearthing.

"Good morning."

Ishmael was soundless. His observation required nearly every breath he took. There was no room for words.

"Coffee?" I asked, turning my nose upward.

He shook his head.

"Not for drinking."

I'd succeeded in extracting words from him.

"Motivation."

"Motivation?" Chuckling, I pulled the cover closer to my chin.

I wasn't ready for the day. I wasn't sure when I would be.

Ishmael shrugged.

"To not return to bed and spend the day wrapped in your walls."

"That doesn't sound like a bad idea."

"You have work to do, Royce. So do I."

"Yes. I knoooooow," I groaned, placing a hand on my forehead. "I need to make some calls before nine."

"It's almost eight. You have an hour."

"Can you pass me my phone?"

"Your phone is in the trash that was picked up by the city this morning."

He leaned over, sliding a new iPhone from his pants.

"Ishmael. What ha–"

"Nothing more than you have done, my baby."

I was immediately reminded of the phone of his I'd destroyed. Karma was nasty in the morning.

"Where's my phone?"

Ignoring me, he continued, "I took the liberty of giving you a new cell, one that is free of dating apps and message threads from niggas with targets on their backs now. You won't be needing either of those."

"You went through my phone?" My breath hiked in my chest.

"I'm many things, my baby, but stupid is not one of those. I won't ever search through your cell. I trust you'll tell me whatever it is I need to know."

"And vice versa?"

He nodded.

"And vice versa."

I sighed, running my hand through my messy hair. It was a disaster. It was evident that I'd been thoroughly fucked and fulfilled. So was my morning breath that both Ishmael and I disregarded. So was my bare face. Unclothed body. And dry mouth.

"Is there anyone special I should know about?"

"You."

I pulled my lip in, sinking my teeth into it.

"Here. There are no codes set or nothing beyond the transferred SIM card."

"Thank you."

I accepted the cell and slid it underneath the cover with me.

"Do you really have to leave?"

"I wish I didn't," he breathed out, placing the coffee cup to his lips.

He grunted as he sipped.

"Awful."

His nose was scrunched and his lips were turned upward.

"Then why are you drinking it, silly?"

"I've told you already, my baby. Every syllable from your mouth brings me closer to the danger zone."

"You should leave."

"I should," he agreed.

Yet, his legs never moved. Neither did his hands. Or his eyes.

I melted against his sheets.

"Don't look at me that way."

"You leave me no choice. I'm fascinated. Admittedly, I'm in disbelief."

"How so?"

"I'm trying my hardest to understand why God didn't sit you in my path long ago. I could've used your presence. Would've saved me so much ene-"

"Timing is everything, Ishmael."

He nodded. "It is."

We embraced the comforting silence. Two full minutes passed before my lips parted again.

"Leave before I beg you to stay."

"Begging wouldn't be necessary."

"No?"

"I don't need much convincing, Royce."

Ishmael placed the cup of coffee on the dark wood nightstand. He kneeled beside the bed, his face near mine. I covered my mouth with the cream sheet.

"I have morning breath."

Ishmael pulled the cover from my face, tucking it under my chin. He placed a hand around my neck and leaned forward. When our lips touched, my eyes closed.

It was the natural reaction to his closeness. He felt so much like a figment of my imagination that I struggled to keep my eyes open with him near. This didn't feel like reality. Though he'd reiterated the fact that he no longer wanted to participate, he still felt make-believe.

Otherwise, there was no perspicuous explanation for his perfection. Lucidity failed me with matters concerning Ishmael. He stripped me of my brilliance. And, for all the right reasons.

"You were mistaken if you assumed I gave a fuck, my baby."

He wiped remnants of me from his mouth as he pulled backward. He stood, towering over me. Discomfort stirred me awake completely. I tossed my legs over the bed, unprepared for Ishmael's departure.

He dug into the pocket of his blazer and removed a sleek, black and gold YSL wallet. He removed the glistening card and shoved it in my direction.

"I'm not sorry for fucking your hair up, but I regretted the decision shortly after it had been made."

"Did you?"

He nodded.

"Only because I liked the way it looked from my favorite spot."

I clenched, pressing my walls together.

"Where could that be?"

"Face wedged between your thighs."

My cheeks flushed as my smile reached my eyes.

"Go get your shit fixed, my baby. And, whatever else your heart desires, *on me*."

My fingers curled around the thickness of his AMEX.

"Well aren't you kind. I was beginning to think you assumed your business bill and bedroom bill were combined."

Ishmael tossed his head back in laughter. It was the sweetest sound known to mankind. My heart skipped a beat. And then another.

Flutters danced around my stomach.

"Nah. No sweat, my baby. I'm no fool."

"Good then. That means this stays with me?" I needed clarity.

He lifted his hands, surrendering.

"It stays with you."

"Well, now that that's clear, we can discuss authorized user accounts."

"It's your world, Royce. I'll get it worked out."

I pursed my lips. He leaned in, first placing a kiss on my forehead. He, then, lowered his eyes to mine and pressed his lips against mine.

His arms engulfed me. So did his aroma.

"Take care of yourself, love. Everything is on me."

Ishmael vanished. However, his scent lingered on my skin and on the sheets. Parts of me went missing along with him. I wanted them back. I wanted him back.

I tossed the cover over my disheveled mane and kicked my legs. A low squeal erupted from my body as I tried suppressing the exhilaration flowing through me.

"Ahhhhhhhhhhh!"

I felt like a high school girl with a crush on the star quarterback who'd just acknowledged my existence with a mere head nod.

But I was no high school girl. And, Ishmael was not the starting quarterback. He'd done far more than acknowledge my presence. He'd acknowledged my heart, my desires, my fears, my transgressions, my frustrations, my bad parts, my good parts, and his interest in it all.

"Your front door is ajar. Disarm now. Disarm now. Disarm now."

I closed the door of the condominium, quieting the sound of the lawnmowers manicuring the lawn of the complex.

Twenty-seven.

Twenty-six.

Twenty-five.

I counted down the seconds until the alarm began blaring.

Twenty-four.

Twenty-three.

Twenty-two.

7662.

I entered the code Mercer had given me. Offering his sanctuary during my Berkeley visits was another way of keeping me close. Mercer wasn't a man of too many words, but one could feel everything he was thinking from his actions.

Vallei added the perfect touch to the pad. Her signature was scribbled all over the furnishings and fixtures. She'd designed their hideaway so beautifully.

"It's nothing special, but it's a safe place to lay your head when you're here. Vallei goes to clear her head every so often. Vallei is where I clear my head, so I'm not there unless she needs me to be."

His words replayed as I stood in front of the central hub for the alarm.

"He's happy," I whispered.

"System disarmed."

I placed a hand on my heart and pulled in fresh air. Everything Mercer needed, Vallei had to give. The two complemented each other well.

"Good evening, baby."

My eyes blossomed. My fingers gripped the threads of my fabric. My heart tried escaping my chest.

"Chemistry!"

"You're slipping," he chastised, kissing the skin of his teeth.

His disappointment led me to follow him. I hated it. The thought of it.

"The alarm was– and then Mercer was on my mi– I–"

"Slipping."

I sighed, dropping my shoulders. Chemistry opened the fridge and removed a bottle of water. He, then, rounded the counter and slid the second drawer out. He dipped his hand inside and removed a long packet.

"Not exactly."

"Excuses aren't necessary, Royce."

He poured the orange powder into the water, capped it, and then shook the mixture.

"I don't have any," I admitted, shrugging.

"They're useless, anyhow."

I rolled my eyes, hating how he was always right and how much I missed him at the same time. His presence was a gift I didn't mind receiving repeatedly.

"You don't make this easy."

"Life isn't easy, baby. Drink up. You're dehydrated."

"Ted–"

"Drink."

"How do you figure I'm dehydrated?"

He grabbed my wrist, extending my arm.

"There isn't a vein in sight, Royce. Drink."

He shoved the bottle in my direction.

"Voluntarily or involuntarily."

I snatched the bottle. Chemistry nearly took my fingers off.

"Ouch." I chuckled.

"Your head is as hard as they come."

"So I've heard."

I sipped from the bottle as I observed his posture. He surveyed our surroundings as if they were unfamiliar to him. I was no fool. He'd visited. The moment he discovered this was where I'd be frequenting during my stays, he'd visited.

I knew Chem by heart because for the longest, he was my heart. Jru forced me to make room for others. So did his first-born son. And Psalem. And Prince. And Malaya.

Ishmael required room now. It was no struggle creating it. My heart was expanding with each thought of him, mention of him, or sight of him.

"Are you comfortable here?"

I nodded.

"Yes."

He tilted his head, waiting for more to escape my mouth.

"I'm comfortable, Teddy. I'm not here much. I–"

"You've made a choice, baby. Even if you're not here

much now, you will be here more often than not. Your comfort is priority."

"*His.*"

He nodded.

"Maybe one day. But, today, it's mine. Always have been."

It didn't surprise me that Ishmael was the topic of our conversation. Chemistry's presence was a result of our arrangement.

He placed both hands behind his back. His chin lifted. His chest protruded. There was so much on his mind. So many words that would remain unsaid. However, I still read them. Read him. Like the open book he wasn't.

"It –" I paused, running my finger around the rim of the water bottle, "It was supposed to b– it was suppos–"

"But it's not."

I shook my head.

"No. It's not."

"And your apprehension?"

"Public eye. Publicity in general," I scoffed. "We've been thro–"

"Does he make you smile, baby?"

I nodded.

"Does he make you laugh?"

I nodded.

"Does he consider you in everything he does?"

I nodded.

"Do you feel like a burden?"

I shook my head.

"Do you listen?"

I tucked my bottom lip inside of my mouth. The smile forming threatened to tear the corners of them.

I moved my hand from side to side, pulling that bright smile of Teddy's from that dark place that often consumed him.

"Then that's all that matters."

I couldn't hold back that laughter.

"Richie said that if–" I hesitated, feeling my heart ache at the sound of my father's name.

"He sai–" I cleared my throat, unable to continue.

"Richie was right, baby."

I sighed.

"Yeah. He was always right."

"We don't choose who we love, Royce. I wasn't the exception to that rule. Should you be in the public eye, *no*. Is it risky, *yes*. But what's life without risk, baby? I risked everything for the woman I love. And, if I had the choice to do it all again... I wouldn't change one thing. Make your bed and lay in that motherfucker."

"It's not me I'm worried about."

He shook his head, shrugging his shoulders.

"I can handle myself, baby. I'm not an assignment of yours. I can't be handled. Don't try."

I took another sip, needing to clear the thickness in my throat. So many emotions were toying with my heart.

"And–" I asked.

"And?"

"Teddy."

I didn't realize my feet had stomped the ground and my lips were poking out until Chemistry's thumb and index fingers squeezed his nose. His shoulders squared immediately after.

"You've done well, Royce."

"Yeah?"

His approval lifted my eyebrows and widened my nostrils. Chemistry nodded.

"He's solid, baby."

"Rugger told m–"

"Rugger knows. Rugger definitely knows."

"You look well," he paused, taking a good look at me. His hand landed on his chest.

"Is it the children?"

"The children?"

"That have you showing a little emotion these days."

He tilted his head and then lifted it as quickly.

"Jru misses you."

"I miss her more."

"Then tell her."

His message was clear. He wanted me in St. Catana.

"I'll be there. As soon as all of this is over."

He stared, unblinking. Unmoving.

"Promise."

"Bring your newest experiment."

I chortled. Liquid spilled from my mouth and went up my nose. The burning sensation forced my eyes closed as I waited for the pain to subside.

"Ugh!"

I clipped my nose, hoping to speed the process. Slowly, the burning sensation vanished. I reopened my eyes, fully expecting Chemistry in my line of vision.

Teddy.

I turned around, peering down the hallway toward the door just as it connected with the frame.

I love you, too.

In every lifetime.

Sadness promised to swallow me whole.

I'll find you.

I finished the mixture I'd been tasked with completing and tossed the bottle in the trash. A shower was in my near future. The thought of changing into something more comfortable replaced the bleakness Chemistry's presence left me with. Just as quickly, the thought of bringing the bags inside plagued me.

I dragged my feet across the floor, nearing the door. The bags wouldn't be spending unnecessary hours in the car. I wouldn't rest until they were inside, unpacked, and everything was in its rightful place.

I opened the front door. My right foot collided with the unknown. I lowered my gaze. The bags I was headed to the car to grab were at the door. So were long legs, dark skin, and a handsome face I loved more than my own sometimes.

"I'll be waiting."

My heart's smile reached my lips as I stepped around the bags. My arms snaked Chemistry's frame.

"As long as you're happy, baby, nothing more matters."

He didn't wrap his long arms around me. Neither did he pull me deeper into his chest. He allowed me time to collect myself before demanding space.

Not with words.

His limbs tensed. His breaths grew shallow. His heart rate sped against my ear.

"You want me to let you go, huh?" I chuckled.

"You're acting like a girl, Royce."

"What happened with Derrick?"

"All is well. I'd tell you if it wasn't."

"Good."

"I understand your position here, but make sure you handle your business… you have a job to do."

"He'll win the election."

"He should."

I breathed in his confidence. The fix was needed. Ishmael was rearranging so many things. In all the best ways, but the discomfort was presence, nonetheless. So was the confusion and uncertainty.

"Royce!"

I released him, pushing him in the process. He didn't budge. Not until I was back inside, bags in tow. I appreciated his consideration. I hated to see him leave, so he never forced me to.

Nor Roaman.

Nor Range.

Nor Roulette.

Nor Rugger.

Nor Rather.

And, never Rome.

I reentered the home in better spirits. As I lifted my cell from the counter, heading up the stairs, it vibrated in my hand.

Black hearts lit up the screen. An image of Ishmael and I covered the background. I hadn't saved the contact and neither had I saved the image.

Oh, Mr. Grayson.

"Yes?"

I pressed the phone against my ear as I leaned against the counter. Everything quieted around me, including the lawnmowers outside. All I could hear was him and the beat of my heart.

Boom.

Boom.

Boom.

Boom.

"I miss you," he rushed out, "I couldn't let another second pass without you knowing that."

I gnawed on my bottom lip. On the heel of my right foot, I turned and placed my elbows on the counter.

"I've missed you."

"I hope you chose the black bag."

"Hm?"

"The black Chanel bag. It's never looked better on an arm."

"Are you stalking me?"

"No, but the women of Berkeley are. And, their obsession is growing quicker than mine."

"Was I on television again?"

"Nah. Social media. I've been tagged an obscene amount of times."

Chuckling, I shook my head.

"Sorry."

"There's no need to be sorry. Not unless you didn't make that purchase."

"I have five bags just like that one."

"I want you to have that one... *here.*"

"Good because, I was trying to justify the twelve thousand dollar charge on your card for a bag I already have."

"Doesn't need to be justified, my baby."

"What do you know about fashion?" I questioned.

"Nothing. But, I know what I like when I see it. And, I know what I'd like you in when I see it on you. That's enough."

"I agree."

Silence coated the line. I made circles on the counter with my index finger.

"Be ready at eight."

"For?"

"Be ready, my baby."

The line died. I held the phone in my hand, still trying to wrap my head around the man on the other end. Ishmael was doing things to me that hadn't been done before. He was making me feel things I'd never felt before.

"Ahhhhhhhh," I squealed.

I made note of the time on the phone screen. Three hours. It was just enough time to pull myself together and have an hour nap. I tiptoed up the stairs, hips rolling and hands high in the air.

"I let my thoughts run wild when I'm thinking of you," I sang. "I get to acting like a child when I'm thinking of you."

My cell became the mic and Mercer's condo became the stage I wasn't aware I needed.

"Okay with losing track of time when I'm thinking of you. You say you're on the way. I say baby that's cool."

ELEVEN

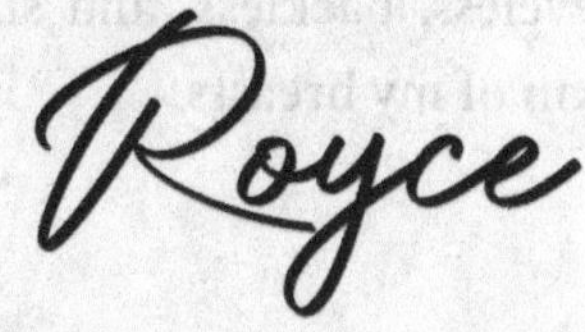

Royce

7:42P

I connected the back of the earring with the fastener. Carefully, I slid the fastener upward, stopping near my earlobe. In the full-length mirror hanging on the wall of the study, I peered at my reflection.

The fresh blow out Flo had worked wonders on was swaying with each turn of my head. The virgin hair was perfect for the style. The ending result belonged in one of the hair magazines from the nineties. My extensions were flourishing.

Ding.

Dong.

Ishmael was eighteen minutes early. So was I.

Anxiousness swelled my chest. I'd been waiting for the moment I saw his handsome face since he vanished into thin air this morning.

I missed him. So did my girl downstairs. She purred at the thought of the time they'd spent together.

In the kitchen.

On the counter.

In the shower.

In the shower again.

And, on the bed.

I was sure the foam remembered me well.

The dress hugged me tightly around the waist and hips. It was sleeveless, backless, and strapless. It was held up by the skin of my breasts.

Click.

Clack.

Click.

Clack.

I stood in front of the alarm's hub. One tap and the front of the condo was in my view. My brows furrowed as I made note of the three figures standing near the door.

The camera's feed wasn't satisfying enough. I needed to lay eyes on the visitors.

Click.

Clack.

I opened the front door and was greeted by a slick smile and open arms.

"Milo!"

His long arms wrapped around me. As he stepped

forward, I stepped back. The door closed shortly after our entrance. I was too wrapped up in his presence to note who had sealed it.

"What's good, sis?"

I was released against my will, but I accepted my fate and fell into a new set of arms.

"Lawe!"

"What's up, cuz?"

He rocked my body from one side to the other before letting me go.

"It's so good to see you."

The third pair of arms remained at their owner's side. His hands were pushed into his pockets. His light skin and pleasant features hardened my nipples. I racked my brain trying to figure out if I was violating some type of unwritten code or rules.

"When you enter someone's home, you open your mouth and speak," I reminded the third guest.

"This ain't your home, love," he reminded me.

He removed a hand from his pocket to twirl the toothpick between his teeth.

"It's mine while I'm in it."

"I'm exempt from hugs and I'm not complaining. Follow suit."

"Fuck you."

"Trust me. If I wasn't madly in love with my wife and you didn't look like family then we could arrange something."

"My nipples don't get hard for family," I told him,

"You're about twelve times removed, anyway. Not exactl–"

"Royce," Milo called out.

"Baisleigh gon' grill your ass like cheese if you keep fucking around."

"She doesn't have to worry," I assured Lawe, "He's safe."

"Am I, *cousin?*"

I tossed a middle finger and turned toward Milo.

"How's Nature? And, the babies?"

"Everybody's good."

"Fuck you headed looking like you have a seat at the Golden Globe?"

I rolled my eyes. Lawe couldn't help himself. The insults were inevitable.

"And, you look like you're headed to a funeral."

"Never know when I might have to send a nigga to meet the Lord, so I'm always dressed for the occasion."

"Headed out?" Milo questioned.

"I am, actually. Date night."

"With that nigga you been all over the news with?" Lawe peered at me with curious eyes. Red surrounded the dark brown circles.

I nodded.

"Ishmael."

Milo said nothing. He stood, waiting for the unknown.

"What?" I sniggered.

"Nothing. You look happy. I'm just here to make sure it's not a facade."

I shook my head. "It's not a facade, Milo."

"Then we won't hold you."

The three of them inched toward the door. They were prepared to leave as quickly as they'd come.

"Tell Malachi and Makai I said–"

"Tell 'em yourself, Royce," Milo yelled over his shoulder. "You're welcomed to our cribs anytime."

"I know."

"Then act like it," Lawe added.

"Why'd you have to bring him?" I laughed.

"He begs to come everywhere like motherfuckers actually want to be around him."

"You're the back up. Makai has fifteen kids. Nigga ain't never free no more, so yo–"

"Just as busy," Milo finished.

Milo was a physician and had two children of his own. He didn't have time for Lawe, but he made time. Makai, on the other hand, didn't care much about Lawe's complaints.

"Goodnight, Milo."

"Goodnight, Royce."

"Goodnight, Lawe. Laike."

"Be careful," Laike murmured as he passed me by.

"Call me if motherfuckers want to jump stupid. I'm laying everything down," Lawe yelled out as he made his way to the car.

"Goodnight."

One final goodnight floated in their direction before I locked myself inside. I pressed my back against the door, trying to recall if Laike had been that glorious the first time I'd met him. I wasn't sure what Baisleigh was feeding him besides pussy, but it had him swollen and scrumptious. I couldn't help but consider how much Luca had changed since I'd last saw him.

I shook them both from my thoughts and stepped away from the door. I spritzed Oak across my body, doubling down on the gorgeous scent. As I recapped it, the door bell chimed again. I tapped the screen of the alarm system.

My lips turned upward.

There he is.

I didn't need another once over. Neither did I need to visit the bathroom again.

Behind the door was a bouquet of red roses. The hate I housed for flowers faded as they touched the skin of my nose.

"You're pretty, my baby."

Hearing his compliments while nose deep in the bouquet helped plead their case.

"And you—*handsome.*"

I straightened my spine.

Ishmael stepped inside. His invitation hadn't come but I doubted he cared. He walked past me, headed for the kitchen as if he'd studied the blueprints of Mercer's place. Like I'd done his.

I turned, admiring his backside as much as I did the front. He was dressed in his signature color. *Black.* It was designed with him in mind. I would confidently bet my last dollar on it.

I didn't deepen my presence. I remained near the

door with the Chanel clutch in front of me, both hands on the handle. Within two minutes, Ishmael rounded the corner, quenching my thirst.

Soothing my soul.

Settling my kitty.

Calming my heart.

His hands flattened against my cheeks. I was casted into the darkness. Naturally, I aimed to savor every moment of us. My body's response to another human was slowly altering my brain chemistry.

Nothing made sense. Yet, everything made perfect sense.

He tasted like the mint still on his tongue. I stole it from his mouth as I tried extracting the flavor from his buds. My nipples pebbled. Butterflies invited an entire exhibit of gentle creatures for a night out with us.

Ishmael. Your perfection is perplexing.

Not until I allowed it did he pull back. A thumb slid across his lip, cleaning the gloss I'd left behind. I rotated the mint on my tongue. The smirk on my face matched the one on his.

He leaned his head leftward, peering at me through a lustful haze. I abandoned his gaze in search of his rigidness. It greeted me behind the zipper of his slacks.

He ran a hand over his head. Decisions were being made internally. The struggle was loud. Obvious. Comical.

At once, Ishmael took me by the hand. He led me toward the front door. I was whisked into the night breeze. It swept across my skin, cooling my temperature.

"Lock the door, Royce."

He stood behind me, observing as I pressed the lock button on the keypad. A Phantom awaited us. Black in color. It blended well with the night. Beside it was an unfamiliar face. I turned to Ishmael for an explanation. He leaned over, mouth near my ear.

"Gibson. Our driver for the night."

I stepped forward, lowering my body onto the seat.

"Good evening, ma'am."

"Good evening."

I settled in. Ishmael did the same. The door closed behind us. Words tumbled from my lips.

"Are you going to tell me where we're headed? And why we need a driver?"

"To dinner. One hosted by one of my largest donors."

"And the driver?"

"I don't plan on making it back home before I get my hands on you, my baby."

His eyes found me as he revealed his truth.

"Ishm–"

"I've dreamt of your lips wrapped around my dick enough times to know what the roof of your mouth feels like against my head. Trust me, my baby, we're not making it home before my dick is down your throat."

His audacity was tantalizing. I straightened my posture, pushing my shoulders backward.

"A wise woman once told me… later isn't promised. Put the dick in your mouth now."

Roulette Childers was the wise woman.

Ishmael's chest imploded.

"We have dinner, Royce. Stop while you're ahead."

His warning never reached me.

"*You* have dinner. I'm just a guest."

"I want you snotty nosed and crying, love. That pretty face of makeup won't survive. Wai–"

In front of Ishmael, I fell onto my knees. His objection was shortened. So was our conversation.

We shared the same dream. I was ready for us to share the same reality.

I unbuckled his belt. Curiosity lifted his eyebrows. I peeled the fabric from around the button of his slacks. Quietly, he watched as I attempted to undress him. I patted his right leg, urging him to lift up.

"Has your head always been this hard?" Ishmael questioned.

He lifted. I pulled downward. I didn't mind ruining my makeup. There was more in my bag. His slacks, however, there weren't a second pair of those in my bag. They had to come down.

"I've been told it's wet… warm… w–"

My jaws nearly touched as my lips folded. I felt like a fish out of water. Puckered lips and bulging eyes.

"Watch your fucking mouth, my baby, before you remind me there are niggas still breathing that didn't treat you the way you should've been treated."

As he loosened his grip, I ran my tongue across my teeth. I tried suppressing the grin. It was useless.

Ishmael's dick sprung from his briefs, serving as the perfect distraction. Its girth was soul-stirring. I wrapped my fingers around it as best I could. I ran the length of his protruding veins. One at a time. Saliva flooded underneath my tongue.

I drew in as much as possible.

"*Spuh.*"

Ishmael's body lifted from the seat slightly. I placed my palm over his head and twirled my hand around, lowering it all the way down his shaft. His head fell backward.

My left hand joined my right hand. Each time I made it to the head, I twisted my palms around it and slid down his length.

"Fuck."

My eyes were on Ishmael. His eyes were low, riddled with need.

"You like that, Ishmael?"

He nodded.

"Use your words, love."

I stole a page from the book of Ishmael.

"Yes."

He didn't attempt to call my bluff. Without a warning, he understood the consequences of him not responding verbally. I'd suffered those same consequences under his ruling.

"Where do you want him?"

"Baby–" he groaned.

"Where do you want him, Ishmael?"

I stroked his dick with closed fists. His shoulders were curled inward. His spine was bent. His eyes had turned to slits.

"Put 'em in your mouth, Royce."

I removed my left hand, replacing it with my tongue. I enclosed him, suctioning his dick until it touched the back of my throat.

"Shit."

In the opposite direction of my hand, I twirled my head as I lifted. I switched directions as I lowered.

"Fuck."

Ishmael tasted so much like mine. His skin pressed against my tastebuds was heartening. My beating red organ slammed against my chest, attempting to free itself.

I rolled my tongue around the tip of Ishmael, harping on his sensitivity. He shuddered. A palm of his rested on my head. Silently, I braced for impact.

"Mmmmm."

Saliva ran down my hand, lubricating his skin. I glided up and down his dick effortlessly. Each time he made contact with the back of my throat, more lubricant was extracted.

"Shit."

Slowly, Ishmael guided my head with a gentle push. He stretched my limits, furthering his reach.

"Ahk. Ahhhhhk."

He tapped against the back of my throat, loosening my restraints. My gag reflex was ignited.

"Urgggggh."

"Don't do that, my baby. Don't fuck up your clothes," he groaned.

"Ahk."

Still, he plunged deeper. Slower. Steadier. Working his way down my throat.

"That's it."

Tears pooled in my eyes.

"Mmmmm."

Ishmael fucked my mouth ever so gently.

"That's it, my baby."

The tears fell down my cheeks. Cream slid from my pussy. I was utterly and unbelievably aroused. Pleasuring Ishmael drove me beyond the point of satisfaction.

His strokes intensified as his grip on my head tightened. I matched his strokes.

"Fuck."

His low grunts were sheer motivation. I dislodged him from my mouth and slid my hands down his shaft. I took his balls into the warmth of my palms—one and then the other.

"Mmm shit."

I massaged his dick with my hand and his balls with my mouth. My tongue slithered between the skin of his dick and my lips, resting against the thin strip just beneath his sack.

His body stiffened. He nearly pulled the threads from my sew-in, twisting my neck in his direction. He leaned forward until his mouth was on mine.

He shoved his tongue into my mouth. Hungrily, I kissed him deeply. Passion radiated from my frame. It rested within his. Ishmael was hot to the touch.

He loosened his grip and released me from his oral inclination. I reclaimed his balls, then his perineum. My strokes matched the rhythm of my tongue. In unison, we strived for his undoing. I wanted Ishmael spineless... boneless... helpless when I finished him.

"Goddamn," he huffed. "Shit."

He disturbed my flow once again, making it evident his ending was approaching. He was prolonging the inevitable. I'd allow it.

For now.

With a hand around my neck, he grunted. I was unmanning him. Right before my very eyes. He wasn't sure how to handle it. How to handle me. But, I surely knew how to handle him and everything that came with him.

"Eyes on me."

My hand never left his shaft. I stroked his dick as I did what I was told. His head was cocked. His lips were pulled back. He wasn't wearing that handsome smile. His face was twisted. His eyebrows were low.

"Make this dick spit up, my baby."

I nodded. A thick strand of slob rubbed across my chest each time I lifted and lowered my head. My eyes burned from the mascara that ran down my face. The back of my throat was sore to the touch. Still, I wasn't ready to part with his pole. Pleasing Ishmael was quickly becoming a passion of mine. It offered me instant, unshakeable gratification.

"Your words, Royce."

"Okay."

I took his dick into my mouth again. I'd missed it much more than I cared to explain. My right hand joined my efforts to disarm the missile at our disposal.

"Urgggh-"

My gag reflex didn't halt my movement. Vomit would have to wait. There was no room for it in my mouth. Not with Ishmael filling it to capacity.

I used my left hand to grab his wrist, guiding his hand back to my head. His guidance wasn't needed, but I craved it like I did my next breath.

"Uhhhhh."

My center was aching with need. Ishmael's semen in my mouth was crucial to my peak. I pushed the fabric of my dress upward and shoved my hand inside my panties. I inserted two fingers inside of me.

"Mmmmm."

"Fuck, my baby."

Ishmael's ending was upon us. I worked my fingers while assaulting my throat with his weapon.

"Mmmmm."

"This motherfucker 'bout to bus' baby. Shit."

His grip on my head tightened. His body stilled. His stomach caved. His breathing changed, nearly stopping completely.

Stars aligned behind Ishmael's head. My eyes were

still on him. Provoking him. Expressing my imminent rapture. I needed him cumming. I needed his semen on my tongue. My lips. My face. Wherever it landed. And, if it happened to be on him, I was prepared to clean the mess I'd made with the tip of every tastebud in my mouth.

"My ba– Urgh. Fuck."

His unearthing was the foundation for mine. My center tingled with numbness as I exploded onto my fingers.

"Uhhhhh!"

Warm semen squirted into my mouth. Hurriedly, I slid backward, allowing the rest to coat my lips and fall onto my chest. Watching Ishmael erupt in high definition rearranged my brain matter.

"Oh God," I moaned, pulling him back into my mouth.

His body pressed into the seat. His grip tightened.

"My baby–*please*."

Only because he'd asked nicely did I release him. My gloss coated his shaft. I rested my lips against it, still looking up into Ishmael's anguished eyes. Whatever dilemma he was facing was written all over his face.

I straightened my spine, allowing his dick to fall between his thighs. My right index finger pushed his remnants of him from the sides of my mouth and my lips. I shoved the finger in my mouth, sure to clean it thoroughly.

I swiped his semen from my chest and placed it at

the tip of my tongue. It vanished in my warmth as I closed my mouth. My smile didn't reach my eyes. They were preoccupied with the greed I suffered at the hands of Ishmael.

"We have arrived, Royce," Ishmael cleared his throat.

Disappointment tiptoed around his statement. He didn't want to attend the dinner. He was fragile. Vulnerable. Open. Exposed.

"We have."

I pulled his pants and boxers toward his waist. A pat on the leg got his body lifted long enough for me to secure them both. As he watched, I zipped his pants and then rebuttoned them. I pulled his belt through the buckle and tightened it.

The Chanel clutch opened with ease. I removed the small pack of wipes and used one to clean my fingers. I, then, used another to swipe the slime from my vulva. In disbelief, Ishmael held me under his watchful eye. I discarded both cloths in the small trash can on the back of the seat.

A dollop of hand sanitizer fell into my palm. I held the bottle over Ishmael's hands. He turned them over. My generosity allowed him to clean his hands without requiring more sanitizer. I rubbed mine together.

"You're makeup," he reminded me.

I opened another pack of wipes and slid the compact mirror out along with it. One side at a time, I cleared my face of the additives. They weren't necessary, neither was reapplication. I finalized the bareness of my appearance with clear KC lip gloss.

"Ready?"

Ishmael sighed with a shake of his head.

He wasn't ready. He wanted to call it a night. He wanted to take me back to his place. He wanted to rip my dress from my body. He wanted to stick his dick inside of me. He wanted me cumming hard and loud– *like he had.*

"Yeah," he lied.

He opened the door. I waited until his feet were planted safely on the ground. He required time to collect himself. He stood on wobbly knees.

Royce." Ishmael extended a hand, welcoming me to join him.

I exited the car, following him like a cat in heat. Cameras began flashing the second we were in full view.

Ishmael leaned closer to my ear. I braced myself for whatever was to come from him. He'd been deep in thought since his semen touched my tongue.

"If you put your mouth on anyone else, I'm going to have to take them motherfuckers off your face," he promised, buttoning the jacket of his suit.

I smiled, turning toward him.

"Jealous much?"

"I don't care how hard your head is, my baby, don't make me prove to you that I am no bluffer."

He pulled me closer, stopping mid-stride for still

images. After five seconds, he pulled me toward the entrance of the large event center.

"I don't bluff either, Ishmael. So, don't force me to pull your card."

I didn't have to explain for him to understand.

"Is that a threat?"

"I don't make threats I can't fall through on."

"Sounds like my type of woman."

We entered the building, hand-in-hand. The coolness sheeted my skin with small bumps. Still, Ishmael kept me warm. His temperature was spiked. His hormones were raging. He had been satisfied, yet he still craved more of me. I, too, needed more of him.

"My dress–" I lied.

"What about it?"

"Come here."

I broke our stride to travel in the direction opposite of the dinner party. Ishmael's mind was elsewhere. He wasn't focused. Every appearance mattered. His head needed to be in the game whenever he was in the public eye. This was our first appearance as a couple. The last thing I needed was my pussy on his mind when the entire room was waiting on him to slip.

"I need you to help me."

I jiggled the door of the first handle I stumbled upon. It was locked. I jiggled the second handle. It, too, was locked. The third door pushed open, allowing both Ishmael and I inside.

"Royce, wha–"

I turned around and unfastened his suit jacket. I slid

it from his shoulders and placed it on the chair behind the desk.

"You hired me for a job that I intend to do well, no matter what we are truly getting ourselves into behind closed doors. You're sexually frustrated, Ishmael. Not because you've been deprived, but because getting your dick sucked only made you want to slide into me even more than you already did before you left your home this morning, while you were at work all day, once you got off, and in the back of the car. Your wish is my command, Ish," I explained, calling him by the name I'd heard his brother utilize.

I shoved his pants down his legs and placed my palms on the desk. With ease, I lifted the bottom of my dress and slid out of my thong. Ishmael was silent, allowing me to vent. Allowing me to give clear instructions so that my job was done well.

"I need your eyes on the prize at all times. Tonight, that's not me. It's Berkeley City's Mayor. I need you sharp and prepared for anything that comes your way. You can't do that with a soft spine and weak knees."

I shoved my panties in his mouth, wadding them until I was certain he wouldn't be heard beyond the walls around us because the walls around him were about to close.

He pushed my body against the desk, holding me by the neck. My desk met the cool surface. They hardened on contact.

He tapped his hard dick against my slit. Up and

down, he rubbed it, lubricating his shaft. And, without warning, he entered me.

"Uhhhhhh–" I moaned, quickly regretting it.

Ishmael's grip tightened, demanding I quiet down.

I stretched my arms across the desk as he stretched my pussy across his dick. On the tips of my toes, I slid my body backward, meeting Ishmael's stroke.

He groaned against the fabric of my panties, reigniting the fire within me. I slid back and forth with ease. My rhythm was in line with his. He refused to have it any other way. He refused to release control. He refused to give me exactly what I was after.

Instead, his pelvic area collided with my backside.

Over.

And over.

And over.

And over.

And over.

"Ishma– uhhhh. Ishhhhhhmael," I begged for consideration.

Whap.

Whap.

Whap.

Whap.

He gave me none. He was relentless with his strokes. My wetness coated us both.

"Plea— uhhh."

He removed the panties from his mouth, never halting his movements or changing his rhythm.

"Shut the fuck up, Royce."

He leaned forward, lifting my right leg. My calf laid against his shoulder, spreading my body wide. He managed to touch my soul from my pussy's portal. I gripped his arm, trying my hardest to keep from tumbling over.

Ishmael's hand was no longer at the back of my neck. It was at the front, squeezing me as I squeezed around him.

"Open your mouth," he demanded.

His words were loaded with tension. I listened. My lips parted and my mouth fell agape.

Huwk.

Spuh.

My eyes closed from the impact of the wind. My body curled toward his. The first wave hit my feminine parts as his spit settled on my tongue. I swallowed.

Hard.

Deep.

Hungrily.

"Again," I begged, mouth wide.

My thirst was beyond my control.

Huwk.

Spuh.

Ishmael's particles slid down my throat as he pulled my face toward him. He buried his tongue in my mouth. I bit down. The intensity of my orgasm was too much to bear alone. I needed somewhere soft to land. There was no better place than him at the moment.

"Mmmmmmm. Yesssss," I murmured. "Yessss."

"Fuck. *Fuck.* Fuck."

I sat across the table from the sexiest man in the room. His eyes were low. His gaze was fixed. His intoxication was evident, but it had little to do with the water he was sipping.

His inhibition was solely due to my influence. My presence. My pussy. My lips and the way they curled around his dick. My mouth and the way it juggled his balls. My warmth and the way it coated him like a blanket in the dead of the winter.

The room blurred around us. It was soundless. I saw nothing but Ishmael. I heard nothing but Ishmael and the beat of my heart. It reminded me that I was still alive. Still well. Still able.

What's the matter? I mouthed.

He tilted his head. I waited with baited breath, hoping he responded. After his shoulders fell flat and his elbows touched the table, displaying his defeat, he made a confession.

I think I'm in love.

I placed a hand over my mouth to conceal my happiness.

You too?

I nodded, sliding my hand down.

Yes. Me, too.

He tipped his head toward the door. I shook my head.

Twenty more minutes.

He frowned, hating that I took my role so seriously. However, we had an election to win. Everything else could wait.

Please.

His eyes were wide with despair. He didn't care to be here. Ishmael wanted to be alone.

Ten more minutes.

"And, that's all thanks to our next mayor, Mr. Grayson. He's been such a beacon for change in our communities in recent years. He's given back to the same communities that raised him to be the man he is today. If there's nothing else I know about this man, it's that he is for the people of Berkeley. Especially the children, because he understands they are our future."

The spotlight shined on Ishmael. He fixed his face, forging a smile. My hands collided, beginning the round of applause he deserved. After a few seconds, he stood, waving his hand around.

"Thank you," he exclaimed. "Thank you."

Though he didn't have a microphone in front of him, everyone knew exactly what he was saying.

"When you visit those polls in November, don't forget to vote Grayson. He's not what Berkeley wants. He's what Berkeley needs."

The spotlight returned to the stage where Velma, the event coordinator and director of The Berkeley City Community Foundation, also known as TBCCF, continued her speech. The fundraiser had pulled in well over a hundred thousand thousand dollars. Each plate was eight hundred and eighty-eight dollars.

There were enough people in the venue to cover one hundred and fifty plates at minimum. It was a great start.

Donations were being taken as well. Ishmael had made a generous donation himself. His love for Berkeley had no limits. He wanted to see the city thrive and the children grow to be responsible, considerate adults.

"Grayson Cares." I leaned over, whispering.

"Hm?"

"Grayson Cares. It has a ring to it. I'm going to start the paperwork for a non-profit."

"Does your mind ever stop working?"

"No. October is coming. It's breast cancer awareness month. You've expressed your concerns for people policing the female body. I think that's right on target for an early detection campaign. In addition, we should start a clothing drive for the children who have been affected by breast cancer.

"When cancer happens, it doesn't just affect the person who is experiencing its symptoms. It changes everyone around them. Children feel it the most when it's a parent or grandparent. Let's not forget those little ones."

Ishmael nodded.

"You, my baby, have a good head on your shoulders."

The grin on his face said more than he was willing to. My trailblazing thoughts weren't the only thing he was referring to.

"Can we leave now?"

I nodded.

"Yes."

Ishmael was up in a flash. He took me by the hand and began the usher wave as we made our way through the dimly lit room. If he wasn't waving, he was shaking a hand. If he wasn't shaking a hand, he was accepting a hug.

It had taken us eight minutes to get from our seats to the backseat of the Phantom. Ishmael's exhaustion weighed him down. His head rested on my shoulder. I ran my fingertips up and down the side of his face.

His head grew heavier as we entered the freeway. His breathing slowed once we were at a pleasant speed.

My baby. I laid my head against the window, admiring the man before me.

He was no soldier at the moment. He was a vulnerable boy with an expanding heart. So much was changing for him. So much of his world was evolving.

I wasn't sure if Ishmael understood yet, but he was safe with me. He would always be safe with me.

[illegible]
[illegible]
[illegible]
[illegible]
[illegible]
[illegible]
[illegible]
[illegible]
[illegible]
[illegible]
[illegible]
[illegible]
[illegible]
[illegible]

TWELVE

Ishmael

THE WEEKS WERE PASSING by like days. I couldn't grasp the concept of time suddenly. Everything was a blur. Everything but *her*.

I unbuttoned the cuffs of my shirt as I watched Royce paint her toenails. She placed a blue light over them each time she finished putting more polish on them. The television's volume was high. Her eyes were on the screen every chance she got.

It was my face that made her teeth show and her eyes bunch in the corners. She was enthralled in the latest updates on the race and my responses to the questions I was asked by the reporters with cameras in my face. A city's historical figure was facing demolishing. I wouldn't stand for it. I was present to show my support and demand a vote from those in the community.

"Exactly," Royce tittered as I concluded my statement.

I sniggered, wondering if this was her routine when she was at my home and I wasn't. She looked up, finally noticing me.

"How long have you been there?" She questioned, placing her chin on her knee and glaring in my direction.

The blue light she held over her toes beeped. It must've been the sound of her freedom, because she was up on her feet in a flash. My white shirt raised along with her arms. She rushed toward me, wrapping them around my body. Her legs joined.

I kissed her lips until she parted them, pulling me into her mouth.

"Hello, my baby," I said, breathlessly.

She'd stolen oxygen directly from my lungs.

"Hi, my love."

Royce's stomach rumbled against my body. She tucked her head, flushed with embarrassment.

"When's the last time you ate?"

She remained silent.

"Royce."

"When you cooked breakfast this morning," she whispered.

I carried her into the kitchen. I placed her body on the cool counter and opened the fridge. A bottle of water was the first thing I grabbed. The sliced turkey meat from the deli was the next. I placed them both beside her and removed my button down.

"Have those and sit your ass right there while I make something for dinner."

"Yes, sir," she joked, placing a hand on her head.

"Remembering to eat shouldn't be so hard."

"I've been swamped with calls and tasks all day."

"So have I, but I still put something on my stomach during lunch hours."

"I wasn't hungry then. I was still full."

I paused, taking a good look at her. As expected, she was wearing a sinister smile.

She'd swallowed every drop of my semen this morning.

And last night.

I was campaigning hard but I was fucking Royce even harder. My hours outside of the office werw spent in her pussy and in her mouth. I loved them both the same almost. However, her pussy had far more power.

Her time was split between Clarke and my home. I hated when she was away, but I loved how much her pussy missed me when she was gone. Her absence was a gift and a curse. When she was waiting for me at home, I couldn't think logically. My mind was at home with her.

"You're ruthless, my baby."

"You love it here."

I nodded.

"You haven't told a lie yet."

She opened the container filled with turkey. She pulled off the first piece and extended it toward me. Her generosity had me by the neck. Royce was selfless. She thought of everyone else, making sure they were okay, before taking care of her own needs. She wasn't the oldest, but it was obvious she wasn't the youngest either. Royce was a caretaker.

Because I knew she needed me to have the piece of meat more than I did, I accepted it. I rolled it up and bit into it.

"Eat."

She nodded, stuffing her mouth with turkey. I watched as she chewed until it was gone.

"How was your day?"

I pulled out all of the ingredients to make spaghetti. I'd purchased the groceries but hadn't gotten around to cooking it. I'd learned a week and a half ago that it was Royce's favorite dish as a kid. Her comfort food.

Time away from her family weighed heavy on her heart. So, to bring her comfort, spaghetti was on the menu tonight.

"Too many questions. Too many words. Too many cameras," I huffed, kissing the skin of my teeth.

"It'll all be worth it."

I agreed. "Yeah."

"I finished the details for the wrap. It's gorgeous."

"For the breast exams?"

She nodded. "Um hm."

"After dinner will you show me?"

"That's the plan."

Our careers took away so much time, we vowed to give each other our undivided attention during the evening hours. During dinner, whether at home or a restaurant of her choice, no phone usage was allowed unless there was an emergency.

"Speaking of plans, my baby. What's our plan for birth control?"

I had refrained from the inquiry as long as I could. My dick was lodged inside of Royce nearly every time it busted. I wasn't being careful. I wasn't being cautious. I was being controlled by our sexual gratification. Nothing else mattered in those moments.

"Do you want children?" She asked, sipping from the water.

I shook my head, "Nah. I never really considered bringing children into this world. I think it's too much of a fucked up place, ya feel me. Sometimes I wonder what the fuck my moms was thinking bringing three boys into this motherfucker."

"You never talk about your brother."

"Indigo?"

She shook her head.

"No. Isaías."

"Out of sight– out of mind. But, he's always in my heart. In the back of my head. In every memory I have as a kid. Just– not so much now."

"Where is he?"

"Probably in the OR at the moment. He drowns himself in work and his studies. He's reserved and very military. His time over there altered so much of him, sometimes I wonder if my actual brother is still overseas."

"Yeah. It does that. Most soldiers suffer a great deal when they return."

"Understood, which is why I give him his space. When he wants me around, I'm there. And, if he needs me, I'm there. He knows it."

"I'm sure he cherishes your time together."

"He can't stand Indigo's playful ass though. Runs Isaías' ass hot every fucking time he's around."

"But he loves him."

"Without a doubt."

"How does your mother handle the distance?"

I shrugged.

"It's like he's still in the service. That's how she thinks of it. That's how we all think of it."

"That's a good way to deal with it."

"How do you deal with it?"

"With what?"

"Your brother's distance?"

Her shoulders sagged. She chewed slower, trying to conjure the words to express her feelings. I didn't know much, but I knew enough about their family to decipher who was around and who wasn't.

"He's never too far away," she revealed. "He's always right there when we need him. There are miles between us but there's no distance. There's never distance."

"Understood."

"How do you know the owner of The M?"

"He's my brother."

"No shit?"

She nodded.

"Yes. There's twelve of us. Seven girls. Five boys."

"Big family."

"Really big family."

"You have enough children running around already, huh? Niece and nephews."

She sighed. "Not really. I don't see the ones that live here enough. They hardly know me. I'm going to do better. Nine nieces and nephews here. From my brothers, of course.

"My sisters– none of us really ever wanted children. We didn't dream of big families because we've always had one. To be honest, we prefer small units. We grew up with twelve siblings and a total of four parents. Two lost their lives early on, but still. That would've made sixteen of us."

"Lost their lives?"

"To a mental illness."

I noted the somberness of her tone. Death was a heavy load to carry. It stuck with you. The grief didn't know when to shake loose. It lingered for years, never giving you a chance to fully recover before it reminded you of what you'd lost again.

I stopped dicing the vegetables and grabbed the hand towel to dry my damp hands. I'd almost forgotten the most important part of Royce's meals.

"Where are you going?" She chuckled.

"To bring you joy."

I disappeared into the pantry. Beyond its doors, I entered the cellar. Aging wine lined the walls. I didn't bother with the labels or the names. I grabbed the first bottle that caught my eye and made my way back to Royce.

"Oh you're after a girl's heart," she cheered as I rejoined her.

"I think I've already got it, my baby."

THE GREY LIST

I shoved my nose between the pillow and Royce's skin. It was my favorite place to be. She was my favorite place to be. This house was haunted when she wasn't around. It was her presence that quieted the loud silence.

She was home. It didn't matter what structure was above us. Royce was home now. Each day I left her, I couldn't wait to get back to her. Because, with her, I could loosen my grip on life. She untied every knot in my heart. Consumed my worries. Catered to my desires. Sucked the semen from my sack. And, walked alongside of me proudly each time I presented her publicly.

This was no game. I was fully invested. Whether I secured the seat as mayor or not, I'd been gifted a permanent residence in Royce's world. For me, that was paramount.

Her breathing was steady. She was deep in her sleep.

Comfortable.

Comforted.

Content.

Safe.

Still.

Providing a secure environment for my baby wasn't an option for me. It was a priority.

I slid the covers back. Insomnia wouldn't allow me to sleep. I gave up the silent battle. It wasn't worth my sanity.

I stalked the bottom drawer in the kitchen. Pulling it open, I retrieved the pre-rolled spliffs that Indigo had left behind. In my past, I could face three and hardly feel a thing. It had been eight years since I'd placed a blunt to my lips, but tonight would change that.

I wasn't on a mission to get high. I needed coaxing. Everything was becoming a lot. Royce had been my source of relief, but I didn't want to wake her with my troubles. She needed her rest. And, I needed to clear my head.

I searched drawer after drawer, trying to locate a lighter. It wasn't until I pulled out the last drawer that I found one. With it, I made my way through my home, stopping in front of the glass doors that led to the backyard.

The views from up top were immaculate. Berkeley's lights twinkled in the background. The pool glistened in the dark. I turned on the heater, warming the water. It was October and the weather was nice when the sun was up. At night was when the chill settled in.

I landed in the dining room where there was a full-sized bar at the furthest end. The bottom of my chilled glass rested on the treated wood. Cognac melted the frost. I filled it halfway and gripped the sides. My glass, my blunts, and I exited my home shortly after.

The difference in my marble floors and the concrete was striking. I conquered the distance from the sliding doors to the steps of the pool. The water had warmed swiftly. I lowered into the water, sitting on the edge of the third step. Only half my body was in the water.

Flick.

Flick.

I placed the fire at the end of the blunt. It fired up with ease. I pulled in, inviting the smoke into my lungs. Slowly, I exhaled, releasing what was left of it.

I pulled the blunt away from my face, staring at its construction. Indigo was a perfectionist in more departments than he cared to name. I appreciated his skillset, especially at the moment.

A sip from my glass put me closer to where I wanted to be. *Mentally.*

The city of Berkeley needed someone who was truly in their corner. Daniels' greed would be the death of the good in the city. I couldn't watch Berkeley crumble and fall before my very eyes. There was too much good in the city. Daniels was destroying it and erasing our history in the process.

Gentrification was on the rise. Our communities were being torn down and replaced with modern, over-priced housing that forced residents out of their environments because they couldn't afford to live there anymore. Schools were closing every year. The attendance rate was declining. And, children were hungry.

Meanwhile, Daniels' main concern was the New Berkeley. One that didn't include everyone. It included the fittest who survived the changes being made at a rapid rate. It didn't include the elderly, veterans, disabled, or the lower-class.

My mind drifted so far away I could hardly catch my thoughts. It was the end of the blunt and the empty cup that brought me back to reality. Still, I was in no shape to return to bed. Sleep wouldn't greet me at the door. More troubles would. Berkeley's troubles would.

I submerged my body in the water. I didn't plan on coming up for air until something felt better.

"He does it too."

Her voice was the calm I'd been longing for. I heard it through the water in my ears and around my head. I ended my ninth lap to find her near.

Royce bent down, her toes stopping where my hands gripped the end of the pool.

"Who?"

"My brother. When he has too much on his mind and his troubles won't let him get a good night's rest."

"It soothes me."

"So can I."

I couldn't deny her. She stood tall. I watched in amazement as she turned, heading toward the other end of the pool. On the way, her hands lifted over her head, pulling my shirt along with them. By the time she touched the first step, her body was bare. My dick was hard. My troubles were gone.

She lured me with her gaze. Gracefully, she lowered her body. No panties. No bottoms. No top.

"I didn't mean to wake you."

"Sit down, Ishmael."

"Ro–"

"I'm not trying to strip you of your power. I trust your leadership. I trust your guidance. I trust you. But, I need you to sit down. I need you to allow me this moment. I need you to understand that this is where my power lies. And, I won't let you strip that from me. *Or you.*"

My ass was on the concrete and my dick was out of my briefs before she could further explain.

Royce hovered over me. Slowly, she lowered her pussy onto my hardness. I swallowed back the taste of weed. I needed to taste her on my tongue.

"I don't like begging, Ishmael."

"You don't have to for something that is yours."

"It felt like it."

"I'm sorry, my baby. *Fuck.*"

Her shit engulfed me. I rested my head against her chest, unable to maintain my gaze. The sound of her heartbeat lulled me to a safer place. A quieter place. A place where my problems didn't exist.

Royce's ability to govern me so effortlessly when her pussy was exposed and her walls were surrounding me needed to be analyzed. I was powerless. All that I had was transferred the moment our bodies connected.

"Ish," she moaned, grabbing my chin.

We were nose to nose. Mouth to mouth. Eye to eye.

"My baby–"

She rolled her body, tugging on my dick with each stroke of her pussy.

"When I said I'd handle it, I meant you, too."

Her breasts were against my chest. Hard like rocks. Yet soft like pillows.

"Worry me."

She made her mark on my heart.

"Worry me with your troubles."

Her pussy was petitioning for my eruption.

"Worry me with your fears."

She rolled slowly.

"Worry me with your desires."

Her voice cracked with emotion.

"Worry me with your concerns."

Royce was indescribable.

"Worry me. I can handle it."

She released my chin. Her right hand wrapped around the pole beside us. Her feet flattened on the ground beneath us.

"I can handle you."

Up.

Down.

"Slow down, my baby."

Royce didn't listen. That hard head of hers was going to make a soft dick.

"Roy–"

She covered my mouth with hers, stifling my objections and my groans.

"I love you," she mumbled against my lips.

Hearing the words pour from her soul inflated my chest. It was an honor to be loved by someone so special. So ravishing. So remarkable.

I vowed, at that moment, to never break her pretty heart or hurt her pretty head. Royce deserved an uncompromising, uncomplicated love. I'd give her that. I didn't care for her to struggle in order to prove her strength to me. She exposed me to her resilience each day.

"I love you," I breathed against her, "I knew the moment I saw you."

"So much."

Her body bounced, coating me with her creaminess. Her pussy was wetter than the water near us.

"Royce... I'm going to cum, my baby."

"Please," she urged.

"You have–"

"Shhhhhh."

Her strokes quickened. A hand rounded my neck.

"Mmmmmm."

Marry me, my baby.

I closed my eyes, shoving the words back down my throat. I'd known Royce for nearly three months. I couldn't remember a day I didn't imagine her in a ring I'd purchased with promises of forever. I couldn't remember a day I hadn't gazed at her beauty, finding my wife in those eyes. I couldn't remember a day that visions of her in a white dress didn't cross my mind.

She was my destination. I wanted nothing more.

"Fuck."

My toes curled forcefully. My grip around Royce's waist tightened. My semen sprouted from my shaft into her awaiting oasis.

"Fuck, baby."

Her arms rounded my body. She laid her chin on my shoulder. I pulsated inside of her.

"I love it here… in your arms."

I closed my eyes, allowing her words to land right where they belonged.

"Thank you. Thank you for taking a chance on me. Thank you for taking good care of me. Thank you for not running the other fucking way. Thank you for seeing my flaws and my faults and choosing to stay anyway.

"Thank you for sacrificing time with the people you love to be here for me. Thank you for being here when I step through the door. You don't understand, my baby. That shit just does so much for me. To me."

"I've been asking for someone to come into my life

who understands me. I wasn't sure how long that would take. But, that night I met you… I knew I wasn't asking for too much."

"You helped a stranger. Your selflessness wouldn't let me forget you. Even if you hadn't walked in my office days later, I wouldn't have let you slip away. I would've found you. As soon as this shit was over, I would've come for you."

"I know," she admitted.

"I want you to cum, Royce."

"And, I want you to rest. Tonight isn't about me, Ish. It's about you."

"Every night is about you, my baby."

She shook her head. "Not tonight."

My flaccid dick fell from her pussy as she stood.

"I won't fight you on this. I'm tired, Ish. I can't sleep until you can."

I removed my soaked briefs, knowing I wouldn't win this battle.

Royce grabbed ahold of my hand. She led me into the house. I pulled the doors closed as she waited. A yawn pulled her lips apart as our journey to the bedroom continued. As much as I wanted to shower, I knew Royce wouldn't last much longer.

It'll have to wait.

She wanted me in bed… skin to skin. Chest to back. Nose to neck. Deep in my slumber.

I pulled her into me, wrapping my arm around her neck. My lips grazed her ear.

"When I ask you to marry me, my baby, don't deny me."

Chuckling, she responded, "I have no plans to."

THIRTEEN

Royce

4 DAYS UNTIL THE ELECTION...

"And napkins, please."

The cashier grabbed a wad from the stack behind the counter and shoved them into the paper bag.

"Thank you."

Ishmael's days were spent in his office, combing through last minute details and garnering every vote he possibly could. We'd exalted every avenue. Still, he refused to leave any stones unturned. I admired his drive.

The fear had begun to become evident in his fight.

The clock was ticking. Daniels was ahead in the polls by a mere 1.2 points. Early voting had revealed the numbers we'd been waiting for. Admittedly, I expected Ishmael to claim the polls during early voting as well as during election day.

Though perplexed, I wasn't concerned. He would be the mayor of Berkeley. As long as I was in his corner, losing wasn't an option. It was never an option. Second place was too close to last place. And, in this race, second place didn't matter.

Absentmindedly, I massaged my breasts. They were still tender to the touch. The mobile mammogram was a success. Two thousand and twenty six women were examined. Fourteen were advised to see an oncologist for the masses found in their breasts. Twenty-two others were advised to monitor small spots noted in their files in the event they became cancerous.

On the final day of the week-long event, we gifted children of those affected by breast cancer the clothes we'd collected throughout the month of October. Cameras and microphones surrounded us, but there was one I was willing to share a word with or allow Ishmael to do the same. Jasmine Kade. She wrote the front page articles for *Berkeley News*. I wanted Ishmael's face plastered over this morning's paper.

"Do you all have any more of today's papers?"

I was off to a late start this morning. Ishmael had taken off before the sun rose. I cut out of the door around eight. Around seven was when I noticed he hadn't touched a pot or skillet in the kitchen. The jug of orange juice we'd had delivered with the rest of the groceries was still unopened.

Feeding Ishmael was my first order of business. Meeting Maylei was my second. Malachi and Mercer would be under the same roof for the better part of the morning, visiting Pops. I was looking forward to squeezing baby cheeks and being surrounded by Chemistry's love although it wasn't him expressing it. Mercer, Malachi, Makai, and Milo all represented parts of Chemistry that I loved.

"Over there," the cashier pointed toward the stand near the door.

I slid a twenty dollar bill across the counter.

"Keep the change," I told her.

The building Ishmael's office was housed in had the best smoke shop in all of Berkeley. I blamed him for introducing me to the smoked turkey, egg, and cheese taco. I grabbed the bag that held three of them. One for me and one for Ishmael. The third one was for anyone inside of his personal space when I entered with food, just in case their stomachs were touching their back as well.

"Thank you!"

I fixed my eyes on the stand with a single issue of Berkeley news left. As I approached, the bell of the small shop rang. The customer was headed in the same direction. I picked my pace, managing to snatch the paper from the wire rack just before the fragile old man was able to take his sixth step.

Sorry, grandaddy.

I tucked the publication under my arm and exited. My feet didn't stop moving when I entered the lobby, when the metal detector notified the staff of the Glocks I was toting, or as the news reporters beckoned for my attention.

Their presence was unnerving. There was no reason for them to be here. There were still four days until the election and there wasn't a press conference scheduled. Ishmael didn't give a damn about being in front of cameras right now. He wanted to be in front of the people. His people. The people he was running for.

Inside the elevator, I removed the paper from my arm. The weekend anticipation had me on edge. Silently, I studied the front page article. Every part of my body numbed.

My heart slammed against my chest as I read the headline. Every muscle in my face contracted.

MAYOR HOPEFUL: SECRET BABY?

Ping.

The elevator doors opened. My Prada heels collided with the floor. I marched into the office that I'd spent more time at in the last two weeks than I had at my own residence, in a city I saw more of than Clarke since I'd met the man I was in pursuit of.

"Good mor–"

"Morning."

"Good morn–"

"Um– Royce– One second. He's in–" Matte stuttered, stepping in front of Ishmael's office door.

"I don't give a fuck what he's in. Step aside before I shampoo your greasy ass bob with these tacos."

"Yes, ma'am."

Stepping aside, she lifted both hands. With a roll of my eyes, I pushed the door open.

"We're no longer confident in your ability to bring this thing home, Grayson. This is the second sc–"

Conversation halted.

Two men sat in front of Ishmael's desk. I recognized them instantly.

"Your confidence in his ability to bring this thing home has been lost, meanwhile, you were confident enough to pair that midnight blue suit jacket with those black slacks? I am confident you will find a better optometrist in the future. And– Caldwell," I chuckled, placing the brown paper bag on the counter.

"How confident are you that the powder your assistant scores from your favorite dealer on 31st and Sabers isn't laced with the big F? How confident are you that your next toot won't be your last? How confident are you that your nose will be able to withstand even three more years of your addiction? Not a hair inside of it has survived. You're working on the nostrils next?"

Ishmael's sigh was the only thing heard around the room. All eyes were on me. My eyes were on Ishmael.

"He is the best chance Berkeley has. Either watch Daniels destroy this beautiful city or get out there on foot, helping bring these votes in. Sitting here bitching and moaning won't win us this election. Action will.

"No one cares about these scandals. It's all bullshit. I know it and so do you. Your skeletons won't stay in the closet forever. Tread really fucking lightly when it comes to this one. He's mine. And, not even the Lord Himself will be able to save you if you are anything but accommodating until this election is over. Now," I cleared my throat and slammed the day's paper on Ishmael's desk.

"If you'd excuse me. We have things to discuss."

Caldwell was up on his feet in a flash. Henderson was right behind him.

"Oh, and, Henderson," I called out.

He paused, turning around.

"Tell Evelyn and your son, Evan, I said hello. Didn't Evan just celebrate his third birthday?"

Henderson's pale skin turned a shade of red I'd never witnessed before.

"See, the difference between Ishmael and you is—*well*," I paused. "You vowed a life of honesty when you married Torri. You've been living a lie since that very day. You're one family photo away from losing everything you've scammed to become. *This man...* he's nothing like you or anyone else in this political circus.

"Put on your clown suits and prepare to perform, because we're winning this fucking election. I'd drag my naked body over a pool of sharks during my menstrual cycle before seeing Daniels take another term. Goodbye."

I waved them both off. The same hand flattened

against Ishmael's desk. I peered down. He wore his nerves on his sleeves.

"My ba–"

"What the fuck is this, Ish?"

"Royce."

He wasn't talking fast enough. And, I wasn't getting the answer I needed quick enough.

"I asked you– I asked you if there was anyone I had to worry about. You looked me in my face," my voice cracked as the words riddled the room like bullets, "You looked me in my face and said there was no one."

"Because there isn't. There wasn't."

"Then who the fuck is having your baby?"

He shook his head, attempting to rise from his seat. I lifted my skirt and removed my Glock from the holster. I laid it on his desk, never taking my finger off the trigger. He retreated. Hands lifted.

"I don't want no smoke with you, my baby."

"Then you better start talking, Ishmael."

"She's someone I've had relations with."

"Claiming to be eleven weeks pregnant?"

He nodded. "It's fucked up, my baby. I underst–"

"Do you fucking understand? Hm? Because I have been in your life for three fucking months."

"Royce, I'm sorry. I–"

"You're not saying enough right now, and I'm not sure if it's her picture on the front page after all the *good* we did this week or your lack of regurgitation that's making my trigger finger itch the most."

"I know her. Her name is Asia. She lives in the

building next to mine. Whenever I needed someone to satisfy me, she was the person I called. She was mere feet away. Always picked up. Always was prepared to–"

"Until when?"

"My baby."

"Since when, Ish? Since us?"

"I–" He tripped over his words. "It–"

I picked up my gun. His words weren't coming fast enough. My heart was hurting and I needed something of his to feel the same pain.

"Don't do that, my baby. I won't be able to forgive you for that."

"You will. I'm not worried about that. Me forgiving you is what you should be worried about."

"I don't know what you want me to say, Royce."

"Say the truth. That's what I want. We're four days away from voting and the world finds out you're expecting a child. When, Ishmael Samuel Grayson? When was the last time you stuck your dick inside of Asia?"

I lifted the flap on one of the four Chanel bags he'd purchased me in the last two months. I removed the silencer.

"August."

"August when because the math ain't mathing."

"August, Royce."

"August when, motherfucker?"

"The day you walked into my office."

My lips pulled backward. A smirk lined them as I shook my head. Ishmael had stuck his dick inside of another woman and possibly produced a child with every intention of pursuing me. Men were hardly ever different.

They were all the same in so many ways. Though he wasn't mine at the time, he planned to be. That thought alone should've kept his dick in his pants.

"Hmph," I scoffed.

Silently, I screwed on the silencer.

"Royce– what the fuck are you doing?"

"By any means, Ishmael." I sighed.

I placed the nose of my gun to his side and fired a single shot.

"Fuck!"

My eyes rolled upward.

"So dramatic."

He didn't as much as flench. His blood soaked his white shirt, immediately. I wished I had the heart to care or even get him a towel, but I didn't. He'd claimed to want me vulnerable, but he'd forced me to be vicious.

I shoved my weapon in my purse and snatched up the brown paper bag. He didn't deserve my generosity today. Neither did he deserve to eat. I hoped his stomach was the source of his discomfort all day.

"That should put you ahead in the poles."

My right shoulder lifted and fell. I wasn't expecting retaliation. Because, deep down, Ishmael felt like he deserved that bullet as much as I wanted to give it to him.

"Are you fucking insane?"

"Yes. And, to win, you have to be. Tight screws don't leave room for successors. Loose screws do."

I opened the office door with my chin high and my chest swelled. Though it was hurting, I wouldn't let the world know it. I wouldn't even allow Ishmael the pleasure of knowing he'd injured me. The bullet to his waist was the sweet redemption I'd settle for at the moment.

"Oh shoot."

Matte fell inside, landing face first next to my feet.

Pathetic.

She couldn't keep her balance if she was paid to do so.

"Girl, grow a fucking spine."

"Sorry– I– uh–"

"And stop apologizing so much."

"Yes. Right."

I stepped over her thin frame. The sudden silence of the office was loud. Orbs traced every step I made. Still, I continued on my journey until I reached the elevator. I pushed the button, calling for a cart.

Ping.

I stepped inside, finally releasing the breath I'd been holding. My nostrils flared and then shrunk.

Flared and shrunk.

Flared and...

You'd better not. I chastised as the tears stung my eyeballs.

I straightened my posture and collected the parts of me that were prepared to fall apart. I was trained for crisis. What I hadn't been trained for was heartbreak. And, seeing the face of a woman who could be carrying the child of the man I had fallen head first for was enough to break the toughest of soldiers.

Ping.

Cameras greeted me as I stepped off the elevator.

"Vote Grayson November 2nd," I suggested, making my way out of the building.

T H E G R E Y L I S T

A set of keys landed on the counter in the kitchen. An unpleasant fragrance filled the air. Giggles gripped the pieces of my sanity that I had left.

"Alright, girl. I just made it home. I'll talk to you later."

"Okay. I'll text you if I hear something from him. I'm sure I'm in for a long day. He's deep in his feelings."

"You know how men are. Dish it but can't take it."

"At least yours isn't a nutcase."

A chuckle followed.

"That has yet to be determined."

"Right. We'll see soon enough. I'll talk to you later."

"Later, Tish."

The FaceTime call ended. I observed the petite, round-faced woman in a fitted top and pants that matched. Her skin was glistening, a sign she'd just come from the gym.

"Good evening, Asia."

A hand went to her chest. Another hand went to her stomach. A dagger pushed through my heart. I grimaced from the pain.

"Fuck! What are yo– you doing here?"

I placed the glass of wine I'd poured myself on the table.

"I've come to get to the bottom of this–*mess*."

I stood on my feet, bringing my Glock along with me.

"Cheap wine, love. Very cheap. I've left a list of quality reds and whites on the notepad on your counter."

"Wha…"

"Seeing as though this bottle and a few more are in the trash, I suggest you start talking or I start filing paperwork for full custody of the child you're carrying. From the heaviness of that trash bag, it's clear they're going to suffer with basic cognitive functions."

"Excuse me."

"A glass of wine here and there, fine. But, we're talking, mental delays, slobbering, physical challenges, speech impediment, helmet head, diapers until they're fiv–"

"I get your fucking point."

"Good then, I don't have to further explain why I'm holding this."

The pregnancy test rested between my fingers.

"I want you to leave my home. Right now."

"This– uh–" I looked around her indecent pad.

The DIY project was rather grotesque. Toddler art

lined the walls, yet there wasn't a toddler in the home. Neither had she birthed one. Her scribbles told a different story from the one I'd learned over the last six hours.

"Dwelling belongs to Hershel Holdings. And, it is far from a home sweetie. It doesn't even meet the requirements of a house."

"I don't give a f–"

"Lower your voice when you're speaking to me. You're at a ten. I need you to be at a two or I'll be forced to put two in you... giving you something to actually scream about."

Her face was beet red. Veins protruded from her forehead. She was unraveling. Her anger was beginning to peak. I was quiet. Observant. Waiting for the slightest movement in my direction, because she was going to be a dead ass, mad ass bitch.

"You come into my home making demands and you expect me to be calm?"

"I do."

I shrugged, closing the gap between us. It was difficult to maneuver the living room. The brick-hard couch was far too big for the space it occupied.

"And I expect you to bring your sweaty pussy into the bathroom and piss on this stick."

"Get out," she demanded, pointing toward the door.

"This way, Asia."

I nodded toward the guest bathroom.

"Or–"

I pulled the steel of my Glock, placing one in the chamber.

"You can piss yourself right the fuck here. I'm not above catching it on the stick myself."

"I've had it. It's not good enough for you to be risking your freedom for him."

Scoffing, I smiled. "You and me will never have the same dick. Not even if it's on the same nigga. Please know that we are very different, Asia. The dick he gives you is not the same dick he gave me. We don't share the same experience. Hopefully your bird ass brain can comprehend that concept."

I straightened my spine.

"Furthermore, there's nothing a man could ever say or do to have me at the door of a woman he's fucking. This is beyond Ishmael and I. I have a job to do. Unfortunately, you and your drunk fetus are part of that job. Now, to the bathroom. I won't ask again."

Her feet began to move. Her mouth stopped moving. I followed her into the guest bathroom. She pulled the door closed behind her.

"Not today, love."

I pushed the door open, handing her the test. With a roll of her eyes, she grabbed the stick and uncapped it. She laid it on the counter and pulled her pants down.

I admired my frame in the full-sized mirror as she followed instructions. The pain of my heart hadn't reached my eyes. The lines in my forehead settled as I relaxed my facial muscles.

My mascara coated lashes were flourishing. The

chocolate ends of the hair I wore matched perfectly with the chocolate leggings and top I'd traded my skirt and button down for. Clear gloss made my lips glisten.

Range's features were so prominent on my face. Sometimes, I felt like it was her I favored most. Other days, it was Rather I felt I resembled most. Every so often, Roaman was the winner. But, Rhea and Richie were the true champions. They'd meshed well together, making seven versions of the same daughter.

The five foot stature pushed past me. Before she was able to cross the threshold, a hand was around her arm, pulling her back inside.

"Wash your hands, *Ms. Bacteria*."

Asia squirted soap onto her hands from the dispenser. She twisted the knobs on the sink and ran her soapy hands underneath the water. She dried them with the hand towel on the wall.

I guess that wasn't for decoration.

She tried smoothing the wrinkles. She managed to pull the towel from the rack in the process. Frustrated, she folded it up and tried replacing it.

Or. I tilted my head, trying to make sense of her misfortune. *Maybe it is for decoration.*

Baffled, I released the air from my lungs.

Asia disabled the water. She turned to leave. Her departure wouldn't be allowed. I wanted eyes on her at all times until we got to the bottom of this situation.

Ishmael was days away from the biggest fight of his life. Strays were hitting him left and right. He needed a victory. I would ensure he received that before the biggest night of his life.

"One more minute."

Her arms folded over her chest. She pressed her back against the wall. Her body was quivering. She couldn't keep her hands steady. Her nervous system was under attack.

"Is there anything you care to tell me, Asia?"

Silence.

"Suits me."

I smoothed the invisible wrinkles from my shirt. Asia's foot tapped against the tile anxiously. Time was on my side. I was in no hurry.

Still, I was curious of the test results. I stepped closer to the sink, peering down at the window that would determine our fate.

Not Pregnant.

My suspicions were confirmed.

"A Black man is willing to carry Berkeley on his back and halt the destruction of a city that carries so much of Huffington's history–" I paused, kissing the skin of my teeth.

"And, you're willing to help destroy him, his credibility, and his chance at being Mayor for what, Asia?"

Silence.

With a shake of my head, I picked up the pregnancy test.

"Hold it."

I lifted her left hand and shoved the stick between her fingers.

"Wh–"

"Shut the fuck up. I gave you two chances to talk. You don't get a third one."

I lifted her arm, placing the pregnancy test next to her face.

"Smile for the camera."

I long-pressed the camera button. When her face appeared on my screen, I snapped a picture.

And then another one.

And then another one.

"Smile, bitch."

She forged a smile for the camera.

I snapped again.

And again.

And again.

"Now, this will look incredible on the front page."

I removed the test from her hands and placed it on the counter. I took more pictures, sure to capture her lousy bathroom decorations.

"I thought we had something," Asia admitted, beckoning for my attention. "Him and I. We were good when we were together. Fun."

"Nobody ever told you, love? Fun girls are usually good for– well, fun. There's no fun in forever. There's hardships, compromising, consideration, ups, downs, shifts, and a plethora of changes. Occasional fun that doesn't last too long or happen too often."

"It was enough for him."

"Is it air up there? Is that what it is? You're willing to deceive the public because you wa–"

"It wasn't about me."

My brows furrowed. My eyelids pulled closer together. I shoved my phone into the side of my leggings. Asia took a step backward every time I took a step forward. Everything was beginning to make sense.

She ran out of room for movement. The door halted her steps.

"How much?"

"What?"

"How much?"

"How much what?"

"How much did Daniels pay you?"

"Dan– Daniels–"

"Asia, don't piss me the fuck off. You and your invisible fetus have already taken away precious time from my day and made my job a little harder than it should've been. Start talking."

"He didn't tell me I would be on the front paper."

"How much?"

"He said it would just be a rumor. He needed it to stick, so it had to be someone Ishmael was actually involved with. I was upset. Seeing you and him everywhere... all over social media... all over the news stations. I thought him and I were working toward something. You know?"

"How much?"

"One hundred thousand dollars."

I wasn't sure when my hand had rose or when the heel of it crashed into her mouth and nose. The blood that rushed down her face, chin, and chest is what brought me back to reality.

"Cheap piece of shit."

I stepped around her, snatching open her door. My journey to the elevator was eventless. I waited for the moment to release something from my clip into Asia. However, she never appeared in the hallway and I never raised my weapon.

I unlocked my cell and scrolled through my contacts until I found the number I was in search of. After two rings, the line connected.

Silence.

"I need you. How soon can you get to me?"

"Minutes."

I stared at the phone, unsure if I'd dialed the correct number.

"Rugs…"

"Minutes, Ro."

"You're here?"

"The election is days away. I came just in case."

"Just in case what?"

"He needed to keep his hands clean when the race got dirty."

"It's muddy."

"Understood."

"I'll see you soon."

Click. Click.

Clack. Clack.

Click. Click.

Clack. Clack.

Our bodies were in sync. Every turn. Every step. Every move.

Rather stopped prematurely, glaring at the disheveled mayoral candidate. His appearance was deplorable. A smile curled my lips upward.

He'd been the mouthiest candidate of them all. Boisterous. Haughty. Cocky. Disgusting. Dirty. And, so damn crooked.

"Evening, ladies," Rugger called out.

"Evening," Rather breathed out, stepping closer to Daniels.

She placed a hand on his cheek, sliding it down to his chin.

"Who the fuck are you?" He grunted, eyes masked with a black strip of fabric.

"Your wettest dream... prettiest nightmare," Rather confessed.

Her presence was a gift. I hadn't expected her to appear in front of Mercer's door alongside Rugger, but every part of me rejoiced at the sight of her.

"I'm the Mayor of this city. Do you know who you're fucking with?"

"The issue is, I'm not sure you know who you're fucking with," I explained, pulling the black fabric over his head.

"Oooooh... You bitc–"

The butt of Rugger's gun was inches away from his skull.

"Aht. Aht. We need him pretty when he addresses the world after his defeat."

Rugger didn't lower her weapon. She redirected it, landing a blow to the back of Daniels' head. I sighed, understanding it was too much to ask Rugger to keep a level head. Her head was never leveled. Her trigger finger was always itching. Her readiness level should've been studied by people around the world.

"URG."

His face pinched together. The restraints on his arms and hands restricted his movements. He couldn't stop the blood running down the back of his neck. His shirt did as best it could.

"Goddamnit. Grayson won't see another podium in his life as long as I'm living."

"Your death can be arranged," Rugger promised, stepping around to face Daniels. "She wants you alive. I don't."

The barrel of Rugger's Beretta slid Daniels' tongue to the back of his mouth.

"Now that we have the introductions out of the way... Let's get down to business so we can all go on about our day."

I placed a hand on Rugger's arm. She lowered the gun from his mouth, placing it by her side.

"Grayson—"

"Just a thug from the projects thinking he deserves something that doesn't belong to him."

Though mouthy, Daniels' knees were colliding at a rapid rate. His voice was shaky and his breathing was erratic.

"Has done well making this a clean fight, seeing as though he can get his hands dirty. He is above the games you politicians like to play, but I'm not. When you motherfuckers go low, I go to hell."

I opened the folder and removed the first image from the stack. Daniels' eyes blossomed with fear. His mouth widened and his yellow skin turned pale.

"I would hate to bring Kait into all of this, seeing as though she has a bad heart, but you didn't give a damn about my heart when you broadcasted my pictures all over the news for all of Berkeley to see."

"My wife has not– nothing to do– Where'd you get those?"

"From the escort you hired to fuck your wife while you watched. I don't blame you. He has a gorgeous dick."

I lifted the second photo.

"That Kait loves to suck."

The third image was of Kait on her knees, sucking Lamar's dick with Daniels just feet away with his mini sausage in his hand.

"Kait is innocent."

"Is she?" I chuckled, lifting one photo after the other, slamming them on the table beside Daniels.

Kait was far from innocent. Her affair with Lamar had been going on for two years, now. She'd found her lover with the help of her husband. It was an added bonus that he could please both her and Daniels.

"What do you want from me?" He mustered, unable to look at the images before him.

"But wait– there's more."

I slammed another photo on the table.

Perfect lines of cocaine sat before Daniels. One was already up his nose and entering his system. His smile was wide. His eyes were glossed over. He was surrounded by his team, his brothers, and a large group of exotic dancers.

"Wh– where– where are you ge–" he stuttered. "What is it that you want from me?"

"We have four days until the election. You have two jobs."

"Kait won't survive her face bei–"

"Frankly, I'm above exposing what women do in their personal time. I applaud Kait for taking her happiness into her own hands and sliding down a big, gorgeous dick after years of suffering with your index finger wiggling around her insides every fucking time you're horny."

"Sh–"

"Shut the fuck up," I demanded.

"I–"

"Four days. Two jobs. Your first order of business is to contact your friends in media. The ones you like to dial up when you think you have new leads on Grayson when in actuality it's all just bullshit."

I removed an image of Asia posing with her pregnancy test from the folder.

"Make sure this image is on the front page of Berkeley News in the morning. As well, make sure it comes across *every* news station."

"What is this?"

I removed another image.

"Or, I will make sure this makes the news by noon."

It was Asia's bank statement. He'd wired $100,000 to her account on Friday morning. Her image hit the papers bright and early Monday. She forwarded it to Berkeley News Sunday at nine in the morning. Printing began at noon. The changes were made to the front page between nine and noon.

Had she gotten the image to the publication even an hour later, it wouldn't have been her face on the front page. It would've been the faces of the women who decided to be proactive and strive for early detection for breast cancer.

"Second task. It's fairly simple, right ladies?"

Rather nodded.

Rugger didn't budge. Her eyes were on Daniels, waiting for him to as much as sneeze in my direction.

"Fight clean or your wife will be scrubbing your blood from the tiles of your home until her knees are raw. Do we have an agreement?"

Rapidly, Daniels nodded his head.

"Yes. Yes. We have an agreement."

"Good."

"Now, if that front page isn't pleasing tomorrow,

understand I won't be the one visiting your home tomorrow. She will."

I pointed at Rugger.

"And seeing her means your date with death has come. Understood?"

His head never stopped moving. He was still nodding, still agreeing.

"Tell Kait I said congratulations."

"Congratulations?"

"On the baby."

I removed the final image, sitting it on the table. Lamar and Kait exited the OB/GYN clinic hand-in-hand. Joy was scribed in their postures.

The color drained from his face. His body slumped with defeat. He didn't share children with Kait. He had a son with his first wife. Since, he'd been trying for a child, but couldn't produce one.

It made him question the paternity of his son. Test results revealed he wasn't the father. However, he never shared the news with Tammy, his ex-wife. Neither had he shared the news with his son, who was now an adult. I discovered the results from my extensive search, digging up any and everything I could on Daniels.

"Karma is a bad bitch, but Royce is badder." I chuckled. "That's what you should've been hollering at the podium instead of making false claims about Ishmael and I. Every lie you've told on him is your truth. I wish you nothing but hell. Good fucking night you fat back, micro dick, powder snorting, booty eating, slew-footed, knock-kneed, viagra popping piece of shit."

Click.

Clack.

Click.

"Arrrrrrrgh!"

Daniel's screams throughout the empty space halted my stride. I turned to find Rugger with the butt of her gun to Daniel's temple.

"Now why'd you do that?"

Rather sniggered, unable to contain herself. Asking Rugger to behave herself was far too much.

"He said you were selling pussy," Rugger murmured.

I quickly recalled the nasty remarks he'd made about me months prior.

"You know what—" I nodded.

"Exactly," Rather agreed.

I removed Rugger's gun from her hand and returned to Daniels' side. He deserved everything that was coming to him, including the headache he'd wake up with in the morning.

Ishmael

SHE WAS FURIOUS. *The fire danced in her eyes. I observed as she reached for the Glock 19.*

Special forces.

Mk27

Trijicon RMR red dot sights

Threaded barrel

Enhanced triggers

Polymer

Enhanced magazines

16 rounds

Ambidextrous capabilities

Lightweight

She was as pretty as her handler.

I'd used the same weapon twenty times or more in the field. It was a well-oiled machine. Slightly compact. Easy to conceal. Easy to carry. But, it packed power.

"Don't do that, my baby. I won't be able to forgive you for that."

"You will. I'm not worried about that. Me forgiving you is what you should be worried about."

"I don't know what you want me to say, Royce."

"Say the truth. That's what I want. We're four days away from voting and the world finds out you're expecting a child. When, Ishmael Samuel Grayson? When was the last time you stuck your dick inside of Asia?"

A silencer appeared from her handbag. A handbag I'd insisted she purchase. The beautiful piece fit the barrel like a glove. They were a perfect match.

I closed my eyes, accepting my fate. It wasn't the first time I'd been on the opposite side of the trigger. Though I'd put that life behind me, I was still certain it wouldn't be my last. Especially not if I kept pissing my baby off.

"August."

"August when because the math ain't mathing."

Her mind was made up. She was ready to burn down the bridge we were building and I would be tasked with rebuilding it.

"August, Royce."

"August when, motherfucker?"

"The day you walked into my office."

She smirked. I braced for impact, knowing it would come.

"Hmph," she scoffed.

Silently, she screwed on the silencer. I released a deep breath.

"Royce– what the fuck are you doing?"

"By any means, Ishmael.," she sighed.

She aimed at my side, firing a single shot.

"Fuck!" The grunt escaped me though it was no indication of how I truly felt.

Her eyes rolled upward.

"So dramatic."

I didn't take my eyes off Royce. She was a mad woman, but she was my mad woman. I'd experienced her vulnerability and I'd experienced her viciousness. I wasn't sure which one made me fall deeper or which made me fall faster.

She concealed her Glock and snatched the brown paper bag from my desk. In awe of her audacity, I observed every move she made.

"That should put you ahead in the polls," she tittered with a shrug.

"Are you fucking insane?"

"Yes. And, to win, you have to be. Tight screws don't leave room for successors. Loose screws do."

She stomped toward the door with her chest out and her chin up. As she opened it, Matte fell through.

I placed a hand on my forehead, rubbing the worry lines that creased it.

"Oh shoot."

"Girl, grow a fucking spine," Royce demanded.

"Sorry– I– uh–"

"And stop apologizing so much."

"Yes. Right."

Matte regained her balance and stood on both feet.

"Is everything okay?"

She approached my desk, completely baffled.

"Oh God, Mr. Grayson. You're bleeding! Oh God! Oh God."

I placed a finger over my mouth as I stood from my chair. It wasn't until then that I surveyed the damage.

"Oh God. What should I do? Should I call the police?"

I shook my head.

"No. Don't make any calls. Find us a way out of here without detection. There's a media storm downstairs and I need to get to Berkeley medical."

I unbuttoned my shirt and wrapped it in a ball. I pressed it against my wound and waited for Matte's feet to move.

"But– but why aren't you– doesn't it– are you sure you don't need me to call you a medic?"

"I need you to do what I've asked of you. I can handle the rest."

"Right. Right."

"This isn't my first rodeo, Matte. It won't be my last."

I didn't need Berkeley City Medical. Neither did I need Matte's assistance. I could remove the shell, clean, bandage, and stitch. But, I wasn't sure if Royce would put another hot one in me if I didn't find my way to the hospital. She was pulling the sympathy card. Though I despised it, I wouldn't hinder her plans.

THE GREYLIST

The weight of my world rested on my shoulders. The weight of her world rested on my shoulders. The weight of us... our world... her pain. Rested on my shoulders. It was heavy, but I carried it without complaint. I didn't have room to moan or mumble or grumble. I'd made a mistake and Royce had every right to demand payment for it.

Twenty-four hours had escaped without me hearing her voice, touching her body, or feeling her against my skin. Withdrawals led me to Clarke. Desperation led me to her door. Desire forced me to knock. And, regret forced me to stay even after she refused to let me in.

Rain poured from the skies, signaling my despair. I pressed the doorbell a third time and stepped backward. Nothing was right without baby girl in my corner. I'd much rather crawl into an early grave than to go another day without her at the center of my universe.

Royce's home was beautiful. There was over ten thousand square feet of silence. I was certain her thoughts were echoing in the silence. Aside from them, all she heard was the sound of her heartbeat. My heartbeat. If there was nothing else I'd learned about her, it was that she hated being alone. It hadn't always been this way, but as life progressed, so did her urge for companionship.

I peered at my cell. A full two minutes passed.

Open up, my baby.

I pressed the doorbell a fourth time. Instead of

waiting for the inevitable, I unlocked my screen and dialed the digits that would connect us.

"Go home, Ishmael."

Her voice appeared on the line almost instantly. The pain in my chest thickened. Sadness sat between each syllable she released. So did strength.

"I'm at home, my baby. I just need you to let me in."

Silence constricted my heart.

"Royce."

"Goodnight."

The line died. So did something inside of me. The disappointment in her tone was devastating. I needed to repair what I'd broken. I needed to bring peace to the war I'd caused inside of her.

I shoved my cell in my pocket. The bouquet of flowers in my hand was restricting. I set them next to her door.

Suit yourself, my baby.

The edges of the hoodie I wore were last to climb over my head. I wrapped the fabric around my knuckles as I observed the lovely front door before destroying its beauty.

WHAM.

I launched my fist into the fourth square of glass, shattering it on contact. The hoodie slid from my skin with ease. I stuck my hand inside of Royce's home and twisted the lock on the handle. The door opened with ease.

Commiseration forced me inside. As quickly as I'd

entered, I remembered I was leaving so much behind. I exited.

The bouquet of flowers rested on my arm. The large Hermès dangled from my hand. With my right foot, I closed the door behind me. Pausing briefly, I twisted the small button on the knob to lock it.

As if I'd stalked her floors a hundred times, I widened the distance between me and the door. Warmth engulfed me. The smell of well-seasoned food lured me through the foyer.

Beige.

Brown.

Black.

Gold.

I took note of every aspect of Royce's residence. The study was the first room I approached. Directly across the hall was another room, one filled with packages, mail, and shelves to keep them in order.

The room next to the study connected by a sliding door. Books lined shelves that filled nearly every inch of the cases.

Her library.

On the other side, just feet away from the mail room was a stair stepper, treadmill, ab cruncher, weights, pilates machine, spin bike, and a television that nearly filled every inch of the wall it was on. Mirrors lined the back walls. A water station hid in the corner.

Go Girl. was scribed in swirly letters on the wall, lined with a strip of light that was a golden white.

Around it, in different spots, were affirmations that would surely keep her moving during sessions.

Her gym.

A long stretch of hallway and a single left turn led me to the openness of her home. Two sets of stairs raced to the second floor. Beyond the stairs was more footage, free of furniture. And, beyond the stretch was the dining area. A table for twelve was perfectly centered with chocolate chairs surrounding it.

There was a plate setting in front of each. Yet, only one chair was occupied. The head of the table, closest to the dining room wall.

There goes my baby.

Fear and fascination gripped me simultaneously. I released my frustrations and embraced whatever was to come of my intrusion. Silently, I asked God to keep her finger off that fucking trigger. But, should she decide to send another hot one through my ass, I'd be back at her front door as soon as they patched me up.

Just like tonight.

Just like any other night she wanted me to pay for the pain I caused. I'd accepted my fate. I knew who I'd laid down with. I didn't want to wake up. I wanted everything that came with Royce, even if that meant an occasional bullet. I'd slid into her pussy. I knew it was worth the ER visits. My body would sort itself out. My heart couldn't if she wasn't in my world.

Slowly, Royce slid her Glock across the table, drawing it closer to her chest. Still, her fork entered her broccoli and brought it to her mouth.

My mouth.

I blinked away the images of what she loved to do with that motherfucker. How wet it was. How skillful it was. How warm it was. How good it felt.

"I come in peace, my baby."

I lifted my hands, gifts in tow.

"You can't come in any other fashion," she assured me.

In a house slip, she was stunning. Her nipples pressed against it, hardening as I closed the gap between us. Royce was utterly alluring. My feet weren't moving because of me.

It was Royce. It was always Royce. Without words, she demanded so much of me.

My stomach rumbled as I drew closer. She'd prepared dinner, but my hunger was mostly due to her absence. I needed a serving of Royce.

Her voice.

Her laughter.

Her pussy.

The way she put that motherfucker on me so effortlessly.

Her confidence.

Her care.

Her.

"I'm starving, Royce."

"Food is in the kitchen. Fix your own plate."

Her voice was cold. She'd iced that pretty heart of hers.

"Not for food, my baby."

Silence.

"Royce—"

"You break into my house... you disturb my dinner... and continue to call my fucking name as if I can't hear. Ishmael, I'm trying really hard not to put one in your arm. Your healing won't take too long."

"If that is the first step to forgiving me, then let that motherfucker rip, Royce."

Silence.

I grimaced. The pain of her silence was far more excruciating than a flesh wound.

"Talk to me."

I pulled out the chair next to her and slid it across the floor. I winched, remembering the first bullet she'd lodged in my side.

"Please."

I sat down, placing the bouquet of flowers on the table and sitting the bag beside the chair.

Silence.

I removed the Birkin from the box, placing it in front of her. I shoved my hand inside, removing a stack of hundreds. A band of white paper with ten thousand dollars written on it kept the money from falling apart.

"Please, my baby."

Silence.

Her eyes were on me. My eyes were on her.

I removed a second one.

"Talk to me."

Silence.

A third stack slammed against the table.

"I despise your silence."

Silence.

A fourth topped the pile.

"It's heinous."

Silence.

A fifth stack met the table linen.

"It makes me feel things I don't want to feel."

Silence.

A sixth fell on top of the fifth.

"When all I want to feel is you."

Seven.

Silence.

"I miss you, my baby."

Silence.

Eight.

Pausing, I watched Royce's eyes glisten.

"I'm sorry. I was an impatient man.

Nine.

Ten.

Silence.

"A foolish man. A coward."

Eleven.

Twelve.

Silence.

"I should've waited, Royce.

Thirteen.

Fourteen.

Silence.

Money filled the gaps on her table.

"I had no business giving someone else what I knew belonged to you."

Fifteen.

Silence.

"But, I don't want to suffer. I can't stand it."

Sixteen.

Seventeen.

"I can't stand not hearing your voice or seeing your face or knowing I've hurt your feelings."

Silence.

Eighteen.

"I love you. I love you, Royce. I love you."

I scooted closer. I needed her to understand every word coming from my mouth.

"I don't want to suffer no more. The last twenty four hours have been the rougest fucking twenty-four hours of my entire life."

Silence.

Nineteen.

"So, please, my baby."

Silence.

Twenty.

I stood on my feet. My right hand was around her neck in a flash. Through anguished eyes, she looked up at me.

"I'm sorry. Just talk to me. Cuss my Black ass out. Tell me how much you wish you'd never given me a chance. Tell me how you should've looked the other way. Tell me you hate me. Tell me all the things you need to tell me to break my fucking heart. But, talk to me."

I lowered my lips to hers.

'Cause, I can't take no more of this shit, Royce."

"I wanted you to be different," she forced out.

I felt the weight lift from her shoulders.

"I am. Don't ever group me with other niggas, because I'm nothing like nobody. No fucking body."

Silence.

"I'm sorry."

"That's not enough," she whispered, briefly placing her eyes on the bills.

"Then tell me how much and it's yours."

Royce could have whatever the fuck Royce wanted as long as I could have her.

"Unlimited access."

I shrugged.

"Unlimited access is yours, my baby."

I, too, wanted unlimited access. *To her body. Her heart. Her mind. Her soul. Her.*

Silence.

"What else will make this right, Royce?"

"You."

I lifted her from the chair.

"You have me."

I sat her body on the table, pushing her food away in the process. Her legs fell to the side of her. Her arousal widened my nostrils.

"All of you," she clarified.

"You have it."

I wasn't sure how much of me she thought was mine, but her assumptions were inaccurate. Everything was hers to have. Nothing belonged to me anymore.

The black shirt I wore bunched in her fist as she pulled me forward. The shift was coming. I permitted it. My baby craved control of something, whether it be her emotions, her body, her heart, or me. She deserved it and could have it.

Anything for you, my baby.

"I've missed you," I admitted.

"Don't make a fool of my heart."

I shook my head.

"I'm a lot of things, Ish, but I'm human underneath it all."

I nodded.

Her layers were so plentiful and so beautiful. Her tough exterior was shelter for the softest parts of her. Royce was a lover. Royce was a fucker. Royce was a listener. Royce was a caretaker. Royce was a resource. Royce was a big ball of fluff. Soft to the touch.

"I love you."

Her voice was cracked with emotion. She closed her eyes, briefly.

"I love you," I responded. "I'm sorry."

"But, I won't give you the chance to break everything I've built. I won't let you, Ishmael. So tell me right now– is this what you truly want? Is this what your heart needs? Is this too much for you to handle? Will this still be enough for you twenty years down the line? Or am I just something to do for now? Someone to keep space. Someone to keep your dick wet. Your thoughts occupied?"

"I want this, my baby. Not for now. Forever."

"I can't deal with heartbreak. I won't be responsible for my actions."

"Bury me next to the biggest fool in the cemetery, Royce. Because the second I break your heart, I would have become an even bigger fool."

Silence.

She searched my eyes for a reason to doubt me but all she found was the regret from my actions and the parts of my soul she'd uprooted with her weariness.

"Don't be mad with me," I pleaded.

"I'm not. I'm sad with you."

I closed my eyes and released my next breath.

"How can I fix it?"

"Put your tongue on my pussy."

I opened my eyes, staring into those mirroring dark orbs.

"Anything else?"

Her requests would be granted. All she had to do was say the fucking word.

"Your phone."

I winced from the pain of loosening my grip. There was nothing more I wanted at the tips of my fingers than Royce. Still, I fought through the aches to retrieve my cell. She removed it from my fingers and typed in the code I'd never given her but had never hid from her either.

"Ishmael."

Her legs widened. Her elbows carried her weight.

Taking heed to her warning, I pulled up the chair I'd lifted her from. Dinner was ready.

I buried my head between her legs. Her arousal was potent. Her pussy was precious. Her vulva was soaking.

Deprivation was an issue for us both.

"Mmmm."

My tongue touched Royce's clit. Greed wouldn't allow me to ease into the assignment. I pulled her into my mouth, sucking on her sensitivity.

The sound of a connecting FaceTime call didn't halt my movement. I slid my index and middle fingers inside of her.

"Uhhhhh. Yessss."

"Hello?"

Asia's voice registered immediately. Royce was playing dirty, but I admired her game, nonetheless. The woman on the phone had put an unnecessary stain on my campaign. Her jealousy could easily be the end of my run. It could be the reason I wasn't victorious at the polls.

And it was all due to her jealousy. She's birthed false narratives in her head, forcing herself to believe we had something we didn't. Asia had never been more than a piece of pussy for me. Nothing more had ever been evident. Boundaries were clear. So were roles. Asia knew hers.

It was Royce who confused her. Her presence. Her power. Her proximity. It turned wheels in her head that should've remained still.

"Ishmael?"

I massaged my baby's insides.

"Mmmmm."

She rolled her hips, feeding me that pussy on a fucking spoon.

"Yesssss."

"Hello?"

My dick stretched in my briefs. Royce's goodness was indescribable. Her mercy didn't exist. I was hanging on her ledge, and didn't want to be rescued. Not now. Not ever.

I released her clit from my mouth. Her inclination was near. However, prolonging her pleasure was far too satisfying to let her have what she wanted. We were both in need. Compromise and consideration was key.

"My baby."

Royce's creaminess coated my tongue and lingered on my lips.

"Ishmael," she moaned.

"Ishmael!" Asia yelled.

"Tell me you forgive me."

"Forgive you fo—mmm. For what?"

"Putting my dick in places it didn't belong."

I massaged her pussy. Her walls clamped around my fingers.

"Even before I'd had the chance to know you."

"Because—"

"Because I knew I was yours all along."

I pressed my thumb against her slipperiness.

"Uhhhh."

"Tell me."

"What the hell is happening here?" Asia grumbled.

"My baby—"

Royce was addictive. She gripped the back of my head, pushing it back between her legs.

"I need a little– a li– uhhh more time to– Mmmmm."

I stroked her with my tongue, flattening it against her clit. A foot lifted to my shoulder. Royce pushed her body forward, deepening her pussy in my mouth.

"Uhhh. Fuck."

Her ass lifted off the table, evidence of her pending pinnacle. She was near the top. I beckoned for her gratification, bending my fingers inside of her.

"Yesss. Yesss. Just like— Ohhhh God."

Her body plummeted, colliding with the tabletop.

"That's it, my baby. Let that shit go."

"Ishma– Uhhhhh."

I forced my pants down my legs. My dick sprang from my bottom, ready for total consumption. I removed my fingers from Royce's pussy and wrapped them around her legs.

"Mmmm."

I pulled her body to the edge of the table.

"Ishhhhhh."

I returned home. My chest deflated as I settled on my property.

"Fuck."

Her pussy pulsated around me.

"Goddamn."

I wouldn't be long. Her wetness wouldn't allow it. Her warmth wouldn't allow it. Her snugness wouldn't allow it. Her gushiness wouldn't allow it.

I was lost at sea, not wanting to be saved. Not by a passing ship. Not be the coast guard. Not by any fucking body or any fucking thing.

"I love you, my baby." I breathed out, managing the first stroke. "Fuck, I love you, girl."

Royce's strength was garnered from my words. Her spine straightened with a slight curve in the middle. I shoved her hand, occupied with my cellular device, to the side. Her slip lifted with a slight tug. I gripped her right breast. Her nippled disappeared in my mouth.

Chocolate.

She reminded me of my favorite Hershey's bar. The left breast was just as impressive.

"Fuuuuuck."

Royce was regaining her momentum. Her strength was evident in her core. When her body twirled around, keeping me inside of her, I was partly surprised. In all her glory, her ass greeted me. With her back arched and my cell pushed all the way to the end of the table, she pushed into me.

"Don't do that. Don't fuc– don't do that, Royce."

She was on a mission to end it all. I grabbed her hair, twisting until her eyes were on me.

"You trying to make my nut all up in this motherfucker?"

"Umm hmmm," she groaned, thrusting her body into mine.

"Fuck."

Smack.

Smack.

Smack.

Smack.

Her skin slapped against mine. Her wetness made us both sticky to the touch.

"Royce."

My pleas fell on death's ear.

"Fuck me back, Ishmael."

Her eyes were still on me. Her hair was still in my hands. Her back was still arched. Her pussy was still suffocating me.

I stabilized her body with my left hand. Her right nipple was my anchor. I drove into Royce until her eyeballs disappeared behind her eyelids.

"Uhhhhh."

Pleasure and pain mingled somewhere in her center. Retracting and reinserting myself, not halting until I was balls deep.

"Uhhhh."

Royce was the culprit of her despair. She provoked everything that was coming to her.

"Uhhhh."

I found my rhythm.

Back.

Forth.

Back.

Forth.

I plummeted. I retracted. I plummeted. I retracted.

"Fuck. I'm cumming. I'm cum– Uhhhhh!"

Me, too, my baby.

I released my seeds in her garden, hoping they

didn't result in growth. But, as our connection progressed, I was beginning to wonder which of us our daughter would favor and who our son would cling to most. Still, I wanted to respect her wishes and her womb. It was her body. *Her choice.*

"Go away with me."

"The election is in three days."

"I just need one, Royce. No cameras. No scandals. No phones. No media. Just you. And me. I'm tired of sharing you with Berkeley. I'm tired of you having to share me with Berkeley."

"Where to?"

"Someone near… Secluded. I don't want to spend all of our time in the air."

Silence.

"I don't mind tying your mean ass up."

"You don't have to."

"So, that's a yes?"

"That's a yes, Ishmael."

I dislodged from her pussy. Remnants of us fell onto the screen of my phone. I couldn't wait to put that motherfucker back on my face. The call had ended and so did Royce's reel.

I sat her down at the edge of the table. My body parted her legs.

"Are you okay, my baby?"

She nodded. "Yes."

I smoothed her hair down.

"Good then. Let's get dressed. We're leaving. No need for clothes. You won't have them on where we're headed. We won't be gone long enough for you to change successfully."

T H E **G R E Y** L I S T

Glorious.

Gracious.

Gorgeous.

Royce's natural beauty was radiant. *Refreshing*. With the pencil pressed against the sketch pad, I tried my damndest to capture every detail of her essence. Rest was her wheelhouse. Her retreat was required to power her presence.

I admired her most when she was recharging. Women carried such heavy loads. No man could ever truly understand their inherent nature. And, though I didn't understand the daily struggles of womanhood, I acknowledged them. I knew they existed and I refused to ignore them.

Royce could sleep for days and I wouldn't wake her. I craved her rest as much as her body. She was better when exhaustion wasn't altering her cognitive functions.

My cell vibrated against the cushion of the couch. I peered at the screen, finding my mother's image filling the background. My heart expanded another inch.

"Good afternoon, Mother."

"Ishmael." She sighed.

I straightened my spine and lowered the pencil.

"Is everything okay?"

"Yes. Yes. Everything is fine. I'm just worried. I'm worried about you, Son. You've been so—so distant lately."

"Not my intention. Never my intention. I apologize if it has been this way for you."

"I'm just worried. I want to make sure this campaign isn't getting the best of you."

"Nah. Not the campaign."

There was a long, pregnant pause.

"Ishmael?"

"Her name is Royce, Mother. She's getting the best of me."

"Son…"

I looked over the sketchbook, prayerful I hadn't awakened my baby.

"Yes?"

"I felt it—"

"Felt what?"

"She's lovely."

"She is."

"I knew from the moment Indie told me it was all a— I— Ishmael."

I could hear the fluttering of her heart through the line.

"Yes?"

"She's beautiful."

"Inside out…"

"Yeah?"

"A little crazy, but—"

"Love makes you that way. If she isn't a little crazy then you worry."

I chuckled, rubbing a hand down my head.

"Is that right?"

"Yes. This is such good news, Son. I want to meet her."

"I want you to meet her. She's a little pissed off at me right now."

"Don't mess this up for me!"

"For you?"

"Yes."

"Was Indigo with you when the news aired last night?"

My face was all over the stations, claiming I'd been assaulted with a deadly weapon. Their ignorance was comical.

I am the deadly weapon.

Aside from Royce, no man would be able to walk the same planet as me after firing his weapon at me. His bullet didn't have to cut through me. Even an aim in my direction would end his entire bloodline.

"Yes."

"Good."

"This is all so much, son."

"It was Royce."

"Hm?"

"It was– who– *Ishmael*. What did you do that warranted a bullet to your body? And, you'd better be glad she didn't kill you. You can't be playing with women's feelings. Not all of them will turn the other cheek or walk away peacefully. I'm glad you're okay. I don't know what I'd do if something happened to you."

I chuckled.

"And you're laughing?"

"Because she's crazy, Ma. And, somehow that makes me love her even more."

"Well, good for you, *I guess*."

"She just wants to make sure I win the election."

Though I knew Royce had to do her job, that bullet had little to do with it. That was more personal than it was business.

"By shooting you?"

"By any means," I quoted Royce verbatim.

I sighed, releasing my transgressions.

"She believes in me, Ma."

Royce's body was in full view. That's where I wanted her forever.

"And, that feels good to me. She feels good to me."

"Then do right by her."

I nodded as if she was in the same room.

"I will. Hurting her hurts too much. I can't do that to my baby."

"Don't."

"Are we still scheduled for dinner."

"Yes. That's another reason I was calling. Are you still coming?"

"I wouldn't miss it for the world."

"I'll see you then, Son."

"I'll see you then."

"I love you and worry not. This is in God's hands."

"I love you, too."

I ended the call.

My mother had raised us all on the same belief system. We fully understood the importance of remaining neutral in matters of the heart. Because, it didn't matter how upset the partner of someone you loved made you, they wouldn't stop loving them because you told them they should. In fact, your opinion was more likely to drive them into their lover's arms faster.

My mouth twisted rightward. I shook my head at the realization that it was hardly anything anyone could tell me about Royce right now. She had my head so far in the clouds that I didn't care what motherfuckers on the ground was talking about. God, Himself, would have to tell me she was no good for me when she sent my Black ass to heaven. Until then, I was fully invested in what we were becoming.

"Good morning."

My body stilled. I searched for those big, wondrous eyes. I couldn't find them. Not until Royce slid her arm down her face, revealing parts of her I obsessed over. The detailed sketch on my pad was proof of Royce's reign.

"Good afternoon," I corrected.

She sat up straight, glancing in my direction. Her hair was wild. My thoughts were wilder.

"Afternoon?"

"It's nearing the one o'clock hour."

"But—plans. We had plans. I've slept the day away."

"No plans, my baby," I assured her with a shake of my head. "I'm listening to your body, not a made up itinerary."

"Ish."

So much of our twenty-four hours had passed us by. In five hours, we'd be on the boat. In five and a half hours, we'd be on the plane again. I didn't consider a second of our trip wasted. We didn't have to leave the room. The noise of the election was obnoxious. Royce was the only one to quiet it. Being with her, no matter what we were doing, was enough.

"You needed rest."

She pushed out a weighty breath and slid both hands down her face.

"I didn't sleep."

Sympathy was the catalyst for my disappointment. I had altered her in ways I never wanted to. My teeth pressed against each other.

"Me either."

"You've been there all morning?"

I nodded.

"Keeping myself busy."

I lifted the sketchpad. The woman resembled Royce though the picture was far from finished.

"You draw?" Her hand laid against her bare chest.

"When I'm inspired enough."

Her nipples were like buttons. They hardened as her fingertips ran along her chest.

She took her eyes off me. A smile began to form slowly as she admired the sea life around us. Large turtles. Fish of all colors. Dolphins. Colorful coral reefs.

"And I thought it was beautiful at night."

We'd reached the boat near midnight. The thirty-six minute ride placed us at the entrance of our villa by twelve-thirty.

"I can't believe it's all underwater."

Royce stood up in bed and extended the hand she lowered from her chest. Her long frame stretched to meet the top of the tank. The bed's height assisted.

"It's so beautiful."

She was a woman with everything... one who had witnessed so much in life. And, one who had experienced even more. Discovering a place she hadn't meant a lot to me.

"Was it me or them?"

"You or them?"

"Your inspiration?"

I hesitated, watching her twirl so carelessly on the bed. Her smile was bright. So were her eyes. The weight and the worries were gone. A gentler version of Royce had replaced the cold, calculated woman I encountered last night. Though I loved her too, this was who I'd been after.

"Both."

"Hmm. Understandable." She paused to catch her breath. Her orbs were on me again. "You look like you have something to say. What is it?"

I folded the cover over the sketch pad and set it

beside me. When time permitted, I would finish. For now, Royce had my undivided attention.

"What are your views on marriage?"

She looked in both directions, never turning her head. Wheels were in motion, although her body had stilled.

"What do you mean?"

"Do you want to be a wife, Royce?"

Slowly, she nodded. Her hands went on her hips as she pondered her response. It wasn't long before the words in her head met her lips.

"I do. I haven't always known I wanted to be or that I would be. I've always known, however, that I was not like most women. I'm different. Not in the sense– you know– I'm wired differently. I was raised differently. My emotions were shoved to the back of my mind and heart since I was a little girl. In the business I'm in, they mean you no good.

"Not having them at the forefront helped me compartmentalize so much better. Because, it's required in my line of work. But, life happened for so many people I love. I began to feel like I was ready for it to happen to me. Slowly, I began to revisit that room I tucked my feelings in. Every time I came out, I noticed something different about myself. Yet and still, I kept those things hidden from view.

"I wanted to spend as much time with them as I could… making sure I wanted to unleash those parts of me. The loneliness began to creep in. It began to reserve space in my everyday life. And, eventually my cravings for companionship arose. And blossomed. And spilled over to the point of seeking love.

"Dating apps became a thing. So did accepting dinner invitations from people I'd turned away before I started visiting that room in my head. The yearning for partnership was the first sign that I wanted a husband. But, admittedly, it wasn't until I met you that I realized I wanted to be a wife. It's not the glitz of marriage I aspire to have. It's the longevity. The stability. The safety. The security."

"Do you feel safe with me?"

She tucked her bottom lip in her mouth and nodded.

"Yes. And, quite honestly, it scares me to give up so much control."

"Is that why you demand it during itima—"

"Yes. It's then when I am most empowered. I can't give that away, too."

"I won't require it."

"Thank you."

"Do you feel stable?"

Her eyes rested on my wound. Wrinkle lines creased her forehead.

"For the most part."

It was her chortling that forced a laugh from me. I loved when she did that. When she parted heaven to bring me life with her laugh.

"I deserved it."

"You did."

Shrugging, I straightened my face and ran a hand down my neck.

"Do I offer you the security you desire?"

She nodded, again.

"Undoubtedly."

"If I asked, would you leave your Glocks at home?"

"You wouldn't ask," she responded.

"I wouldn't," I agreed.

"And that's part of the security you offer."

I understood her well. There was no need to explain further. I allowed Royce to be herself. Still, she knew that I wouldn't allow anything to happen to her on my watch.

"Longevity. Am I a nigga you can rumble with for the rest of your life?"

"The only place we rumble is in the bedroom, Ish. Maybe in the car. The closet. A restroom. And an office, occasionally, but I don't see us fighting."

I shook my head.

"You'll win." I lifted my hands. "You'll leave the earth undisputed if I have anything to do with it."

There it was again. That smile of hers.

"But answer me, my baby."

"Yes. If there's anyone I'm shooting, I'd want it to be you." She sighed. "Deal?"

I couldn't help it. She was magnetic. She was magic. She was mystical. She'd shot me right in the heart with her bow and I didn't have the strength to remove it.

"I want you to be my wife, Royce."

I watched her chest swell with air.

"Ish."

"It doesn't have to be today. It doesn't have to be tomorrow. But, I'm warning you now. I will ask. And, it won't be about me and what I want or what I think you want. I'd rather you tell me."

She paused, plopping down on the bed. Her feet touched the floor. Her body lifted. Each step she took brought her closer to me.

"Privacy."

"Private proposal, it is."

"And for the ring," she paused, lowering her naked body onto me, "I want a band of diamonds. Not two. A single band. And, one diamond in the center. No halo. No diamonds around it. A single stone. A blinding stone. Nothing too large. Something that reeks of elegance and charm."

"Simple?"

She kissed my lips.

"Simple."

I lifted slightly, pushing my pants down far enough to give my baby what she'd come for. Her eyes lit up at the sight of him. My heart expanded at the thought of her.

And the ring.

And the wedding.

And the stability.

And the safety.

And the security.

And the longevity.

And the lifetime.

FIFTEEN

Royce

I WAS BEGINNING *to wonder if regal could perfectly describe him anymore. His hair was freshly cut. His line seemed to have been marked by a scientist who'd done extensive research and took new measurements every three business days to ensure accuracy.*

He rubbed his hand down his beard. His fingers tapped against the screen of his iPad. He was fighting the urge to unlock the screen and respond to the emails flooding his inbox. Apprehension plagued him.

I stretched an arm across my body, hooking my fingers on my shoulder. The air was rigid in the cabin. Fine bumps raised my skin.

"Come 'er, my baby."

Ishmael patted the seat beside him. I gravitated toward him. Naturally. Instinctively. Without thought. Without contemplation. Without hesitation.

The seat next to him felt so many miles away. Instead, I removed his iPad from his lap and placed it beside him. My body fit against his like a puzzle piece. My head rested against his chest. My legs stretched across him.

His lips touched my forehead.

Once.

Twice.

"A penny for your thoughts."

"Where to?"

"The water, love."

"And you?"

He sighed.

"Your thoughts?"

His chest vibrated each time he spoke. With each breath he took, it lifted. He laced his fingers through mine and closed his hand around them.

"My thoughts are with you, Royce."

"How so?" I yawned.

"One day without you nearly killed me. I couldn't imagine more."

"She's not pregnant."

"It was in the papers today. I figured that was all you."

I nodded.

"It was."

"Still, I don't have good feelings about you havin–"

"Ish."

"Yes, my baby?"

"That's over."

"Yeah. It is."

"And, your wound."

"You are something else, Royce." He chuckled.

"What?"

"They were waiting on me when I arrived at Berkeley Medical."

"Good."

"The way your mind works– it's fascinating. Politicians would do themselves a solid by acquiring you the second they decide running is in their future."

"I don't like politicians."

Silence coated the cabin.

"Yet you're sitting on my lap."

"You're part politician. And, something leads me to believe I'd hardly have a choice."

"You wouldn't," he admitted.

"Yeah, you give stalker."

"I'm a lot of things, my baby, but a stalker ain't one. Maybe a kidnapper. I'll take that."

"As if it's any better."

"It is, because who has time to waste? Waiting. Watching. Shit is weird. Especially when I could just snatch your fine ass up and have you for breakfast by sun up."

Sniggering, I wrapped my arms around Ishmael's body. I was so safe here.

"I have a gun. You are aware, right?"

"And that motherfucker is not a prop." He chortled.

I quieted and allowed my heart to feel things my head was still waiting for. I wasn't regretful of my actions. Neither *was I remorseful. Ishmael had been warned. He'd played a very stupid game and gotten a very stupid prize as a result.*

I didn't give a damn that things between us were unofficial. If his plan was to pursue me, his dick belonged to me the second the plan was made. Giving that away, and possibly procreating, was a violation.

"Did it hurt?"

"Not as much as hurting you did."

He pulled my hand to his mouth.

Muah.

Muah.

"Not nearly as much," Ishmael mumbled.

Our flight landed in the middle of nowhere. Ishmael never released my hand. He led me down the stairs and down the dock to the awaiting boat.

"Careful, love."

I stepped on, finding the smell of the ocean to be soothing. Ishmael pulled me along until we reached our seats. Heat blew through the vents, warming us instantly. Our positions on the boat didn't differ much from the plane. I rested my head on his chest. He closed his hand around mine.

"I'm sleepy," I confessed, another yawn tearing my mouth open.

"Thirty-six minutes, my baby. Your rest is waiting."

THE GREY LIST

Take me back. My mind drifted.

With my head pressed against the door, I watched

as Ishmael made his way down the cement path. His landscaper was a scientist in his past life. The greenery was plentiful, but so well-manicured that you hardly noticed it didn't belong, had been planted, and didn't come from the soil beneath it.

"I miss you already."

Gloom danced around me, promising despondency if I didn't keep busy. Both Ishmael's absence and presence were punishment, because each second I had him around I was dreading the second he wouldn't be.

He halted. His body turned a hundred and eighty degrees. Black adorned his frame. I fought the urges stemming from my center.

"How much, my baby?"

I lifted the cropped baby tee I was wearing, exposing my firm nipple.

"This much."

In a flash, Ishmael was before me. His hands were around me. One on my breast and one on my waist, making me feel so small. He lowered his mouth onto my breast.

"Mmmm."

He released me before taking me into his mouth again. Our tongues touched. So did our lips. And our chest. And our noses.

"I love you, my baby."

"I love you."

He tilted his head sideways, analyzing me thoroughly.

"You make it hard to leave," he murmured, hand squeezing my breast.

"Then don't."

He sighed, regretfully. "Berkeley needs me."

I ironed the creases of his suit with my hands.

"I know. I know."

I raised up on the tips of my toes and pecked his lips.

"Good day, Mr. Grayson."

Chuckling, Ishmael stole parts of me I had yet to secure myself.

"Good day, Mrs. Grayson."

My cheeks fluffed. Flattery was etched in each movement. My lashes batted. My weight was shifted from one foot to the other. I couldn't help myself.

"It has a ring to it."

"It will, my baby. It will have a fucking rock to it soon enough."

"Later, baby."

"Later, my love. Dinner at seven."

"Dinner at seven."

I closed the door behind me. My body slid down the hard surface, landing on the floor in his black briefs. I pulled my knees to my chest and placed my chin between them.

Proper love hurts so good.

I mustered the strength to stand. Up on my feet, I made my way through Ishmael's lovely home.

"Ahhhhhhh."

My hands covered my mouth. I shook my head

from side to side. So much was right in my world. Almost too much was right in my world.

I slid my phone from the counter and dialed the number of the woman whose voice I missed something awful.

The call connected. I popped a piece of the turkey sausage Ishmael had prepared for breakfast into my mouth as the phone rang. It wasn't until the third ring that the difference in time registered with me.

Shit.

"Hello?" Grogily, she answered.

"I'm sorry. You're sleeping. I didn't realize what time it was."

"No. No. It's fine."

"I can call back lat–"

"Royce. I'm awake now."

I peered down at my feet. Ishmael's slides covered parts of my feet, protecting it from the cold floor. Regret filled me. I wanted my mother to rest.

"And, it's because *I want to talk to you*. So, fix your face."

I smiled. She knew her children well. Each of us.

"Now, talk to me. You have something to say."

"I do."

"Then, let me hear it."

"I met someone."

"Ishmael."

"Who have you been talking to?"

"My children."

"Teddy?"

She quieted.

"It was him."

"Why does it matter who told me?" she laughed.

"Because, he's always been vocal when it concerns me."

"Is that a problem?"

"No. It's not. Not at all. Sometimes I just wonder– you know."

"Wonder what?"

"Why?"

"As much as you wonder, he worries."

"He doesn't have to. I'll be fine."

"He knows that. But he also knows that things changed for you when Richie died. Your father was your rock. Your stability. Your safety net. It was pulled from under you with hardly a warning. Simultaneously, Teddy was away. He still hasn't forgiven himself for not being here."

"He should."

"I tell him every day, but his head is as hard as yours. He just won't admit it."

I let my thoughts roll in. Neither of us said anything as they registered.

"He's good to me."

"He doesn't have much of a choice, baby."

I cringed as I nodded. The blood that soaked his white button down was fresh on my brain.

"He doesn't."

I chewed another piece of turkey as I waited for

more words to appear. After swallowing, they finally materialized.

"How did it feel?"

I shifted my weight from one side to the other.

"With Dad?"

"Like a Sunday morning. Every morning, Royce."

My mother and father had met early in adulthood and never spent another day without each other. Richie didn't have to question anything when it came to my mother. She was the one thing in life he was certain of.

"What about a Friday night? When the world has been exhausting and there's only one pair of arms you want to fall into? Or when you're at the bottom of your bottle of wine and there's only one person you care to call? Or when the noise has been so loud that you need them to quiet it all?"

"Friday night... Saturday morning... Sunday morning... Tuesday. Thursday. It doesn't matter, Royce. As long as it doesn't feel like the Monday blues. Or the hump you just need to get over Wednesday."

"He doesn't give me the blues. Neither does he feel like an obstacle."

"Then the rest is manageable."

"He'll be the mayor of Berkeley in the next forty-eight hours."

"And he found time to have you blushing on this line this morning?"

"He makes time for me. Always."

"A man after your heart."

"He has it."

"And that makes me so happy, Royce. I've heard your change of tone over the last few months. I admire the peace his presence has brought you."

"I've been wanting to tel–"

"I'm your mother, baby. I birthed six of your best friends. Catherine bore the first. I have come to terms with the fact that I'm the last one to get news and I'm okay with that. It's working out exactly how I planned."

"I haven't seen much of the girls." I sighed. "I've been so tied up with Ishmael and his campaign. I feel awful."

"You spent your entire childhood with your sisters and most of your adulthood. You think those girls are worried about you not seeing much of them lately? They have so much going on in their worlds. I'm sure they haven't noticed much."

"You're right."

"If there's nothing more I've taught you, it's to always give yourself grace. Your sisters abide by the same rule."

"Yeah."

My heart was getting heavier.

"I guess I just miss them."

"Which is understood. I'm sure they share the same feelings."

Pivoting was the solution. I headed toward the bedroom where I wanted to fall deep into the sheets. However, there was work to be done. Votes to secure. Adjustments to be made. And a day-long beauty marathon that I wasn't looking forward to.

"I'm meeting his mother tonight. We have dinner at seven."

"She'll love you."

"I'm not sure that I care if she doesn't," I confessed.

Chuckling, my mother choked on her spit.

"Royce."

"It's true."

"I know and that's what's hilarious."

"But, it would be nice and much easier to navigate shared spaces if she does."

"She will."

"But if she does–" I joined my mother in laughter. "I have a mother, six sisters, and five whole brothers. There's more than enough love amongst us."

"You're absolutely right, baby."

"You're still laughing."

"Because you are your father's child."

"Yeah? How so?"

"He didn't care, Royce. He didn't care about much when it came to anyone. He saved all of that energy for the children he created. Aside from Pops, Catherine, Maurice and I... you all were all that he cared to make a good impression on.

His life revolved around your views of him. He moved with all of you in mind. He wanted to be good at three things in life. Co-parenting. Being a husband. And, raising girls. He didn't care if he sucked at everything else."

"I don't believe that's entirely true. Richie was a perfectionist."

My father approached everything with his best foot forward.

"He was naturally gifted, Royce. He didn't have to try for much else. Everything came naturally to him. Perfectionism only applied to things that involved the three things he wanted to be proficient in. To be a good husband, father, and co-parent, he had to be a provider.

"For two households. Sometimes three. That made him approach business differently. It also required him to be a protector. He wasn't always the calculated man you knew. That's who he became. And a little more with each birth. Oh Royce," she breathed. I could hear the smile in your voice.

"Your father was beyond this world. He taught me that a man ready for change will. No coaxing. No asking. No bribing. The desire will consume all else. Your father was enough as he was. Still, he wanted to be more.

"Not just for me but for all of you. And for the woman he knew so well once. Though his heart was with me, he mourned Catherine long before her death. He'd lost someone that meant so much to him to something he couldn't see. We couldn't see.

"But all felt the effects of. He wanted to be more for Maurice. He wanted to be more for the boys. He wanted to be more for Pops. And when it all came crashing down, he wanted to be more for Chemistry."

"How did he handle their deaths?"

"It broke his spirit. I'd never seen my husband so fragile. Not even before his death. Catherine and

Maurice were his friends. They were my friends. I wouldn't be exaggerating if I claimed them as the best of friends for us. That was the first time I seen tears fall from his eyes. Until Chemistry's arrest, it was the only time."

"Like Rugger."

"Just like Rugger. Richie lives through that girl. She is everything he was and everything he wasn't. Psalem is shaping up to be more like them than either of us will be able to grasp."

"With Psalms and Rugger as his parents, I don't think he could be any other way."

"He's special."

I agreed.

"I need to spend more time with them."

"The children?"

"No," I pushed out a shaky breath. "Mercer, Malachi, Makai, and Milo."

"You should. I'm sure they're happy to have you near."

"It feels–I feel like–"

"Like he's still around?"

I nodded as if she could see me.

"It doesn't matter how much time passes. I miss having him around. Sometimes I need that hug."

"The one he hates?"

"Yes, but can't resist. That one. And his wisdom. I miss seeing him whenever I needed. Whenever I wanted."

"He misses it, too. As happy as he is, he's just as sad.

His children are out in the wild without him."

"His children. Funny, girl."

"You know he believes you are. I don't think he knows Richie and I are your parents. I believe we're surrogates in his mind."

"That sounds about right."

"He visited."

"Of course."

"Ishmael loves the water, too. He reminds me of Teddy in many ways."

"So does Priest, Psalms, and Israel. Saint is–"

"Perfect for Rome."

"Yes. Because, as much as we'd like to believe otherwise, she is too much like him."

"She's his baby."

"She's his baby," my mother repeated.

"He wants to win this election fairly."

"Let him."

"It won't work out in his favor if he does. They need him, Mom."

It wasn't often I used the term, but it was sweet on my tongue each time I tasted it.

"They don't always know what's good for them."

"His opponent plays dirty. He's such a fucking pig. He's going to drain Berkeley of its beauty. My brothers were born here. This is home for them. I can't watch someone destroy it the way Daniels plans to."

"Then don't."

"The second Ishmael put me on his team, Daniels'

run was over. He's still here for the plot. Nothing more."

"That's the spirit."

Ding.

Dong.

My brows scrunched as I turned toward the door. As if I could see through the walls, I stared, waiting for the identity of the visitor to magically appear.

"Royce?"

"I'm not expecting anyone."

I rushed toward the bed, retrieving my weapon in the process. Time was of the essence. I made my way to the kitchen, stopping at the screen displayed on the wall next to the breakfast nook.

Ding.

Dong.

I tapped the doorbell camera. The darkness that followed was alarming. I pressed the microphone icon.

"Unless you want to spend your morning at the morgue, remove your hand from the camera and expose yourself."

Chuckling followed.

My hand fell from the screen. My Glock sounded against the marble countertop. Pieces of my heart that had been growing heavier with each day were now as light as a feather.

I knew that laugh. It warmed me all over.

"I don't want to spend my morning at the morgue, sister. I was hoping to spend it with you."

Rome's gentleness patched the holes in my heart.

"Not she ready to shoot somebody at eight in the morning. Girl, open this fucking door." Roulette was such a problem that I didn't think she noticed it anymore.

"That's why we're not getting in right there." Range sighed.

"Does she not know we shoot back?" Rugger asked.

"Please, ladies," Roaman begged.

"I have to use the bathroom, Royce. Open up." I could hear the anxiousness in Rather's tone.

I headed toward the door with my mother still on the line.

"You knew, huh?"

"I tried staying awake. My eyes were too tired."

"I'll call you later. They've made it and we have so much catching up to do."

"I love you, baby, in every lifetime."

"Wait for me if you make it there first. I'll come and find you."

I ended the call and pulled the door open. Simultaneously, I fell into my sisters' arms. There was no place like home.

"Who sent you?" I pulled back, adjusting the skimpy clothing I was wearing.

As the words escaped my mouth, Rome opened a greeting card with black hearts covering the front. Baylee Paper Co. was written on the back.

"My Baby," Rome paused, taking a peek over the card.

"Though the next few days will be the most complicated days of my life, I couldn't go without reminding you how easy you have made this journey. From the moment you stopped in front of my whip, I knew the woman you were. I knew who you belonged to. And, I knew where you belonged.

"Now that you're here, I promise not to forget all you're sacrificing to be here. That includes time with the people you love most. I admired the relationship you have with your siblings. I'm no stranger to what distance does to the heart.

"So, I sent for your people. And, with their help, I've scheduled a day full of pampering for all of you. Should you get tired of the AMEX, the feisty one has a gift for you. I love you. See you at eight. Ishmael."

Roulette held open her LV duffle. Bills were stuffed inside. My face parted with a smile.

"I like him, Sister," she proclaimed.

"For other reasons, but–" Rugger admitted, pushing her way inside.

"Well, he's sweet. I like that," Rome added.

"Come inside! I need to do something with myself and then we can head out."

My sisters filed inside. My heart was full. Ishmael had a way with words. He also had a way with me. It was the reason he could have his way with me.

T H E G R E Y L I S T

I can't believe I let her talk me into this.

I tugged at the red dress. Though it was beautiful, it was bold. And, it had Roulette's name written all over it. Letting her choose my dinner dress was a foolish mistake.

"Hey. Hey," Ishmael called out, stopping inches shy of his mother's front door.

He pulled me closer, placing a hand on my neck. His fingers laid against my jaw. His hands were massive. I was putty in them.

"You look lovely, my baby. If you tug any harder, you'll rip the dress off and we'll never make it inside. I'll have to have you right here. Right now."

"I let Roulette talk me into this dress," I complained.

"And I'm glad you did. It's stunning. You're stunning, love."

I didn't doubt it. But, red wasn't my color. It was hers.

"Thank you."

"Now, come on. My stomach is touching my back."

He kissed my forehead and then my cheek. I closed my eyes, embracing for impact. When his lips touched mine, I forced myself to disengage. Or, he'd be right. We wouldn't make it inside. I'd have to have him. Right here. Right now.

Hand-in-hand, we entered the modest home. The savoriness of the prepared dishes spread my nostrils. My mouth watered as we approached the dining room where three seats were already occupied. Feet shuffled as everyone stood, acknowledging our presence.

"Hello," I addressed the room.

At the very end of the table was a thin woman with golden skin and long legs. Her natural hair hung down her back. Gray covered nearly every thread. However, it was the only evidence of her birth year. Her skin was glowing. She was aging well.

"Ishmael, Royce," she greeted us.

"Royce, my mother, Janis. Indigo. And, Isaías."

Indigo was no stranger. As he approached me, I extended my hand. Indigo ignored my request and wrapped his hands around me. The smell of marijuana was potent. It lingered on his black hoodie, jeans, and skin. He pulled away with a smirk on his handsome face. Gold teeth flashed, exposing a diamond-encrusted smile.

"What's up, Sis-law?"

"Good evening, Indigo."

I turned toward Isaías, still on Indigo's side of the table. He didn't hesitate to take my hand. His orbs were desolate, but on me, nonetheless.

"Grayson," he informed me. "Isaías Grayson."

After a curt nod he released my hand. I continued toward Ishmael's mother. She was magnetic, pulling me in deeper with each breath she took. I didn't extend a hand. I didn't keep my distance. I didn't abide by the personal space rules my mother had instilled in me.

"It's so good to meet you."

Her arms were around me. My arms were around her. And, my heart was heavy.

I miss my mother. I noted.

"You smell divine."

"I'll be sure to gift you a bottle."

"*Please.*"

We parted, but my heart was still with her. Ishmael's hand lowered to my waist.

"This way," he instructed.

We stopped in front of the hand sink in the corner of the dining room. Ishmael pumped soap into my palm and placed my hands together.

I chuckled. "I can manage."

"I didn't ask."

My claim didn't hinder his plan. He rubbed my hands together until they were clean. Ishmael repeated the same steps for himself as I dried my hands with the paper towel he gave me.

Silently, he guided me to our seats. I was the first to sit. He pushed my chair up to the table and slid his back. He never scooted toward the table. He angled his chair toward mine and closed the gap between us. A hand rested on my thigh.

"Are you okay?" he whispered.

I turned to face him, running a hand down the side of his face. He leaned in, kissing my fingers.

"Yes," I murmured.

Though he masked it well, I could feel the uneasiness under the layers of polish he coated his presence with each day.

"Everything is ready for consumption," Janis announced.

Ishmael stood. So did Indigo. So did Isaías. One by one, they removed the tops from the dishes, exposing the food beneath them. My stomach ached with hunger as I observed each option carefully.

Smothered chicken.

Steak tips covered in brown gravy.

Mashed potatoes.

Cauliflower.

Green beans.

Wild rice.

Cabbage.

Dinner rolls.

"Do you have a preference or would you like everything?" Ishmael leaned in to ask.

"Chicken. Potatoes. Cauliflower. Cabbage. Rice."

He lifted both plates from the setting in front of me. One by one, he filled them with the choices I'd made. Indigo did the same for his mother. Isaías' palms were against the table until our plates were returned. Simultaneously, the three of them began to pile their plates.

"Let me get some chicken, big throat," Indigo exclaimed, shoving Isaías' hand.

"If you don't want your throat shoved down your stomach, I suggest you refrain from putting–"

"Hey. Hey!" Janis called out.

"That's this nigga, acting like he been in the field eating them pouches full of that bul–"

"Indigo," Ishmael warned.

"Aight. Aight. I'm done."

"You're lying." Ishmael eased into his seat.

"I am, but that's nothing new." Indigo shrugged.

I suppressed my laughter. It was obvious who was

in charge. It was just as obvious who was the most problematic.

"Next time you invite me, don't invite him."

"Nigga, why are you here anyway? We ain't seen you in five months of Sundays. It's been peaceful."

"That's extremely hard to believe unless you were absent yourself."

"Yeah, whatever. Answer the question."

"I'm here to support my brother," Isaías revealed. "This is about him. Not me."

"Fine time to support. You marched for this fucked up ass country but ain't been to one door to ask for support from the voters."

Isaías forked his food.

"We can take it outside, Indigo."

"My heat on me right now. Why we going outside? I can light you up in here."

"Is your weapon your only line of defense?"

"Indigo! Isaías! We have a guest."

"I have six sisters and five brothers. This is not—"

"Damn, your people was doing a lot a fucking," Indigo shrieked.

"Watch your mouth, Son!"

"My bad," he apologized.

"Twelve children amongst four adults. Not that I'm explaining the size of my family. Whatever they were doing was their business. Not mine. Not yours."

"I—" Indigo started.

"Some people don't spend their entire adulthood chasing people they aren't genuinely interested in or have no plans to properly pursue for marriage. How old are you, Indigo?"

"Thirty-two."

"No wife? No children?"

"Nope."

"Seems to me as all you're doing is–*excuse me, Ms. Janis*," I paused, "Fucking."

Ishmael, Isaías, and Janis were unable to contain their sniggers.

"Luckily for me that coochie only a couple hundred. I can't say the same for everybody." He laughed, eyes trained on Ishmael.

My lips turned upward into a smile.

"Which lets me know that you aren't ready for a woman of my caliber. Because you'd understand that the two point five million Ishmael paid for my services was a discounted rate. A friend of the family rate of sorts, you know. He has the rest of our lives to settle the rest of his debt. From my understanding, it is the best investment he's made to date."

Janis' fingers snapped as she nodded. Isaías remained silent, eyes twice their size.

"I like her," Janis blurted. "I like her a lot, son."

"Me too," Indigo admitted. "She ain't afraid to rumble."

"I don't rumble, Indigo. And, you won't need to head outside to figure out why. I will heat you up right where you're seated. Concierge came with my Glock. Courtesy of my clip."

"Royce," Ishmael mumbled, squeezing my thigh. His sniggers didn't go unnoticed.

"According to your aim, I don't thin–"

"There's nothing inaccurate about my aim. I've never missed a target I intended to hit. Exactly where I wanted to hit them."

"Why was my son your latest target?"

I tilted my head and took in a deep breath. The truth was never hard to come by. It was always at the tip of my tongue, yet, I didn't want to be the bearer of bad news. Ishmael was Janis' son. And, if it were me, I'd have him walking in the opposite direction. We were different, though, in almost every aspect of our lives.

"Because, your son was warned. He put his penis in a place it didn't belong. Should he find himself in questionable territory again, I won't hesitate to remind him of his shortcomings."

Gasps rounded the table.

"*And,* he was down in the polls. I'm certain his misfortune has put him ahead of Daniels. I am here to ensure Ishmael wins this election. Failure is not an option. He has to win. He's going to win. I won't rest until he does."

Janis' lips rolled between her teeth, forming a smile.

"I don't think he will need another reminder. And, I look forward to seeing him make his post-election speech, declaring his victory over Daniels."

"Me, too."

Food and drinks flowed freely around the table. Though reserved, Isaías loosened the straps of his boots slightly. Indigo didn't give him much of a choice. Janis reminded me so much of Roaman. Yet, just like Roulette, she was the ultimate host.

I learned about her past through stories she'd told a hundred times or more but the boys still loved to hear. There was hardly a whisper about Ishmael's father. When his name was mentioned in a retelling, Janis quickly skated over the details and his involvement.

She was still anguished by his absence. She'd loved once and had been handed dead flowers as a consolation prize. Since then, she vowed to never give her heart to another man. There was no room. She saved everything she had for her boys.

I witnessed it in the way they looked at her. The way they waited on her. The way they quieted when she spoke. The way they made room for her.

"You good, my baby?"

Ishmael's hand hardly left my thigh. Not inside his mother's home and not in the car on the way to his home.

"Yes."

Mentally, I began organizing my calendar to include a week-long visit to the island. Everything needed to be rearranged.

"She's lovely," I yawned.

"My mother?"

I nodded.

"Yes."

"She is."

. . .

I wasn't sure when I'd fallen asleep. Neither was I sure how long I'd been asleep. Soft tunes played in the background. The car's engine was still running. However, we weren't moving.

I lifted my seat using the button on the side. The point of the trip where I'd reclined was blurry. I didn't remember lowering the seat.

"Hey?" I groaned, peering at Ishmael.

We faced the brick home with a perfectly manicured yard. My surroundings were familiar. So was the man beside me. He stared straight ahead in deep thought.

"Is everything okay?"

Ishmael shrugged.

"What's the matter?"

"I'm beginning to wonder if this race was truly for Berkeley to meet their next mayor or for me to meet you."

"Is—"

"Since that night, Royce, I've faced one deterrent after the other. While my confidence in my ability to lead Berkeley hasn't wavered, my confidence in the voters have. It doesn't matter how much good I've done or how much I've invested in the youth of this city, they'll only remember those headlines.

"*False accusations*. And, quite honestly, the work I do won't change. It won't. No matter if I'm in office or just a nigga who cares. The work won't stop. It won't change. So, again, I've been wondering if his race was for Berkeley or just a part of our fate."

"Both. What if it's both?"

I lifted a hand to his chin and pulled it in my direction.

"It can be both, baby."

"I've been trying to go about this the right way. I don't think I've ever fought fair in my lifetime. Daniels is no saint, which makes this shit even more challenging. He's killing our neighborhoods and the children's chance at a bright future.

"He's going to be the death of Berkeley. I can't let that happen, Royce. I won't. Should he win, retirement won't be able to keep me grounded."

"He won't win."

Ishmael nodded. "He won't."

SIXTEEN

Royce

"Shhhhhh! Everybody shut the fuck up!" Indigo yelled.

"You shut the fuck up, toothpick!" Roulette's rebuttal caused us all to chuckle.

"Where y'all get her from and do they make more of her?"

"I hope your mother can make more of you," Israel cleared his throat.

"We not gon' beef 'bout no pussy on election night," Indigo claimed.

"And no other night," Israel confirmed. "Keep pushing if you care to keep breathing."

"Impressive, Ish. Even if you don't win this motherfucker, you've won my heart. You have introduced me to some vicious motherfuckers. I love that for me."

Drunkenly, Indigo peered around the room.

"Yeah. Definitely love that for me."

The room at Ishmael's home was full of strangers, friends and family. The watch party was in full swing. The polls had closed. The votes had been tallied and within seconds, we'd know the results.

"How are you feeling?"

With folded hands, Ishmael rested his elbows on his knees. He hadn't cracked a smile. He hadn't taken a sip from the drink I'd made him. He hadn't said as much as four words since greeting guests. His edginess was agonizing. I missed his voice. His whittiness. His wisdom.

"I'm good, my baby."

I rubbed a hand up and down his back as I lowered my eyes to his.

"I love you."

There it was. That smile.

"Thank you. Thank you for loving me."

"I wouldn't have it any other way," I explained, shaking my head.

"You think I got this shit?" His smile was weak, but his confidence was still intact.

"I know you got this shit."

"That's my baby."

"There's no person who deserves this more than you. There's nothing to worry abo–"

"Uh ohhh. Here we go. Here we fucking go," Indigo chanted, hiking the volume on the television.

My eyes found Mercer. In the corner with Vallei pressed against him, he ran a hand down his head. It was obvious he was familiar with Indigo's vast personality. It was also obvious how much of a nuisance he was when they were counting down the days until their releases.

"The city of Berkeley has chosen their next mayor," Caldwell revealed, adjusting his microphone. Cameras flashed simultaneously. Reporters chanted in the distance.

"4% of voters were in favor of Nate Echols. 45% of voters were in favor of Evan Daniels. 51% of voters were in favor of Ishmael Grayson, making Grayson the new mayor of Berkeley City. Congratulations, Grayson. Your fight continues. *Grayson Cares* continues."

Cheers erupted.

Pop!

Pop!

Pop!

Pop!

Champagne showers were predicted and the forecast hadn't failed us. Ishmael's arms surrounded me. He pulled my body from the seat I'd occupied for the last six minutes.

"Fuck, my baby. I did it."

"You did it!"

His hands were no longer around my body. They were on my face, holding me still. Holding me close. Holding me tight.

Telling me everything I already knew. Telling me that all Ishmael saw was me. Telling me that nothing else mattered in the moment. Telling me he didn't see or hear anyone but me. Telling me that he needed this moment as much as he needed me.

"My baby… my baby."

His lips pressed against mine. He parted my mouth with his tongue. I opened for him. Like I always would.

"My brother the mayor of this BITCH!" Indigo screamed, pouring the bubbling liquid over Ishmael's head.

Laughter pulled us apart, but he didn't venture far. Our separation was his attempt to keep the champagne from raining down onto me and ruining my hair and makeup. His consideration didn't go unnoticed.

Indigo's arm went around Ishmael, pulling him into his chest.

"I love you, my brother! This is only the mother-fucking beginning."

He looked toward me, holding the bottle in the air.

"Sis-law! This nigga won! This nigga fucking won!"

"Yes." I laughed, feeling my heart swell with pride. "He did."

"We just young Black niggas from the 'jects!" he shouted. "They ain't expect us to be in these rooms."

I shook my head. "They didn't."

He released Ishmael. His brother's win was liberating. Not only for Indigo, but for us all. My hands collided. Joy spilled from my eyes.

Relief consumed Ishmael. He didn't stray away. He stayed near my side.

"I'm the motherfucking mayor, my baby."

"Yes you are." I laughed, unable to contain my gratitude.

"This is all you," he told me, pulling me in front of him. "My anchor. You held shit down. Made sure I came out on top."

"Second place is last place, Ish."

"Damn right."

His arm was pulled in so many different directions. But, he didn't budge. He didn't move. His eyes were on me. Mine were on him.

"I want you beside me."

"I am. Always."

"Tomorrow."

"Tomorrow?"

"When I'm in front of that podium addressing everyone that believed in me enough to give me a chance, I want the woman who believes in me beside me for the world to see this is no joke. We're no hoax. I'm real. You're real. And, what we share is real. Can you do that for me, my baby?"

"I can."

"Good, Mrs. Grayson," he replied, his smile big and bright.

Darkness obstructed my view. Foreboding

followed. In a room nearly full of strangers, I was leery of everyone's presence. Ishmael knew his guests. I'd hardly gotten a chance to meet most of them. Besides my sisters and Mercer, I was swimming in a pool of unfamiliar faces.

Ishmael's spine straightened. He pulled his suit together by the jacket, buttoning it as he pulled me into his side. I settled in uncertainty as I found my footing. The abrupt turn was uprooting.

"Ishmael. Ishmael Grayson."

He didn't extend his hand, but neither did the person he was introducing himself to.

My person.

"Chemistry. Chemistry Childers."

My breath was stuck in my throat. But, still, I found the strength to analyze the room. My heart was exposed. Out in the open. Around people that knew his face and his history. Around people that could make one call and have him sent away for the rest of our lives. Around people I was afraid of him being in the same room with, which was why I was hesitant to give parts of me to Ishmael.

But his presence.

His presence was his love language. It was his way of letting us know he was in support of us. And that he was standing ten toes behind us. And that he loved us. And that nothing mattered more than our happiness.

"Teddy," I gasped.

"The phone lines are jammed. All cameras have

been confiscated. No one can enter. No one can exit. I'm safe, baby."

Nothing was the same. Rugger stood near the exit of the living room. Rome was mere feet away. Her smile assured Teddy he was in the clear. Roulette stood beside the coffee table that was littered with cellular devices. Rather held four cameras in her hand.

Roaman leaned against the wall with the official photographer's attention. His camera was near his side. Range quietly acquired signatures of everyone in attendance. I didn't have to read what was on the pages of the paper pinned to the clipboard to know they were Non-Disclosure forms.

"But–"

"But this is a victorious night. I'm here in support of everything you two have accomplished."

"Appreciate that," Ishmael cleared his throat.

"This city raised me," Teddy explained, "Don't let it fall under."

"This city raised me as well. If it falls under, it means I've taken my last breath."

"Rhea is home. We're expecting you for dinner tomorrow."

I could feel my eyes grow in my skull. While I'd been planning to travel across the water, my mother had been doing the same.

"Your mother?"

I turned to face Ishmael. Nodding, I confirmed.

"Yes."

"The trip to visit her will have to wait, I guess."

I agreed.

"It will."

Turning back to Teddy, I parted my lips to inquire about the details.

"I–"

Nothing was left of him. Not even his scent. The room felt cold at once. My chest imploded before expanding. His absence never got old. The pain never dulled. It was still sharp and overwhelming.

"My baby."

Ishmael's hand on my arm brought me back to life. Something inside of me died every time he vanished. I closed my eyes, remembering happier times. When there was Richie and Chemistry, and I didn't have to watch him leave. And, our time together wasn't brief. He could stay longer. He could stay forever.

"Are you okay?"

I shook my head, turning into his chest. "No. I'm not. But, I will be."

"Talk to me."

He pulled my chin toward him.

"Another day, Ish. Today is your day."

"For you," Roulette said, handing me a glass of champagne. "And for you."

She handed Ishmael a glass. He accepted it.

"You're drinking now?" I chuckled.

"I'm drinking now, my baby."

"Good for you."

"Alright everyone," Cameron called over the loud chatter. "I would like to start this toast by congratulating the new mayor of our city. A beacon for change. A trailblazer. A waymaker. A selfless, genuinely caring man. I don't think I could ask for a better boss. Thank you for giving me the opportunity to work alongside of you. Matte–"

Matte raised her glass. Thankfully she didn't attempt to put one foot in front of the other. She kept her back against the wall as she began.

"Mayor Grayson has shown me that nothing is impossible. I've worked the hardest in the last few months than I have in my entire life and it was because I knew this man deserved this spot more than anyone else on the ledger. It brings me great joy that we were able to make that happen for him. Our work doesn't end here. Congratulations, Mayor Grayson… Royce–"

With wide eyes, I pursed my lips. Sensing my uneasiness, Ishmael positioned me in front of him.

"I–uh– I hardly believe anything is a coincidence. Ishmael has perfect vision, so him almost running me over feels more like fate than a mistake on his part."

Giggles filled the space my words hadn't.

"Nevertheless, I noticed so many special components about him then. One look into those big, dark eyes and something happened to my heart. I mean– it was immediate. He didn't feel like a stranger."

I pushed my emotions down my throat.

"He felt sacred. And, I felt like I'd been tasked with his safety. I had to take care of him. I had to help him handle things. I had to help him find his way. As much as I tried dismissing the urge, it stuck to me like glue.

"Shortly after our encounter, I was asked for a favor from someone I love dearly. If he asked, then the job was already done. It was that simple. To my surprise, I walked into the office of the man I'd been trying to rid my thoughts of since that perfectly imperfect night.

"And, I discovered why he felt sacred. I discovered why I'd been tasked with his safety. I discovered why I had to take care of him. I discovered why I needed to help him take care of things. I discovered why I was tasked with helping him find his way. And, I also discovered why the urge stuck to me like glue.

"Because, in the midst of my tasks, he had some of his own. He, too, felt as though I was sacred. He, too, had been tasked with my safety. He, too, felt as though he had to take care of me. Take care of my things. Help me find my way. His urge wouldn't allow our rough beginning be our ending.

"Ishmael is something fresh out of a dream. My dream. And, because he is so good to me, I don't doubt for a second that he won't be as good to Berkeley. He's exemplified it time and time again. His commitment to the city is commendable.

"The time he spends with his boots on the ground is commendable. The passion and devotion to the youth is commendable. The love he has for single mothers is commendable. His knowledge is commendable. His head is in the right place and Berkeley is blessed to have him. So– cheers to you, *my baby*. Cheers to Mayor Grayson."

"To Mayor Grayson."

My glass touched Ishmael's glass. However, it never touched my lips. He did. As quickly as he'd spun me around, he turned me back around. Positioning me on his rigidness.

"You got my dick hard, my baby."

He slid his arm around my waist.

"Can you put 'em down for me?"

I sipped champagne.

"I'm not above begging," he groaned against my ear.

I threaded my fingers through his. One foot in front of the other, I pushed through the room full of champagne flutes. My legs didn't stop moving until I reached Ishmael's bedroom. I pushed my haltered dress toward the floor. It slid from my body with ease. Range had done well. She'd chosen a beautiful gown for the night. I was reminded to thank her again once we were alone.

I turned to find Ishmael's eyes on me. I unbuttoned his suit jacket and pushed it from his shoulders.

"A dream?" He asked, finishing the champagne in his flute. I handed him mine.

"Drink up, baby."

I wanted him nice and tipsy. The difficult part was over. He was mayor.

"A dream, my baby?" He asked again after sitting the empty glasses on the nightstand.

I shoved his pants down his legs. I fell to my knees as they hit the floor.

Ishmael's dick was warm to the touch. Hesitancy wasn't an issue of mine. I consumed him. As much of him as I could, eyes still on him. Once his shaft was wet from my saliva, I removed him from my mouth.

"My dream."

I shoved him in my mouth again. He touched the back of my throat, initiating my gag reflex. My pussy salivated. Intoxication was in our favor. It wasn't the champagne that had driven us to the point of inebriation. It was each other.

SEVENTEEN

Ishmael

"TO THE CITY OF BERKELEY, I am honored to serve you. I will continue to hold the citizens near to my heart. You've given me the chance of a lifetime. I am forever indebted. My gratitude exceeds me. It is immeasurable. So is my love for this great city. There's no place like home.

"To everyone who went out to the polls, whether you voted for me or my opponents, thank you for exercising your right. Your voice matters. To my team… we fought a good fight and were victorious. Thank you. To my family, your support hasn't gone unnoticed. To the beautiful woman beside me–"

I paused. All eyes were on me. My eyes were on her.

Royce was stunning in the black dress and long black boots that reached her thighs. She didn't attempt to conceal her personality with boring ass fashion often displayed in political spaces.

"I couldn't have done this without you, my baby. Thank you for believing in me. For being the stability I needed when the ship started rocking. Thank you for your thoughtfulness. Your will. Your dedication. Your drive. And, your unwavering spirit. We did it, love."

A gentle squeeze from Royce was all the reassurance I needed.

"Have a blessed day, Berkeley."

I took off toward the exit. Royce's grip on my hand tightened as I slowed near the stairs, helping her down. I placed a hand on her waist once she'd made it on leveled ground. Together, we made our way out of the door.

The doors of the Rolls Royce parted. Royce slid inside. I settled beside her, leaving the cameras and questions behind. When the doors closed, the noise toned down.

"Ish."

When Royce opened her mouth, it disappeared completely.

"Yes, my baby?"

"That was good. Really good."

"I could spend the next three months without speaking another word."

"I know, but it's all been worth it."

"I need something stiff. Is the plane stocked?"

She nodded. "Without question. The libations are waiting."

I rested my left hand on her thigh as the wheels began to turn. It was the first week of November. In twenty-six days, Royce would be a year older. The election was behind me. I was ready to show Royce why she'd agreed to give me pieces of her that had never belonged to anyone else.

"I have something for you."

Excitement was etched in her voice. She'd already given me the gift of a lifetime.

"Your presence alone is a gift, Royce. What more could you have for me?"

"Close your eyes."

Her smile was bright. Her cheeks were fluffy. Her teeth were on full display. My baby was beautiful. There wasn't a flaw present.

"You're so fucking incred–"

"Close your eyes, Ishmael."

"Okay."

Sighing, I pressed my eyelids together. Silently, I was preparing to reimburse Royce for whatever she'd purchased me. I didn't want her spending her money. The moment I entered her life, she became my responsibility. I wanted to provide for her. Fully. It didn't matter that she could take care of herself. I *needed* to take care of her. It brought me great joy to do so.

One.

Two.

Three.

Four.

An automatic timer sounded off in my head. Just before I reached the next number, Royce's voice ended the count.

"Open them."

I opened my eyes, finding a yellow gold Patek Philippe. The diamond dial was accented by emerald hour markers. The same diamonds marked the bezel and center links.

"How much do I owe you, my baby?"

"Nothing."

"How much?"

"It's a gift, Ish. A celebratory gift."

"How much?"

"You've already settled your debt. It's paid for with your two–"

"Still, how much?"

"One hundred and sixty."

I nodded, knowing the watch had cost a pretty penny. My baby had done well. I loosened the Rolex and peeled it from my skin.

"I thought it fit you well."

"You have exquisite taste, love."

"I assume that means you like it?"

"It does. Thank you."

She removed it from its case and slid it on my wrist. I admired the new piece while admiring the woman who'd gifted it. They were both one of a kind.

. . .

Time escaped us. It was passing us by rapidly. Thirty minutes felt like ten. Before Royce and I were comfortable in our seats, we were exiting the vehicle. I was the first on my feet. She took my hand, accepting my assistance as she slid to the edge of the seat.

"Well don't you look darling?" Range greeted Royce with a hug.

"Thank you."

"The boots are giving bad bitch energy," Roulette claimed.

"Hi," the youngest, Rome, greeted Royce, tossing her arms around her.

"Hey, Ro."

"We should get going. Dinner is waiting," the oldest suggested.

"Ish. I haven't introduced you to the men in my family."

I remembered one of them from last night. The others I was unfamiliar with.

"Israel, Roulette's other half. He was with us last night. Psalms, Rugger's husband. Priest, Rather's husband. Saint, Rome's fiancé."

"What's good?"

"Congratulations."

"Welcome to the family."

Psalms was silent. No introduction was needed. He was no stranger and neither was I. Though we'd never crossed paths, we never intended to. It was best in our line of work.

"Alright. Enough of the introductions. Let's head up!" Rather instructed, taking Priest by the hand."

"Ladies first," he reminded her.

One after the other, the women took the stairs and entered the aircraft. I wasn't the last to enter the spacious cabin. Neither was I the first of the men. I fell in between the assembly line, eventually getting back to my bit of peace. Back to her.

Pop!

Pop!

Roulette was the first to pop the iced champagne. Rather followed.

"Champagne?" Royce asked, holding an empty glass in my direction.

"Nah, my baby."

"Something stronger?"

I nodded.

"Yeah."

As the word left my mouth, a chilled glass of brown liquor was passed to me. Psalms tipped his head toward me and rejoined his wife just a few feet away. Her eyes were trained on me. So were his. I didn't take offense to their curiosity. It was expected.

I observed as the women poured one glass after the other. Every male in the cabin declined the bubbly and opted for brown. It didn't matter what kind of brown as long as it didn't fizzle and pop.

Royce settled beside me, resting her back against the seat. Her legs crossed mine.

"Are you okay?"

"I've never been better."

"What's with that look?"

"What look?"

"That look."

She pulled her lips into her mouth.

"Of adoration? Of contentment? Or admiration? Or obsession? Or utter allurement? Which one? Or are they all obvious?"

"Is that how you feel, Royce?"

She lifted her chin and then dropped it.

"It is."

"Penny for your thoughts."

The way her attention was undivided when I spoke drove me to the point of no return. Everyone around us vanished.

"I'm listening, *my baby*."

I felt my cheeks rise and my smile attempt to touch my ears.

"I'm my baby, now?"

I loved to hear it roll off her tongue.

"Um hm."

I sipped from my glass, choosing my words carefully. Once upon a time, I hadn't been a man of many. But, between Royce and the race, I had been vomiting at the mouth for months.

"Are you happy? *With me?*"

I watched her inhale deeply. She released a shaky breath before swallowing.

"I'm my happiest with you."

She paused, placing a hand on my cheek.

"I was lost, Ish. I knew I wanted something… someone. I just– I just didn't know what or who. I'm no regular girl. I struggled with the idea of someone being able to handle me. I'm so accustomed to handling everything and everybody else. Then you came. My connection to you was instant. What I did for you the first night we met, I don't–"

She shook her head.

"I've never done that for anyone. Not without payment first. Not unless they were kin to me. Not unless I loved them. And, since that night, I've been wondering how it happened so fast. How my heart knew you were worthy of my love? How I knew that you were someone special to me? I haven't found the answers, so I've decided to stop searching. I don't need an explanation for falling for the perfect stranger. It was meant to be. That's it. Nothing more."

"You've got my shit all fucked up, up here."

I pointed to my chest.

"Nothing ever hurt and healed me at the same time like this."

I cleared my throat, moving closer.

"You make me consider things I've never considered. Want things I've never wanted."

"Care to elaborate?"

I hesitated, unsure if it was my heart or my head influencing me most.

"Ish."

"I want to make you my wife, Royce. But, beyond our bond, I want to create another one. One that continues our love and our legacies. Someone to inherit my fortune."

"Baby–"

"Lately I've been feeling differently. Feeling like I can't spend all of this shit while I'm here. And, I can't take this shit to the grave with me. I want hands to put it in. Hands that resemble mine. And yours. I want to make you a wife, my baby. But, just as much, I want to make you a mother."

The silent stare was torturous.

"Words, Royce."

"Okay."

"Okay?"

"Yes."

"That simple?"

"Whatever you want, Ish."

"But what do you want?"

"To make you happy."

"My baby, will that make you happy, though?"

"I've dreamt of your eyes on my son's face. Your lips on my daughter. I've never considered myself as the motherly type. But, just like you've been feeling things– I've been feeling things too. I've never wanted a child. Yet, I want yours."

"Yeah?"

She nodded. "Yes."

"How many?"

"One." She chuckled, scrunching her nose.

"They'll need someone to play with. You know... so they're not lonely."

"You're pushing it."

"You had six."

"You're right. I couldn't imagine life as an only child."

"Two."

"Two," she agreed.

"If it happens. No pressure."

"No pressure."

"A wife first."

"A few years of marriage?"

"Agreed."

"When we're ready to try, it has to be communicated."

I nodded. "Agreed."

"Only then will I remove my birth control."

It wasn't until that moment that I realized she never answered my question.

"Has that been our lifesaver all this time?"

Smiling, she responded, "Yes. Of course."

"I feel like shit for not asking again."

"By now I'd be swollen and off my feet." She giggled like a school girl.

I brought her closer. I couldn't stomach the distance though she was still near.

"Yes, my baby. Yes, you would be."

I kissed her lips, leaving with traces of her lip gloss.

"I'm so in love with you," I confessed. "You feel so much like home."

"I am. Rest in me. Reset with me. Build with me. Bond with me. Just don't break me."

I shook my head. "I won't. I won't. As long as I'm breathing, your heart will remain intact."

"I love you."

"I love you."

"I have a confession," she revealed.

"Talk to me."

"I'm Clarke to my core."

"Understood."

"How do we marry the two? My home and yours?"

"I'm not asking you to give up your world to join mine. I want us both to be part of each other's. You know where to find me, my baby, when your pussy is purring and your heart is heavy. When everything becomes too much, I know where to find you. I also know how to put you on a plane and get you straight to me. We don't have to complicate it.

"Neither do we have to model our relationship after anyone's before ours. We make our own rules. We create our own dynamic. Different homes. Different cities. Different states. It doesn't matter. As long as you're mine and I'm yours."

She patted my chest, running her hand along my abs.

"Are you real, sir?"

Chuckling, she lowered her hand to my bulge.

"Yes. Yes. You're definitely real."

"I'm real. So are we. I'm not tripping on shit. I know where home is. It's wherever you are. Whether Clarke or Berkeley, I'm coming home, my baby. Every fucking chance I get."

Black trucks lined the driveway. I buttoned the jacket of my suit, squaring my shoulders. Royce's hand gravitated toward mine. They were cold to the touch. Mentally, I noted her need for leather gloves in the upcoming weeks. The weather was breaking. The chill was upon us.

The door swung open. A chocolate, unbelievably gorgeous woman appeared with a child on her hip. Without question, I quickly determined her position in the family.

Mrs. Chemistry Childers.

The diamonds dancing on her skin wasn't enough evidence. All the women were dripping in jewels. It was the child in her arms. He had taken after his father and aunts.

"Evening everyone."

We filed into the spacious dwelling. Royce stopped in front of the curious boy, planting a kiss on his forehead.

"Égée."

She kissed him again. Her words were weighted. She wrapped her hands around him. He turned, placing his hands around her head.

"Oh my goodness. Tee Royce missed you, handsome."

I leaned in, grabbing her purse to free both hands. She took her nephew into her arms. Silently, I sketched the image in my head, waiting for the moment I could put it on paper. I'd saw it in my head a hundred times, but seeing Royce with a child in her hand was confirmation for me. I'd make her a wife. I'd also make her a mother.

"Egypt, this is Ishmael. Ishmael, this is my sister, Egypt, Chemistry's wife."

"Pleasure to meet you."

I stepped forward, taking her hand into mine.

"With all due respect, I can't pass you by without acknowledging your beauty. Are all of you this damn pretty around here?"

Royce's smile was bright.

"She gets that often."

"So do they," Egypt responded.

"Come on. Rhea is waiting. She's been at the stove all day."

We followed the rest of the crew into the dining room that was fit for the large family and had room for growth. Within the next five years, I fully intended to occupy more space with my wife and children.

The aroma made my stomach howl. I hadn't eaten as much as a cracker since breakfast. It was imperative that I got food in my system soon.

Royce rounded the table. I never left her side. Her legs didn't stop moving until she was in front of an equally beautiful woman. Her eyes brightened at the sight of Royce. She took her daughter and grandchild into her arms.

"Ro—I've missed you."

"I've missed you more. I'm elated you decided to visit."

"I felt it was reason enough to celebrate. And, it was about time we dined together. All of us. Here in Clarke. Just like we used to."

Royce's chest caved. Her eyes glossed over. Her thoughts were with the man she admired most. I placed a hand on her back. She leaned into me.

"It's okay, Royce. I'm fine. We're all fine. Grieving continues tomorrow. Today, we embrace what we've always known. *Happiness.*"

She stepped aside.

"Rhea… this is Ishmael. Ishmael, this is my mother. Rhea."

I stepped forward. Rhea's arms were around me in an instant.

"Let that man go before you bring Richie from his grave."

With a hearty laugh, Rhea loosened her grip.

"Quiet, Chem." She waved him off before taking her seat.

"Teddy," Royce breathed out.

"What's up, baby?"

She pushed past her siblings to reach her brother. His son was the first in his arms. Royce was next. From the agony on his face, I knew he'd prefer she not throw her body into his. Still, he accepted her display of affection.

"Good evening, Mayor Grayson."

He pushed Royce away as if she was a germ. I

couldn't help myself. I chuckled, it reminded of Indigo and Isaías.

"Good evening."

"Sit down, Royce."

"Where's Jru?" She ignored his request.

"She's struggling with the time difference. She is asleep."

"So is Psalem," Rugger added.

"Prince? Malaya? Where are you all hiding the children?"

"With my parents," Priest revealed.

"Malaya is at a sleepover," Roulette groaned.

Israel shook his head. "If she makes it through the night."

"*If* is accurate because if I even see a gray bubble pop up I'm going to get her."

"She drove, Princess."

"She won't drive back if I have anything to do with it."

"Leave her alone, Rou. She'll be fine."

"I don't know. She still doesn't know how to fight. We're working on it."

"Shooting is an easier lesson. Aim. Fire." Rugger shrugged.

Simultaneously, Psalms and I nodded. It was true.

"No." Israel wasn't interested in the theory. "She'll be fine. Roulette isn't concerned with her safety or she wouldn't have allowed her to go. She's bitter because she wants to be Malaya's only and best friend."

"I'm the only one without other motives."

"Fair argument."

"My sisters are my friends. Everyone else is questionable."

"Facts," Range blurted.

"Malaya is an only child," Israel reminded them all.

"I'm with Roulette," Royce clarified. "Teenagers are not to be trusted."

With a roll of her eyes, she returned to my side. She scanned the large table setting, trying to find a place for us. Space was plentiful. She didn't have to search for long. We settled beside Range.

"Heads bowed."

My chin fell. Darkness welcomed me back.

"Dear God, thank you for this day. Thank you for bringing us together to celebrate the most gracious gift one could ever receive... life. I pray for peace, continued love, light, and protection. Keep us. Teach us. Lead us. Bless the food we are prepared to receive. Bless our minds. Bless our hearts. Amen."

"Amen."

"Amen."

"Amen."

"Amen."

As our heads lifted and eyes opened, two servers appeared with dishes balanced on their palms. No one stood. No one reached. No one moved. Conversation continued as our plates were piled with savory servings of the dishes Rhea had prepared.

Lamb.

Lobster.

Steak.
Broccoli.
Stuffed bell peppers.
Fully loaded baked potatoes.
A creamy seafood sauce.
Mixed veggies.

I leaned in, nudging Royce.

"Baby, between your mother and mine, I'm going to have to hit the gym twice a day."

"Or let me work you out."

"In that case, I'd better eat up, huh?"

"Please do. But, not too much, because your dessert will be waiting."

"There's always room for that, my baby."

For the next two hours, plates were emptied and bellies were filled. Water was replaced with wine and Cognac and Hennessey and Crown. The options were endless. So was laughter. Connections were made. Bonds were strengthened.

And, little by little, the crowd dispersed. The women slowly exited, one by one, leaving the men to their common interests and conversation. It wasn't until I was ready for something sweet that I stood from my seat in search of my dessert.

I was ready for our night to end. The day had been long and there was an even longer day ahead of me. I would be on the first thing smokin' in the morning. The city of Berkeley was waiting.

"Excuse me, gentleman. It's been great."

"Getting out of here?" Saint asked.

"If I can manage to convince Royce. Have to head back to the city first thing in the morning."

"Understood. Tell Royce to holler at me. Next time you're in town, I'll put you on the list. Come watch some ball."

"Aight. I will. That sounds like a plan."

One by one, I slapped palms with the men around the table. It wouldn't be long before they were all finding their way out. Exhaustion was weighing on us all.

My search for Royce was initiated the second I stepped out of the dining room. The kitchen was the first stop. There was no sign of her.

"Everything alright?" Her mother asked.

"It will be once I find her."

Smiling, she nodded. "I know that feeling."

"A beautiful one."

"Yes, it is. Hold on to it. Don't believe the people telling you it'll fade. It won't. Not when you've chosen well."

"I've chosen well, Mrs. Childers."

"You have. It's up to you to make more great choices."

"I felt that heat she carry around. I don't want that kind of trouble. Royce has nothing to worry about."

"Don't do it for Royce, Ishmael. Do it because it's the right thing to do. Do it for you."

"Understood."

"She and the girls are in the family room. I'm sure of it."

"Thank you."

"Of course."

I pulled my bottom lip as I tried to narrow down the location of the family room. The home gave no clues. Its vastness was unforgiving.

Quieting my thoughts, I listened for the sound of joy that was oozing from my baby. With each step I took, I could feel her more. I could hear her more. I took the steps and passed three doors before laughter nearly stopped my heart.

There was something about a woman's merriment that lulled me. It didn't have to be my woman. Any woman. Any Black woman.

"Let's not act like you haven't been whipped. Still is whipped. If Israel tells you to jump, your only question is how fucking high?"

Snickering followed Royce's observation.

"Don't act like you're not above doing a few tricks for the dick," Roulette countered.

I tapped on the door, hoping not to cause too much of a disturbance.

"I'm not. I fixed an entire election for mine. I have a few more tricks up my sleeve if need be."

Rome appeared behind the door. Pity covered her pretty face.

"Okay!" Range lifted a hand.

"Ro–" she called out to Royce, widening the door.

I was immobile. My voice was ripped from my cords.

Royce's mouth widened with regret. Silence grew louder as the seconds passed us all by.

"Ish."

It was her voice that brought life to my limbs. I retraced my steps.

"Ishmael."

Royce was closer. I could smell the floral perfume she'd sprayed on this evening. But, it was her arousal that I smelled the most. I clipped my breaths, knowing that I wouldn't be able to deny her. Her desires overwhelmed me. It didn't matter much once they were discovered.

"Ishmael, wait."

She reached the bottom of the steps just as I pulled open the front door. I was met by two niggas dressed in black, both with questionable looks.

"Royce?"

"It's fine, August."

I didn't care to explain myself to a fucking stranger. Neither did I care to halt so Royce could catch up to me. Still, she managed. With all her might, she pulled me toward her.

"Ishmael."

Face to face.

Chest to chest.

Nose to nose.

My eyes on her. Her eyes on me.

My chest heaved. Hers rose and fell.

Still, no words were exchanged. I stilled. So did Royce. As much as I wanted to forget her, I wanted to remember her. As much as I wanted to punish her, I wanted to marry her. As much as I wanted to hurt her, I wanted to heal her. As much as I wanted to ignore her, I wanted to hear her. Hug her. Kiss her.

She's dangerous. I concluded. *For me.*

I was too far gone. Royce was a liability. My feelings ran too deep. I had no limits. I had no boundaries. I only had fears. Fears of not having her in my world. And the thought of it crippled me.

"I'm sorry."

I didn't have any words. All there was was feelings. They silenced me. I left her where she stood, desperately needing to put distance between us.

EIGHTEEN

Royce

I FORKED the greens on my plate. The bleakness was consuming. Still, it wasn't as heinous as the pain.

I pushed the food down my throat. I could feel the disgust displayed on my bare face. Makeup was a luxury at this point. So was getting dressed. And thinking. And living.

Ishmael's absence was damning. I'd gone my entire life without him. It was baffling how difficult navigating the last two days in the wake of his absence were.

Grief had me by the neck. It stole my joy. It stole my happiness. It stole my strength. It stole my will. It stole my Ishmael.

"Girl eat your fucking food and go get your nigga back. I'm so tired of you looking ugly. And raggedy."

"Leave her alone, Rou. She's going through something," Rome chastised.

"Something is going through her. Who let her come outside dressed like this?"

I was clothed in a crewneck, sweats, and a pair of furry slides.

"You look fine," Roaman argued.

"Don't lie to her." Roulette sipped from her drink.

"Must I remind you how sad you were when Israe–"

"Sad and ugly are two different things. So are sad and poorly dressed. It's never that serious. The dick isn't dead. It's just upset. There's always a chance if it's still alive."

"I agree," Range protested.

"He needs time."

"He told you that?" Range asked.

"Yes."

"And since when did we start listening to niggas?" Roulette wanted to know.

I shrugged.

"You talked to him?" Rather inquired.

"I've called. He sent me to voicemail. Hours later he texted. Said he's busy. Needs time."

"Then give him time. I imagine it was not easy finding out–"

"He hired her. Then he fell in love with her. He's not upset with her for doing her job. She promised him the election and kept her promise. It's something deeper.

Something he's dealing with. And until he's dealt with it, he will require time. Allow it. But, not too much time," Roaman expressed.

"Or you could go get your man," Roulette emphasized.

"Voluntarily or involuntarily." Rugger lowered her fork onto her plate.

I shook my head.

"I agree with Roaman. He had to have known I would do everything in my power to get him in that office. We fell in love in the process. Still, I had a job to do. Even if that meant hurting his feelings."

I lifted the martini to my lips and sipped.

"It's just that I'm ovulating and– the dick… I need it more than my next breath."

Cackling broke out around the table. Now, everyone understood my pain a bit more. We were women in our thirties, most of us at least, we understood the torture of ovulation.

THE GREY LIST

I rubbed a hand across my chest, hoping the pain would subside. Ishmael's face flashed before me as I closed my eyes. The anguish in his eyes. The disappointment on his face. The defeat in his stride.

My yearning cut me deeper every day. Whatever was happening between us, I despised. My calls were no longer going through. Neither were my texts.

I missed his voice. His touch. His laughter. His hands on my body. His head against my heart. Six days felt like a lifetime of silence.

"Ro?" Range called out. "Are you asleep?"

I wasn't sure if the film was watching me or I was watching it.

"No."

My bed reminded me of Ishmael's absence. I crawled into Range's night after night.

"Are you okay?"

I sucked in air and released it slowly.

"No. No, I'm not," I admitted.

My eyes burned with tears. I wiped them away before they could fall.

"Aw, babe. You want to talk about it?"

Shrugging, I revealed, "I'm not sure there's anything to talk about."

"How you're feeling... your plan... how you'll handle this just like you handle everything else."

"This is different, Range. He is different. I've never felt anything remotely close to what I feel for Ishmael. I feel awful for disappointing him, but I do not regret my decisions. Berkeley needed him. I couldn't chance him not winning. He had to. The second he wired that money, the election was fixed. I'm a fixer. It's what I do."

"He understands that."

"Then why are we at odds?"

"I don't know, baby."

"He's never been upset with me. If this is how it feels, I never want him to be."

"I hope you don't chew me out for saying it, but–" Range paused, "I understand him."

"Me too. I do. I jus– I want to talk about it. I want to work through it. I want to apologize for not being more transparent. I don't want to be here while he's there with all of this on his conscience."

"He's settling into his new position. I say give it another week. Give him the space we both know he could use. If he hasn't cooled down, then go for what we know. Don't give him a choice. Force him to acknowledge what's happening between you two."

"Yeah."

"That's all you can do."

"You're tired of me crawling in your bed, huh?"

"No. It gives the illusion that I'm not alone."

"But when I leave?"

"I'll have to face the music," she admitted.

"Is it music you can get used to or a sound you hope to change?"

She sighed, pulling her knees up to her chest.

"I've been wanting to change the station forever, Ro. But, it's not that simple, you know?"

"I do."

"We're not like the others. The average man wouldn't know what to do with me. And, he'd probably run the other way once he meets my family."

"Teddy is intimidating." I chuckled.

"Exactly. I'm ready for a person. But, it must be the right person. My person."

"It'll come. You've put it into the universe. He'll come."

"You sound so sure."

"Before Ishmael... I mean right before Ishmael... I wanted to change the station too. I was taking on date after date, hoping someone would adjust the nob. It wasn't happening. Chem appeared. Wanted to know what was occupying my thoughts. I was honest. I shared my feelings.

"I told him how lonely I felt and how much I wanted someone to share my time with. Hours later, I walked into Ishmael's office. It wasn't the first time I'd saw his face. But, I knew then that it wouldn't be the last. I'd have the privilege for the rest of my life.

"It didn't happen until I was honest with myself and said it out loud. Like you just did. It's coming, baby. He's coming. And, he will be a brave fella. A fine fella. One who can handle you and everyone that comes with you. Don't worry, Range."

"When you put it that way, I guess I'd better get my shit together."

"You're as put together as put together gets, honey."

Range laughed, pulling the blanket over her body.

"I don't disagree. I don't."

"Because you can't."

She tossed her hands up, surrendering.

THE GREYLIST

I gripped the lime between my fingers, holding the small glass steady in the other hand. There were so many reasons to celebrate. I couldn't allow my transgressions to deplete me. In a single month, my mother had birthed three girls.

November 06 was Roulette's day.

November 16th was Range's day.

November 29th was my day.

We chose to celebrate together. With Range's birthday mid-month, our celebration fell closer to her born day by default.

"To Range."

"And Rou."

"And Ro."

Clink.

Clink.

Clink.

Our glasses touched and then hit the table simultaneously. I kissed the rim, flipping the glass over until the contents were emptied. I followed up with the lime, squeezing it into my mouth.

"Argh," I groaned, hating the taste of tequila flowing down my throat, but loving the effects on my nervous system.

It numbed the pain. One week of not hearing from or seeing Ishmael had turned into two. I didn't have the gumption to fly to Berkeley and demand his time or his love or his energy. The fear of returning alone was too crippling. So, I stayed. I stayed where I was loved, cherished, understood, welcomed, and supported.

"Ahhhhh!" Tiana squealed.

August's position altered immediately. He obliterated the space between them. I observed as he leaned over, whispering the unknown in her ear. The smile on her face revealed the nature of his words.

A pain soared through me. Drunken nights weren't meant to end alone. Neither were they meant to end in your sister's bed. Drunken nights were meant for dick sucking and riding my man into oblivion. My mouth watered at the thought of Ishmael. Post-period hormones were raging. My center was throbbing.

I slid my phone from my purse and unlocked the screen. Instagram was my destination. I played the story I'd posted an hour ago. It wasn't the video I was interested in. It was the viewers. I swiped up, scanning the long list until the names began to blur.

"Shit."

I stopped scrolling when the familiar profile image appeared. The handle I'd created was next to it. Bold. Black. Breathtaking.

Ishmael.

I quickly added him to my close friends. I cleared the other names on the list, promising to add them all later. Those women were amongst me. They knew exactly what I was doing and how I was feeling. I didn't need to document it for them.

I scanned my images for the one Range had

snapped of me after entering our section. In the silk number trimmed in lace and pumps with a feathery strap to match, I held my hand toward the camera, reaching for it. The flash was low, giving it a soft yet vintage vibe that I loved so much.

I tapped the screen to add text. My fingers moved a mile a minute. The music drowned out in the background. So did everything and everyone around me. Ishmael wasn't taking my calls. Neither was he accepting my texts. However, I was still on his heart. He was still on mine.

Loving comes so naturally I almost forget that there are other feelings just as potent. Like, missing you. It's taxing. So is your absence. I wake up wanting you. I lay down wanting you. My heart is hanging on by a piece of nylon thread. Though strong, I doubt it can keep bearing the weight of us. Come get me. Come love me. I don't like it out here. It's cold. Come home.

I uploaded the image without a tune to match. I didn't need distractions. I needed understanding. And, I needed my man.

Once the image had been uploaded, I shoved my phone in my purse. The night was about life, but I couldn't forget my love. It was in shambles.

Up on my feet, I pulled Roulette closer. Both of our hands went in the air. She bent over, exposing parts of her that belonged to Israel. She hardly cared. Neither did he. She wasn't a fool.

"I got a ass so big like the sun–" we sang in unison. "Hope you got a mile for a dick, I wanna run."

Roulette dropped to the floor, slowly pulling her body up.

"Slap it in my face. Shove it down my throat!"

I leaned over, placing a hand around the back of her neck.

"Nigga where your blunt? I can make this pussy smoke."

"I know how to fuck. I know how to ride!" Rather yelled over the music.

"I can spin around and keep the dick still inside," I followed up with.

In unison, we matched Trina's flow, not missing a syllable.

A black tray landed on the table. The drinks we'd ordered when the shots were delivered had finally come.

"Here, babe." I handed Roulette her drink.

"Rome."

She'd requested a margarita. I was almost certain she wouldn't finish it. She'd sip on it for the rest of the night.

"Tiana."

Without a doubt, she'd put her martini down and work on half of another round. August was waiting, and from the looks of it, she was ready.

"Range, this is yours, baby."

The rest of the drinks had already been taken by their rightful owners. I wrapped a napkin around the lemon drop I'd settled on. I didn't want to wake up hungover from mixing liquor.

"Got one baby mama. No bitch. No wife. Like Pac, you need a thug in your life," I rapped along with Jeezy, swaying my hips and rolling my body.

As the liquid slid down my throat, I released my inhibitions, promising to make the best of the night. I'd face my troubles in the morning.

THE GREYLIST

I'd lost track of time. I'd lost track of how many drinks I'd had. I'd lost track of the shots I tossed back. I'd lost track of myself.

We'd reached the R&B set. With a nearly empty cup, I tried keeping my balance.

"I have to go to the restroom," Range revealed.

"Once you break your seal—" I reminded her.

"I know."

"We won't be much longer. If you feel like you can't hold it, then we can go now."

She shook her head.

"I can wait."

"Let me know if you change your mind. I'll go with you."

"Okay."

Tiana's hand went around my shoulders as she

sang.

"Loooooooooove."

The tune changed just as she was beginning to feel herself.

"You say you're searching for a nigga that'll take you out and do you right," Usher's voice came over the loud speakers.

"Well, come here baby, and let daddy show you what it feels like."

My hands were in the air again. My body twirled. I lowered my head, placing both hands on my thighs.

As Usher promised a good time, I was reminded of my good time. With my eyes closed, I moved in sync with the music. I felt everything and nothing at once.

My body dropped, nearing the floor. Without haste, I grinded my way back up. Legs spread, ass in the air, I swirled my hips.

A hardness pressed against me. Familiarity surrounded me. Rigidness comforted me.

Myrrh. It humbled me.

"Let's go, Royce, before I lay out every nigga in this bitch," Ishmael growled.

His fingers gripped the back of my neck, lifting my body and straightening my spine.

"What the fuck do you have on?" He questioned.

"Clothes," I spat.

"Don't make me set this motherfucker ablaze."

"I didn't think you had fingers or a fucking voice or legs–"

"I got a dick and that motherfucker hard, so let's go."

I turned, heading in the opposite direction. The grip he'd loosened, he regained in a millisecond. Pulling me into his chest.

Roulette moved her head from side to side, snapping her finger. I pushed my tongue out of my mouth, allowing the smirk to widen my face momentarily. Ishmael's anger was exhilarating. So was his presence. And his hand around my neck. And his lack of patience. And his hard dick.

His lips touched my ear. I could smell the mint on his breath. He was sober.

"You don't run shit, Royce. Either walk out of this bitch like you have some sense or I'm putting you over my shoulder and shooting every nigga who dares to look in your direction."

"You won't have enough bullets."

"It's enough motherfuckers with enough guns around us. I won't run out of bullets before this club runs out of niggas."

I loved hearing him speak.

"I–"

"Shut up."

He pushed me forward. Range's chuckles reminded me of the tab we'd run through. Everybody was intoxicated.

I lifted my brows and hands by my shoulders, bouncing them as Ishmael led me toward the door. He removed the glass from my hand and placed it on the table.

"Get them to the house," he demanded, pointing to August and Koen.

"Suck that dick tonight, sis. I know I am. One band, one sound!" Roulette yelled.

"One band, one sound," I repeated.

The chill of the night grabbed me by the arms as we exited. Ishmael's hoodie slid down my body. He leaned down and swooped me into his arms. It wasn't until I wasn't on my feet that I realized how much they hurt.

Our journey to the car wasn't long. The unfamiliar set of wheels was right outside of the establishment. The engine was still running. Ishmael lowered me into the seat and closed the door behind me. He was in the driver's seat within seconds. And we were off the parking lot seconds later.

The silence was agonizing.

His beauty was enthralling.

I was utterly and shamelessly obsessed.

I watched him collect himself. Collect his thoughts. Meanwhile, I was falling apart.

"Ish."

Silence.

"Ishmael."

Silence.

"Did you come all this way not to talk to me?"

Silence.

I didn't want to fight. I wanted to talk. I wanted to apologize. Make things right between us.

"I came all this way because I love you, Royce. And, no matter how fucking pissed I am, I can't stand the thought of another day without you. I came all of this way because my heart left me no choice. I am a fool in love. I don't care what you have to say. Neither do I care to hear it tonight. Just sit back. Try not to puke all over this car. And, save your explanation for another day."

"It doesn't work that way."

"How does it work? Hm?"

"When situations arise, we handle them."

"Like you handled the election?"

I nodded. "Yes. Like I handled the election."

There was no need to avoid the elephant in the car. It wouldn't vanish because of it.

The wheels came to a screeching halt. Ishmael maneuvered in his seat, pinning his eyes on me.

"We're in the middle of the street."

"Do you not believe in me?"

"Ishmael."

"Do you not believe in me, Royce?"

"Is–"

"Because it seems as if I was sadly mistaken to think you did."

"I do!" I yelled, feeling my emotions topple over. "I believe in you. I believe in you so fucking much that I couldn't bear the thought of Berkeley breaking your heart. So I took the fall. That's how much I believe in you. I believe that you're better than them all. Smarter than them all. More qualified than them all.

"But all they saw were your faults. All they saw was the news stations, the blogs, and the papers. They didn't see you in the field… at your best. It was all overshadowed by the location of your dick at every waking moment. Did I make a difference?

"Yes. And we had a fighting chance, Ishmael. But, then came Asia. It fucked up everything we'd worked hard to undo. It didn't matter that it was a lie. It didn't matter once it covered that front page. I knew then we'd lost. We lost!

"Not because I didn't believe in you, but because they did too. Daniels did. That's why he tried his hardest to put you under. You would've swept him without question. He was playing dirty. You wanted to keep your hands clean. Those aren't my hands, Ishmael. When motherfuckers go low, I meet them in hell. I am a handler. I handle shit. It's my fucking job.

"You can't destroy us because you can't handle what comes with that. The moment you hired me, your fate was sealed. I'm not a loser. I do not lose! As long as you're with me, you will not lose. It's unacceptable. I will fix every fucking election you apply to if I have to. That's how I operate. If you want it, it's yours.

"You're no different. If I want it, no matter what it is, it's mine. That's how we are built. That's how we will build our family. And that's how we will build our legacy. You've made promises. Promises you can't take back. Or, I swear to God, you won't be able to shit out of your own ass. You don't get to quit me. I do the quitting.

"Unless you want Janis cleaning your shit bag for the rest of your life, then I suggest you come home. I suggest you accept my apology. I suggest you get it through your skull that I'm for you. I'm in your corner. I'm not starting over with anyone else, Ishmael. So be upset. Be pissed. But, be home before the street lights come on or I'm coming to find you. I won't be empty-handed."

"You've betrayed my trust, my baby."

"Then punish me. But, not with your silence. You're killing me, Ishmael."

"You're killing me." He sighed.

"I'm sorry."

"I just need you to believe in me. Don't hide shit from me. If that was your plan all along, then you should've told me. Instead, you're hiding shit. Making me think I've won this from a fair fight. That couldn't be the furthest from the truth.

"I feel like a fucking fool. Like I can't trust you, Royce. I don't like that feeling. So, spit. I don't want to be in the dark about shit. If there's anything you're hiding, tell me right now. Wipe our slate clean. No more secrets."

I inhaled.

"Ishmael, please."

"I'm in no mood, my baby."

"We're in the middle of the street."

"And motherfuckers better move."

He slammed his hand against the dashboard, cutting on the hazard lights.

"Talk."

I shook my head.

"Ish."

"Talk."

"Just know that I believe in you. And, if I've lost your trust, I will work to regain it."

"Nah. Tell me what's on your dome."

Silently, I ran a hand across my lips.

"I'm listening."

"Now is not the time."

"Now is the perfect time."

I swallowed the lump in my throat.

"Royc–"

"Daniels wired two hundred and fifty dollars to your father's bank account the day before the images of us released. It wasn't a stranger. It wasn't a random guy. It was your father. The meeting was nothing more than a set up. He wasn't sure how your night would unfold, but he was certain you'd end up on the street where we met."

The tires were rolling again. Ishmael listened, taking in the new information.

"He also knew what type of women walked that street. And what kind of transactions were made. The address he gave you was for the building on the next street from where I stood. He'd given you the hotel's name but the address wasn't accurate.

"He's in debt. Gambling debt. Three hundred and twenty-six thousand dollars worth of debt. Daniels' payment didn't settle that debt. It lessened it, not settled it. Which means... more than likely..."

"He's plotting again."

I nodded.

"And, I can bet my last dollar you're his victim. Again. He's playing on your vulnerability. He wanted you to lose. I couldn't let him win, Ishmael. I couldn't. He didn't deserve that victory. When I say that I am for you," I choked. Tears cascaded down my cheeks.

"I mean it. I mean it, Ish. Maybe my methods are unorthodox. Maybe I don't go about things the right way. But, don't even question my loyalty to you. I'm for you. I've been for you since the night I met you and I didn't even know you.

"I only want what's best for you. Best for us. I'm sorry I wasn't more transparent. I'm sorry I hid things from you. I'm sorry you had to find out the way you found out. But, I am not sorry for putting you in a position to win. I will do it again and again and again."

Everything hurt at once.

"I've never been so invested in someone. I've never been so deeply moved, deeply loved. Or so deep in my feelings. Not like I am with you. The thought of not having you breaks me to pieces. I have so much shit with me, Ishmael, but I am good. I am good for you."

I couldn't contain my emotions. I was a blubbering wreck.

"I'm not used to feeling this way. And, I don't like it. The last two weeks have been hell for me. I hate waking up without you beside me or on my cell. Sleep has been impossible. My world has been flipped upside down.

"I don't want to fight, Ishmael. I just want you next to me. I don't want you to walk away. I don't want to walk away. I'm ready for all that comes with us. We're not perfect people. Things will arise. But I'm here. I want this. I want you."

The wheels stopped. I peered up at my home, baffled.

"I don't want to be here."

"You have no choice."

I didn't care to hear his explanation. I bolted from the car, forgetting I was shoeless.

The struggle to keep my balance was counterproductive. Still, I managed to close the door behind me.

"Bullshit," I fussed.

"My baby–" Ishmael called out to me.

I pushed forward, determined to reach my door.

"I'm not in the business of begging niggas. Go home, Ishmael."

"I am home."

"Fuck you."

"I was hoping you would, but I need you to make up your mind."

He pushed my body up against the car.

"One minute you sending cryptic messages on Instagram, telling me to come get you with your location attached, knowing damn well I was getting on the PJ no matter what hour of the day it was. Next you're trying to escape me.

"Then you're threatening to put me in a shit bag if I leave you. Crying telling me how much you want to work through our shit and can't live without me. Now you're not begging niggas and its fuck me. What you want, my baby?"

He made it hard for me to breathe. He was too close. He felt too good against my body.

"I don't want to sleep in my bed. I want to sleep in yours."

"We're hours away from my bed."

"Does it look like I give a damn?"

He tilted his head and inhaled deeply.

My phone vibrated in my purse. I stuck my hand inside, removing it. Roulette's name appeared on the screen. I turned around, not interested in the denial I knew was coming from Ishmael.

"Hello?"

His body pressed against mine. His hands pushed my dress up my body.

"Just making sure you made it home safely, babe."

"We're worried!"

"Your man came to get you. I know that's the fuck right."

"I–"

Ishmael pulled my thong aside. We were both drenched, my panties and I.

"Put that pussy on him, tonight. Tomorrow is not promised," Roulette slurred.

"Twin!" Tiana yelled.

He slid into me with ease, forcing both hands

against the hood of the car. Its warmth fought against the November chill.

"Fuuuuck."

I lowered my cell onto the car, ending the call in the process. Ishmael's body was against mine. He straightened my spine. His lips rested against my ear. His hand snacked up my dress, grabbing ahold of my nipple. He squeezed.

"Uhhhhhh."

"This what the fuck you been wanting, my baby?"

"Uhhhhhh."

"This why you acting up?"

He pushed me forward, taking hold of my hair. Stepping back, slightly, he gave our bodies the room they required.

Forward.

He drove into me.

Backward.

He retracted.

"I missed this pussy," he groaned.

Backward.

Forward.

"Yesssssss."

Backward.

Forward.

"This my shit."

Backward.

Forward.

"I don't give a fuck how hard we beefing."

Backward.

Forward.

"You belong to me."

Backward.

Forward.

"This pussy belongs to me."

Backward.

Forward.

"This dick belongs to you."

Backward.

Forward.

"Fuck. Shit so wet."

Backward.

Forward.

Ishmael lifted my upper half.

"Uhhhh."

He was leaving no room to wonder who was in control.

"Stop fucking playing with me, Royce."

Backward.

Forward.

Backward.

Forward.

"Understand?"

Backward.

Forward.

"Yesssssss."

His strokes quickened. Hard. Long. Relentless.

Backward.

Forward.

Backward.

Forward.

My body quivered with content. My orgasm traveled, starting near my chest. It reached my pussy without mercy.

"Is– Ishhhhh– Uhhhhh."

"That's it, my baby. Cum on this motherfucker."

***

Ishmael's lips landed on the back of my hand. I fought to stay awake. He didn't power up the plane. Ishmael made the decision to make the drive back to Berkeley.

He longed for the silence. He longed for the solitude. He longed for the stretch of the road to clear his head. He longed for more time with me.

"You can go to sleep."

I shook my head, yawning.

"Not yet."

"Then when?" He chuckled.

"I don't know. Just not now."

"Why not now?"

"Too much on my mind," I admitted.

"Us."

"What about us, my baby?"

"I'm worried."

"For what?"

"The last two weeks have been scary."

"For us both. But, there's nothing to worry about. I was in my head. Admittedly, my heart was broken. I wanted to win it, Royce, no bullshit. You know. But, the odds were stacked against me."

"They knew you'd crush it. They knew you had voters where you needed them. They weren't running an honest race, Ishmael. You couldn't either. Once they began they wouldn't have stopped until Daniels was back in office."

"I understand that now."

"I'm sorry I hurt your heart."

"It was nothing compared to the pain of your absence. I never want to feel that shit again. Not as long as there's breath in my body."

"I don't either."

"Let's agree to not walk away. To never walk away. To never lay down without fixing our shit. I can't go through what we just went through again."

"Promise."

I held out the pinky of my left hand. Ishmael uncurled the rest. He took his eyes off the road briefly as he slid the diamond onto my finger. Slowly, I sat up in my seat, admiring the stone while attempting to make sense of the moment.

"Promise," he replied.

"Ish."

"Marry me, my baby."

"Ishmael!"

I stared at my hand, feeling myself coming unglued. I was ripping at the seams.

"Marry me."

"Baby!"

"Marry me."

He brought my hand to his mouth.

"I've never been more sure about anything in my life. I'm sure 'bout you, my baby. Marry me."

I nodded.

"Yes."

"Yes?"

"Yes." I repeated. "Yes."

His palm collided with the steering wheel.

"That brings me joy, baby. So much joy."

"Don't ever take that long to come get me."

I punched him in his arm. He rubbed the spot.

"I won't have to come get you because I won't go to sleep with that heavy of a heart. I won't let you either."

"Good, because I hate begging niggas."

Chuckling, he glanced at me and then the road.

"You ain't gon' let me live that down, huh?"

"I'm not."

"I done did some begging, my baby. It's okay. I'm prepared to beg for the rest of my life."

"Whatever it takes."

"Whatever it takes," he joined. "I love you."

"I love you." I sighed, unable to keep my eyes off the diamond causing commotion on my hand and in my heart.

It was perfect. A single diamond-encrusted band with a single stone to top it off.

In every lifetime, my baby.

Ishmael

18 MONTHS LATER...

"Thank you, Matte."

"Of course, Mayor Grayson. Need anything else?"

"For you to close my door and confirm the six players on the opposing team of the game at the community center. Not that it matters. No one remembers the losers."

Chuckling, Matte agreed. "Right. But, I will confirm."

My team was set. I doubted anyone got past six niggas over six feet who were Berkeley Bred and had the city waiting on a win. Indigo, Milo, Mercer, Sharpe, Cameron, and I met at the rec weekly for the last four weeks, getting familiar with each other's style of ball handling. The results were pleasing.

"Thank you."

As the door touched the frame, I tapped the screen of my cell. The FaceTime call connected. I twirled my wedding band around my finger. If there was nothing more in life I was anxious for, it was always her.

"Hi."

Royce brought a smile to my face. I released my wedding band from the trenches.

"Good morning, my baby. Did I wake you?"

She nodded.

"I'll call you bac–"

"Nooo. Nooo. I need to get up."

"Did you sleep well?"

She shook her head.

"Not exactly, but much better than last night."

"I guess it's a win."

"Yes. A small victory, but a victory, nonetheless."

"How are you feeling?"

Yawning, she responded, "Like I'm carrying a watermelon around in my crotch."

"Not a watermelon." Pregnancy humor was her latest discovery.

"A very determined little girl."

We'd learned of our pregnancy at nearly sixteen weeks. There were hardly any signs of our daughter's presence. And, Royce had yet to remove her birth control.

Twelve months into our marriage, a visit to the doctor to remove the contraception led to the discovery. Izzy wasn't planned. Neither were we prepared for her entrance. However, over the last three months, we'd been making the necessary changes to welcome our sweet girl.

"My mother wants us to drop by after our appointment. She prepped your meals for this week."

Janis was over the moon. Every Monday, she spent half the day preparing meals for Royce to keep her off her feet as much as possible. I understood the concept, but I don't think my mother understood who her daughter-in-law was.

Royce had time on her hands she'd never had before. She was utilizing every moment that didn't require rest.

Mondays and Wednesdays were dedicated to pregnant pilates. Tuesdays and Thursdays, she was in Clarke, in hot yoga with her sisters. Fridays, she made her way to the kitchen, determined to have dinner on the table by the time I walked through the door.

Walking through that door filled me with so much pleasure. So did bending her over the counter, dicking her down, and sending her to the table with a wet pussy while I fixed our plates.

"Yeah. I know. She texted me."

Royce was now up on her feet. Her natural hair was

pinned up into a ponytail. A wild one that showcased all of her features. Her beautiful features.

"I'm a mess."

She sat her phone on the bathroom counter and tugged at the band on her hair. It fell down onto her shoulders.

"A pretty mess."

"Our appointment is at one-thirty."

"I'm aware."

"It's noon."

"I'm aware."

"Then where are you?"

Her hands fell to her sides. The frown on her face was evidence of what we both knew.

"You miss me?"

"Yes."

Pregnancy hormones were another discovery of ours. She placed her hands over her face. From the sinking of her chest, I knew what was to come.

"Don't do that, my baby. I'm getting up now. I'm coming. I'll be there."

I stood, rearranging everything I'd touched on my desk.

"But my hair."

"Your hair is fine. I like it just the way it was."

"When I raise my hands above my head, I feel like I can't breathe."

"Then don't. Just wait on me. I'm coming."

"Okay."

"Get in the shower if you had plans on it. You

bathed last night, but maybe it will help. I'll be there by the time you're out. I'll help you with your hair. I'll help you get dressed. Aight?"

"Okay."

"I love you. I'll be there shortly."

"I love you."

I didn't want to end the call. I didn't want to leave Royce to worry. However, I was on my way and the quicker we got off the phone, the quicker I could get to her.

THE GREY LIST

I entered our home with fruit roll ups and a stuffed bear I'd picked up along the way. Silence haunted me. I needed to see Royce's face.

To make sure she was okay.

To make sure everything was right in her world.

Only then would everything be right in mine.

I ended my quest at the door of our bedroom. I pushed it open, finding Royce inside. She was in a pair of panties that matched the color of her skin. Hadn't I taken enough pairs off, I would've assumed she wasn't wearing any.

"There goes my baby," I sang, capturing Royce's attention.

"Shhhhh."

She aimed the remote at the television and hiked

the volume. I stood beside her, eyes glued on the screen.

"...a gunshot wound to the head. Unfortunately, he succumbed to his injuries. Daniels was the mayor of Berkeley for three years. He will be greatly missed. According to sources, there are no leads. If you have any information about this incident, please contact authorities. That's your Berkeley City News."

Royce wasted little time retrieving her cell. The line connected and the ringing began. She paced the floor waiting for someone to pick up.

"Speak." Rugger groaned.

"Was it you?" Royce questioned.

"Me?"

"Daniels?"

"No."

Click.

Royce ended the call. Silently, she turned to face me.

"You weren't with Indigo last night, were you?"

"Briefly, yes."

"And then?"

"And then I went to handle some unfinished business."

"In other words, you went to Daniels' home?"

I shook my head. "No. I didn't go to Daniels' home."

"Then expla–"

"A block away."

"Baby. What if someon–"

"I was made the mayor of Berkeley. I was born to

kill. It's not a skill I needed training for. It came to me. *Naturally.* His contact crossed the network. I didn't hesitate to take it."

"You cut your ties with the network."

"I did."

"But–"

"I know a person."

In deep thought, she placed a hand on her hip. The wheels were turning.

"Rugger?"

I shook my head.

"No."

"Psalms."

"We're going to be late if we don't get you dressed and your hair u–"

"Were you careful?"

"As I could be. Don't worry, Royce."

"I can't help myself. I've been holding my breath, somehow knowing this moment would come. I just wasn't sure if it would be you or her."

"Her?"

"Rugger."

"He called you shit I couldn't let slide. I have killed for less. He was a dead man the minute he put your name in his mouth."

Nodding, Royce pulled her lips together and pushed them out.

"You have a point."

It was inevitable. Daniels' head was on the chopping block the moment Royce entered the race. He was playing dirty not knowing I was the dirtiest. I didn't mind laying with the worms until I hit my target. I'd placed a dot on his head in August. It was an added bonus I was paid to push his shit back. The funds would be donated to the same youth whose future he attempted to kill.

"Good, now let's go, my baby."

I slapped her ass and placed my lips on top of hers. Right where she wanted them. Right where I needed them. With her hand in mine, I led Royce down the steps of our shared dwelling.

Let that nigga be a lesson. Don't put your mouth on shit that belongs to me or I'll wear the same black suit you last saw me in to your funeral.

One down. **One to go**.

The end.

If you are suffering from a **Huffington Hangover**, read *Ishmael,* the extension of Royce.

please *consider*

If you've enjoyed this story as much as I loved writing it, **please consider taking the time to leave a review.**

Reviews are beneficial for Black independent authors because they help push our work. The recommendations put our work in front of eyes we aren't automatically pushed in front of under large publishing houses.

So, log on to leave a review. Not just for Grey Huffington books, but **for all Black indie authors.** We appreciate it much more than you understand.

huffington*news*

Join over 13,000 honorary Huffington residents for monthly broadcasts delivered right to their preferred devices.

Broadcasts include but aren't limited to:

- A beautiful monthly newsletter detailing everything happening in Huffington
- Snippets of upcoming projects
- Release day reminders that include links (to remove the guest work from searching for books online)
- Exclusive discounts + offers for Huffington residents

Ready to become a resident?
Click here.
[https://huffingtonnews.ck.page/4693a79283]

huffington*catalog*

Find the entire collection of Grey Huffington titles below. Titles in the catalog are available in eBook (amazon.com, + ghuffington.com), paperback (ghuffington.com), or audiobook (audible + ghuffington.com) formats.

Syx + the City

Syx + the City 2

Syx Thirty Seven

Syxth Giving

Syx Whole Weeks

Wilde + Reckless

Wilde + Relentless

Wilde + Restless

Mr. Intentional

Unearth Me

My Person
The Realm of Riot Thimble
Whose Love Story is it Anyway?
Unhand Me

Home*
Blues*
31st*
Now That We're Here.*

Then Let's Fuck About It*
Giving Thanks

A Month of Sundays Ep 1
A Month of Sundays Ep 2
A Month of Sundays Ep 3
Dinner at Ever + Luca's
Saylah
The Mayor's Ball
Elm
Temple
Aug

THE EINSENBERG EFFECT
Luca
Lyric
Ever*
Laike
Baisleigh*

Liam
Keanu

THE DOMINO EFFECT
Ledge
Halo*
Lawe
Kleuless*

BERKELEY BRED
Malachi
Anna*
Milo
Makai
Glacier*
Mercer
Vallei*

THE GREY LIST
Chemistry
"The Chemist"
Egypt*
Rather
"The Therapist"
Priest*
Rugger
"The Huntress"
Psalms*
Roulette
"The Madam"

Israel*
Rome
"The Ballerina"
Saint*

---

* signifies the publication is available EXCLUSIVELY on ghuffington.com.

Prefer Audiobooks?

Did you know **there's a library FULL of audiobooks on ghuffington.com** for the lovers who listen?

Audiobooks Available (**exclusively on GHuffing ton.com**)

Egypt
Ever
Baisleigh
Halo
Kleuless
Anna
Glacier
Vallei
Elm.
Egypt

Priest
Psalms
Israel
Saint
And more